CHILLING
Ghost
Stories

CHILLING
Ghost Stories

Edited by **Stefan Dziemianowicz**

FALL RIVER PRESS

New York

FALL RIVER PRESS

New York

An Imprint of Sterling Publishing Co., Inc.
1166 Avenue of the Americas
New York, NY 10036

ISBN 978-1-4351-7103-9

Distributed in Canada by Sterling Publishing Co., Inc.
c/o Canadian Manda Group, 664 Annette Street
Toronto, Ontario M6S 2C8, Canada
Distributed in the United Kingdom by GMC Distribution Services
Castle Place, 166 High Street, Lewes, East Sussex BN7 1XU, England
Distributed in Australia by NewSouth Books
University of New South Wales, Sydney, NSW 2052, Australia

For information about custom editions, special sales, and premium
and corporate purchases, please contact Sterling Special Sales at
800-805-5489 or specialsales@sterlingpublishing.com.

Manufactured in the United States

2 4 6 8 10 9 7 5 3 1

sterlingpublishing.com

Cover design by Elizabeth Mihaltse Lindy
Interior design by Rich Hazelton

CONTENTS

CONTENTS

INTRODUCTION

Ghost stories have been with us ever since human beings began pondering the significance of death and wondering whether there might be an afterlife in which vestiges of mortal existence persist. It wasn't long before the more imaginative among us—the poets, the playwrights, the novelists, and short-story writers—began working their conceptions of ghosts, spirits, and the dear departed into works of fiction. So it was that the ghost moved from the realm of metaphysics and into the canon of literature.

Although ghosts have haunted the literature of all nations for thousands of years, the ghost story as a form of popular fiction first came into vogue in the late eighteenth century, when the gothic novel flourished and specters of the dead were just one of many affronts to the rational conjured in tales of supernatural horror. The era of traditional gothic fiction peaked in the early 1800s before giving way to other literary fads, but the ghost story lived on and flourished in the flickering shadows of the gothic twilight.

Indeed, in the introduction to his anthology *Lost Souls*, ghost-story scholar Jack Sullivan states unequivocally that "the first modern short stories in English were ghost stories." By way of illustration, he points to American author Edgar Allan Poe and his Irish contemporary J. Sheridan Le Fanu, both of whom were publishing fiction in the 1830s, and notes that in their tales of the supernatural one found "the unity of mood and economy of means" that we associate with the short stories of their distinguished literary successors. "There are more ghost stories with unity of tone than any other kinds of early stories," Sullivan continues, "precisely because mood is so basic to the genre." It's not that ghost-story writers were trying consciously to invent a new literary form, but that they were doing what they knew intuitively was the best way to tell their stories for maximum effect.

Chilling Ghost Stories draws from the century of ghost fiction written between the late-nineteenth and early-twentieth centuries—arguably the golden age of the ghost story, and certainly the era in which modern ghost fiction acquired the shape and structure that it has today. In keeping with this book's title, the majority of this book's selections were chosen in acknowledgment of the guidelines set down by master ghost-story writer M. R. James, who, in the preface to his collection *More Ghost Stories of an Antiquary* (1911), outlined basic tenets for an effective ghost story. The first was that "the setting should be fairly familiar and the majority of the characters and their talk such as you may meet or hear any day." To James's way of thinking, the contemporary reader who appreciated the familiarity of the setting and characters in a ghost story was more likely to feel that "If I'm not very careful, something of this kind may happen to me!" Perhaps even more important, James stressed the importance of ghosts being "malevolent or odious." "Amiable and helpful apparitions are all very well in fairy tales or in local legends," he wrote, "but I have no use for them in a fictitious ghost story."

There are ghosts in this volume to suit every taste and temperament. So settle into your chair, draw close to the fire, and turn the page. It could be that what sounds like the tread of footsteps in the shadows beyond the light is just a creaking floorboard, or that the gossamer feel of an unseen hand brushing your face is just a nervous twitch. But then again, it might not be. You don't *have* to believe in ghosts to enjoy these stories—but you dismiss their power to chill your blood at your own peril.

—Stefan Dziemianowicz
New York, 2020

Black Tancrède

Henry S. Whitehead

It is true that Black Tancrède did not curse Hans De Groot as his mangled body collapsed on the rack, and that he did curse Gardelin. But, it must be remembered, Governor Gardelin went home, to Denmark, and so escaped—whatever it was that happened to Achilles Mendoza and Julius Mohrs: and Black Tancrède, who always kept his word, they said, had cursed three!

The Grand Hotel of St. Thomas in the Virgin Islands glistens in the almost intolerable brilliance of the Caribbean sunlight, because that great edifice is whitewashed in every corner, every winter. Built somewhat more than a century ago, it is a noble example of that tropical architecture which depends, for its style, upon the structural necessity for resistance to summer hurricanes. Its massive walls of stone, brick, and heavy cement are thick and ponderous. The ceilings of its huge, square rooms are eighteen feet high. Despite its solidity, the 1916 hurricane took the top story off the main building and this has never been replaced. The fact that the hotel is now uniformly a two-story structure somewhat mars its original symmetry, but it is still as impressive as in the days when the Danish Colonial High Court sat in one of its sections; when its "slave-pens" were especially noted for their safety.

Built alongside the great courtyard which its bulk surrounds, and toward the harbor, once the crater of a volcano in that era when Atlantis and its companion continent, Antillea, reared their proud civilizations in the central Atlantic, stand two houses, added, it is believed, some time after the construction of the original building. On this point the St. Thomas wiseacres continue to dispute. Nevertheless, under the house nearest to the hotel, and built with connecting steps leading to its great gallery, are those very slave-pens, converted nowadays into one enormous workroom where the hotel washing and ironing goes on, remorselessly, all the year round. During its early history, the hotel was called "Hotel du Commerce."

In that nearer, and slightly smaller of the two houses, I was installed for the winter. I took this house because I was accompanied that winter by Stephen de Lesseps, my young cousin, a boy of fourteen. Stephen's parents (his mother is my cousin Marie de Lesseps) had persuaded me to take him with me for the change of climate. Stephen is an agreeable young fellow. I gave him daily "lessons" and he read much himself, so that his education out of books was not neglected, and that major portion derived otherwise was enhanced. Stephen turned out on close association to be so manly, sensible, and generally companionable, that I congratulated myself upon yielding to my cousin Marie's suggestion.

In the middle of that winter, Marie and her sister Suzanne paid us a visit of a month. Mr. Joseph Reynolds, the American proprietor of the Grand Hotel, assigned them Room 4, a huge, double room, opening off the enormous hotel ballroom in which the major social functions of the Virgin Island capital are usually held. I am obliged to mention this background for the extraordinary story I have to tell. If I had not had Stephen along, I should not have remained in St. Thomas. I did so on his account. The capital, rather than my beloved island of Santa Cruz, was a better place for his education. Don Pablo Salazar, a famous teacher of Spanish, is resident there; the director of education lived in the neighboring house—there were many reasons.

And, if I had not had Stephen with me, Marie and Suzanne would not have made that visit, and so could not have spent a month in Number 4, and so this tale would never, perhaps, have been told.

The ladies arrived early in January, after a sweeping tour of "the lower islands"—those historic sea-jewels where England and France fought out the supremacy of the seas a century ago. They were delighted with Number 4. They slept on vast mahogany four-posters; they were entertained by everybody; they patronized St. Thomas' alluring shops; they reveled in the midsummer warmth of midwinter in this climate of balm and spice; they exclaimed over Stephen's growth and rejoiced over the fine edge with which one of the world's politest communities had ornamented the boy's naturally excellent manners. In brief, my lady cousins enjoyed their month tremendously and went home enthusiastic over the quaint charm and magnificent hospitality of the capital of the Virgin Islands, our Uncle Sam's most recent colonial acquisition, once the historic Danish West Indies.

Only one fly, it appeared, had agitated the ointment of their enjoyment. Neither, they eventually reported, could get proper sleep in Number 4 in spite of its airiness, its splendid beds, and its conveniences. At night, one or the other, and, as I learned later, sometimes both simultaneously, would be awakened out of refreshing sleep at that most unpropitious of all night hours, 4 o'clock in the morning.

They said very little of this to me. I found out later that they were extremely chary of admitting that anything whatever had been interfering with their enjoyment of my hospitality. But later, after they were gone, I did recall that Suzanne had mentioned, though lightly, how she had heard knocks at the double-doors of their big room, just at that hour. It had made little impression upon me at the time.

Long afterward, questioning them, I discovered that they had been awakened nearly every morning by the same thing! They had mentioned it to their room-maid, a black girl, who had appeared "stupid" about it; had only rolled her eyes, Marie said. They tried several explanations— brooms carelessly handled in the early morning; a permanent early "call" for some guest, perhaps an officer of marines who had to get to his duties very early. They rejected both those theories, and finally settled down to the explanation that some pious fellow-guest was accustomed to attend the earliest religious service of the day, which, in both the Anglican and Roman Catholic churches in St. Thomas, is at 5:00 in the morning. They knew, because they had several times answered the knocks, that there was never anybody at the door when they opened it. They reconciled their ultimate explanation with the discrepancy that the knocks were on *their* door, by the supposition that there was involved some strange, auditory illusion.

As I have said, these ladies were fascinated with St. Thomas, and they did not allow one minor disturbing element to interfere with their enjoy- ment of its many strange sights; the weird speech of the blacks; the magnif- icent hospitality; the Old World furniture; the street lamps; the delightful little vistas; the Caribbean's incredible indigo; especially, I think, with the many strange tales which they heard more or less incidentally.

For St. Thomas, the very home and heart of old romance, is full of strange tales. Here, in September, 1824, the pirate Fawcett with his two mates was publicly hanged. To this very day, great steel doors guard most St. Thomas stores, and particularly the funds of the Dansk Vestindiske Nationalbank, from marauders, as anciently those same doors guarded them from the frequent raids of the buccaneers. St. Thomas' streets have more than once run red with human blood; for, like Panama, it is a town which has been sacked, though never burned like Frederiksted on the neighboring island of Santa Cruz.

Among these many tales was that of Black Tancrède. This negro, a Dahomeyan, so said tradition, had lived for a while in one of those very slave-pens under my house. He had been, strangely enough, a Haitian refugee, although a full-blooded black African. Many Caucasian refugees from Haiti had come to St. Thomas in the days of Dessalines, Toussaint l'Ouverture, and Henry Cristophe, the black king of Northwestern Haiti, the bloody days of that wise despot whose marvelous citadel still towers incredibly on the hills behind Cap Haitien and who is chiefly remembered for his tyrannies, but who is probably the only person who ever made millions out of the "free" labor of his fellow blacks!

Tancrède had, so said tradition, incurred the enmity of Cristophe, and that in the days of his power was a fearsome thing for any man. But, unlike other known unfortunates who had risked that terrible anger, Tancrède had escaped Cristophe's executioner. That personage boasted that he had had so much practice with the broadsword that he could remove a head without soiling the victim's collar!

By some hook or crook, hidden probably in the stinking, rat-infested hold of some early Nineteenth Century sailing-vessel, perhaps buried under goat-hides or bales of *bacalhao*, Tancrède had shivered and sweated his way to the Danish refuge of St. Thomas. There he fell swiftly into inescapable debt, for he was a fighting-man from a warlike tribe, and no bargainer. Therefore he had become the property of one Julius Mohrs, and because of that his connection with the old hotel had begun. Black Tancrède had been lodged, for safekeeping, in one of those same slave-pens under my house.

He had soon escaped from that servitude, for his strong, bitter soul could not brook it, and made his way to the neighboring Danish island of St. Jan. There he is next heard of as a "free laborer" on the sugar estates of Erasmus Espersen. In the "Rising" of 1833 he was prominent as a leader of those who revolted against the harsh laws of Governor Gardelin. Later, whether by the French troops from Martinique who came in to help the Danes put down their Slave War, or by the Spanish troops from Porto Rico, Black Tancrède had been captured alive, which was a grave error of judgment on his part, and brought back to St. Thomas in chains, there to be tortured to death.

That sentence was delivered in the Danish colonial high court, sitting in its own quarters in the hotel, by Governor Gardelin's judge.

First Black Tancrède's hands had been cut off, one a day. Then he suffered the crushing of his feet (after "three pinches with a hot iron instrument"), a punishment consummated with a heavy bar of iron in the hands of Achilles Mendoza, the executioner, himself a black slave. The iron sheared through his leg-bones, and he was "pinched," and his hands chopped off, because he had been so unfortunate as to be caught in insurrection, bearing weapons, and he was therefore to be made an example by a governor whose name is even now execrated among the black people.

With his last expiring breath Black Tancrède cursed his tormentors. He cursed Achilles Mendoza. He cursed Julius Mohrs. He cursed Governor Gardelin. They buried his shattered body in quicklime in the courtyard of the fort, and with it went his left hand, which was clutched so firmly about the wooden crossbar of the rack that it could not be pried loose. Mendoza therefore broke off the crossbar with the hand attached, and threw it into the limepit. The other hand, chopped off the day before, had disappeared, and no effort was made to recover it. Such items in those "good old days" were not infrequently picked up and kept by onlookers as interesting souvenirs.

Four months after the execution, Julius Mohrs was found strangled in bed one morning. Even the lash failed to elicit any testimony from his household. No one has ever known who committed that murder. Mohrs, like Govenor Gardelin, had the reputation of being harsh with slaves.

Achilles Mendoza died "of a fit" in the year 1835, in the open air. He was, in fact, crossing the courtyard of the hotel at the time and was not more than a few steps from the doors leading into the slave-pens. Many bystanders saw him fall, although it was at night, for the full moon of the Caribbee Islands—by whose light I have myself read print—was shining overhead. Indeed, so much light comes from the Caribbean moon that illuminates these latitudes—degree seventeen runs through Santa Cruz, eighteen through St. Thomas—that on full moonlight nights in the "good old days," the capital itself saved the cost of street-lights; and that is the custom even today in the Santa Crucian towns.

Some of the black people at first believed that Mendoza had strangled himself! This foolish idea was doubtless derived from the fact that both the executioner's hands had gone to his throat even before he fell, gasping and foaming at the mouth, and they were found clasped unbreakably together, the great muscles of his mighty arms rigid in death with the effort, when his now worthless body was unceremoniously gathered up and carted away for early morning burial.

Naturally, everybody who remembered Black Tancrède and his curses, and his character—that is, everybody who believed in black magic as well as in Black Tancrède—was certain that that malefactor, murderer, leader of revolt, had consummated a posthumous revenge. Perhaps Julius Mohrs, too—

The Danes pooh-poohed this solution of the two unaccountable deaths in the capital of their West Indian colony, but that did not affect black belief in the slightest degree. Black Quashee was in those days only a generation removed from Black Africa, where such matters are commonplaces. Such beliefs, and the practises which accompany them, had come in through Cartagena and other routes, deviously and direct, into the West Indies from the Gold Coast, from Dahomey and Ashantee and the Bight of Benin—all the way, indeed, from Dakar to the Congo mouth regions—into the West Indies indeed, where Quashee's sheer fecundity, now that the "good old days" are no more, and Quashee is a Christian of one kind or another, and often a high school or even a college graduate, has caused him vastly to outnumber his erstwhile white masters. White people are now Quashee's masters no longer, though they still live beside him in the West Indies, in a constantly diminishing proportion, under that same bright moon, that same glowing sun, in the shade of the mighty tamarinds, beside the eye-scorching scarlet of the hibiscus, the glaring purple and magenta of the bougainvillea.

Governor Gardelin returned to Denmark very soon after the Slave War of 1833, where, so far as one may know from perusal of the old records, he died in his bed full of years and honors.

As I have mentioned, my cousins, Marie and Suzanne, returned to the continental United States. They left about the tenth of February, and Stephen and I, regretting their departure, settled down for the rest of that winter, planning to return the middle of May.

One morning, a few weeks after their departure, Reynolds, the proprietor, asked me a question.

"Did you hear the uproar last night, or, rather, early this morning?"

"No," said I. "What was 'the uproar'? If it was out in the streets I might have heard it, but if it happened inside the hotel, my house is so detached that I should probably have heard nothing of it and gone right on sleeping."

"It was inside," said Reynolds, "so you probably wouldn't have noticed it. The servants are all chattering about it this morning, though. They believe it is another manifestation of the Jumbee in Number 4. By the way, Mr. Canevin, your cousins were in that room. Did they ever mention any disturbance to you?"

"Why, yes, now that you speak of it. My cousin Suzanne spoke of somebody knocking on their door; about four in the morning I believe it happened. I think it happened more than once. They imagined it was somebody being 'called' very early, and the servant knocking on the wrong door or something of that kind. They didn't say much about it to me. What is 'the Jumbee in Number 4'? That intrigues me. I never happened to hear that one!"

Now a "Jumbee" is, of course, a West Indian ghost. In the French islands the word is "Zombi." Jumbees have various characteristics, which I will not pause to enumerate, but one of these is that a Jumbee is always black. White persons, apparently, do not "walk" after death, although I have personally known three white gentlemen planters who were believed to be werewolves! Among the West Indian black population occurs every belief, every imaginable practice of the occult, which is interwoven closely into their lives and thoughts; everything from mere "charms" to active necromancy; from the use of the deadly *Vaudoux* to the "toof from a dead," which last renders a gambler lucky! Jumbee is a generic word. It means virtually any kind of a ghost, apparition, or *revenant*. I was not in the least surprised to learn that Number 4, Grand Hotel, had its otherworldly attendant. My sole ground for wonder was that I had not heard of it before now! Now that I recalled the matter, something *had* disturbed Marie and Suzanne in that room.

"Tell me about it, please, Mr. Reynolds," I requested.

Mr. Reynolds smiled. He is a man of education and he, too, knows his West Indies.

"In this case it is only a general belief," he answered. "The only specific information about 'the Jumbee in Number 4' is that it wakes occupants up early in the morning. There has, it seems, 'always been a Jumbee' connected with that room. I daresay the very frying-pans in the kitchen have their particular Jumbees, if they happen to be old enough! That rumpus this morning was only that we had a tourist, a Mr. Ledwith, staying overnight—came over from Porto Rico in the *Catherine* and left this morning for 'down the islands' on the *Dominica*. He came in pretty late last night from a party with friends in the town. He explained later that he couldn't sleep because of somebody knocking on his door. He called out several times, got no answer; the knocking went on, and then he lost his temper. He reached out of bed and picked up the earthenware water-jug. His aim was excellent, even though he may have had a drop too much at his party. He hit the door-handle, smashed the jug into fragments, and then, really aroused, got up, flung open the door, found nobody there, and took it into his head that somebody was having a joke on him. Absurd! The man was a total stranger to everybody in the hotel.

"He raged around the ballroom and woke up the Gilbertsons and Mrs. Peck—you know they have rooms on that side—and at last he awakened me and I got up and persuaded him to go back to bed. He said there were no more knocks after that. I was afraid it might have disturbed you and Stephen. I'm glad it didn't. Of course such a rumpus is very unusual in the hotel at any time."

"Hm," said I, "well, well!" I had been thinking while Mr. Reynolds made this long speech about the nocturnal activities of the unknown Mr. Ledwith. I could not talk with him. He had already sailed that morning.

I was really intrigued by now—that occurrence coupled with the experience of my cousins! Of course I knew very little about that, for they had said almost nothing. But it was enough to arouse my interest in "the Jumbee in Number 4."

That was the only time Mr. Reynolds and I spoke of the matter, and for some time, although I kept my ears open, I heard nothing further about Number 4. When the "trouble" did start up again, I was in Number 4 myself. That came about in this manner.

An American family named Barnes, permanent residents of St. Thomas—I believe Barnes was a minor official of the public works or the agricultural department of the Virgin Island government—let their house-lease expire and decided to move into the hotel at family-rates-by-the-month for the convenience. Mrs. Barnes had two young children, and was tired of household cares. She had employed, I think, some rather inferior servants, which always means a heavy burden in the West Indies. One of the two hotel houses would suit them exactly. The other was occupied, by the year, by the director of education and his family, delightful Americans.

It was the first of May, and as Stephen and I were booked to sail on the twelfth for New York, I proposed to Mr. Reynolds that we give up our house to Mr. and Mrs. Barnes, and he could put us into one of the huge double rooms for the remainder of our stay. Mr. Reynolds put us into Number 4, probably the best of all the rooms, and which was, fortunately, vacant at the moment.

It happened that on our first night in our new quarters, I was out very late. I had gone, with the colonel in command of the naval station marines and his wife, to meet an incoming ship on which a certain Major Upton was returning to St. Thomas from a month's leave. Two days before the arrival of the ship, a cable had informed the colonel of Mrs. Upton's sudden death in Virginia. We did not know whether or not Upton had learned of his unexpected bereavement by wireless aboard ship, and we rather thought he had not. The ship was reported due at 1:00 A.M. She came in a little after 2:00, and after meeting Upton—who had, fortunately, received a wireless—and making his arrival as pleasant as we could for him under the circumstances, I got back to the hotel about 3:30 in the morning.

I came in at the side door, which is always open, walked softly along the great length of the ballroom, and very quietly opened the door of Number 4. By the streaming moonlight which was pouring in through the open jalousies of the great room, I could see Stephen's outlines, dimly, through the cloud of mosquito-netting which covered his enormous four-poster. I undressed silently, so that I should not disturb my young cousin. I was just ready to turn in, my soiled drill clothes in the washbag, my white buckskin shoes neatly treed, my other things laid away where they belonged—for I am a rather fussy fellow about such matters—and it was within a minute or two to 4:00 o'clock in the morning; I know I was beastly tired; when, just beside me, on the door leading in from the ballroom, came an abrupt, unmistakable rap-rap-rap!

There could be no possible doubt about it. I was standing within three feet of the door at the moment the raps were delivered. I, Gerald Canevin, am a teller of the truth. I admit that I felt the cold chills which are characteristic of sudden, almost uncontrollable, paralyzing fear, run swiftly up and down my spine; that acute prickling at the hair roots which is called one's "hair standing on end."

But, if Gerald Canevin is a trifle old-maidish about the arrangement of his personal belongings, and, even damagingly, truthful, he may boast, and justly, that no man living can call him a poltroon.

I took one firm step to that door and flung it open, and—so help me God!—as I turned the small, old-fashioned brass knob, the last of the raps— for the summons was repeated, just as the convivial Ledwith had alleged— sounded within three inches of my hand, on the other side of the door.

The great, ghostly still ballroom stood silent and empty. Not a sound, not a movement disturbed its early-morning, dead, serene emptiness. I raked the room with my scrutiny. Everything was visible because the vivid moonlight—the moon had been full two nights before—came flooding in from the gallery with its nine Moorish arches, overlooking the harbor.

There was nothing—absolutely, literally, nothing—to be seen or heard. I glanced back over my shoulder along the wall through which the door of Number 4 opens. What was that? I could feel my heart skip a beat, then start pounding. A dim something, the merest shadowy outline, it seemed, in the form of a gigantic negro was moving along the wall toward the passageway, curtained from the ballroom, which leads to the main entrance of the hotel below.

Even as I looked, the strange form seemed to melt and vanish, and there came a hard, dull thud from the direction where I imagined I had seen it slipping furtively along the wall.

I looked narrowly, my heart still pounding, and there, on the floor moving rapidly from me in the same direction I had imagined that sinister figure following, and with a queer, awkward movement suggestive of a crab's sidelong gait, but moving in utter silence, there ran along the bare floor something about the size of a baseball.

I was barefooted and in thin. China-silk pajamas, but I started, weaponless, after the thing. It was, I surmised, the biggest tarantula I had ever seen in or out of the West Indies. Certainly it was no crab, although its size and even its gait would suggest one of our boxlike, compact landcrabs. But a crab, running away like that, would make a distinctive, identifying, hard rattle with its shell-covered feet on that hard, wooden floor, and this thing ran silently, like velvet.

What I should do with, or to, the tarantula if I caught it, I did not stop to consider. I suppose it was a kind of instinct that sent me in pursuit. I gained on it, but it slipped past the curtains ahead of me and was lost to sight in the broad passageway on the other side at the stairs' head. As soon as I had passed the curtain I saw that any attempt to catch the thing would be an impossibility. There would be innumerable hiding-places; the main entrance doors were closed tight down below there, and the stair-well was as dark as the inside of Jonah's whale.

I turned back, perforce, and re-entered Number 4, shut the door quietly behind me, and turned in upon my own gigantic four-poster and tucked the mosquito-netting under the edge of the mattress. I slept at once and did not awaken until five and one-half hours later, at 9:30 in the morning. The excellent Stephen, realizing the situation, had repaid my pussyfooting in his interest of the earlier morning by getting dressed in silence and ordering my breakfast sent in at this hour.

That was Saturday morning, and there were no lessons for Stephen. I took advantage of that fact to put in a very much occupied day at my type-writer, and I got such a start on what I was then engaged in writing that I determined, if possible, to finish it the next day in time for the New York mail which goes out through Porto Rico every week. A brief, unaccustomed siesta Saturday afternoon helped make up for some lack of sleep. I decided to get up and go to that horribly "early" service at five on Sunday morning. That would give me a reason for early rising—which I have always secretly abominated!—and a good day's start. Stephen and I retired that evening as soon as he returned from his moving-pictures at the naval station; that was, about 9:30.

I must have grown wearier than I had realized, sitting up for Major Upton's ship, and accompanying him to the colonel's quarters afterward; for I slept like the dead, and had my usual fight with myself to get up and shut off an insistent alarm-clock at 4:15. I got to church in time, and was back again a few minutes before 6:00. It was barely dawn when I came in at the side entrance and up the stairs.

As I walked along the still dim ballroom toward Number 4, the tarantula, or land-crab, or whatever the thing might prove to be, came sidling in that same awkward fashion which I had noted along the edge of the side-wall, toward me this time. It was as though the creature were returning from the hiding-place whither I had chased him Saturday morning.

I was carrying a tough, resilient walking-stick, of native black wattle, cut by myself on Estate Ham's Bay, over on Santa Cruz, two years before. I stepped faster toward the oncoming thing, with this stick poised in my hand. I saw now in the rapidly brightening dawn what was wrong with the spider—it was obvious now that it was no land-crab. The thing was maimed. It had, apparently, lost several of its legs, and so proceeded in that odd, crablike fashion which I had noted before. A spider should have eight legs, as most people know. This one came hunching and sidling along on five or six.

The thing, moving rapidly despite its paucity of legs, was almost at the door to Number 4. I ran toward it, for the door stood slightly open, and I did not want that horrible creature to go into my room on account of Stephen. I struck at it, viciously, but it eluded my black wattle and slipped in under the conch-shell which served as a door-chock.

Conchs have many uses in the West Indies. In the Bahamas their contents serve as a food-staple. They occasionally yield "pearls," which have some value to jewelers. One sees the shells everywhere—bordering garden paths, outlining cemetery plots, built, with cement, into ornamental courses like shining pink bricks. In the Grand Hotel every door has a conch for a chock. The one at my door was a very old one, painted, in a dark brown color, to preserve it from disintegration due to the strong, salt air.

I approached the shell, now covering the huge tarantula, with some caution. The bite of our native tarantulas in St. Thomas is rarely or never fatal, but it can put the human victim into the hospital for several days, and this fellow, as I have said, was the largest I had ever seen, in or out of St. Thomas. I poked the end of my stick under the lip-edge of the shell, and turned it suddenly over. The spider had disappeared. Obviously it had crawled inside the shell. There is a lot of room inside a good-sized conch. I decided to take a chance. I did not want that thing about the place, certainly.

Keeping my eye on the upturned shell, I stepped over to the center of the ballroom and picked up a week-old Sunday supplement rotogravure section of one of the New York newspapers, crumpled it, folded it into a kind of wad, and with this, very gingerly—for the tarantula is a fighter and no timid beast—effectually stopped up the long triangular entrance to the shell's inside. Then, picking it up, I carried it outside onto the stone-flagged gallery.

Here things were appreciably lighter. The dawn was brightening into the tropic day every instant, and I could now see everything clearly.

I raised the conch-shell and brought it down crashing on the tessellated floor.

As I had expected, the old shell smashed into many fragments, and I stood by, my black wattle raised and ready to strike at the tarantula as it attempted to run away. I had figured, not unnaturally, that the experience of having its rocklike refuge suddenly picked up, carried away, and then crashing to pieces about itself, would, from the tarantula's viewpoint, prove at least momentarily disconcerting, and I should have a chance to slay the loathsome thing at my leisure. But, to my surprise, nothing ran out of the shattered shell.

I bent and looked closer. The fragments were relatively both large and small, from powdery dust all the way to a few chunks as big as my two fists. I poked at one of these, of an extraordinary and arresting shape, a strangely suggestive shape, though colored a dirty pink like the rest of the couch's lining. I turned it over with the end of my stick.

It was the hand of a negro, which, lying palm upward, had at first seemed pink. The palm of the hand of the blackest of black Africans is pink. So is the sole of the foot. But there was no mistaking the back of that sooty, clawlike thing. It was a severed hand, and it had originally grown upon an owner who had no admixture of any blood other than that of Africa. The name "Tancrède" leapt to my mind. Had he not, even among his fellow slaves, been called "Black Tancrède"? He had, and my knowledge of that ancient tale and the sooty duskiness of this ancient relic conspired forthwith to cause me to leap to that outrageous, that incredible conclusion. The hand of Black Tancrède—this was a right hand, and so, said tradition, was the one which had first been severed and then disappeared—or, at least, the veritable hand of some intensely dark negro, lay there before me on the gallery floor, among the debris of an ancient conch-shell.

I drew a deep breath, for it was an unsettling experience, stooped, and picked the thing up. It was as dry and hard as so much conch-shell and surprisingly heavy. I looked at it carefully, turning it about and examining it thoroughly; for I was alone on the gallery. Nobody was stirring in the hotel; even the kitchen was silent.

I slipped the hand into the pocket of my drill jacket, and returned to Number 4. I laid the hand down on the marble-topped table which stands in the room's center, and looked at it. Stephen, I had noted at once, was absent. He had got up, and was now, doubtless, in his shower-bath.

I had not been looking at it very long, before an explanation, too far-fetched to be dwelt upon or even to be seriously entertained, was invading my dazed mind. Something on five or six "legs" had run under that conch-shell. Nothing, save this, had been there when I smashed the shell. There were the surface facts, and I was my own witness. There was no hearsay about it. This was no black Quashee tale of marvels and wonderment.

I heard a pad-pad outside, like slippered feet, and I had the thing in my pocket again when Stephen came in, glowing from his shower. I did not want to explain that hand to the boy.

"Good morning. Cousin Gerald," said Stephen. "You got off early, didn't you? I heard your alarm-clock but I turned over and went to sleep again."

"Yes," I answered. "You see, I have a lot of work to get through with today."

"I'd have gone with you," continued Stephen, half-way into his fresh clothes by now, "if you'd waked me up! I'm going to 6:00 o'clock church if I can make it."

He dressed rapidly, and with another pleasant, hasty word or two, the boy was off, running. The "English Church" is quite near by.

I got up, left Number 4 empty, crossed the ballroom diagonally, and entered Mr. Reynolds' sanctum at its western extremity. I had thought of something. I *must* do what I could to clear up. or put away forever, if possible, that explanation, the details of which were invading my excited mind, pressing into it remorselessly.

I went to the lowest shelf of one of his bookcases, and took out the three heavy, calf-bound, ancient registers of the Hotel du Commerce. I must find out, on the off-chance that the room numbers had not been changed since then, who had occupied Room 4 at the time of Black Tancrède's execution and cursings. That, for the moment, seemed to me absolutely the salient fact, the key to the whole situation. . . .

I could hardly believe my eyes when the faded entry, the ink brown, the handwriting oddly curleycued, jumped out at me.

For all of the year 1832, 1833, and most of 1834 besides, Room 4, Hotel du Commerce, Raoul Patit, proprietor, had been occupied by one Hans de Groot. Hans de Groot had been Governor Gardelin's judge of the Danish Colonial high court. Hans de Groot had condemned Black Tancrède to death, by amputation of hands, pinching, and breaking on the rack.

I had my explanation. . . .

If only this were a romance, I should proceed to tell how thereafter I had applied, in the traditional method for the laying of this kind of ghost—a ghost with an unfulfilled desire, promise, or curse—how I had applied for permission to restore the hand to the resting-place of Black Tancrède. I should recite the examination of old records, the location of the limepit in the Fort yard; I might even have the horrible thing which lay in my jacket pocket "escape" to wreak devastation upon me after unavailing efforts on my part to avoid destruction; a final twist of luck, the destruction of the hand. . . .

But this is not romance, and I am not attempting to make "quite a tale" of these sober facts.

What I did was to proceed straight to the hotel kitchen, where fat Lucinda the cook was cutting breakfast bacon at a table, and two dusky assistants preparing grapefruit and orange-juice against the hour for breakfast.

"Good morning, Lucinda," I began; "is your fire going?"

"Marnin', Mars' Canevin, sar," returned Lucinda, "hot, good'n hot, sar. Is yo' desirous to cook someting?"

Both handmaidens giggled at this, and I smiled with them.

"I only have something I wish to burn," said I, explaining my early-morning visit.

I approached the glowing stove, anticipating Lucinda, and waving her back to her bacon-cutting, lifted a lid, and dropped the horrible, mummified thing into the very heart of a bed of cherry-colored coals.

It twisted in the heat, as though alive and protesting. It gave off a faint, strange odor of burning, like very old leather. But within a few moments the dry and brittle skin and the calcined bones were only scraps of shapeless, glowing embers.

I replaced the stovelid. I was satisfied. I would now satisfy Lucinda, if not her very natural curiosity. I handed her with an engaging smile one of the small, brown, five-franc currency bills which are still issued by the Dansk Vestindiske Nationalbank, and are legal tender in our Uncle Sam's Virgin Islands.

"Many t'anks, sar; Gahd bless yo'. Mars' Canevin, sar," muttered the delighted Lucinda.

I nodded to them and walked out of the kitchen reasonably certain that the Jumbee of Number 4 would trouble guests no more at 4:00 o'clock in the morning, nor at any other hour; that eternity had now swallowed Black Tancrède, who, tradition alleged, was a very persevering man and always kept his word. . . .

It is true, as I remarked at the beginning of this narrative, that Black Tancrède did not curse Hans de Groot, but that Governor Gardelin went home to Denmark and so escaped—whatever it was that happened to Achilles Mendoza and Julius Mohrs. Perhaps the persevering shade of Black Tancrède was limited, in the scope of its revengeful "projection" through that severed hand, to the island on which he died. I do not know, although there are almost fixed rules for these things; rules in which Quashee believes religiously.

But, since that morning, I, truthful Gerald Canevin, confess, I have never seen any large spider without at least an internal shudder. I can understand, I think, what that strange mental aberration called "spider fear" is like. . . .

For I *saw* that thing which ran along the floor of the Grand Hotel ballroom like a maimed spider—I saw it go under that conch-shell. And it did not come out as it went in. . . .

OUT OF THE DEEP

Walter de la Mare

The steely light of daybreak, increasing in volume and intensity as the East grew larger with the day, showed clearly at length that the prodigious yet elegant Arabian bed was empty. What might tenderly have cradled the slumbers of some exquisite Fair of romance now contained no human occupant at all. The whole immense room—its air dry and thin as if burnt—was quiet as a sepulchre.

To the right of the bed towered a vast and heavily carved wardrobe. To the left, a lofty fireplace of stone flanked by its grinning frigid dogs. A few cumbrous and obscure oil paintings hung on the walls. And, like the draperies of a proscenium, the fringed and valanced damask curtains on either side the two high windows, poured down their motionless cataract of crimson.

They had been left undrawn over night, and yet gave the scene a slight theatricality, a theatricality which the painted nymphs disporting themselves on the ceiling scarcely helped to dispel.

Not that these coy and ogling faces suggested any vestige of chagrin at the absence of the young man who for some weeks past had shared the long nights with them. They merely smiled on. For, after all, Jimmie's restless head upon the pillow had never really been in harmony with his pompous inanimate surroundings—the thin high nose, like the beak of a small ship, between the fast-sealed lids and narrow cheekbones, the narrow bird-like brow, the shell of the ear slightly pointed. If, inspired by the distant music of the spheres, the painted creatures had with this daybreak broken into song, it would certainly not have been to the tune of "Oh where, and oh where is my little dog gone?" There was even less likelihood of Jimmie's voice now taking up their strains from out of the distance.

And yet, to judge from appearances, the tongue within that head might have been that of an extremely vivacious talker—even though, apart from Mrs. Thripps, its talk these last few days had been for the most part with himself.

Indeed, as one of his friends had remarked: "Don't you believe it. Jimmie has pots and pots to say, though he don't say it. That's what makes him such a damn good loser." Whether or not; if Jimmie *had* been in the habit of conversing with himself, he must have had odd company at times.

Night after night he had lain there, flat on his back, his hands crossed on his breast—a pose that never failed to amuse him. A smooth eminence in the dark rich quilt about sixty inches from his chin indicated to his attentive eye the points of his toes. The hours had been heavy, the hours had been long—still there are only twelve or so of utter darkness in the most tedious of nights, and matins tinkles at length. Excepting the last of them—a night, which was now apparently for ever over, he had occupied this majestic bed for about six weeks, though on no single occasion could he have confessed to being really at home in it.

He had chosen it, not from any characteristic whim or caprice, and certainly not because it dominated the room in which his Uncle Timothy himself used to sleep, yes, and for forty years on end, only at last to expire in it. He had chosen it because, when its Venetian blinds were pulled high up under the fringed cornice, it was as light as a London April sky could make it; and because—well, just one single glance in from the high narrow doorway upstairs had convinced him that the attic in which he was wont to sleep as a small boy was simply out of the question. A black heavy flood of rage swept over him at sight of it— he had never before positively realised the abominations of that early past. To a waif and stray any kind of shelter is, of course, a godsend, but even though this huge sumptuous barrack of a house had been left to him (or, rather, abandoned to him) by his Uncle Timothy's relict. Aunt Charlotte, Jimmie could not—even at his loosest—have been described as homeless.

Friendless rather—but that of his own deliberate choice. Not so very long ago, in fact, he had made a clean sweep of every single living being, male or female, to whom the term friend could, with some little elasticity, be applied. A little official affair, to put it politely, eased their exit. And then, this vacant hostel. The house, in fact (occupied only by a caretaker in the service of his Aunt's lawyers) had been his for the asking at any time during the last two or three years. But he had steadily delayed taking possession of it until there was practically no alternative.

Circumstances accustom even a young man to a good many inconveniences. Still it would have been a little too quixotic to sleep in the street, even though his Uncle Timothy's house, as mere "property," was little better than a white and unpleasing elephant. He could not sell it, that is, not *en masse*. It was more than dubious if he was legally entitled to make away with its contents.

But, quite apart from an extreme aversion to your Uncle Timothy's valuables in themselves, you cannot eat, even if you can subsist on, articles of *virtu*. Sir Richard Grenville—a hero for whom Jimmie had every respect—may have been accustomed to chewing up his wine-glass after swigging off its contents. But this must have been on the spur of an impulse, hardly in obedience to the instinct of self-preservation.

Jimmie would have much preferred to balance a chair at the foot of his Uncle's Arabian bed and salute the smiling lips of the painted nymphs on the ceiling. Though even that experiment would probably have a rather gritty flavour. Still, possession is nine points of the law, and necessity is the deadly enemy of convention. Jimmie was unconscious of the faintest scruples on that score.

His scruples, indeed, were in another direction. Only a few days ago—the day, in fact, before his first indulgence in the queer experience of pulling the bell—he had sallied out with his Aunt Charlotte's black leather dressing bag positively bulging with a pair of Bow candlesticks, an illuminated missal, mutely exquisite, with its blues and golds and crimsons, and a tiny old silver-gilt bijouterie box. He was a young man of absurdly impulsive aversions, and the dealer to whom he carried this further consignment of loot was one of them.

After a rapid and contemptuous examination, this gentleman spread out his palms, shrugged his shoulders, and suggested a sum that would have caused even a more phlegmatic connoisseur than his customer's Uncle Timothy to turn in his grave.

And Jimmie replied, nicely slurring his r's, "Really Mr. So-and-so, it is impossible. No doubt the things have an artificial value, but not for me. I must ask you to oblige me by giving me only half the sum you have kindly mentioned. Rather than accept *your* figure, you know, I would—well, perhaps it would be impolite to tell you what I would prefer to do. *Dies irae, dies ilia*, and so on."

The dealer flushed, though he had been apparently content to leave it at that. He was not the man to be easily insulted by a good customer. And Jimmie's depredations were methodical. With the fastidiousness of an expert he selected from the rare and costly contents of the house only what was light and portable and became inconspicuous by its absence. The supply he realised, though without any perceptible animation, however recklessly it might be squandered, would easily last out his lifetime.

Certainly *not*. After having once made up his mind to accept his Uncle Timothy's posthumous hospitality, the real difficulty was unlikely to be a conscientious one. It was the attempt merely to accustom himself to the house—the hated house—that grew more and more arduous. It falsified his hope that, like other experiences, this one would prove only the more piquant for being so precarious. Days and moments quickly flying—just his one funny old charwoman, Mrs. Thripps, himself, and the Past.

After pausing awhile under the dingy and dusty portico, Jimmie had entered into his inheritance on the last afternoon in March. The wind was fallen; the day was beginning to narrow; a chill crystal light hung over the unshuttered staircase. By sheer force of a forgotten habit he at once ascended to the attic in which he had slept as a child.

Pausing on the threshold, he looked in, conscious not so much of the few familiar sticks of furniture—the trucklebed, the worn strip of Brussels carpet, the chipped blue-banded ewer and basin, the framed illuminated texts on the walls—as of a perfect hive of abhorrent memories.

That high cupboard in the corner from which certain bodiless shapes had been wont to issue and stoop at him cowering out of his dreams; the crab-patterned paper that came alive as you stared; the window cold with menacing stars; the mouseholes, the rusty grate—trumpet of every wind that blows—these objects at once lustily shouted at him in their own original tongues.

Quite apart from themselves, they reminded him of incidents and experiences which at the time could scarcely have been so nauseous as they now seemed in retrospect. He found himself suffocatingly resentful even of what must have been kindly intentions. He remembered how his Aunt Charlotte used to read to him—with her puffy cheeks, plump ringed hands, and the moving orbs of her eyes showing under her spectacles.

He wasn't exactly accusing the past. Even in his first breeches he was never what could be called a nice little boy. He had never ordered himself lowly and reverently to any of his betters—at least in their absence. Nevertheless, what stirred in his bosom as he gazed in on this discarded scene was certainly not remorse.

He remembered how gingerly and with what peculiar breathings, his Uncle Timothy used to lift his microscope out of its wooden case; and how, after the necessary manipulation of the instrument, he himself would be bidden mount a footstool and fix his dazzled eye on the slides of sluggish or darting horrors of minute magnified "life." And how, after a steady um-aw-ing drawl of inapprehensible instruction, his uncle would suddenly flick out a huge silk pocket handkerchief as a signal that little tongue-tied nervous boys were themselves nothing but miserable sluggish or darting reptiles, and that his nephew was the most deplorable kind of little boy.

Jimmie remembered, too, once asking the loose bow-shaped old gentleman in his chair if he might himself twist the wheel; and his Uncle Timothy had replied in a loud ringing voice, and almost as if he were addressing a public meeting: "Um, ah, my boy, I say No to that!" He said No to most things, and just like that, if he vouchsafed speech at all.

And then there was Church on Sundays; and his hoop on weekdays in the Crescent; and days when, with nothing to do, little Jimmie had been wont to sit watching the cold silvery rain on the window, the body he was in slowly congealing the while into a species of rancid suet pudding. Mornings, too, when his Aunt Charlotte would talk nasally to him about Christianity; or when he was allowed to help his Uncle and a tall scared parlourmaid dust and rearrange the contents of a cabinet or bureau. The smell of the air, the check duster, the odious *objets d'art* and the ageing old man snorting and looking like a superannuated Silenus beside the neat and frightened parlourmaid—it was a curious thing; though Death with his louring grin had beckoned him off: there he was—alive as ever.

And when amid these ruminations, Jimmie's eyes had at last fixed themselves on the frayed dangling cord that hung from the ceiling over the trucklebed, it was because he had already explored all that the name Soames had stood for. Soames the butler—a black-clothed, tub-bellied, pompous man that might have been his Uncle Timothy's impoverished first cousin or illegitimate step-brother: Soames: Soames.

Soames used frequently to wring Jimmie's then protuberant ears. Soames sneaked habitually; and with a sort of gloating piety on his drooping face, was invariably present at the subsequent castigation. Soames had been wont to pile up his plate with lumps of fat that even Destiny had never intended should consort with any single leg of mutton or even sirloin of beef—jelly-like, rapidly cooling *nuggets* of fat. And Soames invariably brought him cold rice pudding when there was hot ginger roll.

Jimmie remembered the lines that drooped down from his pale long nose. The sleek set of his whiskers as he stood there in his coat-tails reflected in the glass of the sideboard, carving the Sunday joint.

But that slack green bell-cord!—his very first glimpse of it had set waggling *score* of peculiar remembrances. First, and not so very peculiarly, perhaps, it recalled an occasion when, as he stood before his Aunt's footstool to bid her Good-night, her aggrieved pupils had visibly swum down from beneath their lids out of a nap, to fix themselves and look at him at last as if neither he nor she, either in this or in any other world, had ever so much as seen one another before. Perhaps his own face, if not so puffy appeared that evening to be unusually pasty and pallid—with those dark rings which even to this day added vivacity and lustre to his extremely clear eyes. And his Aunt Charlotte had asked him why he was such a cowardly boy and so wickedly frightened of the dark.

"You know very well your dear Uncle will not permit gas in the attic, so there's no use asking for it. You have nothing on your conscience, I trust? You have not been talking to the servants?"

Infallible liar, he had shaken his head. And his Aunt Charlotte in return wagged hers at him.

"It's no good staring in that rebellious sullen way at me. I have told you repeatedly that if you are really in need of anything, just ring the bell for Soames. A good little boy with nothing on his conscience *knows* that God watches over him. I hope you are at least trying to be a good little boy. There is a limit even to your Uncle's forbearance."

It was perfectly true. Even bad little boys might be "watched over" in the dead of night, and as for his Uncle Timothy's forbearance, he had discovered the limitations of that fairly early in life.

Well, it was a pity, he smiled to himself, that his Aunt Charlotte could not be present to see his Uncle Timothy's bedroom on that first celebration of their prodigal nephew's return. Jimmie's first foray had been to range the house from attic to cellar (where he had paused to rest) for candlesticks. And that night something like six dozen of the "best wax" watched over his heavy and galvanic slumbers in the Arabian bed. Aunt Charlotte, now rather more accustomed to the dark even than Jimmie himself, would have opened her eyes at that.

Gamblers are naturally superstitious folk, he supposed; but that was the queerest feature of the whole thing. He had not then been conscious of even the slightest apprehension or speculation. It was far rather a kind of ribaldry than any sort of foreboding that had lit up positive constellations of candles as if for a Prince's—as if for a princely Cardinal's—lying-in-state.

It had taken a devil of a time, too. His Uncle Timothy's port was not the less potent for a long spell of obscure mellowing, and the hand that held the taper had been a shaky one. Yet it had proved an amusing process, too. Almost childish. Jimmie hadn't laughed like that for years. Certainly until then he had been unconscious of the feeblest squeamish inkling of anything—apart from old remembrances—peculiar in the house. And yet—well, no doubt even the first absurd impulsive experiment that followed *had* shaken him up.

Its result would have been less unexpected if he hadn't made a point and almost a duty of continually patrolling the horrible old vacant London mansion. Hardly a day had lately passed—and there was nothing better to do—but it found him on his rounds. He was not waiting for anything (except for the hour, maybe, when he would have to wait no more). Nevertheless, faithful as the sentinel on Elsinore's hoary ramparts, he would find himself day after day treading almost catlike on from room to room, surveying his paradoxical inheritance, jotting down a list in a nice order of the next "sacrifice," grimacing at the Ming divinities, and pirouetting an occasional long nose at the portraits on the walls.

He had sometimes had a few words—animated ones, too—with Mrs. Thripps, and perhaps if he could have persuaded himself to talk "sensibly," and not to gesticulate, not to laugh himself so easily into a fit of coughing, she would have proved better company. She was amazingly honest and punctual and quiet; and why to heaven a woman with such excellent qualities should customarily wear so scared a gleam in her still, colourless eyes, and be so idiotically timid and nervous in his company, he could not imagine.

She was being paid handsome wages anyhow; and, naturally, he was aware of no rooted objection to other people helping themselves; at least if they managed it as skilfully as he did himself. But Mrs. Thripps, it seemed, had never been able in any sense at all to help herself. She was simply a crape-bonneted "motherly" creature, if not excessively intelligent, if a little slow in seeing "points." It was, indeed, her alarm when he asked her if she had happened to notice any young man about the house that had irritated him—though, of course, it was hardly fair not to explain what had given rise to the question. That was perfectly simple. It was like this. . . .

For years—for centuries, in fact—Jimmie had been, except in certain unusual circumstances, an exceedingly bad sleeper. He still hated sleeping in the dark. But a multitude of candles at various degrees of exhaustion make rather lively company when you are sick of your Uncle Timothy's cellar. And even the best of vintage wines may prove an ineffectual soporific. His, too, was a wretchedly active mind.

Even as a boy he had thought a good deal about his Uncle and Aunt, and Soames, and the house, and the Rev. Mr. Grayson, and spectres, and schoolmasters, and painted nymphs, and running away to sea, and curios, and dead silence, and his early childhood. And though, since then, other enigmas had engaged his attention, this purely automatic and tiresome activity of mind still persisted.

On his oath he had been in some respects and in secret rather a goody-goody little boy; though his piety had been rather the off-spring of fear than of love. Had he not been expelled from Mellish's almost solely for that reason? What on earth was the good of repeatedly thrashing a boy when you positively knew that he has lied merely from terror of your roaring voice and horrible white face?

But there it was; if there had been someone to talk to, he would not have talked so much to himself. He would not have lain awake thinking, night after night, like a rat in a trap. Thinking was like a fountain. Once it gets going at a certain pressure, well, it is almost impossible to turn it off. And, my hat! what odd things come up with the water!

On the particular night in question, in spite of the candles and the mice and the moon, he badly wanted company. In a moment of pining yet listless jocosity, then, he had merely taken his Aunt Charlotte's advice. True, the sumptuous crimson pleated silk bell-pull, dangling like a serpent with a huge tassel for skull over his Uncle Timothy's pillow, was a more formidable instrument than the yard or two of frayed green cord in the attic. Yet they shared the same purpose. Many a time must his Uncle Timothy have stretched up a large loose hand in that direction when in need of Soames's nocturnal ministrations. And now, alas, both master and man were long since gone the way of all flesh. You couldn't, it appeared, pull bells in your coffin.

But Jimmie was not as yet in his coffin, and as soon as his fingers slipped down from the smooth pull, the problem, in the abstract, as it were, began to fascinate him. With cold froggy hands crossed over his beautiful puce-patterned pyjamas, he lay staring at the crimson tassel till he had actually seen the hidden fangs flickeringly jet out at him.

The effort, then, must have needed some little courage. It *might* almost have needed a tinge of inspiration. It was in no sense intended as a challenge. He would, in fact, rather remain alone than chance summoning—well, any (once animate) relic of the distant past. But obviously the most practical way of proving—if only to yourself—that you can be content with your own reconnaissances in the very dead of night, was to demonstrate to that self that, even if you should ask for it, assistance would not be forthcoming.

He had been as fantastic as that. At the prolonged, pulsating, faint, distant tintinnabulation he had fallen back on to his pillow with an absurd little quicket of laughter, like that of a naughty boy up to mischief. But instant sobriety followed. Poor sleepers should endeavour to compose themselves. Tampering with empty space, stirring up echoes in pitch-black pits of darkness is scarcely sedative. And then, as he lay striving with extraordinary fervour not to listen, but to concentrate his mind on the wardrobe, and to keep his eyes from the door, that door must gently have opened.

It must have opened, and as noiselessly closed again. For a more or less decent-looking young man, seemingly not a day older than himself was now apparent in the room. It might almost be said that he had insinuated himself into the room. But well-trained domestics are accustomed to move their limbs and bodies with a becoming unobtrusiveness. There was also that familiar slight inclination of the apologetic in this young man's pose, as he stood there solitary in his black, in that terrific blaze of candle light. And for a sheer solid minute the occupant of the Arabian bed had really stopped thinking.

When indeed you positively press your face, so to speak, against the crystalline window of your eyes, your mind is apt to become a perfect vacuum. And Jimmie's first rapid and instinctive "Who the devil. . . ?" had remained inaudible.

In the course of the next few days Jimmie was to become familiar (at least in memory) with the looks of this new young butler or valet. But first impressions are usually the vividest. The dark blue-grey eyes, the high nose, the scarcely perceptible smile, the slight stoop of the shoulders—there was no doubt of it. There was just a flavour, a flicker, there, of resemblance to himself. Not that he himself could ever have cut as respectful and respectable a figure as that. And the smile!—the fellow seemed to be ruminating over a thousand dubious, long-interred secrets, secrets such as one may be a little cautious of digging up even to share with one's self.

His face turned sidelong on his pillow, and through air as visibly transparent as a sheet of glass, Jimmie had steadily regarded this strange bell-answerer; and the bell-answerer had never so much as stirred his frigid glittering eyes in response. The silence that hung between them produced eventually a peculiar effect on Jimmie. Menials as a general rule should be less emphatic personally. Their unobtrusiveness should surely not emphasise their immanence. It had been Jimmie who was the first to withdraw his eyes, only once more to find them settling as if spellbound on those of his visitor.

Yet, after all, there was nothing to take offence at in the young man's countenance or attitude. He did not seem even to be thinking back at the bell-puller; but merely to be awaiting instructions. Yet Jimmie's heart at once rapidly began to beat again beneath his icy hands. And at last he made a perfectly idiotic response.

Wagging his head on his pillow, he turned abruptly away. "It was only to tell you that I shall need nothing more to-night," he had said.

Good Heavens! The fatuity of it! He wanted, thirsted for, scores upon scores of things. Aladdin's was the cupidity of a simpleton by comparison. Time, and the past, for instance, and the ability to breathe again as easily as if it were natural—as natural as the processes of digestion. Why, if you were intent only on a little innocent companionship, one or two of those nymphs up there would be far more amusing company than Mrs. Thripps. If, that is, apart from yearning to their harps and viols, they could have been persuaded to scrub and sweep. Jimmie wanted no other kind of help. There is a beauty that is but skin-deep.

Altogether it had been a far from satisfactory experience. Jimmie was nettled. His mincing tones echoed on in his mind. They must have suggested that he was unaccustomed to men servants and bell-pulls and opulent surroundings. And the fellow had instantly taken him at his word. A solemn little rather agreeable and unservile inclination of the not unfriendly head—and he was gone.

And there was Jimmie, absolutely exhausted, coughing his lungs out, and entirely incapable of concluding whether the new butler was a creature of actuality or of dream. Well, well, well: that was nothing new. That's just how things do take one in one's weak moments, in the dead of night. Nevertheless, the experience had apparently proved sedative. He had slept like an infant.

The morning found him vivacious with curiosity. He had paused to make only an exceedingly negligent toilet before beginning his usual wanderings about the house. Calm cold daylight reflection may dismiss almost any nocturnal experience as a dream, if, at any rate, one's temperature in the night hours is habitually above the norm. But Jimmie could not, or would not, absolutely make up his mind. So clear a picture had his visitant imprinted on his memory that he even found himself (just like a specialist sounding a patient in search of the secret ravages of phthisis)—he had even found himself stealthily tapping over the basement walls—as if in search of a concealed pantry! A foolish proceeding if one has not the least desire in the world to attract the attention of one's neighbours.

Having at length satisfied himself in a rather confused fashion that whatever understudy of Soames might share the house with him in the small hours, he must be a butler of the migratory order. Jimmie then began experimenting with the bells. Mounted on a kitchen chair, cornice brush in hand, he had been surprised by Mrs. Thripps, in her quiet boots, as he stood gently knocking one by one the full eighteen of the long greened crooked jingle row which hung open-mouthed above the immense dresser.

She had caught him in the act, and Jimmie had once more exercised his customary glib presence of mind.

"They ought to be hung in a scale, you know. Oughtn't they, Mrs. Thripps? Then we could have 'Home, sweet Home!' and a hunting up and a hunting down, grandsires and treble bobs, and a grand maximus, even on week days. And if we were in danger of any kind of fire—which *you* will never be, we could ring them backwards. *Couldn't* we, Mrs.

Thripps? Not that there's much quality in them—no medieval monkish tone or timbre in *them*. They're a bit mouldy, too, and one can't tell t'other from which. Not like St. Faiths's! One would recognise that old danker in one's shroud, wouldn't one, Mrs. Thripps? Has it ever occurred to you that the first campanologist's real intention was not so much to call the congregation, as to summon—well—what the congregation's after?"

"Yes, sir," Mrs. Thripps had agreed, her watery grey eyes fixed largely on the elevated young man. "But it don't matter which of them you ring; I'll answer *hany*—at least while I'm in the house. I don't think, sir, you rest your mind enough. My own boy, now: *he's* in the Navy. . . ."

But with one graceful flourish Jimmie had run his long-handled brush clean East to West along the clanging row. "You mustn't," he shouted, "you shouldn't. Once aboard the lugger, they are free! It's you *mothers*. . . ." He gently shook his peculiar wand at the flat-looking little old woman. "No, Mrs. Thripps; what I'm after is he who is here, *here! couchant, perdu, laired*, in these same subterranean vaults when you and I are snug in our nightcaps. A most nice- spoken young man! *Not* in the Navy, Mrs. Thripps!"

And before the old lady had had time to seize any one of these seductive threads of conversation, Jimmie had flashed his usual brilliant smile or grimace at her, and soon afterwards sallied out of the house to purchase a further gross or two of candles.

Gently and furtively pushing across the counter half a sovereign— not as a douceur, but merely as from friend to friend—he had similarly smiled back at the secretive-looking old assistant in the staid West End family-grocer's.

"No, I didn't suppose you *could* remember me. One alters. One ages. One deals elsewhere. But anyhow, a Happy New Year to you—if the next ever comes, you know."

"You see, sir," the straight-aproned old man had retorted with equal confidentiality, "it is not so much the alterations. They are what you might call un-cir-cum-ventible, sir. It's the stream, sir. Behind the counter here, we are like rocks in it. But even if I can't for the moment put a thought to your face—though it's already stirring in me in a manner of speaking, I shall in the future, sir. You may rely upon that. And the same, sir, to you; and many *of* them, I'm sure."

Somehow or other Jimmie's vanity had been mollified by this pleasing little ceremoniousness; and that even before he had smiled yet once again at the saffron young lady in the Pay Box.

"The truth is, my dear," he had assured himself, as he once more ascended into the dingy porch, "the truth is when once you begin to tamper, you won't know where you are. You won't, really."

And that night he had lain soberly on, in a peculiar state of physical quiescence and self-satisfaction, his dark bright eyes wandering from nymph to nymph, his hands folded over his breast under the bedclothes, his heart persisting in its usual habits. Nevertheless, the fountain of his thoughts had continued softly to plash on in its worn basin. With ears a-cock, he had frankly enjoyed inhaling the parched, spent, brilliant air.

And when his fingers had at last manifested the faintest possible itch to experiment once more with the bell-pull, he had slipped out of bed, and hastily searching through a little privy case of his uncle's bedside books, had presently slipped back again, armed with a fat little copy of *The Mysteries of Paris*, in its original French.

The next day a horrible lassitude descended upon him. For the better part of an hour he had stood staring out of the drawing-room window into the London street. At last, with a yawn that was almost a groan, and with an absurdly disproportionate effort, he turned himself about. Heavily hung the gilded chandeliers in the long vista of the room; heavily gloomed the gilded furniture. Scarcely distinguishable in the obscurity of the further wall stood watching him from a mirror what might have appeared to be the shadowy reflection of himself. With a still, yet extreme aversion he kept his eyes fixed on this distant nonentity, hardly realising his own fantastic resolve that if he did catch the least faint independent movement there, he would give Soames Junior a caustic piece of his mind. . . .

He must have been abominably fast asleep for hours when, a night or two afterwards, he had suddenly awakened, sweat streaming along his body, his mouth stretched to a long narrow O, and his right hand clutching the bell-rope, as might a drowning man at a straw.

The room was adrowse with light. All was still. The flitting horrors between dream and wake in his mind were already thinning into air. Through their transparency he looked out once more on the substantial, the familiar. His breath came heavily, like puffs of wind over a stormy sea, and yet a profound peace and tranquillity was swathing him in. The relaxed mouth was now faintly smiling. Not a sound, not the feeblest distant unintended tinkling was trembling up from the abyss. And for a moment or two the young man refrained even from turning his head at the soundless opening and closing of the door.

He lay fully conscious that he was not alone; that quiet eyes had him steadily in regard. But, like rats, his wits were beginning to busy themselves again. Sheer relief from the terrors of sleep, shame of his extremity and weakness, a festering sense of humiliation—yes, he must save his face at all costs. He must put this preposterous spying valet in his place. Oddly enough, too, out of the deeps a peculiar little vision of recollection had inexplicably obtruded itself into consciousness. It would be a witticism of the first water.

"They are dreadfully out of season, you know," he began murmuring affectedly into the hush, "dreadfully. But what I'm really pining for is a bunch of primroses. . . . A primrose by the river's brim . . . *must* be a little conservative." His voice was once more trailing off into a maudlin drowsiness. With an effort he roused himself, and now with an extremely sharp twist of his head, he turned to confront his visitor.

But the room was already vacant, the door ajar, and Jimmie's lids were on the point of closing again, sliding down over his tired eyes like leaden shutters which no power on earth could hinder or restrain, when at the faintest far whisper of sound they swept back suddenly— and almost incredibly wide—to drink in all they could of the spectacle of a small odd-looking child who at that moment had embodied herself in the doorway.

She seemed to have not the least intention of returning the compliment. Her whole gaze, from out of her fair flaxen-pigtailed face, was fixed on the coarse blue-banded kitchen bowl which she was carrying with extreme care and caution in her two narrow hands. The idiots down below had evidently filled it too full of water, for the pale wide-petalled flowers and thick crinkled leaves it contained were floating buoyantly nid-nod to and fro as she moved—pushing on each slippered foot in turn in front of the other, her whole mind concentrated on her task.

A plain child, but extraordinarily fair, as fair as the primroses themselves in the congregation of candlelight that motionlessly flooded the room—a narrow-chested long-chinned little creature who had evidently outgrown her strength. Jimmie was well accustomed to take things as they come; and his brief sojourn in his uncle's house in his present state of health had already enlarged the confines of the term "things." Anyhow, she was a relief from the valet.

He found himself, then, watching this new visitor without the least trace of astonishment or even of surprise. And as his dark eyes coursed over the child, he simply couldn't decide whether she most closely "took after" Soames Junior or Mrs. Thripps. All he could positively assure himself of was just the look, "the family likeness." And that in itself was a queerish coincidence, since whatever your views might be regarding Soames Junior, Mrs. Thripps was real enough—as real, at any rate, as her scrubbing-brush and her wholesome evil-smelling soap.

As a matter of fact, Jimmie was taking a very tight hold of himself. His mind might fancifully be compared to a quiet green swarming valley between steep rock-bound hills in which a violent battle was proceeding—standards and horsemen and smoke and terror and violence—but no sound.

Deep down somewhere he really wanted to be "nice" to the child. She meant no ill; she was a demure far-away harmless-looking creature. Ages ago . . . On the other hand he wished to heaven they would leave him alone. They were pestering him. He knew perfectly well how far he was gone, and bitterly resented this renewed interference. And if there was one thing he detested, it was being made to look silly—"I hope you are trying to be a good little boy? . . . You have not been talking to the servants?" That kind of thing.

It was, therefore, with mixed feelings and with a tinge of shame-facedness that he heard his own sneering toneless voice insinuate itself into the silence; "And what, missikins, can I do for you? . . . *What*, you will understand; not *How*?" The sneer had degenerated into a snarl.

The child at this had not perceptibly faltered. Her face had seemed to lengthen a little, but that might have been due solely to her efforts to deliver her bowl without spilling its contents. Indeed she actually succeeded in so doing, almost before Jimmie had time to withdraw abruptly from the little gilt-railed table on which she deposited the clumsy pot. Frock, pigtail, red hands—she seemed to be as "real" a fellow creature as you might wish to see. But Jimmie stared quizzically on. Unfortunately primroses have no scent, so that he could not call on his nose to bear witness to his eyes. And the congested conflict in the green valley was still proceeding.

The child had paused. Her hands hung down now as if they were accustomed to service; and her pale blue eyes were fixed on his face in that exasperating manner which suggests that the owner of them is otherwise engaged. Not that she was looking *through him*. Even the sharpest of his "female friends" had never been able to boast of that little accomplishment. She was looking into him; and as if he occupied time rather than space. Or was she, sneered that weary inward voice again, was she merely waiting for a tip?

"Look here," said Jimmie, dexterously raising himself to his elbow on the immense lace-fringed pillow, "it's all very well; you have managed things quite admirably, considering your age and the season, and so on. But I didn't ask for primroses, I asked for violets. That's very old trick—very old trick."

For one further instant, dark and fair, crafty and simpleton face communed, each with each. But the smile on the one had fainted into a profound childlike contemplation. And then, so swift and imperceptible had been his visitant's envanishment out of the room, that the very space she had occupied seemed to remain for a while outlined in the air—a nebulous shell of vacancy. She must, apparently, have glided *backwards* through the doorway, for Jimmie had assuredly not been conscious of the remotest glimpse of her pigtail from behind.

Instantly on that, the stony hillside within had resounded with a furious clangour—cries and shouts and screamings—and Jimmie, his face bloodless with rage, his eyes almost blind with it, had leapt out of the great bed as if in murderous pursuit. There must, however, have been an unusual degree or so of fever in his veins that night so swift was his reaction. For the moment he was on his feet an almost unendurable self-pity had swept into possession of him. To take a poor devil as literally as that! To catch him off his guard; not to give him the mere fleck of an opportunity to get his balance, to explain, to answer back! Curse the primroses.

But there was no time to lose.

With one hand clutching his pyjamas, the other carrying the bowl, he poked forward out of the flare of the room into the cold lightlessness of the wide stone staircase.

"Look here," he called down in a low argumentative voice, "look here. You! You can cheat and you can cheat, but to half strangle a fellow in his sleep, and then send him up the snuffling caretaker's daughter— No, No. . . . Next time, you old makebelieve, we'd prefer company a little more—a little more *congenial*."

He swayed slightly, grimacing vacantly into the darkness, and listening to his speech as dimly as might a somnambulist to the distant roar of falling water. And then, poor benighted creature, Jimmie tried to spit, but his lips and tongue were dry, and that particular insult was spared him.

He had stooped laboriously, had put down the earthenware bowl on the Persian mat at the head of the staircase, and was self-congratulatorily re-welcoming himself into the scene of still lustre he had dared for that protracted minute to abandon, when he heard as if from beneath and behind him a kind of lolloping disquietude and the sound as of a clumsy-clawed, but persistent animal pushing its uncustomary awkward way up the soap-polished marble staircase.

It was to be tit for tat, then. The miserable ménage had let loose its menagerie. That. They were going to experiment with the mouse-cupboard-and-keyhole trickery of his childhood. Jimmie was violently shivering; his very toes were clinging to the mat on which he stood.

Swaying a little, and casting at the same time a strained whitened glance round the room in which every object rested in the light as if so it had rested from all eternity, he stood mutely and ghastly listening.

Even a large bedroom, five times the size of a small boy's attic, affords little scope for a fugitive, and shutting your eyes, darkening your outward face, is no escape. It had been a silly boast, he agreed—that challenge, that "dare" on the staircase; the boast of an idiot. For the "congenial company" that had now managed to hoof and scrabble its way up the slippery marble staircase was already on the threshold.

All was utterly silent now. There was no obvious manifestation of danger. What was peering steadily in upon him out of the obscurity beyond the door, was merely a blurred whitish beast-like shape with still, passive, almost stagnant eyes in its immense fixed face. A perfectly ludicrous object—on paper. Yet a creature so nauseous to soul and body, and with so obscene a greed in its motionless pig-like grin that with one vertiginous swirl Jimmie's candles had swept up in his hand like a lateral race of streaming planets into outer darkness.

If his wet groping fingers had not then encountered one of the carved pedestals of his uncle's bedstead, Jimmie would have fallen; Jimmie would have found in fact, the thing's physical level.

Try as he might, he had never in the days that followed made quite clear in his mind why for the third time he had not made a desperate plunging clutch at the bell rope. The thing *must* have been Soames Junior's emissary, even if the bird-faced scullery maid with the primroses had not also been one of the "staff."

That he had desisted simply in case she should herself have answered his summons and so have encountered the spurious animal as she mounted the dark staircase seemed literally too "good" to be true. Not only was Jimmie no sentimentalist, but that particular kind of goodness, even in a state of mind perfectly calm and collected, was not one of his pleasanter characteristics.

Yet facts are facts—even comforting ones. And unless his memory was utterly untrustworthy, he had somehow—somehow contrived to regain his physical balance. Candelabrum in hand, he had actually, indeed, at last emerged from the room, and stooped his dark head over the balusters in search of what unaccountably had not awaited his nearer acquaintance. And he had—he must have—flung the substantial little blue-banded slop-basin, primroses and all, clean straight down in the direction of any kind of sentient target that happened to be in its way.

"You must understand, Mrs. Thripps," he had afterwards solemnly explained, "I don't care to be disturbed, and particularly at night. All litter should, of course, be immediately cleared away. That's merely as things go in a well-regulated household, as, in fact, they *do* go. And I see you have replaced the one or two little specimens I was looking over out of the cabinet on the staircase. Pretty things, too; though you hadn't the advantage of being in the service of their late owner—my uncle. As *I* was. Of course, too, breakages cannot be avoided. There, I assure you, you are absolutely free. Moth and rust, Mrs. Thripps. No; all that I was merely enquiring about at the moment is that particular pot. There was an accident last night—primroses and so on. And one might have expected, one might almost have sworn, Mrs. Thripps, that at least a shard or two, as the Psalmist says, would have been pretty conspicuous even if the water *had* completely dried away. Not that I heard the smash, mind. I don't go so far as that. Nor am I making any insinuations *whatever*. You are the best of good creatures, you are indeed—and it's no good looking at me like Patience on a monument; because at present life is real and life is earnest. All I mean is that if one for a single moment ceases to guide one's conduct on reasonable lines—well, one comes a perfectly indescribable cropper, Mrs. Thripps. Like the pot."

Mrs. Thripps's grey untidy head had remained oddly stuck out from her body throughout this harangue. "No, sir," she repeated once more. "High and low I've searched the house down, and there isn't a shadder of what you might be referring to, not a shadder. And once more, I ask you, sir; let me call in Dr. Stokes. He's a very nice gentleman; and one as keeps what should be kept as close to himself as it being his duty he sees right and proper to do. Chasing and racketing of yourself up and down these runs of naked stairs—in the dead of night—is no proper place for you, sir, in *your* state. And I don't like to take the responsibility. It's first the candles, then the bells, and then the kitching, and then the bason; I know what I'm talking about, sir, having lost two, and one at sea."

"And suppose, my dear," Jimmie had almost as brilliantly as ever smiled; "suppose we are all of us 'at sea.' What then?"

"Why then, sir," Mrs. Thripps had courageously retorted, "I'd as lief be at the bottom of it. There's been as much worry and trouble and making two ends meet in my life not to make the getting out of it what you'd stand on no ceremony for. I say it with all decent respect for what's respectful and proper, sir; but there isn't a morning I step down those area steps but my heart's in my mouth for fear there won't be anything in the house but what can't answer back. It's been a struggle to keep on, sir; and you as generous a gentleman as need be, if only you'd remain warm and natural in your bed when once there."

A little inward trickle of laughter had entertained Jimmie as he watched the shapeless patient old mouth utter these last few words.

"That's just it, Mrs. Thripps," he had replied softly. "You've done for me far more effectively than anyone I care to remember in my insignificant little lifetime. You have indeed." Jimmie had even touched the hand bent like the claw of a bird around the broom-handle. "In fact, you know—and I'm bound to confess it as gratefully as need be—they are all of them doing for me as fast as they can. I don't complain, not the least little bit in the world. All that I might be asking is, How the devil—to put it politely—how the goodness gracious is one to tell which is which? In my particular case, it seems to be the miller that sets the wind: not, of course, that he's got any particular grain to grind. Not even wild oats, you funny old mother of a youthful mariner. No, no, no. Even the fact that there wasn't perhaps any pot after all, you will understand, doesn't positively prove that neither could there have been any primroses. And before next January's four months old we shall be at the end of yet another April. At least"—and a sort of almost bluish pallor had spread like a shadow over his face—"at least you will be. All of which is only to say, dear Madam, as Beaconsfield remarked to Old Vic., that I am thanking you *now*."

At which Mrs. Thripps immediately fell upon her knees on her housemaid's pad and plunged her hands into her zinc pail—only instantly after to sit back on her heels, skinny hands on canvas apron. "All I says, sir, is. We go as we go; and a nicer gentleman, taking things on the surface, I never worked for. But one don't want to move too much in the Public Heye, sir. Of all the houses below stairs I've worked for and all alone in I don't want to charnst on a more private in a manner of speaking than this. All that I was saying, sir, and I wouldn't to none but you, is the life's getting on my nerves. When that door there closes after me, and every day drawing out steady as you can see without so much as glancing at the clock—I say, to myself, Well, better that pore young gentleman alone up there at night, cough and all, than *me*. I wouldn't sleep in this house, sir, not if you was to offer me a plateful of sovereigns . . . Unless, sir, you *wanted* me."

On reflection Jimmie decided that he had cut almost a gallant figure as he had retorted gaily—yet with extraordinary sobriety:—"You shall have a whole dishful before I'm done, Mrs. Thripps—with a big scoop in it for the gravy. But on my oath, I assure you there's absolutely nothing or nobody in this old barn of a museum except you and me. Nobody, unless, of course, you will understand, one happens to pull the bell. And that we're not likely to do in broad daylight. Are we, Mrs. Thripps?" Upon which he had hastily caught up his aunt's handbag and had emerged into a daylight a good deal bleaker if not broader than he could gratefully stomach.

For a while Jimmie had let well alone. Indeed, if it had been a mere matter of choice, he would far rather have engaged in a friendly and jocular conversation of this description with his old charwoman than in the endless monologues in which he found himself submerged on other occasions. One later afternoon, for instance, at half-past three by his watch, sitting there by a small fire in the large muffled drawing room, he at length came definitely to the conclusion that some kind of finality should be reached in his relations with the Night Staff in his Uncle Timothy's.

It was pretty certain that *his* visit would soon be drawing to a close. Staying out at night until he was almost too exhausted to climb down to the pavement from his hansom—the first April silver of dawn wanning the stark and empty chimney-pots—had proved a dull and tedious alternative. The mere spectator of gaiety, he concluded, as he stared at the immense picture of the Colosseum on his Uncle Timothy's wall, may have as boring a time as must the slaves who cleaned out the cages of the lions that ate the Christians. And snapping out insults at former old cronies who couldn't help their faces being as tiresome as a whitewashed pigsty had soon grown wearisome.

Jimmie, of course, was accustomed to taking no interest in things which did not interest him; but quite respectable people could manage that equally well. What fretted him almost beyond endurance was an increasing inability to keep his attention fixed on what was really *there*, what at least all such respectable people, one might suppose, would unanimously agree was there.

A moment's fixture of the eyes—and he would find himself steadily, steadily listening, now in a creeping dread that somewhere, down below, there was a good deal that needed an almost constant attention, and now in sudden alarm that, after all, there was absolutely nothing. Again and again in recollection he had hung over the unlighted staircase listening in an extremity of foreboding for the outbreak of a rabbit-like childish squeal of terror which would have proved—well, what *would* it have proved? My God, what a world! You can prove nothing.

The fact that he was all but certain that any such intolerably helpless squeal never had wailed up to him out of its pit of blackness could be only a partial consolation. He hadn't meant to be a beast. It was only his facetious little way. And you would have to be something pretty piggish in pigs to betray a child—however insubstantial—into the nausea and vertigo he had experienced in the presence of that unspeakable abortion. The whole thing had become a fatuous obsession. If, it appeared, you only remained solitary and secluded enough, and let your mind wander on in its own sweet way, the problem was almost bound to become, if not your one and only, at least your chief concern. Unless you were preternaturally busy and preoccupied, you simply couldn't live on and on in a haunted house without being occasionally reminded of its ghosts.

To dismiss the matter as pure illusion—the spectral picturing of life's fitful fever—might be all very well; that is if you had the blood of a fish. But who on earth had ever found the world the pleasanter and sweeter a place to bid good-bye to simply because it was obviously "substantial," whatever *that* might mean? Simply because it did nothing you wanted it to do unless you paid for it pretty handsomely; or unless you accepted what it proffered with as open a hospitality as Jimmie had bestowed on his pilgrims of the night. Not that he much wanted—however pressing the invitation—to wander off out of his body into a better world, or, for that matter, into a worse.

Upstairs under the roof years ago Jimmie as a small boy would rather have died of terror than meddle with the cord above his bed-rail—simply because he knew that Soames Senior was at the other end of it. He had hated Soames; he had merely feared the nothings of his night hours. But, suppose Soames had been a different kind of butler. There must be almost as many kinds as there are human beings. Suppose his Uncle Timothy and Aunt Charlotte had chosen theirs a little less idiosyncratically; what then?

Well, anyhow, in a sense, he was not sorry life had been a little exciting these last few weeks. How odd that what all but jellied your soul in your body at night or in a dream, might merely amuse you like a shilling shocker in the safety of day. The safety of day—at the very cadence of the words in his mind, as he sat there in his aunt's "salon," his limbs huddled over Mrs. Thripps's fire, Jimmie's eyes had fixed themselves again. Again he was listening. Was it that, if you saw "in your mind" *any* distant room of place, that place must actually at the moment contain you—some self, some "astral body?" If so, wouldn't, of course, you *hear* yourself moving about in it?

There was a slight whining wind in the street outside the rainy window that afternoon, and once more the bright idea crossed Jimmie's mind that he should steal upstairs before it was dark, mount up on to the Arabian bed and just cut the bell-pull—once for all. But would that necessarily dismiss the Staff? Necessarily? His eye wandered to the discreet S of yet another bell-pull—that which graced the wall beneath the expansive white marble chimney-piece.

He hesitated. There was no doubt his mind was now hopelessly jaundiced against all bell-ropes—whether they failed to summon one to church or persisted in summoning one to a six-foot hole in a cemetery. His Uncle Timothy lay in a Mausoleum. On the other hand he was properly convinced that a gentleman is as a gentleman does, and that it was really "up to you" to treat *all* bell-answerers with decent courtesy. No matter who, when, where. A universal rule like that is a sheer godsend.

If they didn't answer, well, you couldn't help yourself. Or rather, you would have to.

This shivering was merely physical. When a fellow is so thin that he can almost hear his ribs grid one against the other when he stoops to pick up a poker, such symptoms must be expected. There was still an hour or two of daylight—even though clouds admitted only a greyish light upon the world, and his Uncle Timothy's house was by nature friendly to gloom. That house at this moment seemed to hang domed upon his shoulders like an immense imponderable shell. The flames in the chimney whispered, fluttered, hovered, like fitfully-playing, once-happy birds.

Supposing if, even against his better judgment, he leaned forward now in his chair and—what was infinitely more conventional and in a sense more proper than summoning unforeseen entities to one's bedside—supposing he gave just one discreet little tug at that small porcelain knob; what would he ask for? He need ask nothing. He could act. Yes, if he could be perfectly sure that some monstrous porcine caco-demon akin to the shapes of childish nightmare would come hoofing up out of the deeps at his behest—well, he would chance it. He would have it out with the brute. It was still day.

It was still day. But, maybe, the ear of pleasanter visitors might catch the muffled tinkle? In the young man's mind there was now no vestige of jocularity. In an instant's lightness of heart he had once thought of purchasing from the stiff-aproned old assistant at his Aunt Charlotte's family grocer's, a thumping big box of chocolates. Why, just that one small bowl in *famille rose* up there could be bartered for the prettiest little necklet of seed pearls. She had done her best—with her skimpy shoulders, skimpier pigtail and soda-reddened hands. Pigtail! But no; you might pull real bells: to pull dubiously genuine pigtails seemed now a feeble jest. The old Jimmie of that kind of facetiousness was a thing of the past.

Apart from pigs and tweeny-maids, what other peculiar emanations might in the future respond to his summonings, Jimmie's exhausted imagination could only faintly prefigure. For a few minutes a modern St. Anthony sat there in solitude in the vast half-blinded London drawing-room; while shapes and images and apparitions of memory and fantasy sprang into thin being and passed away in his mind. No, no.

> Do to the Book; quench the candles;
> Ring the bell. *Amen, Amen.*

—he was done with all that. Maledictions and anathemas; they only tangled the hank.

So when at last—his meagre stooping body mutely played on by the flamelight—he jerked round his dark narrow head to glance at the distant mirror, it must have been on the mere after-image, so to speak, of the once quite substantial-looking tweeny-maid that his exhausted eyes thirstily fixed themselves.

She was there—over there, where Soames Junior had more than once taken up his obsequious station. She was smiling—if the dusk of the room could be trusted that far; and not through, but really *at* Jimmie. She was fairer than ever, fairer than the flaxenest of nymphs on his uncle's ceiling, fairer than the saffronest of young ladies in the respectablest of family grocers, fairer even then—

Jimmie hung on this simple vision as did Dives on the spectacle of Lazarus in bliss. At once, of course, after his very first sigh of relief and welcome, he had turned back on his lips a glib little speech suggesting forgiveness—Let auld acquaintance be forgot; that kind of thing. He was too tired even to be clever now. And the oddest of convictions had at once come into his mind—seemed almost to fill his body even—that she was waiting for something else. Yes, she was smiling as if in hope.

She was waiting to be told to go. Jimmie was no father. He didn't want to be considerate to the raw little creature, to cling to her company for but a few minutes longer, with a view to returns in kind. No, nothing of all that. "Oh, my God; my God!" a voice groaned within him, but not at any unprecedented jag or stab of pain.

The child was still waiting. Quite quietly there—as if a shadow, as if a secret and obscure ray of light. And it seemed to Jimmie that in its patient face hung veil upon veil of uncountable faces of the past—in paint, stone, actuality, dream—that he had glanced at or brooded on in the enormous history of his life. That he may have coveted, too. And as well as his rebellious features could and would, he smiled back at her.

"I understand, my dear," he drew back his dry lips to explain. "Perfectly. And it was courtesy itself of you to look in when I didn't ring. I *didn't*. I absolutely put my tongue out at the grinning old knob . . . But no more of that. One mustn't talk for talking's sake. Else, why all those old Trappists . . . though none of 'em such a bag-of-bones as me, I bet. But without jesting, you know. . . ."

Once more a distant voice within spoke in Jimmie's ear. "It's important"; it said. "You really must hold your tongue—until, well, it holds itself." But Jimmie's face continued to smile.

And then suddenly, every vestige of amusement abandoned it. He stared baldly almost emptily at the faint inmate of his solitude. "All that I have to say," he muttered, "is just this:—I have Mrs. Thripps. I haven't absolutely cut the wire. I wish to be alone. But *if* I ring, I'm not *asking*, do you see? In time I may be able to know what I want. But what is important now is that no more than that accursed Pig were your primroses 'real,' my dear. You see things *must* be real. And now, I suppose," he had begun shivering again, "you must go to—you must go. But listen! listen! we part friends!"

The coals in the grate, with a scarcely audible shuffling, recomposed themselves to their consuming.

When there hasn't been anything there, nothing can be said to have vanished from the place where it has not been. Still, Jimmie had felt infinitely colder and immeasurably lonelier when his mouth had thus fallen to silence; and he was so empty and completely exhausted that his one apprehension had been lest he should be unable to ascend the staircase to get to bed. There was no doubt of it: his ultimatum had been instantly effective. The whole house was now preternaturally empty. It was needless even to listen to prove that. So absolute was its pervasive quietude that when at last he gathered his bones together in the effort to rise, to judge from the withering colour of the cinders and ashes in the fireplace, he must have been for some hours asleep; and daybreak must be near.

He managed the feat at last, gathered up the tartan travelling shawl that had tented in his scarecrow knees, and lit the only candle in its crystal stick in his Aunt Charlotte's drawing-room. And it was an almost quixotically peaceful though forebodeful Jimmie who, step by step, the fountain of his thoughts completely stilled, his night-mind as clear and sparkling as a cavern bedangled with stalagmites and stalactites, climbed laboriously on and up, from wide shallow marble stair to stair.

He paused in the corridor above. But the nymphs within—Muses, Graces, Fates, what not—piped in vain their mute decoy. His Uncle Timothy's Arabian bed in vain summoned him to its downy embraces. At the wide-open door he brandished his guttering candle in a last smiling gesture of farewell: and held on.

That is why when, next morning, out of a sounding slanting shower of rain Mrs. Thripps admitted herself into the house at the area door, she found the young man, still in his clothes, lying very fast asleep indeed on the trucklebed in the attic. His hands were not only crossed but convulsively clenched in that position on his breast. And it appeared from certain distressing indications that he must have experienced a severe struggle to refrain from a wild blind tug at the looped-up length of knotted whipcord over his head.

As a matter of fact, it did not occur to the littered old charwoman's mind to speculate whether or not Jimmie had actually made such a last attempt. Or whether he had been content merely to wait on a Soames who might, perhaps, like all good servants, come when he was wanted rather than when he was called. All her own small knowledge of Soameses, though not without comfort, had been acquired at second-hand.

Nor did Mrs. Thripps waste time in surmising how Jimmie could ever have persuaded himself to loop up the cord like that out of his reach, unless he had first become abysmally ill-content with his small, primitive, and belated knowledge of campanology.

She merely looked at what was left of him; her old face almost comically transfixed in its appearance of pity, horror, astonishment, and curiosity.

THE TOWER

Barry Pain

In the billiard-room of the Cabinet Club, shortly after midnight, two men had just finished a game. A third had been watching it from the lounge at the end of the room. The winner put up his cue. slipped on his coat, and with a brief "Good-night" passed out of the room. He was tall, dark, clean-shaven and foreign in appearance. It would not have been easy to guess his nationality, but he did not look English.

The loser, a fair-haired boy of twenty-five, came over to the lounge and dropped down by the side of the elderly man who had been watching the billiards.

"Silly game, ain't it, doctor?" he said cheerfully. The doctor smiled.

"Yes," he said, "Vyse is a bit too hot for you, Bill."

"A bit too hot for anything," said the boy. "He never takes any trouble; he never hesitates; he never thinks; he never takes an easy shot when there's a brilliant one to be pulled off. It's almost uncanny."

"Ah," said the doctor, reflectively, "it's a queer thing. You're the third man whom I heard say that about Vyse within the last week."

"I believe he's quite alright—good sort of chap, you know. He's frightfully clever too—speaks a lot of beastly difficult Oriental languages—does well at any game he takes up."

"Yes," said the doctor, "he is clever; and he is also a fool."

"What do you mean? He's eccentric, of course. Fancy his buying that rotten tower—a sweet place to spend Christmas in all alone, I don't think."

"Why does he say he's going there?"

"Says he hates the conventional Christmas, and wants to be out of it; says also that he wants to shoot duck."

"That won't do," said the doctor. "He may hate the conventional Christmas. He may, and probably will, shoot duck. But that's not his reason for going there."

"Then what is it?" asked the boy.

"Nothing that would interest you much, Bill. Vyse is one of the chaps that want to know too much. He's playing about in a way that every medical man knows to be a rotten, dangerous way. Mind, he may get at something; if the stories are true he has already got at a good deal. I believe it is possible for a man to develop in himself certain powers at a certain price."

"What's the price?"

"Insanity, often as not. Here, let's talk about something pleasanter. Where are you yourself going this Christmas, by the way?"

"My sister has taken compassion upon this lone bachelor. And you?"

"I shall be out of England," said the doctor. "Cairo, probably."

The two men passed out into the hall of the club.

"Has Mr. Vyse gone yet?" the boy asked the porter.

"Not yet, Sir William. Mr. Vyse is changing in one of the dressing-rooms. His car is outside."

The two men passed the car in the street, and noticed the luggage in the tonneau. The driver, in his long leather coat, stood motionless beside it, waiting for his master. The powerful headlight raked the dusk of the street; you could see the paint on a tired woman's cheek as she passed through it on her way home at last.

"See his game?" said Bill.

"Of course," said the doctor. "He's off to the marshes and that blessed tower of his to-night."

"Well, I don't envy him—holy sort of amusement it must be driving all that way on a cold night like this. I wonder if the beggar ever goes to sleep at all?"

They had reached Bill's chambers in Jermyn Street.

"You must come in and have a drink," said Bill.

"Don't think so, thanks," said the doctor; "it's late, you know."

"You'd better," said Bill, and the doctor followed him in.

A letter and a telegram were lying on the table in the diminutive hall. The letter had been sent by messenger, and was addressed to Sir William Orsley, Bart., in a remarkably small hand-writing. Bill picked it up, and thrust it into his pocket at once, unopened. He took the telegram with him into the room where the drinks had been put out, and opened it as he sipped his whisky-and-soda.

"Great Scot!" he exclaimed.

"Nothing serious, I hope," said the doctor.

"I hope not. I suppose all the children have got to have the measles some time or another; but it's just a bit unlucky that my sister's three should all go down with it just now. That does for her house-party at Christmas, of course."

A few minutes later, when the doctor had gone, Bill took the letter from his pocket and tore it open. A cheque fell from the envelope and fluttered to the ground. The letter ran as follows:

DEAR BILL,—

I could not talk to you to-night, as the doctor, who happens to disapprove of me, was in the billiard-room. Of course, I can let you have the hundred you want, and enclose it herewith with the utmost pleasure. The time you mention for repayment would suit me all right, and so would any other time. Suit your own convenience entirely.

I have a favour to ask of you. I know you are intending to go down to the Leylands' for Christmas. I think you will be prevented from doing so. If that is the case, and you have no better engagement, would you hold yourself at my disposal for a week? It is just possible that I may want a man like you pretty badly. There ought to be plenty of duck this weather, but Ii don't know that I can offer any other attraction.

Very sincerely yours,
Edward Vyse

Bill picked up the cheque, and thrust it into the drawer with a feeling of relief. It was a queer invitation, he thought—funnily worded, with the usual intimations of time and place missing. He switched off the electric lights and went into his bedroom. As he was undressing a thought struck him suddenly.

"How the deuce," he said aloud, "did he know that I should be prevented from going to Polly's place?" Then he looked round quickly. He thought that he had heard a faint laugh just behind him. No one was there, and Bill's nerves were good enough. In twenty minutes he was fast asleep.

The cottage, built of grey stone, stood some thirty yards back from the road, from which it was screened by a shrubbery. It was an ordinary eight-roomed cottage, and it did well enough for Vyse and his servants and one guest—if Vyse happened to want a guest. There was a pleasant little walled garden of a couple of acres behind the cottage. Through a doorway in the further wall one passed into a stunted and dismal plantation, and in the middle of this rose the tower, far higher than any of the trees that surrounded it.

Sir William Orsley had arrived just in time to change before dinner. Talk at dinner had been of indifferent subjects—the queer characters of the village, and the chances of sport on the morrow. Bill had mentioned the tower, and his host had hastened to talk of other things. But now that dinner was over, and the man who had waited on them had left the room, Vyse of his own accord returned to the subject.

"Danvers is a superstitious ass," he observed, "and he's in quite enough of a funk about that tower as it is; That's why I wouldn't give you the whole story while he was in the room. According to the village tradition, a witch was burned on the site where the tower now stands, and she declared that where she burned the devil should have his house. The lord of the manor at that time, hearing what the old lady had said, and wishing to discourage house-building on that particular site, had it covered with a plantation, and made it a condition of his will that this plantation should be kept up."

Bill lit a cigar. "Looks like checkmate," he said. "However, seeing that the tower is actually there—"

"Quite so. This man's son came no end of a cropper, and the property changed hands several times. It was divided and sub-divided. I, for instance, only own about twenty acres of it. Presently there came along a scientific old gentleman and bought the piece that I now have. Whether he knew of the story, or whether he didn't, I cannot say, but he set to work to build the tower that is now standing in the middle of the plantation. He may have intended it as an observatory. He got the stone for it on the spot from his own quarry, but he had to import his labour, as the people in these parts didn't think the work healthy. Then one fine morning before the tower was finished they found the old gentleman at the bottom of his quarry with his neck broken."

"So," said Bill, "they say of course that the tower is haunted. What is it that they think they see?"

"Nothing. You can't see it. But there are people who think they have touched it and have heard it."

"Rot, ain't it?"

"I don't know exactly. You see, I happen to be one of those people."

"Then, if you think so, there's something in it. This is interesting. I say, can't we go across there now?"

"Certainly, if you like. Sure you won't have any more wine? Come along, then."

The two men slipped on their coats and caps. Vyse carried a lighted stable-lantern. It was a frosty moonlit night, and the path was crisp and hard beneath their feet. As Vyse slid back the bolts of the gate in the garden wall, Bill said suddenly, "By the way, Vyse, how did you know that I shouldn't be at the Leyland's this Christmas? I told you I was going there."

"I don't know. I had a feeling that you were going to be with me. It might have been wrong. Anyhow, I'm glad you're here. You are just exactly the man I want. We've only a few steps to go now. The path is ours. That cart-track leads away to the quarry where the scientific gentleman took the short cut to further knowledge. And here is the door of the tower."

They walked round the tower before entering. The night was so still that, unconsciously, they spoke in lowered voices and trod as softly as possible. The lock of the heavy door groaned and screeched as the key turned. The light of the lantern fell now on the white sand of the floor and on a broken spiral staircase on the further side. Far above one saw a tangle of beams and the stars beyond them. Bill heard Vyse saying that it was left like that after the death in the quarry.

"It's a good slid bit of masonry," said Bill, "but it ain't a cheerful spot exactly. And, by Jove! It smells like a menagerie."

"It does," said Vyse, who was examining the sand on the floor.

Bill also looked down at the prints in the sand. "Some dog's been in here."

"No," said Vyse, thoughtfully. "Dogs won't come in here, and you can't make them. Also, there were no marks on the sand when I left the place and locked the door this afternoon. Queer, isn't it?"

"But the thing's a blank impossibility. Unless, of course, we are to suppose that—"

He did not finish his sentence, and, if he had finished it, it would not have been audible. A chorus of grunting, growling and squealing broke out almost from under his feet, and he sprang backwards. It lasted for a few seconds, and then died slowly away.

"Did you hear that?" Vyse asked quietly.

"I should rather think so."

"Good; then it was not subjective. What was it?"

"Only one kind of beast makes that row. Pigs, of course—a whole drove of them. It sounded like they were in here, close to us. But as they obviously are not, they must be outside."

"But they are not outside," said Vyse. "Come and see."

They hunted the plantation through and through with no result, and then locked the tower door and went back to the cottage. Bill said very little. He was not capable of much self-analysis, but he was conscious of a sudden dislike of Vyse. He was angry that he had ever put himself under an obligation to this man. He had wanted the money for a gambling debt, and he had already repaid it. Now he saw Vyse in the light of a man from whom one should accept a kindness. The strange experience that he had just been through filled him with a loathing far more than with fear or wonder. There was something unclean and diabolical about the whole thing that made a decent man reluctant to question or investigate. The filthy smell of the brutes seemed still to linger in his nostrils. He was determined that on no account would he enter the tower again, and that as soon as he could find a decent excuse he would leave the place altogether.

A little later, as he sat before the log fire and filled his pipe, he turned to his host with a sudden question: "I say, Vyse, why did you want me to come down here? What's the meaning of it all?"

"My dear fellow," said Vyse, "I wanted you for the pleasure of your society. Now, don't get impatient. I also wanted you because you are the most normal man I know. Your confirmation of my experiences in the tower is most valuable to me. Also, you have good nerves, and, if you will forgive me for saying so, no imagination. I may want help that only a man with good nerves would be able to give."

"Why don't you leave that thing alone? It's too beastly."

Vyse laughed. "I'm afraid my hobby bores you. We won't talk about it. After all, there's no reason why you should help me?"

"Tell me just what it is you wanted."

"I wanted you if you heard this whistle"—he took an ordinary police whistle down from the mantelpiece—"any time tonight or to-morrow night, to come over to the tower at once and bring a revolver with you. The whistle would be a sign that I was in a tight place—that my life, in fact, was in danger. You see, we are dealing here with something pre-ternatural, but it is also something material; in addition to other risks, one risks ordinary physical destruction. However, I could see that you were repelled by the sight and sound of those beasts, whatever they may be; and I can tell you from my own experience that the touch of them is even worse. There is no reason why you should bother yourself any further about the thing."

"You can take the whistle with you," said Bill. "If I hear it I will come."

"Thanks," said Vyse, and immediately changed the subject. He did not say why he was spending the night in the tower, or what it was he proposed to do there.

It was three in the morning when Bill was suddenly startled out of his sleep. He heard the whistle being blow repeatedly. He hurried on some clothes and dashed down into the hall, where his lantern lay all ready for him. He ran along the garden path and through the door in the wall until he got to the tower. The sound of the whistle had ceased now, and everything was horribly still. The door of the tower stood wide open, and without hesitation Bill entered, holding his lantern high.

The tower was absolutely empty. Not a sound was to be heard. Bill called Vyse by name twice loudly, and then again the awful silence spread over the place.

Then, as if guided by some unseen hand, he took the track that led to the quarry, well knowing what he would find at the bottom of it.

The jury assigned the death of Vyse as an accident, and said that the quarry should be fenced in. They had no explanation to offer of the mutilation of the face, as if by the teeth of some savage beast.

LOST HEARTS

M. R. James

It was, as far as I can ascertain, in September of the year 1811 that a postchaise drew up before the door of Aswarby Hall, in the heart of Lincolnshire. The little boy who was the only passenger in the chaise, and who jumped out as soon as it had stopped, looked about him with the keenest curiosity during the short interval that elapsed between the ringing of the bell and the opening of the hall door. He saw a tall, square, red-brick house, built in the reign of Anne; a stone-pillared porch had been added in the purer classical style of 1790; the windows of the house were many, tall and narrow, with small panes and thick white woodwork. A pediment, pierced with a round window, crowned the front. There were wings to right and left, connected by curious glazed galleries, supported by colonnades, with the central block. These wings plainly contained the stables and offices of the house. Each was sur-mounted by an ornamental cupola with a gilded vane.

An evening light shone on the building, making the window-panes glow like so many fires. Away from the Hall in front stretched a flat park studded with oaks and fringed with firs, which stood out against the sky. The clock in the church-tower, buried in trees on the edge of the park, only its golden weather-cock catching the light, was striking six, and the sound came gently beating down the wind. It was altogether a pleasant impression, though tinged with the sort of melancholy appropriate to an evening in early autumn, that was conveyed to the mind of the boy who was standing in the porch waiting for the door to open to him.

He had just come from Warwickshire, where, some six months before, he had been left an orphan. Now, owing to the generous offer of his elderly cousin, Mr. Abney, he had come to live at Aswarby. The offer was unexpected, because all who knew anything of Mr. Abney looked upon him as a somewhat austere recluse, into whose steady-going household the advent of a small boy would import a new and, it seemed, incongruous element. The truth is that very little was known of Mr. Abney's pursuits or temper. The Professor of Greek at Cambridge had been heard to say that no one knew more of the religious beliefs of the later pagans than did the owner of Aswarby. Certainly his library contained all the then available books bearing on the Mysteries, the Orphic poems, the worship of Mithras, and the Neo-Platonists. In the marble-paved hall stood a fine group of Mithras slaying a bull, which had been imported from the Levant at great expense by the owner. He had contributed a description of it to the *Gentleman's Magazine*, and he had written a remarkable series of articles in the *Critical Museum* on the superstitions of the Romans of the Lower Empire. He was looked upon, in fine, as a man wrapped up in his books, and it was a matter of great surprise among his neighbours that he should ever have heard of his orphan cousin, Stephen Elliott, much more that he should have volunteered to make him an inmate of Aswarby Hall.

Whatever may have been expected by his neighbours, it is certain that Mr. Abney—the tall, the thin, the austere—seemed inclined to give his young cousin a kindly reception. The moment the front-door was opened he darted out of his study, rubbing his hands with delight.

"How are you, my boy?—how are you? How old are you?" said he—"that is, you are not too much tired, I hope, by your journey to eat your supper?"

"No, thank you, sir," said Master Elliott; "I am pretty well."

"That's a good lad," said Mr. Abney. "And how old are you, my boy?"

It seemed a little odd that he should have asked the question twice in the first two minutes of their acquaintance.

"I'm twelve years old next birthday, sir," said Stephen.

"And when is your birthday, my dear boy? Eleventh of September, eh? That's well—that's very well. Nearly a year hence, isn't it? I like—ha, ha!—I like to get these things down in my book. Sure it's twelve? Certain?"

"Yes, quite sure, sir."

"Well, well! Take him to Mrs. Bunch's room, Parkes, and let him have his tea—supper—whatever it is."

"Yes, sir," answered the staid Mr. Parkes; and conducted Stephen to the lower regions.

Mrs. Bunch was the most comfortable and human person whom Stephen had as yet met at Aswarby. She made him completely at home; they were great friends in a quarter of an hour: and great friends they remained. Mrs. Bunch had been born in the neighbourhood some fifty-five years before the date of Stephen's arrival, and her residence at the Hall was of twenty years' standing. Consequently, if anyone knew the ins and outs of the house and the district, Mrs. Bunch knew them; and she was by no means disinclined to communicate her information.

Certainly there were plenty of things about the Hall and the Hall gardens which Stephen, who was of an adventurous and inquiring turn, was anxious to have explained to him. "Who built the temple at the end of the laurel walk? Who was the old man whose picture hung on the staircase, sitting at a table, with a skull under his hand?" These and many similar points were cleared up by the resources of Mrs. Bunch's powerful intellect. There were others, however, of which the explanations furnished were less satisfactory.

One November evening Stephen was sitting by the fire in the house-keeper's room reflecting on his surroundings.

"Is Mr. Abney a good man, and will he go to heaven?" he suddenly asked, with the peculiar confidence which children possess in the ability of their elders to settle these questions, the decision of which is believed to be reserved for other tribunals.

"Good?—bless the child!" said Mrs. Bunch. "Master's as kind a soul as ever I see! Didn't I never tell you of the little boy as he took in out of the street, as you may say, this seven years back? and the little girl, two years after I first come here?"

"No. Do tell me all about them, Mrs. Bunch—now, this minute!"

"Well," said Mrs. Bunch, "the little girl I don't seem to recollect so much about. I know master brought her back with him from his walk one day, and give orders to Mrs. Ellis, as was housekeeper then, as she should be took every care with. And the pore child hadn't no one belonging to her—she told me so her own self—and here she lived with us a matter of three weeks it might be; and then, whether she were somethink of a gipsy in her blood or what not, but one morning she out of her bed afore any of us had opened a eye, and neither track nor yet trace of her have I set eyes on since. Master was wonderful put about, and had all the ponds dragged; but it's my belief she was had away by them gipsies, for there was singing round the house for as much as an hour the night she went, and Parkes, he declare as he heard them a-calling in the woods all that afternoon. Dear, dear! a hodd child she was, so silent in her ways and all, but I was wonderful taken up with her, so domesticated she was—surprising."

"And what about the little boy?" said Stephen.

"Ah, that pore boy!" sighed Mrs. Bunch. "He were a foreigner—Jevanny he called hisself—and he come a-tweaking his 'urdy-gurdy round and about the drive one winter day, and master 'ad him in that minute, and ast all about where he came from, and how old he was, and how he made his way, and where was his relatives, and all as kind as heart could wish. But it went the same way with him. They're a hunruly lot, them foreign nations, I do suppose, and he was off one fine morning just the same as the girl. Why he went and what he done was our question for as much as a year after; for he never took his 'urdy-gurdy, and there it lays on the shelf."

The remainder of the evening was spent by Stephen in miscellaneous cross-examination of Mrs. Bunch and in efforts to extract a tune from the hurdy-gurdy.

That night he had a curious dream. At the end of the passage at the top of the house, in which his bedroom was situated, there was an old disused bathroom. It was kept locked, but the upper half of the door was glazed, and, since the muslin curtains which used to hang there had long been gone, you could look in and see the lead-lined bath affixed to the wall on the right hand, with its head towards the window.

On the night of which I am speaking, Stephen Elliott found himself, as he thought, looking through the glazed door. The moon was shining through the window, and he was gazing at a figure which lay in the bath.

His description of what he saw reminds me of what I once beheld myself in the famous vaults of St. Michan's Church in Dublin, which possesses the horrid property of preserving corpses from decay for centuries. A figure inexpressibly thin and pathetic, of a dusty leaden colour, enveloped in a shroud-like garment, the thin lips crooked into a faint and dreadful smile, the hands pressed tightly over the region of the heart.

As he looked upon it, a distant, almost inaudible moan seemed to issue from its lips, and the arms began to stir. The terror of the sight forced Stephen backwards and he awoke to the fact that he was indeed standing on the cold boarded floor of the passage in the full light of the moon. With a courage which I do not think can be common among boys of his age, he went to the door of the bathroom to ascertain if the figure of his dreams were really there. It was not, and he went back to bed.

Mrs. Bunch was much impressed next morning by his story, and went so far as to replace the muslin curtain over the glazed door of the bathroom. Mr. Abney, moreover, to whom he confided his experiences at breakfast, was greatly interested and made notes of the matter in what he called "his book."

The spring equinox was approaching, as Mr. Abney frequently reminded his cousin, adding that this had been always considered by the ancients to be a critical time for the young: that Stephen would do well to take care of himself, and to shut his bedroom window at night; and that Censorinus had some valuable remarks on the subject. Two incidents that occurred about this time made an impression upon Stephen's mind.

The first was after an unusually uneasy and oppressed night that he had passed—though he could not recall any particular dream that he had had.

The following evening Mrs. Bunch was occupying herself in mending his nightgown.

"Gracious me, Master Stephen!" she broke forth rather irritably, "how do you manage to tear your nightdress all to flinders this way? Look here, sir, what trouble you do give to poor servants that have to darn and mend after you!"

There was indeed a most destructive and apparently wanton series of slits or scorings in the garment, which would undoubtedly require a skilful needle to make good. They were confined to the left side of the chest—long, parallel slits about six inches in length, some of them not quite piercing the texture of the linen. Stephen could only express his entire ignorance of their origin: he was sure they were not there the night before.

"But," he said, "Mrs. Bunch, they are just the same as the scratches on the outside of my bedroom door: and I'm sure I never had anything to do with making *them*."

Mrs. Bunch gazed at him open-mouthed, then snatched up a candle, departed hastily from the room, and was heard making her way upstairs. In a few minutes she came down.

"Well," she said, "Master Stephen, it's a funny thing to me how them marks and scratches can 'a' come there—too high up for any cat or dog to 'ave made 'em, much less a rat: for all the world like a Chinaman's finger-nails, as my uncle in the tea-trade used to tell us of when we was girls together. I wouldn't say nothing to master, not if I was you, Master Stephen, my dear; and just turn the key of the door when you go to your bed."

"I always do, Mrs. Bunch, as soon as I've said my prayers."

"Ah, that's a good child: always say your prayers, and then no one can't hurt you."

Herewith Mrs. Bunch addressed herself to mending the injured nightgown, with intervals of meditation, until bed-time. This was on a Friday night in March, 1812.

On the following evening the usual duet of Stephen and Mrs. Bunch was augmented by the sudden arrival of Mr. Parkes, the butler, who as a rule kept himself rather *to* himself in his own pantry. He did not see that Stephen was there: he was, moreover, flustered and less slow of speech than was his wont.

"Master may get up his own wine, if he likes, of an evening," was his first remark. "Either I do it in the daytime or not at all, Mrs. Bunch. I don't know what it may be: very like it's the rats, or the wind got into the cellars; but I'm not so young as I was, and I can't go through with it as I have done."

"Well, Mr. Parkes, you know it is a surprising place for the rats, is the Hall."

"I'm not denying that, Mrs. Bunch; and, to be sure, many a time I've heard the tale from the men in the shipyards about the rat that could speak. I never laid no confidence in that before; but to-night, if I'd demeaned myself to lay my ear to the door of the further bin, I could pretty much have heard what they was saying."

"Oh, there, Mr. Parkes, I've no patience with your fancies! Rats talking in the wine-cellar indeed!"

"Well, Mrs. Bunch, I've no wish to argue with you: all I say is, if you choose to go to the far bin, and lay your ear to the door, you may prove my words this minute."

"What nonsense you do talk, Mr. Parkes—not fit for children to listen to! Why, you'll be frightening Master Stephen there out of his wits."

"What! Master Stephen?" said Parkes, awaking to the consciousness of the boy's presence. "Master Stephen knows well enough when I'm a-playing a joke with you, Mrs. Bunch."

In fact, Master Stephen knew much too well to suppose that Mr. Parkes had in the first instance intended a joke. He was interested, not altogether pleasantly, in the situation; but all his questions were unsuccessful in inducing the butler to give any more detailed account of his experiences in the wine-cellar.

We have now arrived at March 24, 1812. It was a day of curious experiences for Stephen: a windy, noisy day, which filled the house and the gardens with a restless impression. As Stephen stood by the fence of the grounds, and looked out into the park, he felt as if an endless procession of unseen people were sweeping past him on the wind, borne on resistlessly and aimlessly, vainly striving to stop themselves, to catch at something that might arrest their flight and bring them once again into contact with the living world of which they had formed a part. After luncheon that day Mr. Abney said:

"Stephen, my boy, do you think you could manage to come to me to-night as late as eleven o'clock in my study? I shall be busy until that time, and I wish to show you something connected with your future life which it is most important that you should know. You are not to mention this matter to Mrs. Bunch nor to anyone else in the house; and you had better go to your room at the usual time."

Here was a new excitement added to life: Stephen eagerly grasped at the opportunity of sitting up till eleven o'clock. He looked in at the library door on his way upstairs that evening, and saw a brazier, which he had often noticed in the corner of the room, moved out before the fire; an old silver-gilt cup stood on the table, filled with red wine, and some written sheets of paper lay near it. Mr. Abney was sprinkling some incense on the brazier from a round silver box as Stephen passed, but did not seem to notice his step.

The wind had fallen, and there was a still night and a full moon. At about ten o'clock Stephen was standing at the open window of his bedroom, looking out over the country. Still as the night was, the mysterious population of the distant moon-lit woods was not yet lulled to rest. From time to time strange cries as of lost and despairing wanderers sounded from across the mere. They might be the notes of owls or water-birds, yet they did not quite resemble either sound. Were not they coming nearer? Now they sounded from the nearer side of the water, and in a few moments they seemed to be floating about among the shrubberies. Then they ceased; but just as Stephen was thinking of shutting the window and resuming his reading of *Robinson Crusoe*, he caught sight of two figures standing on the gravelled terrace that ran along the garden side of the Hall—the figures of a boy and girl, as it seemed; they stood side by side, looking up at the windows. Something in the form of the girl recalled irresistibly his dream of the figure in the bath. The boy inspired him with more acute fear.

Whilst the girl stood still, half smiling, with her hands clasped over her heart, the boy, a thin shape, with black hair and ragged clothing, raised his arms in the air with an appearance of menace and of unappeasable hunger and longing. The moon shone upon his almost transparent hands, and Stephen saw that the nails were fearfully long and that the light shone through them. As he stood with his arms thus raised, he disclosed a terrifying spectacle. On the left side of his chest there opened a black and gaping rent; and there fell upon Stephen's brain, rather than upon his ear, the impression of one of those hungry and desolate cries that he had heard resounding over the woods of Aswarby all that evening. In another moment this dreadful pair had moved swiftly and noiselessly over the dry gravel, and he saw them no more.

Inexpressibly frightened as he was, he determined to take his candle and go down to Mr. Abney's study, for the hour appointed for their meeting was near at hand. The study or library opened out of the front-hall on one side, and Stephen, urged on by his terrors, did not take long in getting there. To effect an entrance was not so easy. It was not locked, he felt sure, for the key was on the outside of the door as usual. His repeated knocks produced no answer. Mr. Abney was engaged: he was speaking. What! why did he try to cry out? and why was the cry choked in his throat? Had he, too, seen the mysterious children? But now everything was quiet, and the door yielded to Stephen's terrified and frantic pushing.

On the table in Mr. Abney's study certain papers were found which explained the situation to Stephen Elliott when he was of an age to understand them. The most important sentences were as follows:

"It was a belief very strongly and generally held by the ancients—of whose wisdom in these matters I have had such experience as induces me to place confidence in their assertions—that by enacting certain processes, which to us moderns have something of a barbaric complexion, a very remarkable enlightenment of the spiritual faculties in man may be attained: that, for example, by absorbing the personalities of a certain number of his fellow-creatures, an individual may gain a complete ascendancy over those orders of spiritual beings which control the elemental forces of our universe.

"It is recorded of Simon Magus that he was able to fly in the air, to become invisible, or to assume any form he pleased, by the agency of the soul of a boy whom, to use the libellous phrase employed by the author of the *Clementine Recognitions*, he had 'murdered.' I find it set down, moreover, with considerable detail in the writings of Hermes Trismegistus, that similar happy results may be produced by the absorption of the hearts of not less than three human beings below the age of twenty-one years. To the testing of the truth of this receipt I have devoted the greater part of the last twenty years, selecting as the *corpora vilia* of my experiment such persons as could conveniently be removed without occasioning a sensible gap in society. The first step I effected by the removal of one Phoebe Stanley, a girl of gipsy extraction, on March 24, 1792. The second, by the removal of a wandering Italian lad, named Giovanni Paoli, on the night of March 23, 1805. The final 'victim'—to employ a word repugnant in the highest degree to my feelings—must be my cousin, Stephen Elliott. His day must be this March 24, 1812.

"The best means of effecting the required absorption is to remove the heart from the *living* subject, to reduce it to ashes, and to mingle them with about a pint of some red wine, preferably port. The remains of the first two subjects, at least, it will be well to conceal: a disused bathroom or wine-cellar will be found convenient for such a purpose. Some annoyance may be experienced from the psychic portion of the subjects, which popular language dignifies with the name of ghosts. But the man of philosophic temperament—to whom alone the experiment is appropriate—will be little prone to attach importance to the feeble efforts of these beings to wreak their vengeance on him. I contemplate with the liveliest satisfaction the enlarged and emancipated existence which the experiment, if successful, will confer on me; not only placing me beyond the reach of human justice (so-called), but eliminating to a great extent the prospect of death itself."

Mr. Abney was found in his chair, his head thrown back, his face stamped with an expression of rage, fright, and mortal pain. In his left side was a terrible lacerated wound, exposing the heart. There was no blood on his hands, and a long knife that lay on the table was perfectly clean. A savage wild-cat might have inflicted the injuries. The window of the study was open, and it was the opinion of the coroner that Mr. Abney had met his death by the agency of some wild creature. But Stephen Elliott's study of the papers I have quoted led him to a very different conclusion.

THE HORSE OF THE INVISIBLE

William Hope Hodgson

When I reached 427, Cheyne Walk, Chelsea, I found Carnacki sitting alone. As I came into the room, he rose with a perceptibly stiff movement, and extended his left hand. His face seemed to be badly scarred and bruised, and his right hand was bandaged. He shook hands, and offered me his paper, which I refused. Then he passed me a handful of photographs, and returned to his reading.

Now, that is just Carnacki. Not a word had come from him, and not a question from me. He would tell us all about it later. I spent about half an hour, looking at the photographs, which were chiefly "snaps" (some by flashlight) of an extraordinarily pretty girl; though, in some of the photographs it was wonderful that her prettiness was so evident; for so frightened and startled was her expression, that it was difficult not to believe that she had been photographed in the presence of some imminent and overwhelming danger.

The bulk of the photographs were of interiors of different rooms and passages, and in every one the girl might be seen, either full length in the distance, or closer, with, perhaps, only a hand or arm, or portion of the head or dress included in the photograph. All of these had evidently been taken with some definite aim, that did not have for its first purpose the picturing of the girl, but obviously of her surroundings; and they made me very curious, as you can imagine.

Near the bottom of the pile, however, I came upon something *definitely* extraordinary. It was a photograph of the girl, standing abrupt and clear in the great blaze of a flashlight, as was plain to be seen. Her face was turned a little upward, as if she had been frightened suddenly by some noise. Directly above her, as though half-formed and coming down out of the shadows, was the shape of a single, enormous hoof.

I examined this photograph for a long time, without understanding it more than that it had probably something to do with some queer Case in which Carnacki was interested.

When Jessop, Arkright, and Taylor came in, Carnacki quietly held out his hand for the photographs, which I returned in the same spirit, and afterwards we all went in to dinner. When we had spent a quiet but profitable hour at the table, we pulled our chairs round, and made ourselves snug; and Carnacki began:—

"I've been North," he said, speaking slowly and painfully, between puffs at his pipe. "Up to Hisgins of East Lancashire. It has been a pretty strange business all round, as I fancy you chaps will think, when I have finished. I knew, before I went, something about the 'horse story,' as I have heard it called; but I had never thought of it as coming my way, somehow. Also, I know now that I had never considered it seriously—in spite of my rule always to keep an open mind. Funny creatures, we humans!

"Well, I got a wire, asking for an appointment, which of course told me that there was some trouble. On the date I fixed, old Captain Hisgins himself came up to see me. He told me a great many new details about the horse story; though, naturally, I had always known the main points, and understood that if the first child were a girl, that girl would be haunted by the Horse, during her courtship.

"It is, as you can see, an extraordinary story, and though I have always known about it, I have never thought it to be anything more than old-time legend, as I have already hinted. You see, for seven generations the Hisgin Family have had men-children for their first-born, and even the Hisgins themselves have long considered the tale to be little more than a myth.

"To come to the present, the eldest child of the reigning family, is a girl, and she has been often teased and warned in jest by her friends and relations that she is the first girl to be the eldest for seven generations, and that she would have to keep her men friends at arm's length, or go into a nunnery, if she hoped to escape the haunting. And this, I think, shows us how thoroughly the tale had grown to be considered as nothing worthy of the least serious thought. Don't you think so?

"Two months ago, Miss Hisgins became engaged to Beaumont, a young Naval Officer, and on the evening of the very day of the engagement, before it was even formally announced, a most extraordinary thing happened, which resulted in Captain Hisgins making the appointment, and my ultimately going down to their place to look into the thing.

"From the old family records and papers that were trusted to me, I found that there could be no possible doubt but that prior to something like a hundred and fifty years ago there were some very extraordinary and disagreeable coincidences, to put the thing in the least emotional way. In the whole of the two centuries prior to that date, there were five first-born girls, out of a total of seven generations of the family. Each of these girls grew up to Maidenhood, and each became engaged, and each one died during the period of the engagement, two by suicide, one by falling from a window, one from a 'broken-heart' (presumably heart-failure, owing to sudden shock through fright). The fifth girl was killed one evening in the park round the house; but just how, there seemed to be no *exact* knowledge; only that there was an impression that she had been kicked by a horse. She was dead, when found.

"Now, you see, all of these deaths might be attributed, in a way—even the suicides—to natural causes, I mean, as distinct from supernatural.

You see? Yet, in every case, the Maidens had undoubtedly suffered some extraordinary and terrifying experiences during their various courtships, for in all of the papers there was mention either of the neighing of an unseen horse, or of the sounds of an invisible horse galloping, as well as many other peculiar and quite inexplicable manifestations. You begin to understand now, I think, just how extraordinary a business it was that I was asked to look into.

"I gathered from the records that the haunting of the girls was so constant and horrible that two of the girls' lovers fairly ran away from their lady-loves. And I think it was this, more than anything else, that made me feel that there had been something more in it, than a mere succession of uncomfortable coincidences.

"I got hold of these facts, before I had been many hours in the house; and after this, I went pretty carefully into the details of the thing that happened on the night of Miss Hisgins' engagement to Beaumont. It seems that as the two of them were going through the big lower corridor, just after dusk and before the lamps had been lighted, there had been a sudden, horrible neighing in the corridor, close to them. Immediately afterward, Beaumont received a tremendous blow or kick, which broke his right forearm. Then the rest of the family came running, to know what was wrong, and the servants. Lights were brought, and the corridor and, afterward, the whole house searched; but nothing unusual was found.

"You can imagine the excitement in the house, and the half incredulous, half believing talk about the old legend. Later on, in the middle of the night, the old Captain was waked by the sound of a great horse galloping round and round the house.

"Several times after this, both Beaumont and the girl said that they had heard the sounds of hoofs near to them, after dusk, in several of the rooms and corridors.

"Three nights later, Beaumont was waked by a strange neighing in the night-time, seeming to come from the direction of his sweetheart's bedroom. He ran hurriedly for her father, and the two of them raced to her room. They found her awake, and ill with sheer terror, having been awakened by the neighing, seemingly close to her bed.

"The night before I arrived, there had been a fresh happening, and they were all in a frightfully nervy state, as you can imagine.

"I spent most of the first day, as I have hinted, in getting hold of details; but after dinner, I slacked off, and played billiards all the evening with Beaumont and Miss Hisgins. We stopped about ten o'clock, and had coffee, and I got Beaumont to give me full particulars about the thing that had happened the evening before.

"He and Miss Hisgins had been sitting quietly in her aunt's boudoir, whilst the old lady chaperoned them, behind a book. It was growing dusk, and the lamp was at her end of the table. The rest of the house was not yet lit, as the evening had come earlier than usual.

"Well, it seems that the door into the hall was open, and suddenly, the girl said:—'S'ush! What's that?'

"They both listened, and then Beaumont heard it—the sound of a horse, outside of the front door.

"'Your father?' he suggested; but she reminded him that her father was not riding.

"Of course, they were both ready to feel queer, as you can suppose; but Beaumont made an effort to shake this off, and went into the hall to see whether anyone was at the entrance. It was pretty dark in the hall, and he could see the glass panels of the inner draught-door, clear-cut in the darkness of the hall. He walked over to the glass, and looked through into the drive beyond; but there was nothing in sight.

"He felt nervous and puzzled, and opened the inner door and went out on to the carriage-circle. Almost directly afterward, the great hall door swung-to with a crash behind him. He told me that he had a sudden awful feeling of having been trapped in some way that is how he put it. He whirled round, and gripped the door-handle; but something seemed to be holding it with a vast grip on the other side. Then, before he could be fixed in his mind that this was so, he was able to turn the handle, and open the door.

"He paused for a moment in the doorway, and peered into the hall; for he had hardly steadied his mind sufficiently to know whether he was really frightened or not. Then he heard his sweetheart blow him a kiss out of the greyness of the big, unlit hall, and he knew that she had followed him, from the boudoir. He blew her a kiss back, and stepped inside the doorway, meaning to go to her. And then, suddenly, in a flash of sickening knowledge, he knew that it was not his sweetheart who had blown him that kiss. He knew that something was trying to tempt him alone into the darkness, and that the girl had never left the boudoir. He jumped back and in the same instant of time, he heard the kiss again, nearer to him. He called out at the top of his voice:—'Mary, stay in the boudoir. Don't move out of the boudoir until I come to you.' He heard her call something in reply, from the boudoir, and then he had struck a clump of a dozen, or so, matches, and was holding them above his head, and looking round the hall. There was no one in it; but even as the matches burned out, there came the sounds of a great horse galloping down the empty drive.

"Now, you see, both he and the girl had heard the sounds of the horse galloping; but when I questioned more closely, I found that the aunt had heard nothing; though, it is true, she is a bit deaf, and she was further back in the room. Of course, both he and Miss Hisgins had been in an extremely nervous state, and ready to hear anything. The door might have been slammed by a sudden puff of wind, owing to some inner door being opened; and as for the grip on the handle, that may have been nothing more than the sneck catching.

"With regard to the kisses and the sounds of the horse galloping, I pointed out that these might have seemed ordinary enough sounds, if they had been only cool enough to reason. As I told him, and as he knew, the sounds of a horse galloping, carry a long way on the wind; so that what he had heard might have been nothing more than a horse being ridden, some distance away. And as for the kiss, plenty of quiet noises—the rustle of a paper or a leaf—have a somewhat similar sound, especially if one is in an over-strung condition, and imagining things.

"I was preaching this little sermon on common-sense, versus hysteria, as we put out the lights and left the billiard-room. But neither Beaumont nor Miss Hisgins would agree that there had been any fancy on their parts.

"We had come out of the billiard-room, by this, and were going along the passage; and I was still doing my best to make both of them see the ordinary, commonplace possibilities of the happening, when what killed my pig, as the saying goes, was the sound of a hoof in the dark billiard-room, we had just left.

"I felt the 'creep' come on me in a flash, up my spine and over the back of my head. Miss Hisgins whooped like a child with whooping-cough, and ran up the passage, giving little gasping screams. Beaumont, however, ripped round on his heels, and jumped back a couple of yards. I gave back too, a bit, as you can understand.

"'There it is,' he said, in a low, breathless voice. 'Perhaps you'll believe now.'

"'There's certainly something,' I whispered back, and never taking my gaze off the closed door of the billiard-room.

"'H'sh!' he muttered. 'There it is again.'

"There was a sound like a great horse pacing round and round the billiard-room, with slow, deliberate steps. A horrible cold fright took me, so that it seemed impossible to take a full breath, you know the feeling; and then I know we must have walked backward, for we found ourselves suddenly at the opening of the long passage.

"We stopped there, and listened. The sounds went on steadily, with a horrible sort of deliberateness; as if the brute were taking a sort of malicious gusto in walking about all over the room in which we had just been. Do you understand just what I mean?

"Then there was a pause, and a long time of absolute quiet, except for an excited whispering from some of the people down in the big hall. The sound came plainly up the wide stair-way. I fancy they were gathered round Miss Hisgins, with some notion of protecting her.

"I should think Beaumont and I stood there, at the end of the passage, for about five minutes, listening for any noise in the billiard-room. Then I realised what a horrible funk I was in, and I said to him:—'I'm going to see what's there.'

"'So'm I,' he answered. He was pretty white; but he had heaps of pluck. I told him to wait one instant, and I made a dash into my bedroom, and got my camera and flashlight. I slipped my revolver into my right-hand pocket, and a knuckle-duster over my left fist, where it was ready, and yet did not stop me from being able to work my flashlight.

"Then I ran back to Beaumont. He held out his right hand, to show me that he had his pistol, and I nodded; but whispered to him not to be too quick to shoot, as there might be some silly practical-joking at work, after all. He had got a lamp from a bracket in the upper hall, which he was holding in the crook of his damaged arm, so that we had a good light. Then we went down the passage, towards the billiard-room; and you can imagine that we were a pretty nervous couple.

"All this time, there had not been a sound; but, abruptly when we were within perhaps a couple of yards of the door, we heard the sudden clumping of a hoof on the solid *parquet*-floor of the billiard-room. In the instant afterward, it seemed to me that the place shook beneath the ponderous hoof-falls of some huge thing, *coming towards the door.* Both Beaumont and I gave back a pace or two, and then realised, and hung on to our courage, as you might say, and waited. The great tread came right up to the door, and then stopped, and there was an instant of absolute silence, except that, so far I was concerned, the pulse in my throat and temples almost deafened me.

I daresay we waited quite half a minute, and then came the further restless clumping of a great hoof. Immediately afterward, the sounds came right on, as if some invisible thing passed through the closed door, and the ponderous tread was upon us. We jumped, each of us, to our side of the passage, and I know that I spread myself stiff against the wall. The clungk, clunck, clungk, clunck, of the great hoof-falls passed right between us, and slowly and with deadly deliberateness, down the passage. I heard them through a haze of blood-beats in my ears and temples, and my body extraordinarily rigid and pringling and breathless. I stood for a little time like this, my head turned, so that I could see up the passage. I was conscious only that there was a hideous danger abroad. Do you understand?

"And then, suddenly, my pluck came back to me. I was aware that the noise of the hoof-beats sounded near the other end of the passage. I twisted quickly, and got my camera to bear, and snapped the flashlight. Immediately afterward, Beaumont let fly a storm of shots down the passage, and began to run, shouting:—'It's after Mary. Run! Run!'

"He rushed down the passage, and I after him. We came out on to the main landing and heard the sound of a hoof on the stairs, and after that, nothing. And from thence, onward, nothing.

"Down, below us in the big hall, I could see a number of the household round Miss Hisgins, who seemed to have fainted; and there were several of the servants clumped together a little way off, staring up at the main landing, and no one saying a single word. And about some twenty steps up the stairs was old Captain Hisgins with a drawn sword in his hand, where he had halted just below the last hoof-sound. I think I never saw anything finer than the old man standing there between his daughter and that infernal thing.

"I daresay you can understand the queer feeling of horror I had at passing that place on the stairs where the sounds had ceased. It was as if the monster were still standing there, invisible. And the peculiar thing was that we never heard another sound of the hoof, either up or down the stairs.

"After they had taken Miss Hisgins to her room, I sent word that I should follow so soon as they were ready for me. And, presently, when a message came to tell me that I could come any time, I asked her father to give me a hand with my instrument box, and between us we carried it into the girl's bedroom. I had the bed pulled well out into the middle of the room; after which I erected the electric pentacle round the bed. Then I directed that lamps should be placed round the room, but that on no account must any light be made within the pentacle, neither must anyone pass in or out. The girl's mother, I had placed within the pentacle, and directed that her maid should sit without, ready to carry any message, so as to make sure that Mrs. Hisgins did not have to leave the pentacle. I suggested also, that the girl's father should also stay the night in the room, and that he had better be armed.

"When I left the room, I found Beaumont waiting outside the door, in a miserable state of anxiety. I told him what I had done, and explained to him that Miss Hisgins was probably perfectly safe within the 'protection'; but that, in addition to her father remaining the night in the room, I intended to stand guard at the door. I told him that I should like him to keep me company, for I knew that he would never sleep, and I should not be sorry to have a companion. Also, I wanted to have him under my own observation; for there was no doubt but that he was actually in greater danger than the girl. At least, that was my opinion; and is still, as I think you will agree later.

"I asked him whether he would object to my drawing a pentacle round him, for the night, and got him to agree; but I saw that he did not know whether to be superstitious about it, or to regard it more as a piece of foolish mumming; but he took it seriously enough, when I gave him some particulars about the Black Veil case, when young Aster died. You remember, he said it was a piece of silly superstition, and stayed outside. Poor devil!

"As it chanced, the night passed quietly enough, until a little while before dawn when we both heard the sounds of a great horse galloping round and round the house, just as old Captain Hisgins had described it. You can imagine how queer it made me feel, and directly afterward, I heard someone stir within the room. I knocked at the door; for I was uneasy, and the Captain came. I asked whether everything was right; to which he replied, yes; and immediately asked me whether I had heard the sounds of the galloping; so that I knew he had heard them also. 1 suggested that it might be as well to leave the bedroom door open a little, until the dawn came in, as there was certainly something abroad. This was done, and he went back into the room, to be near his wife and daughter.

"I had better say here, that I was doubtful whether there was any value in the 'defense' about Miss Hisgins; for what I term the 'personal-sounds' of the manifestation were so extraordinarily material, that I was inclined to parallel the case with that one of Harford's, where the hand of a child kept materializing within the pentacle, and patting the floor. As you will remember, that was a hideous business.

"Yet, as it chanced, nothing further happened; and so soon as daylight had fully come, we all went off to bed.

"Beaumont knocked me up about midday, and I went down and made breakfast into lunch. Miss Hisgins was there, and seemed in very fair spirits, considering. She told me that I had made her feel almost safe, for the first time for days. She told me also that her cousin, Harry Parsket, was coming down from London, and she knew that he would do anything to help fight the ghost. And after that, she and Beaumont went out into the grounds, to have a little time together.

"I had a walk in the grounds myself, and went round the house, but saw no traces of hoof-marks; and after that, I spent the rest of the day, making an examination of the house; but found nothing.

"I made an end of my search, before dark, and went to my room to dress for dinner. When I got down, the cousin had just arrived; and I found him one of the nicest men 1 have met for a long time. A chap with a tremendous amount of pluck, and the particular kind of man I like to have with me, in a bad case like that.

"I could see that what puzzled him most was our belief in the genuineness of the haunting; and I found myself almost wanting something to happen, just to show him how true it was. As it chanced, something did happen, with a vengeance.

"Beaumont and Miss Hisgins had gone out for a stroll in the dusk, and Captain Hisgins asked me to come into his study for a short chat whilst Parsket went upstairs with his traps, for he had no man with him.

"I had a long conversation with the old Captain, in which I pointed out that the 'haunting' had evidently no particular connection with the house, but only with the girl herself, and that the sooner she was married, the better, as it would give Beaumont a right to be with her at all times; and further than this, it might be that the manifestations would cease, if the marriage were actually performed. The old man nodded agreement to this, especially to the first part, and reminded me that three of the girls who were said to have been 'haunted,' had been sent away from home, and met their deaths whilst away. And then in the midst of our talk there came a pretty frightening interruption;

for all at once the old butler rushed into the room, most extraordinarily pale:—

"'Miss Mary, Sir! Miss Mary, Sir!' he gasped out, using the old name. 'She's screaming . . . out in the Park, Sir! And they say they can hear the Horse—'

"The Captain made one dive for a rack of arms, and snatched down his old sword, and ran out, drawing it as he ran. I dashed out and up the stairs, snatched my camera-flashlight and a heavy revolver, gave one yell at Parsket's door:—'The Horse!' and was down and out into the grounds.

"Out in the darkness there was a confused shouting, and I caught the sounds of shooting, away out among the scattered trees. And then, from a patch of blackness to my left, there burst out suddenly an infernal gobbling sort of neighing. Instantly I whipped round and snapped off the flashlight. The great blare of the light blazed out momentarily, showing me the leaves of a big tree close at hand, quivering in the night breeze; but there had been nothing else; and then the ten-fold blackness came down upon me, and I heard Parsket shouting a little way back to know whether I had seen anything.

"The next instant he was beside me, and I felt safer for his company; for there was some incredible thing near to us, and I was momentarily blind, because of the brightness of the flashlight. 'What was it? What was it?' he kept repeating in an excited voice. And all the time I was staring into the darkness and answering, mechanically, 'I don't know. I don't know.' There was a burst of shouting somewhere ahead, and then a shot. We ran towards the sounds, yelling to the people not to shoot; for in the darkness and panic there was this danger also. Then there came two of the game-keepers, racing hard up the drive, with lanterns and their guns; and immediately afterward a row of lights dancing towards us from the house, carried by some of the men-servants.

"As the lights came up, I saw that we had come close to Beaumont. He was standing over Miss Hisgins, and he had his revolver in his right hand. Then I saw his face, and there was a great wound across his forehead. By him was the Captain, turning his naked sword this way and that, and peering into the darkness; and a little behind him stood the old butler, a battle-axe, from one of the arm-stands in the hall, in his hands. Yet there was nothing strange to be seen anywhere.

"We got the girl into the house, and left her with her mother and Beaumont, whilst a groom rode for a doctor. And then the rest of us, with four other keepers, all armed with guns and carrying lanterns, searched round the home-park. But we found nothing.

"When we got back, we found that the Doctor had been. He had bound up Beaumont's wound, which, luckily, was not deep, and ordered Miss Hisgins straight to bed. I went upstairs with the Captain and found Beaumont on guard outside the girl's door. I asked him how he felt; and then, so soon as they were ready for us, Captain Hisgins and I went into the bedroom, and fixed the pentacle again round the bed. They had already got lamps about the room; and after I had set the same order of watching, as on the previous night, I joined Beaumont, outside the door.

"Parsket had come up while I had been in the bedroom, and between us we got some idea from Beaumont as to what had happened out in the Park. It seems that they were coming home after their stroll, from the direction of the West Lodge; when, suddenly, Miss Hisgins said, 'Hush!' and came to a standstill. He stopped, and listened; but heard nothing for a little. Then he caught it—the sound of a horse, seemingly a long way off, galloping towards them over the grass. He told the girl that it was nothing, and started to hurry her towards the house; but she was not deceived, of course. In less than a minute, they heard it quite close to them in the dark, and they began to run. Then Miss Hisgins caught her foot, and fell. She began to scream, and that is what the butler heard. As Beaumont lifted the girl, he heard the hoofs come thudding right at him. He stood over her, and fired all five chambers of his revolver right at the sounds. He told us that he was sure he saw something that looked like an enormous horse's head, right upon him, in the light of the last flash of his pistol. Immediately afterwards, he was struck a tremendous blow, which knocked him down; and then the Captain and the butler came running up, shouting. The rest, of course, we knew.

"About ten o'clock, the butler brought us up a tray; for which I was very glad; as the night before I had got rather hungry. I warned Beaumont, however, to be very particular not to drink any spirits, and I also made him give me his pipe and matches. At midnight, I drew a pentacle round him, and Parsket and I sat one on each side of him; but outside of the pentacle; for I had no fear that there would be any manifestation made against anyone, except Beaumont or Miss Hisgins.

"After that, we kept pretty quiet. The passage was lit by a big lamp at each end; so that we had plenty of light; and we were all armed, Beaumont and I with revolvers, and Parsket with a shot-gun. In addition to my weapon, I had my camera and flashlight.

"Now and again we talked in whispers; and twice the Captain came out of the bedroom to have a word with us. About half-past one, we had all grown very silent; and suddenly, about twenty minutes later, I held up my hand, silently; for there seemed to me to be a sound of galloping, out in the night. I knocked on the bedroom door, for the Captain to open it, and when he came, I whispered to him that we thought we heard the Horse. For some time, we stayed, listening, and both Parsket and the Captain thought they heard it; but now I was not so sure, neither was Beaumont. Yet afterwards, I thought I heard it again.

"I told Captain Hisgins I thought he had better go back into the bedroom, and leave the door a little open, and this he did. But from that time onward, we heard nothing; and presently the dawn came in, and we all went very thankfully to bed.

"When I was called at lunch-time, I had a little surprise; for Captain Hisgins told me that they had held a little family council, and had decided to take my advice, and have the marriage without a day's more delay than possible. Beaumont was already on his way to London to get a special licence, and they hoped to have the wedding the next day.

"This pleased me; for it seemed the sanest thing to be done, in the extraordinary circumstances; and meanwhile I should continue my investigations; but until the marriage was accomplished, my chief thought was to keep Miss Hisgins near to me.

"After lunch, I thought I would take a few experimental photographs of Miss Hisgins and her *surroundings*. Sometimes the camera sees things that would seem very strange to normal human eyesight. You see what I mean? With this intention, and partly to make an excuse to keep her in my company as much as possible, I asked Miss Hisgins to join me in my experiments. This she seemed glad to do, and I spent several hours with her, wandering all over the house, from room to room; and whenever the impulse came, I took a flashlight of her and the room or corridor in which we chanced to be at the moment.

"After we had gone right through the house in this fashion, I asked her whether she felt sufficiently brave to repeat the experiments in the cellars. She said, yes; and so I rooted out Captain Hisgins and Parsket; for I was not going to take her down even into what you might call artificial darkness, without help and companionship at hand.

"When we were ready, we went down into the wine-cellar, Captain Hisgins carrying a shot-gun, and Parsket a specially-prepared background and a lantern. I got the girl to stand in the middle of the cellar, whilst Parsket and the Captain held out the background behind her.

Then I fired off the flashlight, and we went into the next cellar, where we repeated the experiment.

"Then, in the third cellar, a tremendous, pitch-dark place, something extraordinary and horrible manifested itself. I had stationed Miss Hisgins in the centre of the cellar, with her father and Parsket holding the background, as before. When all was ready, and just as I pressed the trigger of the 'flash,' there came in the cellar that dreadful, gobbling neighing, that I had heard out in the Park. It seemed to come from somewhere above the girl; and in the glare of the sudden light, I saw that she was staring tensely upward at no visible thing. And then in the succeeding comparative darkness, I was shouting to the Captain and Parsket to run Miss Hisgins out into the daylight.

"This was done, instantly; and I shut and locked the door, afterwards making the First and the Eighth signs of the Saaamaaa Ritual opposite to each post, and connecting them across the threshold with a triple line. In the meanwhile, Parsket and Captain Hisgins carried the girl to her Mother, and left her there, in a half-fainting condition; whilst I stayed on guard outside of the cellar door, feeling pretty horrible, for I knew that there was some disgusting thing inside; and along with this feeling there was a sense of half-ashamedness, rather miserable you know, because I had exposed Miss Hisgins to this danger.

"I had got the Captain's shot-gun, and when he and Parsket came down again, they were each carrying guns and lanterns. I could not possibly tell you the utter relief of spirit and body that came to me, when I heard them coming; but just try to imagine what it was like, standing outside of that cellar. Can you?

"I remember noticing, just before I went to unlock the door, how white and ghastly Parsket looked, and the old Captain was grey-looking; and I wondered whether my face was like theirs. And this, you know, had its own distinct effect upon my nerves; for it seemed to bring the beastliness of the thing bash down on to me in a fresh way. I know it was only sheer will-power that carried me up to the door and made me turn the key.

"I paused one little moment, and then with a nervy jerk, sent the door wide open, and held my lantern over my head. Parsket and the Captain came one on each side of me, and held up their lanterns; but the place was absolutely empty. Of course, I did not trust to a casual look of this kind; but spent several hours with the help of the two others in sounding every square foot of the floor, ceiling, and walls. Yet, in the end, I had to admit that the place was absolutely normal; and so in the end we came away none the wiser. But I sealed the door, and outside, opposite each door-post, I made the First and Last Signs of the Saaamaaa Ritual, joining them, as before, with a triple-line. Can you imagine what it was like, searching that cellar?

"When we got upstairs, I inquired very anxiously how Miss Hisgins was, and the girl came out herself to tell me that she was all right and that I was not to trouble about her, or blame myself, as I told her I had been doing. I felt happier then, and went off to wash for dinner; and after that was done with, Parsket and I went off to one of the bathrooms to develop the negatives that I had been taking. Yet none of the plates had anything to tell me, until we came to the one that was taken in the cellar. Parsket was developing, and I had taken a batch of the fixed plates out into the lamplight to examine them.

"I had just gone carefully through the lot, when I heard a shout from Parsket, and when I ran to him, he was looking at a partly-developed negative, which he was holding up to the red-lamp. It showed the girl plainly, looking upward, as I had seen her; but the thing that astonished me, was the shadow of an enormous hoof, right above her, as if it were coming down upon her out of the shadows. And, you know, I had run her bang into that danger. That was the thought that was chief in my mind.

"As soon as the developing was complete, I fixed the plate, and examined it carefully in a good light. There was no doubt about it at all; the thing above Miss Hisgins was an enormous, shadowy hoof. Yet I was no nearer to coming to any definite knowledge; and the only thing I could do was to warn Parsket to say nothing about it to the girl; for it would only increase her fright; but I showed the thing to her father, for I considered it right that he should know.

"That night, we took the same precautions for Miss Hisgins' safety, as on the two previous nights; and Parsket kept me company; yet the dawn came in, without anything unusual having happened, and I went off to bed.

"When I got down to lunch, l learnt that Beaumont had wired to say that he would be in soon after four; also that a message had been sent to the Rector. And it was generally plain that the ladies of the house were in a tremendous fluster.

"Beaumont's train was late, and he did not get home until five; but even then the Rector had not put in an appearance; and the butler came into say that the coachman had returned without him, as he had been called away unexpectedly. Twice more during the evening the carriage was sent down; but the clergyman had not returned; and we had to delay the marriage until the next day.

"That night, I arranged the 'Defense' round the girl's bed, and the Captain and his wife sat up with her, as before. Beaumont, as I expected, insisted on keeping watch with me, and he seemed in a curiously frightened mood; not for himself, you know; but for Miss Hisgins. He had a horrible feeling, he told me, that there would be a final, dreadful attempt on his sweetheart, that night. This, of course, I told him was nothing but nerves; yet, really, it made me feel very anxious; for I have seen too much, not to know that, under such circumstances, a premonitory *conviction* of impending danger, is not necessarily to be put down entirely to nerves. In fact, Beaumont was so simply and earnestly convinced that the night would bring some extraordinary manifestation, that I got Parsket to rig up a long cord from the wire of the butler's bell, to come along the passage handy. To the butler himself, I gave directions not to undress, and to give the same order to two of the footmen. If I rang, he was to come instantly, with the footmen, carrying lanterns; and the lanterns were to be kept ready lit all night. If, for any reason, the bell did not ring, and I blew my whistle, he was to take that as a signal in place of the bell.

"After I had arranged all these minor details, I drew a pentacle about Beaumont, and warned him very particularly to stay within it, whatever happened. And when this was done, there was nothing to do but wait, and pray that the night would go as quietly as the night before.

"We scarcely talked at all, and by about 1 A.M., we were all very tense and nervous; so that, at last, Parsket got up and began to walk up and down the corridor, to steady himself a bit. Presently, I slipped off my pumps, and joined him; and we walked up and down, whispering occasionally, for something over an hour, until in turning I caught my foot in the bell-cord, and went down on my face; but without hurting myself, or making a noise.

"When I got up, Parsket nudged me.

"'Did you notice that the bell never rang?' he whispered.

"'Jove!' I said, 'you're right.'

"'Wait a minute,' he answered. 'I'll bet it's only a kink somewhere in the cord.' He left his gun, and slipped along the passage, and taking the top lamp, tip-toed away into the house, carrying Beaumont's revolver ready in his right hand. He was a plucky chap, as I think you will admit.

"Suddenly, Beaumont motioned to me for absolute quiet. Directly afterwards, I heard the thing for which he listened—the sound of a horse galloping, out in the night. I think that I may say, I fairly shivered.

The sound died away, and left a horrible, desolate, eerie feeling, in the air, you know. I put my hand out to the bell-cord, hoping that Parsket had got it clear. Then I waited, glancing before and behind. Perhaps two minutes passed, full of what seemed like an almost unearthly quiet. And then, suddenly, down the corridor, at the lighted end, there sounded the clumping of a great hoof; and instantly the lamp was thrown down with a tremendous crash, and we were in the dark. I tugged hard on the cord, and blew the whistle: then I raised my snapshot, and fired the flashlight. The corridor blazed into brilliant light: but there was nothing; and then the darkness fell like thunder. I heard the Captain at the bedroom door, and shouted to him to bring out a lamp, *quick*; but instead, something started to kick the door, and I heard the Captain shouting within the bedroom, and then the screaming of the women. I had a sudden horrible fear that the monster had got into the bedroom; but in the same instant, from up the corridor, there came abruptly the vile, gobbling neighing that we had heard in the Park and the cellar. I blew the whistle again, and groped blindly for the bell-cord, shouting to Beaumont to stay in the Pentacle, whatever happened. I yelled again to the Captain to bring out a lamp, and there came a smashing sound against the bedroom door. Then I had my matches in my hand, to get some light before that incredible, unseen Monster was upon us.

"The match scraped on the box, and flared up, dully; and in the same instant, I heard a faint sound behind me. I whipped round, in a kind of mad terror, and saw something, in the light of the match—a monstrous horse-head, close to Beaumont.

"'Look out, Beaumont!' I shouted in a sort of scream. 'It's behind you!'

"The match went out, abruptly, and instantly there came the huge bang of Parsket's double-barrel (both barrels at once), fired (evidently single-handed by Beaumont) close to my ear, as it seemed. I caught a momentary glimpse of the great head, in the flash, and of an enormous hoof amid the belch of fire and smoke, seeming to be descending upon Beaumont. In the same instant, I fired three chambers of my revolver. There was the sound of a dull blow, and then that horrible, gobbling neigh, broke out close to me. I fired twice at the sound. Immediately afterward, Something struck me, and I was knocked backwards. I got on to my knees, and shouted for help, at the top of my voice. I heard the women screaming behind the closed door of the bedroom, and was dully aware that the door was being smashed from the inside; and directly afterwards I knew that Beaumont was struggling with some hideous thing, near to me. For an instant, I held back, stupidly, paralysed with funk; and then, blindly, and in sort of rigid chill of goose-flesh, I went to help him, shouting his name. I can tell you, I did not feel much of a hero. There came a little, choking scream, out of the darkness: and, at that, I jumped forward into the dark. I gripped a vast, furry ear. Then something struck me another great blow, knocking me sick. I hit back, weak and blind, and gripped with my other hand at the incredible thing. Abruptly, I was dimly aware of a tremendous crash behind me, and a great burst of light. There were other lights in the passage, and a noise of feet and shouting. My hand-grips were torn from the thing they held; I shut my eyes stupidly, and heard a loud yell above me; and then a heavy blow, like a butcher chopping meat; and something fell upon me.

"I was helped to my knees by the Captain and the butler. On the floor lay an enormous horse-head, out of which protruded a man's trunk and legs. On the wrists were fixed great hoofs. It was the monster. The Captain cut something with the sword that he held in his hand, and stooped, and lifted off the mask; for that is what it was. I saw the face then of the man who had worn it. It was Parsket. He had a bad wound across the forehead, where the Captain's sword had bit through the mask. I looked bewilderedly from him to Beaumont, who was sitting up, leaning against the wall of the corridor. Then I stared at Parsket, again.

"'By Jove!' I said, at last; and then I was quiet; for I was so ashamed for the man. You can understand, can't you. And he was opening his eyes. And, you know, I had grown so to like the man.

"And then, you know, just as Parsket was getting back his wits, and looking from one to the other of us, and beginning to remember, there happened a strange and incredible thing. For from the end of the corridor, there sounded, suddenly, the clumping of a great hoof. I looked that way, and then instantly at Parsket, and saw a sudden horrible fear come into his face and eyes. He wrenched himself round, weakly, and stared in mad terror up the corridor to where the sound had been; and the rest of us stared, all in a frozen group. I remember hearing vaguely, half sobs and whispers from Miss Hisgins' bedroom, all the while that I stared, frightenedly, up the corridor.

"The silence lasted several seconds; and then, abruptly, there came again the clumping of the great hoof, away up at the end of the corridor. And immediately afterward, the clungk, clunk—clungk, clunk, of mighty hoofs coming down the passage, towards us.

"Even then, you know, most of us thought it was some mechanism of Parsket's still at work; and we were in the queerest mixture of fright and doubt. I think everyone looked at Parsket. And suddenly the Captain shouted out:—

"'Stop this damned fooling at once. Haven't you done enough!'

"For my part, you know, I was frightened; for I had a sense that there was something horrible and wrong. And then Parsket managed to gasp out:—

"'It's not me! My God! It's not me! My God! It's not me!'

"And then, you know, it seemed to come home to everyone in an instant that there was really some dreadful thing coming down the passage. There was a mad rush up the passage, and even old Captain Hisgins gave back with the butler and the footman. Beaumont fainted outright, as I found afterwards; for he had been badly mauled. I just flattened against the wall, kneeling, as I was, too stupid and dazed even to run. And almost in the same instant the ponderous hoof-falls sounded close to me, and seeming to shake the solid floor, as they passed. Abruptly the great sounds ceased, and I knew in a sort of sick fashion that the thing had halted opposite to the open door of the girl's bedroom. And then, you know, I was aware that Parsket was standing rocking in the doorway, with his arms spread across, so as to fill the doorway with his body. I saw with less bewilderment. Parsket showed extraordinarily pale, and the blood was running down his face from the wound in his forehead; and then I noticed that he seemed to be looking at something in the passage with a peculiar, desperate, fixed gaze. But, there was really nothing to be seen. And suddenly the clungk, clunk—clungk, clunk, recommenced, and passed onward down the passage. And in the same moment, Parsket pitched forward out of the doorway on to his face.

"There were shouts from the huddle of men down the passage, and the two footmen and the butler simply ran, carrying their lanterns; but the Captain went against the side-wall with his back, and put the lamp he was carrying over his head. The dull tread of the Horse went past him, and left him unharmed; and I heard the monstrous hoof-falls going away and away through the quiet house; and after that a dead silence.

"Then the Captain moved, and came towards us, very slow and shaky, and with an extraordinarily grey face.

"I crept towards Parsket, and the Captain came to help me. We turned him over; and, you know, I knew in a moment that he was quite dead; but you can imagine what a feeling it sent through me.

"I looked up at the Captain; and suddenly he said:—

"'That— That— That—,' and I knew that he was trying to tell me that Parsket had stood between his daughter and whatever it was that had gone down the passage. I stood up, and steadied him; though I was not very steady myself. And suddenly, his face began to work, and he went down on to his knees by Parsket, and cried like some shaken child. And then, you know, I knew that the women were in the doorway of the bedroom; and I turned away and left him to them, whilst I went over to Beaumont.

"That is practically the whole story; and the only thing that is left to me is to try to explain some of the puzzling parts, here and there.

"Perhaps you have seen that Parsket was in love with Miss Hisgins; and this fact is the key to a good deal that was extraordinary. He was doubtless responsible for some portions of the 'haunting'; in fact, I think for nearly everything; but, you know, I can prove nothing, and what I have to tell you is chiefly the result of deduction.

"In the first place, it is obvious that Parsket's intention was to frighten Beaumont away; and when he found that he could not do this, I think he grew so desperate that he really intended to kill him. I hate to say this; but the facts force me to think so.

"It is quite certain that Parsket was the person who broke Beaumont's arm. He knew all the details of the so-called 'Horse Legend,' and got the idea to work upon the old story, for his own end. He evidently had some method of slipping in and out of the house, probably through one of the many French windows, or probably he had a key to one or two of the garden doors; and when he was supposed to be away, he was really coming down, on the quiet, and hiding somewhere in the neighbourhood.

"The incident of the kiss in the dark hall, I put down to sheer nervous imaginings on the part of Beaumont and Miss Hisgins; yet, I must say that the sound of the horse outside of the front door, is a little difficult to explain away. But I am still inclined to keep to my first idea on this point, that there was nothing really unnatural about it.

"The hoof-sounds in the billiard-room and down the passage, were done by Parsket, from the floor below, by pomping against the panelled ceiling, with a block of wood tied to one of the window-hooks. I proved this, by an examination, which showed the dints in the woodwork.

"The sounds of the horse galloping round the house, was also done by Parsket, who must have had a horse tied up in the plantation, near by, unless, indeed, he made the sounds himself; but I do not see how he could have gone fast enough to produce the illusion, you see?

"The gobbling neighing in the park was a ventriloquial achievement on the part of Parsket; and the attack out there on Beaumont was also by him; so that when I thought he was in his bedroom, he must have been outside all the time, and joined me after I ran out of the front-door. This is probable, I mean that Parsket was the cause; for if it had been something more serious, he would certainly have given up his foolishness, knowing that there was no longer any need for it. I cannot imagine how he escaped being shot, both then, and in the last mad action, of which I have just told you. He was enormously without fear of any kind for himself, as you can see.

"The time when Parsket was with us, when we thought we heard the Horse galloping round the house, we must have been deceived. No one was very *sure*, except, of course, Parsket, who would naturally encourage the belief.

"The neighing in the cellar, is where I consider there came the first suspicion into Parsket's mind that there was something more at work than his sham-haunting. The neighing was done by him, in the same way that he did it in the Park; but when I remember how ghastly he looked, I feel sure that the sounds must have had some quality in them, which frightened the man himself. Yet, later, he would persuade himself that he had been getting fanciful. Of course, I must not forget that the effect upon Miss Hisgins must have made him feel pretty miserable.

"Then, about the clergyman being called away, we found afterwards that it was a bogus errand, or rather, call; and it is obvious that

Parsket was at the bottom of this, so as to get a few more hours in which to achieve his end; and what that was, a very little imagination will show you; for he had found that Beaumont would not be frightened away. You see what I mean?

"Then, there is no doubt at all but that Parsket left the cord to the butler's bell in a tangle, or hitched somewhere, so as to give him an excuse to slip away naturally to clear it. This also gave him the opportunity to remove one of the passage lamps. Then he had only to smash the other, and the passage was in utter darkness, for him to make the attempt on Beaumont.

"In the same way, it was he who locked the door of the bedroom, and took the key (it was in his pocket). This prevented the Captain from bringing a light, and coming to the rescue. But Captain Hisgins broke down the door, with the heavy fender-curb; and it was his smashing the door that had sounded so confusing and frightening in the darkness of the passage.

"The photograph of the monstrous hoof above Miss Hisgins in the cellar, is one of the things that I am less sure about. It might have been faked by Parsket, whilst I was out of the room, and this would have been easy enough, to anyone who knew how. But, you know, it does not look like a fake. Yet, there is as much evidence of probability that it was faked, as against; and the thing is too vague for an examination to help to a definite decision; so that I will express no opinion, one way or the other. It is certainly a horrible photograph.

"And now I come to that last, dreadful thing. There has been no further manifestation of anything abnormal; so that there is an extraordinary uncertainty in my conclusions. IF we had not heard those last sounds, and if Parsket had not shown that enormous sense of fear, the whole of this case could be explained away in the way in which I have shown. And, in fact, as you have seen, I am of the opinion that almost all of it can be cleared up; but I see no way of going past the thing we heard at the last, and the fear that Parsket showed.

"His death— No, that proves nothing. At the inquest it was described somewhat untechnically as due to heart-spasm. That is normal enough, and leaves us quite in the dark as to whether he died because he stood between the girl and some incredible monster.

"The look on Parsket's face, and the thing he called out, when he heard the great hoof-sounds coming down the passage, seem to show that he had the sudden realisation of what before then may have been nothing more than a horrible suspicion. And his fear and appreciation of some tremendous danger approaching was probably more keenly real even than mine. And then he did the one fine, great thing!"

"And the cause?" I said. "What caused it?"

Carnacki shook his head.

"God knows," he answered, with a peculiar sincere reverence. "IF that thing was what it seemed to be, one might suggest an explanation, which would not offend one's reason, but which may be utterly wrong. Yet I have thought, though it would take a long lecture on Thought Induction to get you to appreciate my reasons, that Parsket had produced what I might term a kind of 'induced haunting,' a kind of induced simulation of his mental conceptions, due to his desperate thoughts and broodings. It is impossible to make it clearer, in a few words."

"But the old story!" I said. "Why may not there have been something in *that*?"

"There may have been something in it," said Carnacki, quietly. "But I do not think it had anything to do with *this*. I have not clearly thought out my reasons, yet; but later I may be able to tell you why I think so."

"And the marriage. And the cellar—was there anything found there?" asked Taylor.

"Yes, the marriage was performed that day, in spite of the tragedy," Carnacki told us. "It was the wisest thing to do—considering the things that I cannot explain. Yes, I had the floor of that big cellar up; for I had a feeling I might find something there to give me some light. But there was nothing.

"You know, the whole thing is tremendous and extraordinary. I shall never forget the look on Parsket's face. And afterwards the disgusting sounds of those great hoofs going away through the quiet house."

Carnacki stood up:—

"Out you go!" he said, in friendly fashion, using the recognised formula.

And we went presently out into the quiet of the Embankment, and so to our homes.

The Haunted Organist of Hurly Burly

Rosa Mulholland

There had been a thunderstorm in the village of Hurly Burly. Every door was shut, every dog in his kennel, every rut and gutter a flowing river after the deluge of rain that had fallen. Up at the great house, a mile from the town, the rooks were calling to one another about the fright they had been in, the fawns in the deer-park were venturing their timid heads from behind the trunks of trees, and the old woman at the gate-lodge had risen from her knees, and was putting back her prayer-book on the shelf. In the garden, July roses, unwieldy with their full-blown richness, and saturated with rain, hung their heads heavily to the earth; others, already fallen, lay flat upon their blooming faces on the path, where Bess, Mistress Hurly's maid, would find them, when going on her morning quest of rose-leaves for her lady's pot-pourri. Ranks of white lilies, just brought to perfection by to-day's sun, lay dabbled in the mire of flooded mould. Tears ran down the amber cheeks of the plums on the south wall, and not a bee had ventured out of the hives, though the scent of the air was sweet enough to tempt the laziest drone. The sky was still lurid behind the boles of the upland oaks, but the birds had begun to dive in and out of the ivy that wrapped up the home of the Hurlys of Hurly Burly.

This thunderstorm took place more than half a century ago, and we must remember that Mistress Hurly was dressed in the fashion of that time as she crept out from behind the squire's chair, now that the lightning was over, and, with many nervous glances towards the window, sat down before her husband, the tea-urn, and the muffins. We can picture her fine lace cap, with its peachy ribbons, the frill on the hem of her cambric gown just touching her ankles, the embroidered clocks on her stockings, the rosettes on her shoes, but not so easily the lilac shade of her mild eyes, the satin skin, which still kept its delicate bloom, though wrinkled with advancing age, and the pale, sweet, puckered mouth, that time and sorrow had made angelic while trying vainly to deface its beauty.

The squire was as rugged as his wife was gentle, his skin as brown as hers was white, his grey hair as bristling as hers was glossed; the years had ploughed his face into ruts and channels; a bluff, choleric, noisy man he had been; but of late a dimness had come on his eyes, a hush on his loud voice, and a check on the spring of his hale step. He looked at his wife often, and very often she looked at him. She was not a tall woman, and he was only a head higher. They were a quaintly well-matched couple, despite their differences. She turned to you with nervous sharpness and revealed her tender voice and eye; he spoke and glanced roughly, but the turn of his head was courteous. Of late they fitted one another better than they had ever done in the heyday of their youthful love. A common sorrow had developed a singular likeness between them. In former years the cry from the wife had been, "Don't curb my son too much!" and from the husband, "You ruin the lad with softness." But now the idol that had stood between them was removed, and they saw each other better.

The room in which they sat was a pleasant old-fashioned drawing-room, with a general spider-legged character about the fittings; spinnet and guitar in their places, with a great deal of copied music beside them; carpet, tawny wreaths on pale blue; blue flutings on the walls, and faint gilding on the furniture. A huge urn, crammed with roses, in the open bay-window, through which came delicious airs from the garden, the twittering of birds settling to sleep in the ivy close by, and occasionally the pattering of a flight of rain-drops, swept to the ground as a bough bent in the breeze. The urn on the table was ancient silver, and the china rare. There was nothing in the room for luxurious ease of the body, but everything of delicate refinement for the eye.

There was a great hush all over Hurly Burly, except in the neighbourhood of the rooks. Every living thing had suffered from heat for the past month, and now, in common with all Nature, was receiving the boon of refreshed air in silent peace. The mistress and master of Hurly Burly shared the general spirit that was abroad, and were not talkative over their tea.

"Do you know," said Mistress Hurly, at last, "when I heard the first of the thunder beginning I thought it was—it was—"

The lady broke down, her lips trembling, and the peachy ribbons of her cap stirring with great agitation.

"Pshaw!" cried the old squire, making his cup suddenly ring upon the saucer, "we ought to have forgotten that. Nothing has been heard for three months."

At this moment a rolling sound struck upon the ears of both. The lady rose from her seat trembling, and folded her hands together, while the tea-urn flooded the tray.

"Nonsense, my love," said the squire; "that is the noise of wheels. Who can be arriving?"

"Who, indeed?" murmured the lady, reseating herself in agitation.

Presently pretty Bess of the rose-leaves appeared at the door in a flutter of blue ribbons.

"Please, madam, a lady has arrived, and says she is expected. She asked for her apartment, and I put her into the room that was got ready for Miss Calderwood. And she sends her respects to you, madam, and she'll be down with you presently."

The squire looked at his wife, and his wife looked at the squire.

"It is some mistake," murmured madam. "Some visitor for Calderwood or the Grange. It is very singular."

Hardly had she spoken when the door again opened, and the stranger appeared—a small creature, whether girl or woman it would be hard to say—dressed in a scanty black silk dress, her narrow shoulders covered with a white muslin pelerine. Her hair was swept up to the crown of her head, all but a little fringe hanging over her low forehead within an inch of her brows. Her face was brown and thin, eyes black and long, with blacker settings, mouth large, sweet, and melancholy. She was all head, mouth, and eyes; her nose and chin were nothing.

This visitor crossed the floor hastily, dropped a courtesy in the middle of the room, and approached the table, saying abruptly, with a soft Italian accent:

"Sir and madam, I am here. I am come to play your organ."

"The organ!" gasped Mistress Hurly.

"The organ!" stammered the squire.

"Yes, the organ," said the little stranger lady, playing on the back of a chair with her fingers, as if she felt notes under them. "It was but last week that the handsome signor, your son, came to my little house, where I have lived teaching music since my English father and my Italian mother and brothers and sisters died and left me so lonely."

Here the fingers left off drumming, and two great tears were brushed off, one from each eye with each hand, child's fashion. But the next moment the fingers were at work again, as if only whilst they were moving the tongue could speak.

"The noble signor, your son," said the little woman, looking trustfully from one to the other of the old couple, while a bright blush shone through her brown skin, "he often came to see me before that, always in the evening, when the sun was warm and yellow all through my little studio, and the music was swelling my heart, and I could play out grand with all my soul; then he used to come and say, 'Hurry, little Lisa, and play better, better still. I have work for you to do by-and-by.' Sometimes he said, 'Brava!' and sometimes he said 'Eccellentissima!' but one night last week he came to me and said, 'It is enough. Will you swear to do my bidding, whatever it may be?' Here the black eyes fell. And I said, 'Yes.' And he said, 'Now you are my betrothed.' And I said, 'Yes.' And he said, 'Pack up your music, little Lisa, and go off to England to my English father and mother, who have an organ in their house which must be played upon. If they refuse to let you play, tell them I sent you, and they will give you leave. You must play all day, and you must get up in the night and play. You must never tire. You are my betrothed, and you have sworn to do my work.' I said, 'Shall I see you there, signor?' And he said, 'Yes, you shall see me there.' I said, 'I will keep my vow, signor.' And so, sir and madam, I am come."

The soft foreign voice left off talking, the fingers left off thrumming on the chair, and the little stranger gazed in dismay at her auditors, both pale with agitation.

"You are deceived. You make a mistake," said they in one breath.

"Our son—" began Mistress Hurly, but her mouth twitched, her voice broke, and she looked piteously towards her husband.

"Our son," said the squire, making an effort to conquer the quavering in his voice, "our son is long dead."

"Nay, nay," said the little foreigner. "If you have thought him dead have good cheer, dear sir and madam. He is alive; he is well, and strong, and handsome. But one, two, three, four, five" (on the fingers) "days ago he stood by my side."

"It is some strange mistake, some wonderful coincidence!" said the mistress and master of Hurly Burly.

"Let us take her to the gallery," murmured the mother of this son who was thus dead and alive. "There is yet light to see the pictures. She will not know his portrait."

The bewildered wife and husband led their strange visitor away to a long gloomy room at the west side of the house, where the faint gleams from the darkening sky still lingered on the portraits of the Hurly family.

"Doubtless he is like this," said the squire, pointing to a fair-haired young man with a mild face, a brother of his own who had been lost at sea.

But Lisa shook her head, and went softly on tiptoe from one picture to another, peering into the canvas, and still turning away troubled. But at last a shriek of delight startled the shadowy chamber.

"Ah, here he is! See, here he is, the noble signor, the beautiful signor, not half so handsome as he looked five days ago, when talking to poor little Lisa! Dear sir and madam, you are now content. Now take me to the organ, that I may commence to do his bidding at once."

The mistress of Hurly Burly clung fast by her husband's arm.

"How old are you, girl?" she said faintly.

"Eighteen," said the visitor impatiently, moving towards the door.

"And my son has been dead for twenty years!" said his mother, and swooned on her husband's breast.

"Order the carriage at once," said Mistress Hurly; recovering from her swoon; "I will take her to Margaret Calderwood. Margaret will tell her the story. Margaret will bring her to reason. No, not to-morrow; I cannot bear to-morrow, it is so far away. We must go to-night."

The little signora thought the old lady mad, but she put on her cloak again obediently, and took her seat beside Mistress Hurly in the Hurly family coach. The moon that looked in at them through the pane as they lumbered along was not whiter than the aged face of the squire's wife, whose dim faded eyes were fixed upon it in doubt and awe too great for tears or words.

Lisa, too, from her corner gloated upon the moon, her black eyes shining with passionate dreams.

A carriage rolled away from the Calderwood door as the Hurly coach drew up at the steps. Margaret Calderwood had just returned from a dinner-party, and at the open door a splendid figure was standing, a tall woman dressed in brown velvet, the diamonds on her bosom glistening in the moonlight that revealed her, pouring, as it did, over the house from eaves to basement. Mistress Hurly fell into her outstretched arms with a groan, and the strong woman carried her aged friend, like a baby, into the house. Little Lisa was overlooked, and sat down contentedly on the threshold to gloat awhile longer on the moon, and to thrum imaginary sonatas on the doorstep.

There were tears and sobs in the dusk, moonlit room into which Margaret Calderwood carried her friend. There was a long consultation, and then Margaret, having hushed away the grieving woman into some quiet corner, came forth to look for the little dark-faced stranger, who had arrived, so unwelcome, from beyond the seas, with such wild communication from the dead.

Up the grand staircase of handsome Calderwood the little woman followed the tall one into a large chamber where a lamp burned, showing Lisa, if she cared to see it, that this mansion of Calderwood was fitted with much greater luxury and richness than was that of Hurly Burly. The appointments of this room announced it the sanctum of a woman who depended for the interest of her life upon resources of intellect and taste. Lisa noticed nothing but a morsel of biscuit that was lying on a plate.

"May I have it?" said she eagerly. "It is so long since I have eaten. I am hungry."

Margaret Calderwood gazed at her with a sorrowful, motherly look, and, parting the fringing hair on her forehead, kissed her. Lisa, staring at her in wonder, returned the caress with ardour. Margaret's large fair shoulders, Madonna face, and yellow braided hair, excited a rapture within her. But when food was brought her, she flew to it and ate.

"It is better than I have ever eaten at home!" she said gratefully. And Margaret Calderwood murmured, "She is physically healthy, at least."

"And now, Lisa," said Margaret Calderwood, "come and tell me the whole history of the grand signor who sent you to England to play the organ."

Then Lisa crept in behind a chair, and her eyes began to burn and her fingers to thrum, and she repeated word for word her story as she had told it at Hurly Burly.

When she had finished, Margaret Calderwood began to pace up and down the floor with a very troubled face. Lisa watched her, fascinated, and, when she bade her listen to a story which she would relate to her, folded her restless hands together meekly, and listened.

"Twenty years ago, Lisa, Mr. and Mrs. Hurly had a son. He was handsome, like that portrait you saw in the gallery, and he had brilliant talents. He was idolized by his father and mother, and all who knew him felt obliged to love him. I was then a happy girl of twenty. I was an orphan, and Mrs. Hurly, who had been my mother's friend, was like a mother to me. I, too, was petted and caressed by all my friends, and I was very wealthy; but I only valued admiration, riches—every good gift that fell to my share—just in proportion as they seemed of worth in the eyes of Lewis Hurly. I was his affianced wife, and I loved him well.

"All the fondness and pride that were lavished on him could not keep him from falling into evil ways, nor from becoming rapidly more and more abandoned to wickedness, till even those who loved him best despaired of seeing his reformation. I prayed him with tears, for my sake, if not for that of his grieving mother, to save himself before it was too late. But to my horror I found that my power was gone, my words did not even move him; he loved me no more. I tried to think that this was some fit of madness that would pass, and still clung to hope. At last his own mother forbade me to see him."

Here Margaret Calderwood paused, seemingly in bitter thought, but resumed:

"He and a party of his boon companions, named by themselves the 'Devil's Club,' were in the habit of practising all kinds of unholy pranks in the country. They had midnight carousings on the tombstones in the village graveyard; they carried away helpless old men and children, whom they tortured by making believe to bury them alive; they raised the dead and placed them sitting round the tombstones at a mock feast. On one occasion there was a very sad funeral from the village. The corpse was carried into the church, and prayers were read over the coffin, the chief mourner, the aged father of the dead man, standing weeping by. In the midst of this solemn scene the organ suddenly pealed forth a profane tune, and a number of voices shouted a drinking chorus. A groan of execration burst from the crowd, the clergyman turned pale and closed his book, and the old man, the father of the dead, climbed the altar steps, and, raising his arms above his head, uttered a terrible curse. He cursed Lewis Hurly to all eternity, he cursed the organ he played, that it might be dumb henceforth, except under the fingers that had now profaned it, which, he prayed, might be forced to labour upon it till they stiffened in death. And the curse seemed to work, for the organ stood dumb in the church from that day, except when touched by Lewis Hurly.

"For a bravado he had the organ taken down and conveyed to his father's house, where he had it put up in the chamber where it now stands. It was also for a bravado that he played on it every day. But, by-and-by, the amount of time which he spent at it daily began to increase rapidly. We wondered long at this whim, as we called it, and his poor mother thanked God that he had set his heart upon an occupation which would keep him out of harm's way. I was the first to suspect that it was not his own will that kept him hammering at the organ so many laborious hours, while his boon companions tried vainly to draw him away. He used to lock himself up in the room with the organ, but one day I hid myself among the curtains, and saw him writhing on his seat, and heard him groaning as he strove to wrench his hands from the keys, to which they flew back like a needle to a magnet. It was soon plainly to be seen that he was an involuntary slave to the organ; but whether through a madness that had grown within himself, or by some supernatural doom, having its cause in the old man's curse, we did not dare to say. By-and-by there came a time when we were wakened out of our sleep at nights by the rolling of the organ. He wrought now night and day. Food and rest were denied him. His face got haggard, his beard grew long, his eyes started from their sockets. His body became wasted, and his cramped fingers like the claws of a bird. He groaned piteously as he stooped over his cruel toil. All save his mother and I were afraid to go near him. She, poor, tender woman, tried to put wine and food between his lips, while the tortured fingers crawled over the keys; but he only gnashed his teeth at her with curses, and she retreated from him in terror, to pray. At last, one dreadful hour, we found him a ghastly corpse on the ground before the organ.

"From that hour the organ was dumb to the touch of all human fingers. Many, unwilling to believe the story, made persevering endeavours to draw sound from it, in vain. But when the darkened empty room was locked up and left, we heard as loud as ever the well-known sounds humming and rolling through the walls. Night and day the tones of the organ boomed on as before. It seemed that the doom of the wretched man was not yet fulfilled, although his tortured body had been worn out in the terrible struggle to accomplish it. Even his own mother was afraid to go near the room then. So the time went on, and the curse of this perpetual music was not removed from the house. Servants refused to stay about the place. Visitors shunned it. The squire and his wife left their home for years, and returned; left it, and returned again, to find their ears still tortured and their hearts wrung by the unceasing persecution of terrible sounds. At last, but a few months ago, a holy man was found, who locked himself up in the cursed chamber for many days, praying and wrestling with the demon. After he came forth and went away the sounds ceased, and the organ was heard no more. Since then there has been peace in the house. And now, Lisa, your strange appearance and your strange story convince us that you are a victim of a ruse of the Evil One. Be warned in time, and place yourself under the protection of God, that you may be saved from the fearful influences that are at work upon you. Come—"

Margaret Calderwood turned to the corner where the stranger sat, as she had supposed, listening intently. Little Lisa was fast asleep, her hands spread before her as if she played an organ in her dreams.

Margaret took the soft brown face to her motherly breast, and kissed the swelling temples, too big with wonder and fancy.

"We will save you from a horrible fate!" she murmured, and carried the girl to bed.

In the morning Lisa was gone. Margaret Calderwood, coming early from her own chamber, went into the girl's room and found the bed empty.

"She is just such a wild thing," thought Margaret, "as would rush out at sunrise to hear the larks!" and she went forth to look for her in the meadows, behind the beech hedges, and in the home park. Mistress Hurly, from the breakfast-room window, saw Margaret Calderwood, large and fair in her white morning gown, coming down the garden-path between the rose bushes, with her fresh draperies dabbled by the dew, and a look of trouble on her calm face. Her quest had been unsuccessful. The little foreigner had vanished.

A second search after breakfast proved also fruitless, and towards evening the two women drove back to Hurly Burly together. There all was panic and distress. The squire sat in his study with the doors shut, and his hands over his ears. The servants, with pale faces, were huddled together in whispering groups. The haunted organ was pealing through the house as of old.

Margaret Calderwood hastened to the fatal chamber, and there, sure enough, was Lisa, perched upon the high seat before the organ, beating the keys with her small hands, her slight figure swaying, and the evening sunshine playing about her weird head. Sweet unearthly music she wrung from the groaning heart of the organ—wild melodies, mounting to rapturous heights and falling to mournful depths. She wandered from Mendelssohn to Mozart, and from Mozart to Beethoven. Margaret stood fascinated awhile by the ravishing beauty of the sounds she heard, but, rousing herself quickly, put her arms round the musician and forced her away from the chamber. Lisa returned next day, however, and was not so easily coaxed from her post again. Day after day she laboured at the organ, growing paler and thinner and more weird-looking as time went on.

"I work so hard," she said to Mrs. Hurly. "The signor, your son, is he pleased? Ask him to come and tell me himself if he is pleased."

Mistress Hurly got ill and took to her bed. The squire swore at the young foreign baggage, and roamed abroad. Margaret Calderwood was the only one who stood by to watch the fate of the little organist. The curse of the organ was upon Lisa; it spoke under her hand, and her hand was its slave.

At last she announced rapturously that she had had a visit from the brave signor, who had commended her industry, and urged her to work yet harder. After that she ceased to hold any communication with the living. Time after time Margaret Calderwood wrapped her arms about the frail thing, and carried her away by force, locking the door of the fatal chamber. But locking the chamber and burying the key were of no avail. The door stood open again, and Lisa was labouring on her perch.

One night, wakened from her sleep by the well-known humming and moaning of the organ, Margaret dressed hurriedly and hastened to the unholy room. Moonlight was pouring down the staircase and passages of Hurly Burly. It shone on the marble bust of the dead Lewis Hurly, that stood in the niche above his mother's sitting-room door. The organ room was full of it when Margaret pushed open the door and entered—full of the pale green moonlight from the window, mingled with another light, a dull lurid glare which seemed to centre round a dark shadow, like the figure of a man standing by the organ, and throwing out in fantastic relief the slight form of Lisa writhing, rather than swaying, back and forward, as if in agony. The sounds that came from the organ were broken and meaningless, as if the hands of the player lagged and stumbled on the keys. Between the intermittent chords low moaning cries broke from Lisa, and the dark figure bent towards her with menacing gestures. Trembling with the sickness of supernatural fear, yet strong of will, Margaret Calderwood crept forward within the lurid light, and was drawn into its influence. It grew and intensified upon her, it dazzled and blinded her at first; but presently, by a daring effort of will, she raised her eyes, and beheld Lisa's face convulsed with torture in the burning glare, and bending over her the figure and the features of Lewis Hurly! Smitten with horror, Margaret did not even then lose her presence of mind. She wound her strong arms around the wretched girl and dragged her from her seat and out of the influence of the lurid light, which immediately paled away and vanished. She carried her to her own bed, where Lisa lay, a wasted wreck, raving about the cruelty of the pitiless signor who would not see that she was labouring her best. Her poor cramped hands kept beating the coverlet, as though she were still at her agonising task.

Margaret Calderwood bathed her burning temples, and placed fresh flowers upon her pillow. She opened the blinds and windows, and let in the sweet morning air and sunshine, and then, looking up at the newly awakened sky with its fair promise of hope for the day, and down at the dewy fields, and afar off at the dark green woods with the purple mists still hovering about them, she prayed that a way might be shown her by which to put an end to this curse. She prayed for Lisa, and then, thinking that the girl rested somewhat, stole from the room. She thought that she had locked the door behind her.

She went downstairs with a pale, resolved face, and, without consulting any one, sent to the village for a bricklayer. Afterwards she sat by Mistress Hurly's bedside, and explained to her what was to be done. Presently she went to the door of Lisa's room, and hearing no sound, thought the girl slept, and stole away. By-and-by she went downstairs, and found that the bricklayer had arrived and already begun his task of building up the organ-room door. He was a swift workman, and the chamber was soon sealed safely with stone and mortar.

Having seen this work finished, Margaret Calderwood went and listened again at Lisa's door; and still hearing no sound, she returned, and took her seat at Mrs. Hurly's bedside once more. It was towards evening that she at last entered her room to assure herself of the comfort of Lisa's sleep. But the bed and room were empty. Lisa had disappeared.

Then the search began, upstairs and downstairs, in the garden, in the grounds, in the fields and meadows. No Lisa. Margaret Calderwood ordered the carriage and drove to Calderwood to see if the strange little Will-o'-the-wisp might have made her way there; then to the village, and to many other places in the neighbourhood which it was not possible she could have reached. She made inquiries everywhere; she pondered and puzzled over the matter. In the weak, suffering state that the girl was in, how far could she have crawled?

After two days' search, Margaret returned to Hurly Burly. She was sad and tired, and the evening was chill. She sat over the fire wrapped in her shawl when little Bess came to her, weeping behind her muslin apron.

"If you'd speak to Mistress Hurly about it, please, ma'am," she said. "I love her dearly, and it breaks my heart to go away, but the organ haven't done yet, ma'am, and I'm frightened out of my life, so I can't stay."

"Who has heard the organ, and when?" asked Margaret Calderwood, rising to her feet.

"Please, ma'am, I heard it the night you went away—the night after the door was built up!"

"And not since?"

"No, ma'am," hesitatingly, "not since. Hist! hark, ma'am! Is not that like the sound of it now?"

"No," said Margaret Calderwood; "it is only the wind." But pale as death she flew down the stairs and laid her ear to the yet damp mortar of the newly-built wall. All was silent. There was no sound but the monotonous sough of the wind in the trees outside. Then Margaret began to dash her soft shoulder against the strong wall, and to pick the mortar away with her white fingers, and to cry out for the bricklayer who had built up the door.

It was midnight, but the bricklayer left his bed in the village, and obeyed the summons to Hurly Burly. The pale woman stood by and watched him undo all his work of three days ago, and the servants gathered about in trembling groups, wondering what was to happen next.

What happened next was this: When an opening was made the man entered the room with a light, Margaret Calderwood and others following. A heap of something dark was lying on the ground at the foot of the organ. Many groans arose in the fatal chamber. Here was little Lisa dead!

When Mistress Hurly was able to move, the squire and his wife went to live in France, where they remained till their death. Hurly Burly was shut up and deserted for many years. Lately it has passed into new hands. The organ has been taken down and banished, and the room is a bed-chamber, more luxuriously furnished than any in the house. But no one sleeps in it twice.

Margaret Calderwood was carried to her grave the other day a very aged woman.

THE INTERCESSOR

May Sinclair

I

They had told him that he couldn't miss it. There wasn't another house near it for a good mile. He knew where the bridle-path from the hill road struck the lane in the Bottom. It was down there, with a clump of ash-trees close up against the back of it, trying to hide it.

Garvin followed the path. It went straight over the slope of the fields, hemmed in by stone walls, low and loose piled, part of the enormous network of stone flung across the north country to the foot of the fells.

At the end of the last field a wild plum-tree stood half-naked on a hillock and pointed at the house. All that Garvin could see was a bald gable-end pitched among the ash-trees. It was black grey, like ash bark drenched with rain.

It stood, he now saw, in a little orchard of dead trees, shut in from the fields by walls, low and loose piled, a plot so small that it showed like a loop in a mesh of the stone network.

As he approached the place he had the distinct thrill of fascination that seized him always in the presence of old things.

Garvin was by nature and profession a hunter of old things, of old houses, old churches, old ways and superstitions. He had had his nose in a hundred parish registers, sifting the dust of oblivion for a clue to some forgotten family. He was gifted with an implacable persistence in following up a trail, a terrible and untiring industry in minute research. His almost legal precision had served him well when he left an estate agent's office in Pall Mall to work for the Blackadders on their County History.

The Blackadder enterprise was so vast that Garvin in his operations was a mere fly-wheel of the machinery. But it fired him; it gave him scope. As an estate agent, selling land for building lots, Garvin had done violence to his genius. The dream of Garvin and his passion was for wild open stretches, everlastingly unbuilt on, for moors and fells, for all places that have kept the secret and the memory of the ancient earth. It was this queer, half-savage streak in the respectable Garvin that marked him as the man for the Craven country.

He had travelled the district all summer, working up his notes at night in small humble hotels and wayside inns. But when it came to the actual writing of his section, Garvin had taken rooms in a village in Craven. He had insisted on two things only when he took them, that the house must be old and that there must be no children in it. That was in July. And before August other lodgers had come and had brought many children. Garvin was driven out. He said he *must* have a place to himself, and was told, fairly and squarely, in broad Yorkshire, that he couldn't have it; leastways, not in August. If he wasn't satisfied where he was, he could go to Falshaw's in the Bottom. Likely enough he'd have it to himself there as much as he wanted.

Garvin ignored the hint of perdition. He inquired placably if Falshaw's was an old place, and was told that it was "old enough." He asked also whether at Falshaw's there would be any children. No (this time it was palpable, the sidelong, sinister intention), there wouldn't be; leastways not in August nor yet September—if all went well with Falshaw's wife.

Garvin judged that the state of Falshaw's wife had acted somehow as a deterrent to tourists. It had kept Falshaw's empty. That was good. Anyhow he thought he'd risk it.

It was early evening in the first week of August that he set out for the house in the Bottom.

It didn't strike him (for the approach was sideways through a little gate in the low wall), it didn't strike him all at once that the house was not "old enough." But it struck him very sharply as he entered and took in, slant-ways, its bare rectangular front. So far from being old enough (for Garvin) it was not old at all, if you went by years. He had given it about a hundred at sight, when he came upon its date graved above the lintel of its door: 1800, and the initials of its founder: E. F.

If you went by years—but this gaunt and naked thing had grown old before its years. It wore the look of calamity, of terrible and unforgetting and unforgotten age. What it did was to throw back its century into some tract of dark and savage time.

He stepped back a few paces to get a better look at it. The unsheltered door stood open; its flagged passage, flush with the ground outside it, showed like a continuation of the orchard path. At the further gable- end its wall was broken half-way by the roof of a pent-house. A clump of elder bushes here were the only green and living things about the place. It stood before Garvin, dark and repellent in its nakedness, built from floor to roof of that bleak stone that abhors the sun, that blackens under rain. The light of the August evening was grey round it; the heat of the August day lived only in the rank smell of the elder bushes by the pent-house wall. It seemed to Garvin that the soul of eighteen hundred hung about him in the smell of the elder bushes. He found it in the blurred gleam of the five windows, deep set and narrow, that looked out on the orchard of dead trees. Garvin's delicate sense of time was shaken under their poignant, impenetrable stare, so that the figures 1800 troubled him, stirred in him the innermost thrill of his passion for the past.

He knocked with his stick on the open door. The sounds struck short and hard. Nobody answered. Garvin took another look at the house. The wall-space to the left of the threshold was narrow and had but one window, which he had passed as he entered. The long, two-windowed wall on the right bounded the house place. Garvin saw through the open door that this interior was diminished by two wooden partitions, one of which formed the passage, the other shut off the staircase at the back. The door at the end of the passage was closed. So was the door on his left, leading into the small room he had passed. The door in the partition on his right stood ajar, so that when he knocked again he heard the loud scraping of a chair on the stone floor. Somebody had got up and was probably listening there, but nobody came. He knocked again on the inner door imperiously.

This time he heard footsteps. They advanced heavily to the door and paused there. The door swung to with a click of the latch and the footsteps retreated. They trailed off somewhere into the depths of the house to the back. Somebody called out there to somebody else, "Onny! Onny!" and Garvin waited.

Some moments passed before the door at the end of the passage (the door into the backyard) opened, and a girl, whom he took to be Anny, came to him. She was a young girl, sturdy and full-blown in the body, florid and fair in the face; in all commonplace and a little coarse. She came heavily, with no sign of interest or of haste, but staring at Garvin with her thick grey eyes.

He asked if he could have rooms. Anny didn't know, she was sure.

Would she be good enough to find out?

She didn't know. He could find out himself. Ooncle was in the tool-shed.

With more good-will than her speech indicated she led the way to the shed under the elder bushes.

There was no one there. Anny now reckoned that Ooncle would be in the mist-house.

A gate in the wall behind the elder bushes opened into the mist-house yard. Falshaw was alone there, pitching dung from the cow-shed. At the girl's call he came forward, leaning on his pitchfork. He was a big man, thick in the girth, and fair like his niece, and florid. Garvin reckoned his age at fifty or thereabouts. For in his body, built for power, the muscles had begun to slacken; it was sunken in its secret foundations. Garvin supposed that this was because of Falshaw's age. What baffled him was the contradiction between Falshaw's face and its expression. It was natural that Falshaw should grow old; but what had Falshaw done that his face, formed by nature in an hour of genial grossness, should have all its contours tortured to that look of irreme-diable gloom?

The gloom did not lift as the big man slouched nearer, and (con-temptuous of the stranger's greeting) inquired what Garvin wanted. His manner intimated that whatever it was Garvin would probably have to want it.

As to whether Garvin could put up at Falshaw's, Falshaw, like his niece, didn't know, he was sure. It depended upon whether the missus could "put oop" with Garvin.

Garvin, suddenly remembering what he had heard about Falshaw's wife, protested that his requirements would be slight. Falshaw did not know about that either, he was sure; but he reckoned that Garvin would have to ask the missus. The missus was "oop there," in the house.

He was about to leave Garvin to deal with the situation when he seemed to think better of it, and to have decided that, after all, he would see him through. All this time he had clung to his pitchfork. He now planted it firmly in the earth to await his return. He seemed to leave it with reluctance and regret.

The girl Anny smiled as if she was pleased at the turn affairs were taking. Garvin thought he saw hope for himself in Anny's smile.

As they reached the door that had been shut against Garvin, Falshaw drew himself up and squared his shoulders with a tightening of all his muscles. He seemed to take the young man under his protection with an air of dogged courage in seeing him through. It struck Garvin then that Falshaw was afraid of his wife.

She sat in twilight and slant-wise from the doorway, so that she had her back both to them and to the light. The sound of the lifted latch had been answered by a loud and sudden scraping of her chair; it was like a shriek of fright. She rose as Garvin entered, and turned, as if she suffered the impulse of the pregnant woman to hide herself.

He approached her, uttering some such soft and inarticulate sound as he would have used to soothe a shy animal As she swung heavily round and faced him he saw that he was likely to be mistaken as to Mrs. Falshaw's impulses. Otherwise he would have said that it was she who was afraid. But whatever her instinct was, fear or hostility, it already was submerged in the profound apathy of her gloom.

For the expression on Falahaw's face was a mere shadow fallen on it from his wife's face, where gloom and heaviness had entered into the substance of the flesh and the structure of the bone. Gloom was in the very fibre of her hair, a dull black, rusted.

It was Falshaw, with his air of protection, who put it to her whether it would be possible for them to take Garvin in.

"Ya knaw how *thot'll* end," said she significantly.

Things had happened, then, at Falshaw's. The gloom on Falshaw's face renewed Garvin's impression that Falshaw, perhaps, on account of these things, was afraid of his wife. He looked from her to his niece Anny, who stood leaning awkwardly against the dresser and twisting and untwisting a corner of her apron. There was a queer, half-frightened, half-sullen look on her face. And Garvin received a further impression, that the things that had happened at Falshaw's were connected unpleasantly with Falshaw's niece. It might well be. The girl was coarse.

By way of establishing his own incorruptibly moral character, Garvin drew a portrait of himself as a respectable, intellectual dry-as-dust, alien to human interests and emotions, intolerant of the society of his kind. So much so that he was obliged to stipulate that wherever he lodged there must be no other lodgers, and no children.

"There'll be no other lodgers. You can depend on thot," said Falshaw.

"And—no children?"

The girl Anny stirred uneasily. Her face, florid a second ago, was white as Garvin looked at it. She hid her hands in her apron, turned on her heel abruptly, and left the room.

Then Garvin was sure that he knew. *That* was the trouble in the house. Falshaw's eyes followed his niece as she went out. There was some tenderness in the gross man, and plainly he was sorry for the girl. But his wife's face had tightened; it had grown even more forbidding than it had been. The woman, Garvin judged, had been hard on Anny. He could see Anny being ground under that nether millstone.

Of course they would resent his touching on the sore point, but it happened to be the point on which Garvin himself was uneasy, and he really had to settle it. He approached it gently and with some confusion.

"I was told—" he began, and hesitated.

"What were ya told?" said Falshaw.

"Why—that there weren't any."

"Speak oop. Ah doan' understond ya."

Garvin plunged. "I mean—any children. I say, you know, there aren't any, really, are there?" He plunged deeper. "I mean, of course, in the house." And deeper still. "I mean—at present."

"There's noa fear o' thot—here."

It was Falshaw's wife who spoke.

II

It was as if the heart of her gloom had suddenly found utterance. Silence followed it.

They had seated themselves round the deep open hearth-place, Garvin on the settle facing Mrs. Falshaw, and Falshaw in the middle facing his hearth. His attitude indicated that he was seeing Garvin through, not because he liked him or approved of him, but as a simple matter of justice between man and man.

He did not look at Garvin when he spoke to him. He had not looked straight at him since he had brought him into the house. He seemed unable to face another man fairly and squarely in the presence of his wife. That might be, Garvin supposed, either because he was afraid of her or because his consciousness of approaching fatherhood had made him shy. Now, as his wife spoke, he turned on Garvin a dumb and poignant look that besought his pity and his comprehension. It was as if he had said, "You see what's wrong with her"; as if he were letting him into the secret of her malady, of the gloom that hung about them both. And Garvin understood that the unfortunate woman had fallen into some melancholy incidental to her state. She had got it into her head that the unborn thing had died within her or would die. A curse was on her. She would never be the mother of a living child.

She sat there, leaning forward, propping her weight with hands planted on her thighs, and staring at the hearth, a creature bowed and stupefied with her burden. Her husband leaned forward too, staring as she stared, moved to a like attitude by sympathy. He pushed out his loose lips from time to time, as if he said, "That's how it takes her. That's how it takes her."

Garvin's delicacy prompted him to inquire whether it would be inconvenient for Mrs. Falshaw to take him in.

At this innocent query Falshaw actually smiled. It was the most extraordinary smile. Without altering the expression of his face it went quivering through his whole vast bulk, as if his body were invaded by a malign mirth. It became articulate.

"We woan't," said Falshaw, "put *ourselves* out for anybody."

Garvin took this as an intimation in the northern manner that he was to consider himself at home.

Falshaw now approached his wife so near as to reckon that they could let the yoong mon have the parlour and the back bedroom, and Mrs. Falshaw replied from the depths of her apathy that he, Falshaw, could do as he liked.

A brief inspection showed Garvin that his quarters, though small, were incomparably clean. He moved into them in the afternoon of the next day.

He was pleased with the cool stone-flagged parlour. Its narrow walls concentrated the light in a clear equable stream on his table under the window. He ranged his books on the top of the low cupboard that flanked the fireplace; and, if the room was still cold and strange to him, he had only to look at them to feel instantly at home. Nobody interfered with him.

It was his bedroom that made him realise that Falshaw had meant what he said. They weren't going to put themselves out for anybody, not they. Garvin's expert eye had measured the resources of the house, and he knew that he had got the worst bedroom in it. It was such a room as is only given to a servant even in houses like the Falshaws'. And nobody had turned out of it for him. With all its cleanness, it had the musty smell of long disuse. Garvin, however, preferred this smell to any kindred sign that might suggest recent habitation. Apart from its appearance and the smell, the room inspired him with a profound discomfort and distrust. He prowled about in it for half an hour, searching in vain for possible sources of this feeling.

So little did the Falshaws put themselves out that nobody came upstairs to tell the lodger that his tea was waiting for him in the parlour. He drank it lukewarm and stewed to an abominable blackness. A delicious scent of home-baked bread and hot girdle-cakes came from the Falshaws' kitchen, while Garvin sniffed suspicion at a sour loaf and a slab of salt butter from the village shop. Bacon from the shop appeared at his supper, its rankness intensified by a savour of hot stew wafted through the doorway. He ventured to ask Anny if he couldn't have some of the new bread he had smelt baking, and was told that they only baked once a week for themselves. The idea seemed to be that any food cooked by the Falshaws was sacred to the tribe. He wouldn't be allowed to eat it.

But Garvin was ready to endure any privation of mere appetite in the satisfaction of his passion for peace, and peace (he could feel it) was what he had found at Falshaw's.

Before going to bed he had assured himself that he had his side of the house entirely to himself. He found out that the girl Anny slept with Mrs. Falshaw in the large front room over the kitchen. He supposed that this arrangement was unavoidable if they wanted to keep the young minx out of harm's way. As for Falshaw, he was lodged in a commodious chamber next his wife's, covering both the parlour and the passage. Garvin's room was certainly not commodious. The roof of the house, low and short on the front of it, long and steep-pitched on the back, dwarfed Garvin's room to the proportions of a garret. The space on this side of the house was further taken up by a landing, lighted through a small pane in the slope of the roof.

The doors of the three rooms opened on to the landing. There was also, at the top of a short stair, a fourth door, opposite Garvin's. This door was locked (Garvin in his fastidious curiosity had tried it). But the wall, flanking the well of the staircase, reassured him. There could be no width behind it for anything bigger than a box room. Garvin was certain of his peace.

Oh, certain. At evening an almost unnatural stillness had fallen on the place. It was in the house, in the orchard, and in the yard down there under the ash-trees. It deepened with each hour of the night. He was almost oppressed with his sense of it as he lay in bed, waiting for the sleep which he knew would be shy of visiting him in his strange quarters.

He would have had a better chance—as far as sleeping went—if there *had* been some noise about; some noise, that was to say, outside his own body. For in the silence, Garvin's body, with all its pulses, had become a centre of intolerable clamour.

Garvin's body grew quiet. He was deliciously, delicately aware of the approach of sleep, of sleep entering his veins, of sleep and silence and oblivion flooding his brain, his heart, submerging him, or just submerging, when, with a terrible vain resistance and resentment, he found himself being drawn out of it.

What amazed him as he came up was the slenderness of the thread that drew him, a sound so fragile, so thin, that he was almost unaware of it as sound. His resentment flamed to indignation as the thing became audible and recognisable, distinctly recognisable, as the crying of a child.

It came from one of the upper rooms: it was hardly a crying, a sobbing, a whimpering rather, muffled by closed doors. The wonder was how it could have waked him; the sound was so distant, so smothered, so inarticulate.

It went on for a long time, and Garvin could not say whether it ceased or whether he slept through it. He knew he did sleep.

III

In the morning he was aware that, as the victim of their deception, he was more interesting to the Falshaws than he had been overnight. Returning from a stroll before breakfast, he found Mrs. Falshaw standing in the door of the house and watching him. She slunk away at his approach and shut the kitchen door between them. Falshaw, encountered in the passage, eyed him stealthily with suspicion that turned at close quarters to defiance, as much as to say that, if Garvin was up to anything, he, Falshaw, was ready for him.

Garvin would have dealt with Falshaw then and there but for the presence of the girl Anny, who was stationed in the doorway of the parlour, watching also. She lingered in her waiting on him, and he discerned in her thick eyes a vague animal terror, half-spiritualised by an unspoken, an unspeakable appeal. It was borne in on him that her change of attitude was somehow connected with the disturbance of the night. He gathered from it that if her fear could have spoken it would have besought him to spare her, to say nothing.

His annoyance was accompanied by an inward shrug of cynical comprehension. Nothing more likely, said Garvin in his shrewdness, than that Anny should have borne a child, and that her child should be a shame and a burden to the Falshaws. They couldn't have resented it more than he did; but he meant to wait and see the extent of the nuisance before he made his protest.

All day the inviolate stillness of his solitude was a reproach to the resentment that he felt. The child was kept quiet, smuggled away somewhere out of sight.

But that night and the next night he heard it. And no wonder. He had found that its crying came from the small garret facing his, where apparently it was locked in and left to sleep alone.

It had its trick of waking at the same hour. The crying would begin about eleven and go on till past midnight. There was no petulance in it and no anger; it had all the qualities of a young child's cry, except the carnal dissonances and violences. The grief it uttered was too profound and too persistent, and, as it were, too pure; it knew none of the hot-blooded throes, the strangulated pauses, the lacerating resurgences of passion. At times it was shrill, unbroken, irremediable; at times it was no more than a sad sobbing and whimpering, stifled, Garvin gathered, under the bedclothes. He lay and listened to it till he knew all its changes and inflections, its languors and wearinesses, its piteous crescendos and amazements, as of a creature malignly re-created, born again to its mysterious, immitigable suffering.

As he never slept until it had ceased, Garvin was qualified to witness to the Falshaws' abominable neglect. Nobody came near the poor little wretch to comfort it. It was probably frightened there all by itself. The mere sound of the crying wouldn't have kept him awake but for his pity for the helpless thing that made it. In the daytime he found himself thinking about it. He couldn't get away from the thought of it. He worried over it. He had the horrible idea that the child suffered on his account; that the Falshaws kept it locked up in the garret in the daytime that it might be out of the lodger's way. As this theory was inconsistent with their allowing it to keep the lodger awake at night, he could only suppose that the Falshaws were as indifferent to its suffering as to his. They had more than one devil in their blood. Likely enough, it was the devil of Puritanism that made the man and woman cruel to the child of Anny's sin.

But the girl herself?

He had the very worst opinion of the girl Anny. He was convinced that Anny, and not Mrs. Falshaw, was the mother of the child. Not that he was inclined to think hardly of the girl for having it. What he couldn't stand was her behaviour to it now that she had had it. There was nothing very intimately revealing in Anny's heavy, full-blown face; but Garvin had judged her gross. He saw her now sinning grossly, for the sin's sake, without any grace of tenderness. She was the kind predestined to go wrong. She lacked the intelligence that might have kept her straight. He could see her going to meet her sin half-way, slowly, without any beating of the heart, finding the way by some dull instinct older than her soul.

He was obliged to admit that the poor thing had at any rate let him alone. Probably her instinct sufficed to tell her that he was not her prey. But he had gathered that she was responsible for the Falshaws' unwillingness to take him in; and it was plain enough that they kept a sharp lookout on her. He knew their habits now. He knew, for instance, that Falshaw accompanied his niece on any errand undertaken after dark. Indoors they wouldn't trust her out of their sight a minute on his side of the house. Now he came to think of it, he had never once seen her there in the hours of dusk and dark; he had never found her alone in his room at any hour. Mrs. Falshaw was always hovering somewhere near; her forbidding eye was for ever on the poor girl as she swept and scoured.

This austerity of the Falshaws had its inconveniences for Garvin. He didn't expect a tidy room at bed-time, or hot water, or sheets invitingly turned down. But nobody seemed to think of closing the window when the evening mists came on and settled on his bed, or when the rain beat in and made it damp.

He determined to deal with Anny.

He dealt with her on the morning after his third bad night.

"Look here," he said; "why don't you keep that child quiet?"

Her gross colour fled. And yet she faced him.

"You've heard her, sir?"

"Of course I've heard her."

Her thick eyes stared at him. They were curiously without shame.

"You don't look as if you had," she said.

That and her stare staggered him. Before he could answer her she had given utterance to a still more amazing thing.

"You needn't go," she said. "She won't hurt you."

With that she left him.

IV

That night, his fourth, Garvin found that his nerves were growing so increasingly, so frightfully sensitive to sound that the crying seemed to come from the threshold of his door, from his bedside, from his pillow. It got from his nerves into his dreams, and he woke with the sense of a child's body pressed to his body, the palms of its hands upon his breast, its face hidden against his side, and the vibration of its sobbing above his heart. The thing passed, with a fainter, shivering, vanishing vibration which he felt as somehow external to himself.

He sat up, wideawake, and listened. The crying had ceased. His nerves were all right again.

He supposed he'd have (as Falshaw would have said) to put up with it. He could, after all, reckon on six or seven hours' good sleep, and in the daytime the poor little thing was quiet enough in all conscience. He couldn't very well resent it.

And yet he did resent it. He resented the cruelty of it. So much so that he spoke about it to Mackinnon, the doctor, whose acquaintance he had made when he was lodging up in the village. Mackinnon had called at the house in the Bottom to see how Mrs. Falshaw was getting on. Garvin lay in wait for him and asked him if he couldn't do something. He, Garvin, couldn't stand it.

The doctor was a little Highlander, red haired, fiery, and shrewd. He looked shrewdly at Garvin and told him that if he couldn't stand that his nerves must be in an awful state. And he took him off with him in his motor on a long round that swept the district.

That evening, Garvin, drowsed with the wind of speed, refused the solicitations of the County History and went to bed before ten.

He was in the act of undressing when he heard the child cry.

The sobbing whimper was no longer stifled under bed-clothes; it sounded distinctly from the open landing. Garvin unlatched his door and looked out.

At this hour of the newly risen moon there was light on the landing like a grey day. He saw a girl child standing on the garret stair. It had on a short nightgown that showed its naked feet. It was clinging to the rail with one hand.

Its face was so small, so shrunken and so bleached, that at first its actual features were indistinct to him. What was distinct, appallingly distinct, was the look it had; a look not to be imagined or defined, and thinkable only as a cry, an agony, made visible.

The child stood there long enough to fix on him its look. At the same time it seemed so withdrawn in the secret of its suffering as to be unaware of him.

It descended the stair, went close past him, and crossed the landing to the women's room.

Now on these hot August nights the door was left half-open, leaving a wide passage way into the room. Garvin could see it. He looked for the child to go in where its mother lay. Instead of going in it stood there motionless as if it kept watch.

Then all at once it began crying, crying and beating on the open door with its tenuous hands, beating and pushing as against a door closed and locked.

It was then that Garvin knew.

The creature gave up its efforts at last and turned from the door sobbing. Garvin could not see its face now, for it had raised its arms and held them across its forehead with the backs of the hands pressed against its weeping eyes. Thus blinded, it made its way across the landing towards Garvin's door, and passed by him, still unaware, into his room.

He went in and shut-to the door. The child was standing by the foot of the bed as if it watched somebody who slept there. It stayed, watching, while Garvin undressed and got into bed. Then—Garvin was not frightened nor even surprised at what happened then; he seemed to have expected it—the little creature climbed up the bedside and crept in beside him. He felt, flesh to flesh, its body pressed to his body, the palms of its hands upon his breast, and its face hidden against his side.

V

He knew now what he was in for; he knew what was the matter with house; he knew its secret, the source of what, so far as *he* went, he could only call its fascination. For he could swear to his own state of mind—he was *not* afraid.

On one point only he was uncertain. He did not yet know whether he were alone or not in His experience, whether the Falshaws knew what he knew, and whether it was the things that they knew, that they had heard and seen, their experiences, which accounted for their abiding gloom. Neither they nor anybody else had told him precisely what he would be in for if he insisted on staying at Falshaw's; but there had been (he remembered now) a rather sinister inflection laid on certain words that had been said to him.

They came back to him now. He could have very little doubt that the place had a sinister reputation, and that the Falshaws knew it. He had not understood it at the time, because his mind had been so misled by Falshaw's bodily grossness that it could only form a gross conception of the trouble of the house, of the things that, as they had intimated to him, had happened there. Poor Garvin profoundly repented the infamy of some of his suspicions, those relating to the girl Anny.

He found on the morning of his experience that Falshaw's attitude, like his own, had changed somewhat overnight. The gross man was still suspicious (like Garvin), but there was more solicitude than hostility in his suspicion. He watched Garvin as if he thought he were going to be ill, as if he knew and were on the look out for the symptoms of his malady.

Ill or not (he certainly felt all right), Garvin was an object of even greater interest to his friend Mackinnon. The doctor called that evening with the evident intention of cheering him up. Garvin felt that Mackinnon was on the look out for something too. They talked about the County History and Garvin's part in it, which Mackinnon plainly regarded as conferring lustre upon Garvin. Incidentally he put him in the way of much valuable information, for the doctor knew something (sometimes he knew a great deal) about each house and its family within thirty miles round.

In the pauses of the conversation they could hear Falshaw talking to his wife. The two were sitting up late, and he seemed to be arguing with her.

It was eleven o'clock before Mackinnon went. The clank of the gate behind him was instantly followed by the sound of Mrs. Falshaw's chair scraping on the stone flags of the kitchen and by Falshaw's fist knocking upon Garvin's door.

He was almost respectful as he stood looming before Garvin's writing-table.

"Mr. Garvin," he began, "ah've soommat to saay to you. If you doan't loike what you've found you'd better goa. There's noa call for you to give the 'ouse a bod naame. There's too mooch been saaid. Ah'm dommed if ah'll put oop with it."

"I know the worst," said Garvin quietly, "and *I* can put up with it. How do you know what your next lodger'll do—or say?"

Falshaw's huge bulk seemed to sway there as he placed his balled fists on the table for support. He was silent.

"Mr. Falshaw, I don't know how much you know, or what—but if it happens to be what I know—"

"Ah doan't saay as 'tisn't. What ah saay is that there's noa call for you to stomach it. You can goa."

"I don't want to go. Why should I?"

"You doan't?" He peered at him.

"Of course not."

"Then, sir" (it was the first time that Falshaw had called him "sir"), "you bean't afeard?"

"No more, Mr. Falshaw, then you are yourself."

"Ah've noa cause to be afeard. Ah knaw nothing."

A tremor passed through him as from some centre stirred by utterance. His face quivered. Its brute heaviness was redeemed for a moment by some inscrutable pathos. It was impossible to say whether Falshaw deplored his ignorance or repudiated knowledge.

On the whole, Garvin inclined to think that he *was* alone in his experience.

VI

Three days passed. Night after night Garvin witnessed the same supernatural event.

His senses were now so perfectly adjusted to his experience that he no longer thought of it as supernatural. What struck him as marvellous was the change it worked in the Falshaws now that they knew he had it. He was evidently set apart, consecrated by his experience. He had become for them an object of extraordinary respect—he would almost have said of affection. Whereas they had once disregarded his wishes and treated his little likings and dislikings with an almost insolent contempt, now, everything that he had ever asked for, that he had ever wanted without asking for, was remembered and provided. The fresh home-made bread that he had coveted appeared daily at his table; his meals had a savour and variety which he would have judged beyond the scope of Mrs. Falshaw's art. He could hardly suppose that they did it for the sake of gain; for, poor as they were, they had taken him in under protest and had made no effort to keep him until now.

This change from hostility to the extreme of friendliness dated from the evening when he had declared to Falshaw that he felt no fear.

The statement (he had to own it) required qualification. It was true enough that he felt no fear of the primal, the complete manifestation. That, having all the colours and appearances of flesh and blood, had the value, the assurance, almost the inevitability of a natural thing. It had parted with its horror from the moment when he perceived that it was responsive to his pity and accessible to his succour.

But Garvin, reviewing his experiences, distinguished between the perfect and the imperfect. Beyond the primal haunting, round and about the central figure, the completed vision, he was conscious of a borderland of fear into which he had not yet entered.

It was chiefly present to him as a disagreeable feeling he had about his bedroom—a feeling which little Garvin, as he valued his own manliness, sternly refused to attend to. Still it was there. But for that sense he had, he would have preferred his garret to the long eastern chambers looking on the orchard of dead trees. The branches that hung before his window were alive. At sunset the light ran through their leaves, kindling them to a divine translucent green. And yet he loathed it.

The room had, clearly, some profound significance for the child, since it was always compelled to come there. But the significance was something that Garvin didn't care to explore; he felt it to be part of the peculiar, foggy unpleasantness of the borderland.

It was strange that, while he knew no terror of the perfect apparition, the bedfellow, his fear of the borderland was growing on him. His feeling was that if the things that were *there* became visible they would be more than he could endure.

There were degrees in the clearness of the primal manifestation; degrees which, as he made it out, corresponded to the intensity of the emotion, the suffering behind it. The child's form gathered and lost substance. At times it was of an extreme tenuity, suggesting nothing tangible. At times it had, not only the colour, but the pressure of flesh and blood. At times its face, its hands, and little naked feet had the peculiar vivid whiteness of white skin seen under water. Its feet along the floor were like feet moving through water.

He saw it now by day as well as night. It would pass him in the passage, on the stairs. It lay in wait for him at his door or at its own. He had an idea that it spent hours playing in the backyard under the ash-trees. Once when he looked out of his window he could have sworn that he saw it hanging over the great stone water-tank that stood there at the comer of the wall. He had never once seen it in his sitting-room, and what went on in the Falshaws' kitchen he could not say.

Thrice he saw it in the garden, coming towards him from the back-yard and going to a comer under the orchard wall. As it passed under the trees he could see the grass growing through its feet. It carried in its hand a little cup of water which it emptied there in the corner. It was busy and absorbed, very earnestly and seriously bent upon this act. He noticed that always, out of doors, the appearance was imperfect, but he discerned dimly that, out of doors, it had a happy look.

He examined the corner that it visited. A long flat-faced stone stood upright in the wall there; below it, hidden by the grass, he found a small plot marked out with stones.

A child's garden ruined beyond remembrance. There were gaps in its borders where the stones had been upheaved or buried. In the middle, trampled and beaten into the earth, he came upon the fragments of a broken cup.

It was thus that he began to construct the child's history. He had found that its more complete manifestations occurred indoors, on the landing and after dark, and that they culminated in bodily contact, the pressure of its form—the bedfellow's—against his own. And so he argued that outside, in the open air, it had been happy. It was within the house that the suffering which was its life had come to pass; the suffering was somehow connected with the closing of Mrs. Falshaw's door; it was habitually intenser at night-time, and it had its unspeakable climax, its agony, in Garvin's room.

On all these points he was certain with an absolute and immutable certainty. What baffled him was their date. Things had happened. He had more than a sense, an intolerable sense, of their happening. But when had they happened? To which one of the four generations that the house had known?

He thought he could tell if he could only get into the room where, as far as he could make it out, the whole thing started, the garret opposite his own with the stair before its door. It was the child's room and was bound to contain some sign or trace of the child. He must contrive to get in somehow.

He found a pretext. The parlour was still lumbered with the packing-cases his books had travelled in (Garvin had bruised his shins over them more than once). He approached Falshaw and asked him if he might not store the packing-cases in that box-room that they had upstairs. He supposed it was a box-room.

Falshaw hesitated. His gloom deepened. Presently, with some visible perturbation, he replied. Mr. Garvin might do as he liked. He would give him the key of the room. Mr. Garvin would be so good as to put the packing-cases in the space behind the door, without—Falshaw's trouble grew on him—disarranging anything.

He carried the cases upstairs and left them on the landing after giving Garvin the key of the room. It was evident that nothing would induce him to go in there himself.

Garvin's heart beat thickly as he entered. The room—he could see at a glance—was not used as a box-room. It was not used now for anything at all. It was a long garret, narrowed excessively by the sloping roof, and bare of all furniture but a chest of drawers and a washstand near the window, and, drawn to the far end of the room against the wall, two objects, each covered with a white sheet.

Garvin drew back the sheets. Thrust away, hidden out of sight, shrouded like the dead, were a child's little chair and a child's cot. He could see the slender hollow in the mattress where its body had lain.

He raised the edge of the coarse blue and white counterpane. The pillow beneath was not soiled, neither was it freshly clean. There was a small round patch, slightly discoloured, slightly dinted, by the pressure of a child's head.

For a moment that brought the thing horribly near to him.

He felt the hollows with his hand and found that they were hard. His reason told him that it must have taken more than one generation to make them so. He was, therefore, no surer of his date. The room had given him an uncomfortable sensation, and that was all.

That evening, setting out for his walk, he met Falshaw in the path coming over the brow of the hill. They exchanged a greeting and some remarks about the weather. There was a wind on the hill, and Falshaw advised Garvin not to go far. It was beating up, he said, for rain.

Garvin turned and walked back with him towards the lane. A sudden impulse seized him to make Falshaw talk. They stopped at the rise where the naked plum-tree pointed to the house in the Bottom.

"That's not an old house for these parts, Falshaw. How long have you had it?"

"Ever since ah can remember. Ma faather had it before me, and 'is faather before 'im agen."

"Four generations, then?"

"Three, sir." He added, "There'll be four soon enough if all goas well."

It was his first open reference to his wife's state.

"Why shouldn't all go well?"

"Thot's what I tell the missus. But ah can't move 'er. She's got it into 'er 'ead thot thick," said Falshaw gloomily.

Garvin murmured something vaguely consoling; and all the time his mind was running on his date. He must make Falshaw give it him.

"You see, Mr. Garvin, she's bin, you may say, in a dark state ever since—"

He stopped. Speech was painful and difficult to him.

"Ever since?" For a moment Garvin felt that Falshaw might be giving him the date.

But if Falshaw had hovered on the verge of a confidence he now drew back. All he said was, "It's more soometimes than ah can put oop with."

He meditated.

"And t' doctor, 'e cooms to cheer 'er oop, but 'e can't *do* nowt."

"What does he think?" asked Garvin, recalled to sympathy by the man's misery.

"Think? 'E doan't think. 'E saays it's natch'ral to 'er condition. But—ah doan't remember—"

He stopped again, and fell into the gloom that Garvin recognised as the shadow of his wife's dark state.

"It's a bod job, Mr. Garvin, it's a bod job."

"I wonder," said Garvin, "if I ought to stay much longer. She may be doing too much. Honestly, hadn't I better go?"

Falshaw shook his head.

"Doan't you think thot, sir; doan't you think thot."

"I can't bear," Garvin went on, "to be giving trouble at a time like this."

"Trooble? You call *thot* trooble?"

"Well—"

"You'll bring trooble, Mr. Garvin, if you goa."

"I don't understand."

"And ah doan't understond it neither. But—if you *can* stop, Mr. Garvin, doan't you goa. Doan't you goa."

He paused.

"If she sees you con stond it, maybe she'll mak out thot things can't be so bod."

Things? It was vague; but when it came to the point, to Garvin's point, Falshaw *was* vague. Garvin felt that they were on the verge again. He was determined to find out how much Falshaw knew, or how much he didn't know. He would tackle him there and then. He would tackle him suddenly and straight.

"Things can't be so bad if I can stand them?" he questioned. "And how bad do you think they are yourself, Falshaw?"

"Ah doan't think. And ah *know* nobbut what ah've heard. What you've heard." (He glossed it further.) "What folks saay."

"And these things—that they say, how long have they been said?"

Falshaw winced. "Ah doan't knaw."

There was no doubt that Falshaw repudiated any personal knowledge of the things; but then, Garvin reflected, he might be lying. He pressed it home.

"Before your time?"

"Noa. Not afore *ma* time. Thot couldn't be."

He said it simply and uncontrollably, as if it had been wrung from him, not by Garvin but by the pressure of some suffering of his own. He was profoundly unaware of having given Garvin what he wanted.

"You know *that*," said Garvin, who was for the moment insensible to pity in the excitement of following his trail.

Falshaw rallied. "Ah knaw nothing, ah tell you, but what ah've heard. Nothing but what *you've* heard, Mr. Garvin."

They had come to the stone stile that led into the lane. They stood there facing each other.

"It's not what I've heard," said Garvin. "It's what I've seen." At that Falshaw turned from him and bowed himself upon the stone wall.

VII

Up till that moment Garvin had barely hinted at the nature of his experiences. He was aware that his previous intimations had given Falshaw some uncomfortable emotions; but he was not prepared for the violence of the passion with which his final revelation was received.

He couldn't leave the man there in his agony; neither could he touch him nor speak to him. A certain awe restrained him in the presence of a feeling so tremendous and inscrutable.

It was Falshaw who recovered first, pulling his huge bulk together and steadying himself to speak. It was as if under it all he had not forgotten the consideration due to Garvin, who had become so inexplicably the witness and partaker of his tragedy.

"Mr. Garvin," he said, "ah think ah knaw what you may have seen. And ah tell you you've noa call to be afeard. It woan't harm you."

It was what Army had told him.

"I know," he said, "it won't harm me."

"It wouldn't," Falshaw went on. "There's a soort o' pity in they things."

He paused, feeling for his words.

"They knaw; and they doan't coom to those that are afeard of 'em. They doan't coom so as to be seen."

He paused again, meditating, and fell back upon his phrase, "It's the pity in them."

He climbed the stone stile and went slowly towards his house.

Garvin turned and walked again to the brow of the hill. There he stopped and looked back. Above the stone wall of the orchard, in the corner of the child's garden, he saw Falshaw standing, with his head bowed to his breast.

He said to himself then that he might have known. The child's garden under the orchard grass—*that* belonged clearly to the Falshaws' time. Why—as grass grows—within fifteen, within ten years it would have been buried, grassed over, without a stone to show that it had ever been. It belonged, not to Falshaw's father's generation, nor yet to Falshaw's. but to the generation that his wife bore in her womb.

VIII

The wild plum-tree on the hill rocked in the south-west wind, and pointed, gesticulated at the house.

Garvin's gaze followed the network of stone walls flung over the country. He had a sense of the foregoneness of the things he saw. He saw the network as a system of lines that, wherever you picked it up and followed it, led in some predestined way to the house as its secret and its centre. You couldn't get away from the house.

It was in an effort to get away from it that he walked on towards the fells.

The wind, as Falshaw had warned him, was beating up for rain. The south-west was black with rain. He could see it scudding up over the shoulder of the fell.

Half-way he turned and was blown home before the storm, leaning backwards, supporting himself on the wind. A mile from the Bottom the lain caught him and soaked him through.

Falshaw and Anny stood at the door of the house, watching for him. They were troubled at his drenching. He changed, and threw his dripping clothes down over the stairhead to be dried in the kitchen. He knew that neither Falshaw nor Anny had the nerve to go to his room to fetch them. He was glad to get out of it himself.

Mrs. Falshaw had his supper keeping hot for him by the kitchen hearth. She proposed that he should sit and eat it there while the fire was being lit in the parlour. He had owned to a chilliness.

She had set the lamp on the supper table, and sat in the ring of twilight with darkness behind her. Portions of her face and body thus appeared superficially illuminated, while the bulk of her became part of the darkness. Garvin was deeply aware of her face and of her eyes, which were fixed on him with an intolerable hunger. The face was sombre and sallow; it was hewn with a hard, unrounded heaviness, unlike her husband's. It would have been deadly hard but for the fugitive, hunted look that gave it a sort of painful life in deadness. Whether she sat or stood she was a creature overtaken, fixed in her fear, with no possibility of escape.

There were moments when he thought that she was about to speak, to ask him what he had seen. He felt somehow that she knew. She knew he had seen something. Whatever Mackinnon thought, he, Garvin, knew, and her husband knew, that she suffered no bodily ailment. What weighed on her was her sense of the supernatural, and her fear of it and of its inscrutable work on her, penetrating her flesh and striking the child that was to be born. It had been already brought home to him that his value, his fascination for her lay in his shared sense of it. That was the secret that they kept between them.

It was terrible to have to sit in that tongue-tied communion, and eat, bearing his own knowledge and her sense of it. He was glad when it was over and he was safe in the parlour, a place which he felt to be immune from these influences.

Anny was in there, on her knees by the hearth, trying to coax the fire to draw up the damp chimney. His impulse urged him to talk to Anny as he had talked to Falshaw. He was at that stage when he had to talk to some body; and he wanted to know how much Anny knew.

"Anny," he said, "my bed's damp; why didn't you go up and shut the window?" He knew why.

She rose and stood before him, awkwardly wiping her hands on her rough apron.

"Because I'm afeard, sir."

He looked at Anny. She was coarsely made as to the body, but to his purified perception there seemed to flow from her an almost radiant innocence and probity.

"What are you afraid of?"

She glanced aside miserably.

"You knaw what."

"Yes, I know. But you told me yourself it wouldn't hurt me."

"Hurt you? Little Affy—"

It had a name then, but he hadn't caught it.

"Little—"

"Little Affy."

"Effy," he murmured.

"Yes, sir. Little Affy never 'urt anyone in her life."

He said it over to himself. It touched him even more than Falshaw's "There's a sort of pity in they things." It brought the child nearer to him, poignantly near, in tender flesh and blood. He felt the sting of an intolerable evocation.

It was not yet complete.

"Who *was* little Effy?"

The girl's eyelids flickered and reddened and filled with tears.

"I mustn't talk about her, sir."

"Why not?"

"I promised Ooncle."

"It doesn't matter, does it, as long as I'm not afraid?"

"You're *not* afraid, sir" (she whispered it), "to sleep with her?"

"No, Anny, I'm not afraid."

The girl said "Good night" as if she had said "God bless you," and left him to his thought.

Whatever Anny had or hadn't seen, she knew.

He could not doubt that he was alone in his complete experience, yet he would have said that if ever there was a man and a woman and a girl that were haunted, it was Falshaw and his wife and the girl Anny. He could only suppose that their haunting was vague and imperfect. They lived on the edge of the borderland of fear, discovering nothing clearly yet knowing all. Anny, at any rate, knew the worst.

For he always put it to himself that it was the worst, even while he felt in his flesh the horror of the borderland, his own borderland, beyond.

It was on him that night, though he tried to fortify himself by reiterating that he knew the worst, and that if his nerves could stand that they could stand anything. He was not afraid (as Anny had suggested) to sleep as he had slept; he was not afraid of his bedfellow. He was afraid of his room, and of his bed, of the white sheets and the coarse quilt, of the whole twilight bulk of it, waiting for him in the corner by the window wall.

His sense of terror had defined itself as a sense of evil surpassing the fear of the supernatural. It was borne in on him that some iniquitous thing had had its place in this house and in this room.

He lay awake there, listening to the sounds of the night; to the wind sweeping the ash boughs along the roof above his window; to the drip of the rain in the stone trough beneath. The sounds of the night comforted him; and, before long, his brain became fogged with a grey stupor. But the stupor was like a veil spread over some backward, bottomless pit of fear. Tenuous itself, intangible, it yet held him, perilously it held him, breaking, delaying, lengthening out, moment by moment, his imminent descent.

The air in the dose garret oppressed him to suffocation. He got up and opened the window. The wind and the rain had passed, the ash-trees were still; a clear light, grey as water, filled the room. Things showed in it solid and distinct. Something seemed to shift in Garvin's brain with the sudden shifting of his body, and, as he stood there at the foot of the bed, he was aware of something happening before him.

He couldn't say what it was that happened. He only knew that it was bound to happen; it had been foreshadowed by his fear. He knew what that sudden shifting in his brain meant. He had simply gone over the borderland of fear and was in the gripping centre.

There were two there, a man and a woman. He did not discern them as ordinary supernatural presences; the terror they evoked surpassed all fear of the intangible. Of one thing he was certain—the man was Falshaw. He could swear to that. The woman he had with him was a woman whom Garvin had never seen. He couldn't say what it was he saw, what was done by those two, but he knew that it was evil. He couldn't say whether he really saw it, or whether he apprehended it by some supreme sense more living and more horrible than sight. It was monstrous, unintelligible; it lay outside the order of his experience. He seemed, in this shifting of his brain, to have parted with his experience, to have become a creature of vague memory and appalling possibilities of fear. He had told the truth when he had said that he was not afraid. Until this moment he had never known what fear was. The feeling was unspeakable. Its force, its vividness was such as could be possible only to a mind that came virgin to horror.

The whole thing lasted for a second or so. When it passed and the two with it, Garvin turned and saw the child, in its nightgown and with its naked feet, standing in the middle of the room and staring at the bed as he had stared. The fear on its face was more terrible to Garvin than his own fear. If it *was* his own.

He turned sick and knew nothing. He supposed he must have fainted.

IX

The next day Garvin said to himself that he would see Mackinnon. His nerves had gone to pieces for the time being, and he would have to get Mackinnon to patch them up. He found himself clinging to the thought of Mackinnon.

He spent the morning and afternoon out of doors, as far from Falshaw's as his legs would carry him; and in the evening he went to see Mackinnon.

The doctor was out, and Garvin waited. He hadn't the pluck to go back to Falshaw's without seeing Mackinnon.

By the time Mackinnon appeared (late for dinner) Garvin knew that he hadn't really come there to consult him. He had come to talk to him, to make him tell him what he knew about the Falshaws. He couldn't think why on earth he hadn't done it before; but he supposed Mackinnon must have put him off by the stupid things he had said about his nerves. He didn't mean to be put off to-night, and he wasn't going to talk about his nerves.

Neither was Mackinnon. He only looked at Garvin and said it was odd his being there; for he had just gone round to Falshaw's to see Garvin and bring him back to dine.

They dined alone together (Mackinnon was a bachelor); but it was afterwards in his den, over the cigarettes and whisky, that they talked.

"I say," said Garvin, who began it, "do you know anything about those Falshaws?"

"Oh, as much as I know about most people," said Mackinnon.

"Do you know what's the matter with them?"

"Would you expect me to own it if I didn't?"

"You know as well as I do that there's something wrong with them."

"There's something wrong with Mrs. Falshaw. Melancholy. They get it. She's had it ever since."

"Ever since what? That's what I want to know."

Mackinnon shrugged. "Ever since she began to be—"

"You think *that* accounts for it?"

"Presumably."

"Well—but how about Falshaw? And how about the girl Anny? And if it comes to that—how about *me*?"

"You? I suppose you've been hearing some queer stories. There *are* queer stories."

"I haven't heard one of them," said Garvin.

"Are you quite sure?"

"Positive."

"What *have* you heard, then?"

"I told you the other day."

"Yes," said Mackinnon; "that's one of the stories."

"How do you account for them?"

"The stories?"

"Yes."

"The facts account for the stories right enough."

"You mean they've been fabricated after the fact?"

"That's what happens."

"You forget," said Garvin, "that I haven't heard the stories and that I don't yet know the facts."

"I can give you them if you want them. They're quite as queer as the stories, and more interesting, because more human."

"I think," said Garvin, "you'd better hear *my* story first."

"Haven't I heard it?"

"Not my latest. Do you want it?"

"Well, I'd like to see if it's different from other people's. You know they all say they've *heard* things."

"Do they say they've seen them?"

"No. None of them seem to have gone as far as that."

"Well, I've gone as far as that—farther."

He told Mackinnon as casually as he could what he had seen.

Mackinnon was inclined to be impatient. "Yes, yes—a child that cries—in a nightgown—of course. But can you describe her? Can you give me any details?"

"She was very small; she had short hair—bleached—and pale eyes. The flesh under her eyes wa sunken. Two little pits—just here. Her face was sallow white and drawn a little, by her nostrils—"

"Queer," murmured Mackinnon, "very queer."

Garvin went on till Mackinnon interrupted him again.

"Beating on the door? Which door?"

"The door of Mrs. Falshaw's room."

"All right. Go on."

Garvin went on, to the scene in the orchard. "And I've seen it hanging over that stone tank at the back."

"Good God!" said Mackinnon softly.

Garvin came to his last experience.

"There," he said, "I own I am a bit vague."

"You're certain you saw a man and a woman?"

"Yes. And I'm certain that the man was Falshaw. But the woman I know nothing about. It wasn't Mrs. Falshaw."

"No," said Mackinnon thoughtfully. "Can you describe her?"

"I couldn't see her very well. Falshaw was between us. She was big and young and—that part of it's beastly."

He stopped.

"And the beastliest thing about it is that I didn't understand it, Mackinnon, I didn't understand it—and, frankly, I was in an awful funk."

Mackinnon stared. "You didn't understand it?"

"I'm only talking about what I felt at the time. I'm explaining what made it so horrible. I seemed to have parted with my power of understanding—a whole tract of knowledge—clean gone—"

Mackinnon was silent.

"What room were you in?" he asked presently.

"The small room at the back."

"I know." The doctor shifted his position as if he were trying to shake off something.

"Well," he said, "that yarn of yours would be queer enough if you knew the facts. As it is, I don't mind telling you that it's the queerest yarn I've heard yet."

"Can you account for it?"

"My dear Garvin, you can't live up here, in this country and with these people, and still go about accounting for things. If you're a wise man you accept them."

"You accept my statements then?"

"I have to. They square with the facts. Did you say anything to the Falshaws?"

"A little—to him—and Anny. I can't tell how much they know. They wouldn't say."

"Anny wouldn't?"

"She let out that the child's name was Effy; and then she told me she'd promised Falshaw not to talk about her."

"She isn't allowed to talk about her—because she—*knows*. She didn't tell you that Effy was the Falshaws' child?"

"No."

"She was. Their only child. She died three years ago."

"How?"

"Drowned. In the stone tank under your window."

"She fell in," said Garvin dreamily.

"She fell in. There was nobody about. She must have had some sort of fit, or she could have got out all right."

"Who found her?"

"The woman you saw."

Garvin winced.

"The Falshaws were severely censured at the inquest. You see, the child oughtn't to have been left alone. She'd had one fit about a month before and they knew it."

"And before that?"

"Can't say. Nobody knew. They weren't likely to know. The child was left by herself night and day."

"I see. That's what's the matter with them."

"No doubt it's what's given Sarah Falshaw this idea of hers that the baby will be born dead. Shouldn't wonder if it was. Good thing, too, when you think how the made the other one suffer."

Mackinnon's fire broke out. "Women like that oughtn't to bear children. But they do. They always will do."

"She wants it to live?"

"I can't tell you what she wants—now."

"She didn't want—the other one?"

"Oh, she wanted her well enough. But she wanted something else more. And she had to want. She'd been all right to the child until she found that out; and then she couldn't bear the sight of it."

"She wanted another man, I suppose?"

"Not a bit of it. She wanted her own husband. It isn't a pretty story to tell, Garvin."

X

All the same he told it.

"I'd say she was like an animal, only animals don't carry the thing to the point of insanity. And animals—most of them, at any rate—aren't cruel to their young."

"What did she do to it?"

"She did nothing. That was it. She used to say it was Falshaw's fault that she didn't care for it. Everything, you see, was Falshaw's fault. But she behaved as if it was the child's fault that Falshaw didn't want her. You'd have said she had a grudge against it. Things certainly got worse after it came. But she'd led him a life before that. Lord, what a life a woman can lead a man when she wants him more than he wants her and he lets her know it.

"They'd been all right at first. You wouldn't think it, but Sarah was a fine-looking woman when he married her—one of those hard black and white women who turn yellow when they worry. And Sarah was the sort that worried. She worried the life out of Falshaw. He was a big, strong, full-blooded fellow with a lot of exuberant young animality about him, and look at him now; what aged man do you suppose he is? Fifty, wouldn't you? Well, if you'll believe it, he's only thirty-eight. That's Sarah.

"He was twenty-three when he married her, and Sarah may have been a bit older. And they'd been married five years before the child came. He wasn't a bad sort, Falshaw, and he rubbed along with Sarah and her tongue and her temper for three years or so. He used to say she didn't mean it, and she couldn't help it, and she'd be all right when there was a youngster or two about. I suppose he thought all women were like that when they hadn't any children. The worst of it was she knew he thought it, and it riled her.

"Many a man would have tried to knock it out of her with a stout ash stick, but Falshaw wasn't that sort. He chuckled and grinned at her and reckoned secretly on the baby. And there's something exquisitely irritating, to a woman of Sarah's temperament, in a man who chuckles and grins and reckons on a baby that doesn't come. And long before it came she'd tired him out, and he took up with another woman, a bad lot.

"That was a temporary lapse. Falshaw's heart wasn't in it. And, though I don't suppose Sarah forgave him, she got over it. But she never got over Rhoda Webster.

"Rhoda was a servant girl at the White Hart Inn. I don't blame Falshaw, mind you. When I think what his life was, I'm glad he had that one bright spot of immorality to look back upon. He'd got into the way of going off to the White Hart—a good two miles—to get out of the range of his wife's tongue, and Rhoda wasn't by any means a bad girl—then. She was neither good nor bad; she was just natural, without a bit of art to help her one way or the other. Anyhow, there was so little harm in the girl—then—or in Falshaw for that matter, that nothing happened till he had her in his house after Sarah's child was born. Sarah was laid up for months—that's how it took her—and the man was at his wits' end. Rhoda got restless and left her place, and was always in and out of Falshaw's house looking after Falshaw. She'd walk the two miles from the village and back just to cook his dinner and see him eat it. And when Sarah got about again she wasn't fit for much, and she had to mind the baby. So Falshaw kept on having the girl about the house. He said he had to have someone.

"That went on for months and months. It looked innocent enough; but Sarah began to suspect things. They had a row about it. Sarah said the girl was to go, and Falshaw said she was to stay, and if Sarah didn't like it she could lump it.

"It ended in the girl staying altogether. She slept in the house. Then Sarah found them out. And this time it broke her nerve. If she'd been a woman of any spirit she'd have left him. But she wasn't that sort. The feeling she had for Falshaw wouldn't let her leave him. She had to stay. She wasn't going to leave him to the other woman, and the other woman wasn't going to leave him to her. So there they were all three, shut up in that house, Falshaw carrying on with Rhoda behind his wife's back, and his wife stalking them, and seeing everything and pretending half the time she didn't see. And Rhoda, if you please, amiable, imperturbable, scouring and scrubbing, and behaving as if it didn't matter to her whether Falshaw carried on with her or not. She always had that air of not knowing what Sarah saw to worry about.

"At first, I believe, Falshaw made a great point of not leaving Sarah. But one night he never came near her. And then Sarah turned. The next night was a wet one, and she waited till Rhoda was in the backyard or somewhere, and she locked her out. Up till then Falshaw had chuckled and grinned and gone his own way, reckoning on the child that had come to keep things straight. He excused himself for everything by saying Sarah'd got the child.

"But when he came home that night and found Rhoda standing on the front doorstep in the rain, he went for Sarah there and then and told her that if she did anything more to the girl he'd go out of the house—he and Rhoda—and leave her, as he put it, for good and all. He was sick of her. It was her own doing. She'd driven him to it. It had got to be, and she'd have to 'put oop with it.' Can't you hear him saying it? He hammered it in. She'd got the child. He'd given her the child; and it ought to be enough for her.

"Up till then she might have had some hope of getting him back, but when he began to talk about the child she knew it was the end. And she blamed the child for it. If the child hadn't been born Falshaw's girl would never have got her foot into the house. If the child hadn't been born she'd have had her strength, she could have turned the girl out and made her stay out. If the child hadn't been bom she'd have kept her good looks and had a hold on Falshaw.

"Which," said Mackinnon, "was all perfectly true."

"How old was the child then?" Garvin asked.

"Let me think. It must have been about three."

"It was older than that when *I* saw it," said Garvin.

"Up till then it hadn't suffered," said Mackinnon. "Sarah had been quite decent to it. But when she realised that she'd got it instead of her husband she couldn't bear it near her.

"The first thing she did was to turn it out of the bed where it used to sleep with her. They say she couldn't stand the touch of its body against hers. You see that was how she took it. You may think I'm unjust to the woman—Heaven knows she suffered—but if you'd seen her with that child and how *it* suffered—I've seen passion, animal passion, in unpleasanter forms than you can imagine, and I've seen some very ugly results of its frustration; but that woman showed me the ugliest thing on God's earth—the hard, savage lust that avenges its frustration on its own offspring. If she couldn't have Falshaw with her she wouldn't have the child. That was her attitude.

"When it was older she turned it out of her room—that long room in the front. It had to sleep by itself in some place at the back—"

"I know," said Garvin.

"Not that Sarah was actively or deliberately cruel. It was well-fed and all that. But it loved its mother—and it knew. My God—how she *could*! I've seen the child making love to that woman—making love, Garvin, with its little face and its funny voice and its fingers—stroking her; and if she didn't push it away, she'd sit and take no notice of it. But it went on.

"I've seen that; and I've seen Rhoda kiss it and give it things when its mother wasn't looking. Rhoda was always good to it. But it would go from Rhoda to its mother any day.

"That was when it was little. She'd suckled it, you see, before she took a grudge against it.

"At last she took to locking her door against it. Once Rhoda found it beating on the door and crying the house down, and she took it into her own bed.

"Rhoda slept in the servant's room, the room you have now.

"All this came out at the inquest, mind you, when Rhoda gave evidence. Lots of things came out. It seems that when Falshaw was annoyed with his wife or she with Falshaw, she vented her annoyance on the child. She found out that was the way to hurt him. For instance, Falshaw had dug a little garden for it at the bottom of the orchard. And it made the child happy. She used to go running backwards and forwards from the stone tank to the garden, watering it from a little cup that Rhoda gave her. Rhoda and Falshaw used to play with her there. One day Mrs. Falshaw found them at it. And she took the cup from the child and broke it to pieces in a fury, and stamped on the garden till she'd destroyed it. Just because Falshaw made it. Rhoda took the child into the house so that it mightn't see what its mother was doing. She got that in at the inquest, too. But she shielded Falshaw so well, and made the case so black against his wife, that it was considered to damage her evidence.

"And here's where you come in. When the child couldn't get into its mother's room it used to go across to Rhoda's, and creep into her bed and cuddle up to her for warmth. It was always cold. It fretted, you see, and though it was well-fed its food didn't do it any good. I was always being called in. Once I spoke my mind to Sarah Falshaw, and she told me I didn't know what I was talking about.

"Then, one night, it went into Rhoda's room and found Falshaw there.

"And I'm inclined to think, Garvin, that you saw what it saw. For Falshaw turned round and cursed it. Heaven knows how much it understood. Falshaw may have frightened it. Anyhow, it had some kind of fit—the first, I believe, it ever did have.

"After that it was afraid of Falshaw and of Rhoda, though it had been very fond of both of them. Oddly, enough, it never was afraid of its mother. Account for *that* if you can."

"What happened," said Garvin, who didn't attempt to account for it, "when Effy died?"

"Falshaw sent Rhoda away, wouldn't have anything more to do with her. His wife blamed them both for the child's death, and Falshaw blamed himself. It sobered him. He's been a good husband to that woman ever since.

"It's queer, Garvin—but in one way it hasn't changed him. He still reckons on the child, the child that Mrs. Falshaw insists will be born dead. It may be. But it's far more probable—"

"What is?"

"That Sarah Falshaw will go off her head. That," said Mackinnon, "is what I'm waiting for."

They were silent a long time till Garvin spoke.

"But, Mackinnon, what do you make of it? Of my seeing these things? It's a series of hallucinations, if you like. But a series, and it all tallies. On your own showing it all tallies."

"It does."

"What I can't get at is *why* it tallies—what makes me see?"

Mackinnon brooded, while Garvin excitedly went on.

"Is it, do you suppose, suggestion? Or some influence given off by these people—by their evil consciences?"

"Or," said Mackinnon gravely—"their evil."

XI

It was morning. Garvin was sitting in the field under the plum-tree, staring at the house in the Bottom, the house that seemed to stand always in the twilight, to gather upon its walls a perpetual dusk.

It knew no sun, only degrees of twilight, dark and clear. Yesterday under a grey sky it had been drenched in gloom. To-day, when the south was golden white with the sun, when the hot air quivered like water over the grass tops in the field, the house stood as if withdrawn into its own grey, sub-lucid evening, intolerably secret, intolerably remote.

And now he knew its secret. "Their evil" saturating the very walls, leaking through and penetrating those other walls, the bounds of Garvin's personality, starting in him a whole train of experience not his own.

Their evil. It had been for Mackinnon an immense admission. It went beyond all accepted theories of suggestion; and considering what Mackinnon's information was compared with his, Garvin couldn't see that he could very well have gone further. The doctor had watched the outside of events; whereas he, Garvin, had been taken into the invisible places, into the mystic heart of suffering. He knew the unnamed, unnameable secret of pity and fear.

These things had become the substance of his innermost self.

His knowledge, overlaid by his own adult experience, had been a little tangled and obscure; Mackinnon's revelations had served to make it orderly, dear, complete. From that tale, half-savage, half-sordid, from that tragedy of the Falshaws, from that confusion of sombre lusts, and unclean, carnal miseries, there emerged the figure of the child Effy, tender, luminous, spiritual, unspeakably lovable and pure.

He knew now what had happened to him. He had been made the vehicle of that spirit; he had been possessed, divinely coerced by Effy. What he had seen he had seen with Effy's eyes, with Effy's awful innocence and terror. He had slipped the intangible bonds, to become one (Heaven knew how) with that slender, fragile being, broken by the invasion of a knowledge out of all proportion to its understanding. For Effy's vision of evil had been thus immense and horrible because it had been so obscure, so unintelligible. He could not doubt that he had shared to some extent the child's malady.

But all that had been only for a moment. What really possessed him and remained with him was Effy's passion. Effy's passion (for the mother who had not loved her) was *the* supernatural thing, the possessing, pursuing, unappeasably crying thing that haunted the Falshaws' house. Effy's passion was indestructible. It was set free of time and of mortality. He could not detach Effy from her passion and think of her as in a place apart. Where it was there she was also.

As far as Garvin could make out from his experience, the place of the blessed or of the unblessed was not by any means a place apart. There were no bounds and partitions between flesh and spirit, the visible and invisible. He had seen Effy's spirit as flesh.

He asked himself why he had seen it? Why he and not any of the Falshaws of whose flesh she was? Falshaw and Anny had given him a hint. He saw Effy because he was not afraid to see her. Fear was the great blinder and divider. Falshaw could see that.

But hadn't Falshaw, in his moment of inspiration, seen further? Wasn't it Effy's pity that had spared them? She hadn't hurt them—she had never hurt anyone in her life. She hadn't pressed them hard.

Under Effy's pressure, her continual pursuing of him, Garvin's "Why?" had come to mean "For what reason? To what end?"

Mackinnon's story had enlightened him. He was the intercessor between Effy's passion and the Falshaws' fear.

Effy's suffering had endured with her indestructible, unappeasable passion. It was through him, Garvin, that her passion clamoured for satisfaction and her suffering for rest.

She had come back (so he made it out) to recover the love that had been withheld from her. She pursued them all; but, if her father and Anny were afraid of her, her mother was mortally afraid. And it was her mother that she wanted to get at. She could only get at her mother through Garvin, who had no fear.

It was clear to Garvin that Mrs. Falshaw divined what purpose he had been put to. Her fear divined it. And how, he now asked himself, was he, the intercessor, going to break down her fear? Plainly she, like her husband, was relying on Effy's pity to protect her from the vision of Effy. It was a sort of moral support to her; and morally the woman was already so shattered and undermined that to break any prop might bring down the whole structure. Mackinnon had warned him of that. And there was her state to be considered. He had been at Falshaw's now for nearly a month. It wanted but seven weeks of her time. But it was borne in upon Garvin that if he waited till *afterwards* it would be too late—for Effy.

If he were responsible for Mrs. Falshaw, how about his responsibility to Effy? That—seeing the incredible relation in which he stood to her—was unmistakable; it was supreme. And couldn't he, who knew her, rely upon Effy too?

He watched his opportunity for three days. Then, on the evening of the third day, the last of August, the thing was taken out of his hands. Mrs. Falshaw sent for him of her own accord.

She was sitting in her chair in the kitchen and excused herself from rising as he entered. There was nothing unusual in her appearance— nothing, as far as he could see, premonitory. What he did notice was the unabated fear in her eyes as she fixed them on him. She was holding something hidden in her lap.

A chair had been placed for Garvin close beside her.

"Mr. Garvin," she said, "d'ye knaw it'll be a month to-morrow you've been here? I didn't look for ya to stop soa long."

"Why shouldn't I? You've been very good to me."

"Good to ya? Who wouldn' be good to ya? You're a good man, Mr. Garvin, else you'd a been afeard to stop. You'd 'ave tuk and roon like the rest of 'em."

She brooded. Garvin sought for words to break the intolerable silence, and found none.

"Ah can't blaame 'em. Ah'm afeard myself."

"There's no need. It's not a thing to be afraid of. It's a thing to pity, Mrs. Falshaw—and to love. Such a little thing."

She looked at him. Her obscure soul was at his feet. Up till now she had not known the extent and substance of his knowledge; but now she knew. It was not only that she respected him as one who had seen the thing she feared and had not feared it. She yearned to him; she longed for touch with him, as if through him she reached, unterrified, the divine, disastrous vision.

"It's true what they saay?" she said. "You've heard it?"

"I've seen it."

"Tell me what you've seen?" she whispered.

He told her in a few words. He saw her body stiffen as she braced herself to hear him. She heard him in silence until he began witnessing to Effy's form, her face, her features; then she gave a low moan of assent. "Thot's her. Thot's Affy."

She now uncovered the thing she had held hidden in her lap. "Was it like thot?" she said. "Would you knaw 'er from thot picture?" She gave it him. It was a photograph of a much younger child than Effy as he had seen her.

He hesitated. "Yes. Just. She's a little older than this and thinner—ever so much thinner."

"Thot's Affy at three year old. She was seven when she died. She'd be ten year old to-day. To-day's 'er birthday."

Garvin got on with his tale as far as the child's coming to his bed. He told how he had received the little thing and had warmed it at his side. Hitherto Mrs. Falshaw had sat rigid and constrained, as if she held herself back from realisation of the thing she feared; but at that touch she trembled and broke down.

"You let 'er stay?" she cried. "You didn't send 'er away? You let little Affy stay with you?"

She drew back again and paused.

"She comes to you in 'er little night-shift?"

"Yes."

He wondered why she should ask him that and in that accent of fear made vehement.

"Thot's how ah'm *afeard* of seeing 'er."

She leaned forward to him.

"There's times, Mr. Garvin, when ah'm scairt for ma life o' seeing 'er, any way. And when the fear taks hold o' me, it strikes through, as if it wud kill the child. And so 'twull, so 'twull. 'Tisn' likely as ah should bear a living child. Ah'm not fit to 'ave un."

"Don't think of it," said Garvin.

"Thinking doan't mak' no difference. I doan't care," she cried savagely, "if 'tis killed."

"Don't say that, Mrs. Falshaw. Think of your husband."

That was not judicious of Garvin, as he saw. It stirred Mrs. Falshaw's devil from its sleep.

"Falshaw!" She spat his name out. "'E thinks child-bearing's the only cure for all a woman's suffering."

"He has suffered, too," said Garvin.

She softened. "'E's sot on it," she said. "'E saays if there's a child about the plaace, there'll be an end of the trooble. But I tall 'im if Affy's here, and she knaws, and she sees me takken oop with another child, 'twill be worse trooble for 'er then than 'tis now."

"You know what her trouble was and is."

She said nothing.

"And you know that at this moment, in this room, there's nothing between you and Effy but your fear."

"My little Affy! 'Tis more than that. If ah weren't afeard ah should see 'er, ah knaw. But if ah were a good woman ah shouldn't be afeard."

As she said it Garvin felt a light breath on the back of his neck. He turned and saw the child standing behind his chair. It slid past his shoulder, and he saw it now in the open space between him and the hearthstone, facing Mrs. Falshaw. It advanced, solicitous, adventurous. It put out its hand and, with a touch that must have fallen light as thistle-down, it stroked its mother's face.

Mrs. Falshaw shrank slightly and put up her hands to ward it off, and the child slid back again. Garvin cried out, "Don't send her away—don't, for God's sake, send her away!"

Mrs. Falshaw and Effy seemed both unconscious of his cry.

He saw the child approach again fearlessly. It smiled, as with an unearthly pity and comprehension (he could not tell whether Effy had learnt this sad wisdom on earth, or in the place of the blessed). The look was superhuman. Urged by the persistence of its passion, the child hovered for a moment, divinely coercing, divinely caressing; its touch fell now on its mother's hair, now on her cheek, now on her lips, and lingered there.

And then the woman writhed and flung herself backwards in her chair away from it. Her face was convulsed with a hideous agony of fear. Then, even to Garvin's sight, Effy vanished.

That night Mrs. Falshaw was delivered of a dead child.

XII

That was at midnight.

An hour before, Garvin had been roused out of his bed by Falshaw knocking at His door. He flung on his clothes and went to fetch Mackinnon.

The doctor was up till dawn with Mrs. Falshaw. When he looked in again at noon of the next day he found the woman doing well. Her body, he said, was as strong as any horse.

He took Garvin away with him and put him up at his own house. It was better both for him and the Falshaws that he should be out of the way. Garvin was worrying. He held himself responsible for the event. Having been assured four times that Mrs. Falshaw's body was out of danger, he insisted on his fear as to her mind. Mackinnon had said himself that she would go off her head. Did Mackinnon think now that that was at all likely?

The doctor was cautious. He wouldn't swear to Mrs. Falshaw's mind. It might be better, or it might be worse. So far there had been no disturbing symptoms. She had behaved just like any other woman.

She had asked for the dead baby, and Falshaw had fetched it and put it in her arms. Mackinnon had left her looking at it. There was no distress. On the contrary, she was placid and curiously appeased. The mere act of child-bearing, Mackinnon declared, was sometimes enough to set a woman straight who had been queer before it. And Mrs. Falshaw had been decidedly queer.

Mackinnon was now steeped in the physical aspects of the case; and when Garvin dwelt morbidly on his own possible share in it, he became almost grossly derisive, and refused to listen to any other view. He was fantastically fertile in suggesting things that Garvin might just as well suppose. But when Garvin began to tell him about the latest appearance of the child, he was angry and got up and left him. There was a real child in the village, he said, whom he had to attend to.

That was about nine o'clock in the evening. Garvin had settled himself comfortably in Mackinnon's study with a book, when he was told that Mr. Falshaw was outside and wanted to see him. It wasn't the doctor, it was Mr. Garvin, the maid was sure of it, that he had said he must see.

Garvin went to Falshaw. He was standing in the door of the doctor's house. The lamp-light on his face showed it fallen and undone. He held, half-hidden under his arm, an oblong thing covered with a black cloth.

His wife, he said, wanted to see Garvin. She was in an awful way. They could do nothing with her. She kept on calling for Mr. Garvin. They couldn't get the child away from her to bury it (he glanced at the thing he held under his arm).

Garvin left a message for Mackinnon and went out with Falshaw.

The short cut from the village was a mile and a half by the lane through the Bottom. As they trudged through the dark, Falshaw, between fits of silence, took up his tale. He'd been up to the village to fetch the coffin. The child was to be buried in the morning soon after daybreak. And the trouble was that its mother wouldn't hear of the burying. She'd got the child in the bed with her and she wouldn't let it go. They'd taken it from her when she was asleep and laid it on the cot in the back-room, and the nurse, she'd dressed it pretty. They were at their supper, and the nurse was out of the wife's room but five minutes when Sarah she'd up and she'd got, somehow stealthy, into the backroom and taken the child. And she turned mad-like when they tried to take it from her.

"An' what she saays is, Mr. Garvin, that you knaw all about it."

The high village road dropped to the lane. A mile off a solitary light shone in the Bottom. Coming from the village, they approached the house from the back, and Garvin saw that the light came from the long garret, Effy's garret, where the dead child had been laid.

Falshaw put the coffin in there and took Garvin to his wife's room.

Mrs. Falshaw lay in a big bed facing the door. A candle burned on the table beside her. A nurse sat at the head of the bed and Anny at the foot. Mrs. Falshaw lay slant-wise on her left side with her back turned to them. The candle-light fell full on her and left the watchers in shadow.

Falshaw took Garvin by the arm and led him to the bedside. They stood there without speaking, made dumb by what they saw.

The bed-clothes were turned back a little on this side, and in the uncovered space the dead child, wrapped in a flannel, lay cradled in its mother's left arm. With her left hand she held it tight against her side, with her right she supported her own sagging breast and pressed the nipple to its shut mouth.

Her face, thinned and smoothed, refined beyond Garvin's recognition, brooded over the dead face, in the stillness, the stupefaction, of desire accomplished.

"It's Affy. It's little Affy," she said. "She's afeard to suck."

"Thot's how she keeps on," said Falshaw.

"She's afeard o' me. She's afeard of her mother. You speak to 'er, Mr. Garvin, and tell 'er not to be afeard."

Garvin bent over the body, and she whispered fiercely, "You tell little Affy, sir."

"Let me look," said Garvin.

Mrs. Falshaw closed her eyes. As Garvin laid his hand on the dead child she drew back a little. Her breast dropped from its dead lips.

"Now," he heard Falshaw muttering at his elbow. And some innermost voice in him replied, "Not yet."

"There's Affy now. Standing by the doorway."

Garvin saw her.

It was Anny who had spoken.

She rose, fascinated; and Falshaw turned. They stood motionless, gazing at Effy as she came. Their lips were parted slightly. It was evident that they felt no fear. They were charmed, rather, as at the approach of some wonderful, shining thing. (The nurse sat on, stolidly unconscious.)

"She's gone," said Anny.

She had passed out of their momentary vision. Her business was not with them.

She came—Garvin saw her—no longer solicitous, adventurous, but with a soft and terrible swiftness, an irresistible urgency.

As Garvin stooped suddenly and lifted the dead child from the bed, he saw Effy slide through his hands into its place. In Mrs. Falshaw's eyes there was neither fear nor any discernment of the substitution; yet she saw as he saw. She saw with sanity. Her arms pressed the impalpable creature, as it were flesh to flesh; and Garvin knew that Effy's passion was appeased.

Epilogue

A year later Garvin was on Dartmoor, working up Stone Circles for the County History. A letter from Mackinnon reached him there. It came as an answer to his wonder.

"There's a man in your trade living at Falshaw's. He doesn't see or hear things; and he's there for nerves, too. They tell me nothing has been seen or heard since you left.

"Mrs. Falshaw often talks about you. I saw her the other day, and she desired, almost with tears, to be remembered to you. The point she insists on is that you are a good man. I'm inclined to think, Garvin, that you knew more about that woman than I ever did. She is, I ought to tell you, absolutely sane—has been ever since that night.

"There's a little thing that may interest you. In Mrs. Falshaw's room—you remember it?—they've got a picture, an enlarged photograph of the child Effy, framed and hung on the wall. Under it there's a shelf with her things—a cup she used to drink out of—some tin animals—a doll. They suggest votive offerings on an altar of the dead. What does it mean? Just remembrance? Or—some idea of propitiation?

"You ought to know."

He did.

FROM THE DEAD

E. Nesbit

I

But true or not true, your brother is a scoundrel. No man—no decent man—tells such things."

"He did not tell me. How dare you suppose it? I found the letter in his desk; and she being my friend and you being her lover, I never thought there could be any harm in my reading her letter to my brother. Give me back the letter. I was a fool to tell you."

Ida Helmont held out her hand for the letter.

"Not yet," I said, and I went to the window. The dull red of a London sunset burned on the paper, as I read in the quaint, dainty handwriting I knew so well and had kissed so often—

DEAR,

I do—I do love you; but it's impossible. I must marry Arthur. My honour is engaged. If he would only set me free—but he never will. He loves me so foolishly. But as for me, it is you I love—body, soul, and spirit. There is no one in my heart but you. I think of you all day, and dream of you all night. And we must part. And that is the way of the world. Good-bye!—

Yours, yours, yours,

ELVIRE

I had seen the handwriting, indeed, often enough. But the passion written there was new to me. That I had not seen.

I turned from the window wearily. My sitting-room looked strange to me. There were my books, my reading-lamp, my untasted dinner still on the table, as I had left it when I rose to dissemble my surprise at Ida Helmont's visit—Ida Helmont, who now sat in my easy-chair looking at me quietly.

"Well—do you give me no thanks?"

"You put a knife in my heart, and then ask for thanks?"

"Pardon me," she said, throwing up her chin. "I have done nothing but show you the truth. For that one should expect no gratitude—may I ask, out of mere curiosity, what you intend to do?"

"Your brother will tell you——"

She rose suddenly, pale to the lips.

"You will not tell my brother?" she began.

"That you have read his private letters? Certainly not!"

She came towards me—her gold hair flaming in the sunset light.

"Why are you so angry with me?" she said. "Be reasonable. What else could I do?"

"I don't know."

"Would it have been right not to tell you?"

"I don't know. I only know that you've put the sun out, and I haven't got used to the dark yet."

"Believe me," she said, coming still nearer to me, and laying her hands in the lightest light touch on my shoulders, "believe me, she never loved you."

There was a softness in her tone that irritated and stimulated me. I moved gently back, and her hands fell by her sides.

"I beg your pardon," I said. "I have behaved very badly. You were quite right to come, and I am not ungrateful. Will you post a letter for me?"

I sat down and wrote—

> I give you back your freedom. The only gift of mine that can please you now.
>
> ARTHUR

I held the sheet out to Miss Helmont, and, when she had glanced at it, I sealed, stamped, and addressed it.

"Good-bye," I said then, and gave her the letter. As the door closed behind her I sank into my chair, and I am not ashamed to say that I cried like a child or a fool over my lost plaything—the little dark-haired woman who loved some one else with "body, soul, and spirit."

I did not hear the door open or any foot on the floor, and therefore I started when a voice behind me said—

"Are you so very unhappy? Oh, Arthur, don't think I am not sorry for you!"

"I don't want any one to be sorry for me, Miss Helmont," I said.

She was silent a moment. Then, with a quick, sudden, gentle movement she leaned down and kissed my forehead—and I heard the door softly close. Then I knew that the beautiful Miss Helmont loved me.

At first that thought only fleeted by—a light cloud against a grey sky—but the next day reason woke, and said—

"Was Miss Helmont speaking the truth? Was it possible that—?"

I determined to see Elvire, to know from her own lips whether by happy fortune this blow came, not from her, but from a woman in whom love might have killed honesty.

I walked from Hampstead to Gower Street. As I trod its long length, I saw a figure in pink come out of one of the houses. It was Elvire. She walked in front of me to the corner of Store Street. There she met Oscar Helmont. They turned and met me face to face, and I saw all I needed to see. They loved each other. Ida Helmont had spoken the truth. I bowed and passed on. Before six months were gone they were married, and before a year was over I had married Ida Helmont.

What did it I don't know. Whether it was remorse for having, even for half a day, dreamed that she could be so base as to forge a lie to gain a lover, or whether it was her beauty, or the sweet flattery of the preference of a woman who had half her acquaintances at her feet, I don't know; anyhow, my thoughts turned to her as to their natural home. My heart, too, took that road, and before very long I loved her as I had never loved Elvire. Let no one doubt that I loved her—as I shall never love again, please God!

There never was any one like her. She was brave and beautiful, witty and wise, and beyond all measure adorable. She was the only woman in the world. There was a frankness—a largeness of heart—about her that made all other women seem small and contemptible. She loved me and I worshipped her. I married her, I stayed with her for three golden weeks, and then I left her. Why?

Because she told me the truth. It was one night—late—we had sat all the evening in the verandah of our seaside lodging watching the moonlight on the water and listening to the soft sound of the sea on the sand. I have never been so happy; I never shall be happy any more, I hope.

"Heart's heart," she said, leaning her gold head against my shoulder, "how much do you love me?"

"How much?"

"Yes—how much? I want to know what place it is I hold in your heart. Am I more to you than any one else?"

"My love!"

"More than yourself?"

"More than my life!"

"I believe you," she said. Then she drew a long breath, and took my hands in hers. "It can make no difference. Nothing in heaven or earth can come between us now."

"Nothing," I said. "But, sweet, my wife, what is it?"

For she was deathly pale.

"I must tell you," she said; "I cannot hide anything now from you, because I am yours—body, soul, and spirit."

The phrase was an echo that stung me.

The moonlight shone on her gold hair, her warm, soft, gold hair, and on her pale face.

"Arthur," she said, "you remember my coming to you at Hampstead with that letter?"

"Yes, my sweet, and I remember how you——"

"Arthur!"—she spoke fast and low—"Arthur, that letter was a forgery. She never wrote it. I—"

She stopped, for I had risen and flung her hands from me, and stood looking at her. God help me! I thought it was anger at the lie I felt. I know now it was only wounded vanity that smarted in me. That I should have been tricked, that I should have been deceived, that I should have been led on to make a fool of myself! That I should have married the woman who had befooled me! At that moment she was no longer the wife I adored—she was only a woman who had forged a letter and tricked me into marrying her.

I spoke; I denounced her; I said I would never speak to her again. I felt it was rather creditable in me to be so angry. I said I would have no more to do with a liar and forger.

I don't know whether I expected her to creep to my knees and implore forgiveness. I think I had some vague idea that I could by-and-by consent with dignity to forgive and forget. I did not mean what I said. No, no; I did not mean a word of it. While I was saying it I was longing for her to weep and fall at my feet, that I might raise her and hold her in my arms again.

But she did not fall at my feet; she stood quietly looking at me.

"Arthur," she said, as I paused for breath, "let me explain—she—I—"

"There is nothing to explain," I said hotly, still with that foolish sense of there being something rather noble in my indignation, as one feels when one calls one's self a miserable sinner. "You are a liar and forger, and that is enough for me. I will never speak to you again. You have wrecked my life—"

"Do you mean that?" she said, interrupting me, and leaning forward to look at me. Tears lay on her cheeks, but she was not crying now.

I hesitated. I longed to take her in my arms and say—"Lay your head here, my darling, and cry here, and know how I love you."

But instead I kept silence.

"Do you mean it?" she persisted.

Then she put her hand on my arm. I longed to clasp it and draw her to me.

Instead, I shook it off, and said—

"Mean it? Yes—of course I mean it. Don't touch me, please! You have ruined my life."

She turned away without a word, went into our room, and shut the door.

I longed to follow her, to tell her that if there was anything to forgive I forgave it.

Instead, I went out on the beach, and walked away under the cliffs.

The moonlight and the solitude, however, presently brought me to a better mind. Whatever she had done had been done for love of me—I knew that. I would go home and tell her so—tell her that whatever she had done she was my dearest life, my heart's one treasure. True, my ideal of her was shattered, but, even as she was, what was the whole world of women compared to her? I hurried back, but in my resentment and evil temper I had walked far, and the way back was very long. I had been parted from her for three hours by the time I opened the door of the little house where we lodged. The house was dark and very still. I slipped off my shoes and crept up the narrow stairs, and opened the door of our room quite softly. Perhaps she would have cried herself to sleep, and I would lean over her and waken her with my kisses and beg her to forgive me. Yes, it had come to that now.

I went into the room—I went towards the bed. She was not there. She was not in the room, as one glance showed me. She was not in the house, as I knew in two minutes. When I had wasted a priceless hour in searching the town for her, I found a note on the dressing-table—

"Good-bye! Make the best of what is left of your life. I will spoil it no more."

She was gone, utterly gone. I rushed to town by the earliest morning train, only to find that her people knew nothing of her. Advertisement failed. Only a tramp said he had met a white lady on the cliff, and a fisherman brought me a handkerchief marked with her name that he had found on the beach.

I searched the country far and wide, but I had to go back to London at last, and the months went by. I won't say much about those months, because even the memory of that suffering turns me faint and sick at heart. The police and detectives and the Press failed me utterly. Her friends could not help me, and were, moreover, wildly indignant with me, especially her brother, now living very happily with my first love.

I don't know how I got through those long weeks and months. I tried to write; I tried to read; I tried to live the life of a reasonable human being. But it was impossible. I could not endure the companionship of my kind. Day and night I almost saw her face—almost heard her voice. I took long walks in the country, and her figure was always just round the next turn of the road—in the next glade of the wood. But I never quite saw her—never quite heard her. I believe I was not altogether sane at that time. At last, one morning as I was setting out for one of those long walks that had no goal but weariness, I met a telegraph boy, and took the red envelope from his hand.

On the pink paper inside was written—

Come to me at once. I am dying. You must come.—

IDA

Apinshaw Farm, Mellor, Derbyshire

There was a train at twelve to Marple, the nearest station. I took it. I tell you there are some things that cannot be written about. My life for those long months was one of them, that journey was another. What had her life been for those months? That question troubled me, as one is troubled in every nerve at the sight of a surgical operation or a wound inflicted on a being dear to one. But the overmastering sensation was joy—intense, unspeakable joy. She was alive! I should see her again. I took out the telegram and looked at it: "I am dying." I simply did not believe it. She could not die till she had seen me. And if she had lived all those months without me, she could live now, when I was with her again, when she knew of the hell I had endured apart from her, and the heaven of our meeting. She must live. I would not let her die.

There was a long drive over bleak hills. Dark, jolting, infinitely wearisome. At last we stopped before a long, low building, where one or two lights gleamed faintly. I sprang out.

The door opened. A blaze of light made me blink and draw back. A woman was standing in the doorway.

"Art thee Arthur Marsh?" she said.

"Yes."

"Then, th'art ower late. She's dead."

II

I went into the house, walked to the fire, and held out my hands to it mechanically, for, though the night was May, I was cold to the bone. There were some folks standing round the fire and lights flickering. Then an old woman came forward with the northern instinct of hospitality.

"Thou'rt tired," she said, "and mazed-like. Have a sup o' tea."

I burst out laughing. It was too funny. I had travelled two hundred miles to see *her*; and she was dead, and they offered me tea. They drew back from me as if I had been a wild beast, but I could not stop laughing. Then a hand was laid on my shoulder, and some one led me into a dark room, lighted a lamp, set me in a chair, and sat down opposite me. It was a bare parlour, coldly furnished with rush chairs and much-polished tables and presses. I caught my breath, and grew suddenly grave, and looked at the woman who sat opposite me.

"I was Miss Ida's nurse," said she; "and she told me to send for you. Who are you?"

"Her husband——"

The woman looked at me with hard eyes, where intense surprise struggled with resentment. "Then, may God forgive you!" she said. "What you've done I don't know; but it'll be 'ard work forgivin' *you*— even for *Him*!"

"Tell me," I said, "my wife——"

"Tell you?" The bitter contempt in the woman's tone did not hurt me; what was it to the self-contempt that had gnawed my heart all these months? "Tell you? Yes, I'll tell you. Your wife was that ashamed of you, she never so much as told me she was married. She let me think any-thing I pleased sooner than that. She just come 'ere an' she said, 'Nurse, take care of me, for I am in mortal trouble. And don't let them know where I am,' says she. An' me bein' well married to an honest man, and well-to-do here, I was able to do it, by the blessing."

"Why didn't you send for me before?" It was a cry of anguish wrung from me.

"I'd *never* 'a sent for you—it was *her* doin'. Oh, to think as God A'mighty's made men able to measure out such-like pecks o' trouble for us womenfolk! Young man, I dunno what you did to 'er to make 'er leave you; but it muster bin something cruel, for she loved the ground you walked on. She useter sit day after day, a-lookin' at your picture an' talkin' to it an' kissin' of it, when she thought I wasn't takin' no notice, and cryin' till she made me cry too. She useter cry all night 'most. An' one day, when I tells 'er to pray to God to 'elp 'er through 'er trouble, she outs with your putty face on a card, she doez, an', says she, with her poor little smile, 'That's my god, Nursey,' she says."

"Don't!" I said feebly, putting out my hands to keep off the torture; "not any more, not now."

"*Don't?*" she repeated. She had risen and was walking up and down the room with clasped hands—"don't, indeed! No, I won't; but I shan't forget you! I tell you I've had you in my prayers time and again, when I thought you'd made a light-o'-love o' my darling. I shan't drop you outer them now I know she was your own wedded wife as you chucked away when you'd tired of her, and left 'er to eat 'er 'art out with longin' for you. Oh! I pray to God above us to pay you scot and lot for all you done to 'er! You killed my pretty. The price will be required of you, young man, even to the uttermost farthing! O God in heaven, make him suffer! Make him feel it!"

She stamped her foot as she passed me. I stood quite still; I bit my lip till I tasted the blood hot and salt on my tongue.

"She was nothing to you!" cried the woman, walking faster up and down between the rush chairs and the table; "any fool can see that with half an eye. You didn't love her, so you don't feel nothin' now; but some day you'll care for some one, and then you shall know what she felt—if there's any justice in heaven!"

I, too, rose, walked across the room, and leaned against the wall. I heard her words without understanding them.

"Can't you feel *nothin'*? Are you mader stone? Come an' look at 'er lyin' there so quiet. She don't fret arter the likes o' you no more now. She won't sit no more a-lookin' outer winder an' sayin' nothin'—only droppin' 'er tears one by one, slow, slow on her lap. Come an' see 'er; come an' see what you done to my pretty—an' then ye can go. Nobody wants you 'ere. She don't want you now. But p'r'aps you'd like to see 'er safe underground fust? I'll be bound you'll put a big slab on 'er—to make sure *she* don't rise again."

I turned on her. Her thin face was white with grief and impotent rage. Her claw-like hands were clenched.

"Woman," I said, "have mercy!"

She paused, and looked at me.

"Eh?" she said.

"Have mercy!" I said again.

"Mercy? You should 'a thought o' that before. You 'adn't no mercy on 'er. She loved you—she died lovin' you. An' if I wasn't a Christian woman, I'd kill you for it—like the rat you are! That I would, though I 'ad to swing for it arterwards."

I caught the woman's hands and held them fast, in spite of her resistance.

"Don't you understand?" I said savagely. "We loved each other. She died loving me. I have to live loving her. And it's *her* you pity. I tell you it was all a mistake—a stupid, stupid mistake. Take me to her, and for pity's sake let me be left alone with her."

She hesitated; then said in a voice only a shade less hard—

"Well, come along, then."

We moved towards the door. As she opened it a faint, weak cry fell on my ear. My heart stood still.

"What's that?" I asked, stopping on the threshold.

"Your child," she said shortly.

That, too! Oh, my love! oh, my poor love! All these long months!

"She allus said she'd send for you when she'd got over her trouble," the woman said as we climbed the stairs. "'I'd like him to see his little baby, nurse,' she says; 'our little baby. It'll be all right when the baby's born,' she says. 'I know he'll come to me then. You'll see.' And I never said nothin'—not thinkin' you'd come if she was your leavins, and not dreamin' as you could be 'er husband an' could stay away from 'er a hour—her bein' as she was. Hush!"

She drew a key from her pocket and fitted it to the lock. She opened the door and I followed her in. It was a large, dark room, full of old-fashioned furniture. There were wax candles in brass candlesticks and a smell of lavender.

The big four-post bed was covered with white.

"My lamb—my poor pretty lamb!" said the woman, beginning to cry for the first time as she drew back the sheet. "Don't she look beautiful?"

I stood by the bedside. I looked down on my wife's face. Just so I had seen it lie on the pillow beside me in the early morning when the wind and the dawn came up from beyond the sea. She did not look like one dead. Her lips were still red, and it seemed to me that a tinge of colour lay on her cheek. It seemed to me, too, that if I kissed her she would wake, and put her slight hand on my neck, and lay her cheek against mine—and that we should tell each other everything, and weep together, and understand and be comforted.

So I stooped and laid my lips to hers as the old nurse stole from the room.

But the red lips were like marble, and she did not wake. She will not wake now ever any more.

I tell you again there are some things that cannot be written.

III

I lay that night in a big room filled with heavy, dark furniture, in a great four-poster hung with heavy, dark curtains—a bed the counterpart of that other bed from whose side they had dragged me at last.

They fed me, I believe, and the old nurse was kind to me. I think she saw now that it is not the dead who are to be pitied most.

I lay at last in the big, roomy bed, and heard the household noises grow fewer and die out, the little wail of my child sounding latest. They had brought the child to me, and I had held it in my arms, and bowed my head over its tiny face and frail fingers. I did not love it then. I told myself it had cost me her life. But my heart told me that it was I who had done that. The tall clock at the stairhead sounded the hours—eleven, twelve, one, and still I could not sleep. The room was dark and very still.

I had not been able to look at my life quietly. I had been full of the intoxication of grief—a real drunkenness, more merciful than the calm that comes after.

Now I lay still as the dead woman in the next room, and looked at what was left of my life. I lay still, and thought, and thought, and thought. And in those hours I tasted the bitterness of death. It must have been about two that I first became aware of a slight sound that was not the ticking of the clock. I say I first became aware, and yet I knew perfectly that I had heard that sound more than once before, and had yet determined not to hear it, *because it came from the next room*—the room where the corpse lay.

And I did not wish to hear that sound, because I knew it meant that I was nervous—miserably nervous—a coward and a brute. It meant that I, having killed my wife as surely as though I had put a knife in her breast, had now sunk so low as to be afraid of her dead body—the dead body that lay in the room next to mine. The heads of the beds were placed against the same wall; and from that wall I had fancied I heard slight, slight, almost inaudible sounds. So when I say that I became aware of them I mean that I at last heard a sound so distinct as to leave no room for doubt or question. It brought me to a sitting position in the bed, and the drops of sweat gathered heavily on my forehead and fell on my cold hands as I held my breath and listened.

I don't know how long I sat there—there was no further sound—and at last my tense muscles relaxed, and I fell back on the pillow.

"You fool!" I said to myself; "dead or alive, is she not your darling, your heart's heart? Would you not go near to die of joy if she came to you? Pray God to let her spirit come back and tell you she forgives you!"

"I wish she would come," myself answered in words, while every fibre of my body and mind shrank and quivered in denial.

I struck a match, lighted a candle, and breathed more freely as I looked at the polished furniture—the commonplace details of an ordinary room. Then I thought of her, lying alone, so near me, so quiet under the white sheet. She was dead; she would not wake or move. But suppose she did move? Suppose she turned back the sheet and got up, and walked across the floor and turned the door-handle?

As I thought it, I heard—plainly, unmistakably heard—the door of the chamber of death open slowly—I heard slow steps in the passage, slow, heavy steps—I heard the touch of hands on my door outside, uncertain hands, that felt for the latch.

Sick with terror, I lay clenching the sheet in my hands.

I knew well enough what would come in when that door opened—that door on which my eyes were fixed. I dreaded to look, yet I dared not turn away my eyes. The door opened slowly, slowly, slowly, and the figure of my dead wife came in. It came straight towards the bed, and stood at the bed-foot in its white grave-clothes, with the white bandage under its chin. There was a scent of lavender. Its eyes were wide open and looked at me with love unspeakable.

I could have shrieked aloud.

My wife spoke. It was the same dear voice that I had loved so to hear, but it was very weak and faint now; and now I trembled as I listened.

"You aren't afraid of me, darling, are you, though I am dead? I heard all you said to me when you came, but I couldn't answer. But now I've come back from the dead to tell you. I wasn't really so bad as you thought me. Elvire had told me she loved Oscar. I only wrote the letter to make it easier for you. I was too proud to tell you when you were so angry, but I am not proud any more now. You'll love me again now, won't you, now I'm dead? One always forgives dead people."

The poor ghost's voice was hollow and faint. Abject terror paralyzed me. I could answer nothing.

"Say you forgive me," the thin, monotonous voice went on; "say you love me again."

I had to speak. Coward as I was, I did manage to stammer—

"Yes; I love you. I have always loved you, God help me!"

The sound of my own voice reassured me, and I ended more firmly than I began. The figure by the bed swayed a little unsteadily.

"I suppose," she said wearily, "you would be afraid, now I am dead, if I came round to you and kissed you?"

She made a movement as though she would have come to me.

Then I did shriek aloud, again and again, and covered my face with the sheet, and wound it round my head and body, and held it with all my force.

There was a moment's silence. Then I heard my door close, and then a sound of feet and of voices, and I heard something heavy fall. I disentangled my head from the sheet. My room was empty. Then reason came back to me. I leaped from the bed.

"Ida, my darling, come back! I am not afraid! I love you! Come back! Come back!"

I sprang to my door and flung it open. Some one was bringing a light along the passage. On the floor, outside the door of the death-chamber, was a huddled heap—the corpse, in its grave-clothes. Dead, dead, dead.

She is buried in Mellor churchyard, and there is no stone over her.

Now, whether it was catalepsy—as the doctors said—or whether my love came back even from the dead to me who loved her, I shall never know; but this I know—that, if I had held out my arms to her as she stood at my bed-foot—if I had said, "Yes, even from the grave, my darling—from hell itself, come back, come back to me!"—if I had had room in my coward's heart for anything but the unreasoning terror that killed love in that hour, I should not now be here alone. I shrank from her—I feared her—I would not take her to my heart. And now she will not come to me any more.

Why do I go on living?

You see, there is the child. It is four years old now, and it has never spoken and never smiled.

THE HOUSE OF ILL OMEN

Rosa Campbell Praed

We were all having tea in the hall at Castle Strange. Aunt Felicia sat in her high-backed oak chair looking like an old picture, with a black mantilla draped over her prematurely white hair which was dressed Margarita fashion and only made her look younger and more attractive from the contrast with her brilliant brown eyes and dark pencilled brows and lashes. She was in one of her quiet moods, and her gaze would wander often to Uncle Gaston who had been troubled lately by a sort of sore throat which the local doctor had ordered him to nurse indoors. So he had given up hunting these last few weeks and was horribly bored in consequence. He only brightened up a little now that Aunt Felicia, after telegraphing round the county and up to London, had got together a small house-party which she hoped would amuse him. There were two or three men—a soldier from India, the hero of a frontier fight; a Europeanised Virginian—dilettante artist and a distant connection of Aunt Felicia; Sir Thomas Hathaway, a kindred soul with Uncle Gaston in the matter of short-horns, and Lady Hathaway who cared for nothing but hunting and cards, and who played piquet-bridge had not then arrived when she was not in the saddle, or visualising runs and picking her places in imagination from the seat of an armchair.

Uncle Gaston did not seem in the humour however for short-horns, and to hear about runs made him cross. He was in an aesthetic

mood to-day, and had got out his photographic camera to make pictures of a pretty London woman—a young widow who, with her half-
Oriental father, Bastian Pacha, had come down just before luncheon.
There were only two other guests to arrive, a Colonel and Mrs. Bray.
Uncle Gaston had been making whimsical complaints that the features of Mrs. Maunde, the pretty widow, were of that faultlessly reg-
ular type which lends itself to Madonna effects and will not produce
an artistic surprise.

"Ah, if you want artistic surprises, my dear Gaston," said Aunt Felicia, "you must study Beatrix Bray when she comes this evening."

"Thanks for the opportunity," he returned. "All this time, I have not
been permitted to make the enchantress's acquaintance. My wife has a
way of preparing artistic surprises for me," he added, turning to Bastian
Pacha, "and this is one of them."

"Beatrix Bray? Ah, to be sure! The lady is—" He stopped.

"Mrs. Bray is the wife of Colonel Bray, who was in the Maroons,
and the most charming creature in the world," put in Aunt Felicia. "I
met them at Cannes last winter, and as he was sick of golf and dying, he
said, to follow hounds again in England, I recommended him to take a
house in Elchester. They have been looking at one or two, were to hunt
to-day and come on here after the run."

"Colonel Bray used to come to our house some years ago," said
Bastian Pacha. "I believe that he was in love with Elinor." The old man
glanced over at his daughter upon whose interesting *spirituelle* face
there came a quick blush, and she made a little gesture of repulsion.

"Oh, yes, I know," proceeded the Pacha. "He was too material in his
tastes to please Elinor. And now I hear that he has married the exact
opposite of himself—a Galbraith!"

"A Galbraith ! Ah, that accounts—" began Aunt Felicia, and checked
her speech.

"For a morbid twist in her, you were going to say? Is she also—?" And Uncle Gaston touched his forehead significantly.

"No, no," hastily answered Aunt Felicia. "There never was a brighter creature than Beatrix Bray."

"So was poor Rose Galbraith, her mother," observed Bastian Pacha, "until—" and he too paused.

The eyes of several of us turned towards him expectantly.

"Homicidal mania which developed after the birth of her second daughter," he explained. "The poor Galbraiths had a narrow escape from a bad tragedy. I wonder if Bray knew what he was undertaking? It's a double inheritance, unfortunately. Galbraith married his cousin. Do you happen to know what became of poor Mrs. Galbraith?" Bastian Pacha added. "I heard that she had been put in confinement."

"Poor lady, she is dead," said Aunt Felicia, gently. "I think we should forget that sad episode. I saw nothing in Mrs. Bray that could have suggested such an association."

There was a short silence. Sir Thomas Hathaway broke it. "I remember hunting with Bray in Leicestershire," he observed; "a bit of a brute, but a straight goer. So he's settling in Elchester. I wonder what house they'll take."

"Felicia," broke in Uncle Gaston, "I suppose you know that the House of Ill Omen, as you call it, has been done up again for letting. You'd better warn the Brays not to be caught by its picturesqueness, and inveigled into taking it."

Everybody exclaimed at the name-everybody, except Lady Hathaway and the Virginian gentleman who were absorbed in their piquet. All were anxious to be told the reason for so christening the place. Mrs. Maunde, who looked as if she herself might have psychic experiences, was specially pressing in her inquiries.

"But why—why the House of Ill Omen?" she asked.

"Because of all the dreadful things which have happened in it," returned Uncle Gaston. "Don't you know that there are two houses in Elchester which have a very evil reputation. One belongs to an old lady called Miss Crosson, who is said to deal in familiar spirits, and the other is Kingdon Lodge—the House of Ill Omen."

"Is it haunted?" asked Mrs. Maunde.

"By invisible and inaudible ghosts who prompt to murder and suicide," he replied. "Don't you ever go near the place, or you'll be tempted to kill yourself or the Pacha."

Mrs. Maunde laughed uneasily, as she twisted a long chain which she wore, of gold links and valuable uncut stones. She had much beautiful jewellery.

"If Father Canalis were only anywhere near, I should beg him to go and exorcise the evil spirits," said Aunt Felicia, gravely. "I feel sure that he would be able to do it. But, alas, he is at Cannes, so ill that his doctor will not allow him to come back to England."

"Tell me about the dreadful things that have happened there?" pleaded Mrs. Maunde.

"Nobody ever sees anything, or hears anything," Aunt Felicia began, "but everyone who lives in the house seems to become infected by some horrible influence, which first showed itself, they say, about fifteen years ago—after the sudden death of its owner. I remember well the talk at the time, about the old gentleman and a man-servant who was always in close attendance upon him. At first there was not any suspicion of foul play on the part of the servant, for he had appeared devoted to his master—so much so that the old gentleman's nephew, who came into possession of the property, kept him on in his service. It was noticed, however, that the man fell into great depression after the death of the old gentleman, and a year later he was found dead in his bedroom. He had hanged himself, and left a written confession that he had murdered his master. The whole affair was most odd," proceeded Aunt Felicia. "That servant must undoubtedly have been insane, for in his confession he told that for years he had been haunted by the desire to kill. He was evidently psychic in a peculiar way. He believed that the spirit of some old black magician talked to him, and put homicidal ideas into his head; and apparently he was fairly well educated. He had a passionate love of reading, being particularly fond of out-of-the-way literature. I remember he described having got hold of some queer black-letter books on magic, and practising, from the directions in them, devilish incantations and unholy rites with wax images, and the sacrifice of cats and dogs, in order to bring about the old gentleman's end by sorcery. That accounted for the disappearance of a number of pets which had greatly puzzled the neighbours. Then, not succeeding by these means, the servant related how he had at last yielded to the temptation now become irresistible, and had deliberately done away with his master by a course of slow poisoning."

Mrs. Maunde shuddered, and Bastian Pacha asked whether any further crime had followed the murder.

"The place was shut up for a time," replied Aunt Felicia, "for the owner's wife was so upset by what had happened, that she made her husband take her and their children abroad for a few years. After a while, they came back to inhabit the house, and things went on in an ordinary fashion. There were two schoolboy sons who came home every Saturday to Monday from Westminster where they were being educated, and it was in the summer vacation that the second tragedy took place. One of these boys was delicate and of a morbid turn. He had got into trouble at school and this so preyed upon his mind that he killed himself with a dose of cyanide of potassium. He went in for photography, and that was how he came into possession of the poison. After this, the owner gave up the place, and by and by it was taken by an Elchester solicitor with a large family. I used to see these people occasionally, and never did there appear a healthier or happier set of human beings, with the exception perhaps of the youngest—a boy of about ten, who looked a sickly creature, with big, melancholy eyes and a nervous, shrinking way with him. Well, he was the next victim. His death was looked upon as an accident, but afterwards, people used to say what an odd coincidence it was that for some time before the boy's death, he was always harping upon the thought. He would play games with his sister's dolls, in which he would pretend to kill them in different ways, and he continually asked questions about the boy who had lived in the house before him and who had committed suicide there. Finally, he was one day amusing himself attitudinising before a mirror with a toy-pistol, which, unknown to everyone, was loaded. Suddenly, he exclaimed: 'Now, let us see how people look when they are going to shoot themselves,' put the pistol to his head and pulled the trigger. The tiny bullet killed the poor child. He just lived long enough to say: 'I didn't want to do it, but something came and made me.'"

At that moment, the butler entered with a yellow envelope on a salver, and Aunt Felicia, as she took it, observed, with a rather shaky laugh—

"What is this, I wonder? In the country, after second post, nothing happens except a miracle."

"The Brays are not coming and I am to be cheated out of my artistic surprise," growled Uncle Gaston. "Is that your miracle?"

"No," said Aunt Felicia, putting down the telegram—"though you are partly right. This is from Beatrix Bray saying that her husband has to remain on business at Elchester, but that she is taking the liberty of bringing her sister, Eve Galbraith, instead of him. So, my dear Gaston, it is possible that you may have two artistic surprises, instead of one."

The prospect proved fallacious, however. Miss Galbraith was a disappointment—frightfully shy, with pale yellow hair, pale blue eyes, an immature figure and shrinking carriage. She seemed, in fact, little more than a raw schoolgirl, and looked to Mrs. Bray for her cue in everything.

But Mrs. Bray was artistic and brilliant enough to atone for every shortcoming in her sister, and before many minutes it became clear that Uncle Gaston was enchanted with her. She had a lively, almost volatile and easy manner, so much so that one might have imagined all the men present were her intimate friends. Perhaps they were—I don't know. When we sat down to dinner, the Virginian—Mr. Vignolles—had already arranged to make an impressionist portrait of her, and Uncle Gaston was studying her exhaustively, with a view to a photographic sitting on the morrow. She appeared to take all the admiration with a delightful naturalness, as if it were a mere matter of course, lightly discounting her own attractions.

"Oh, I know I'm not pretty, but I think I'm effective," she said, with a little audacious laugh.

"Nowadays that's about the highest compliment you can pay a woman," said Bastian Pacha, turning to her with a gallant bow.

And certainly as she trailed past me into the drawing-room after dinner, I thought her extraordinarily effective—an immensely tall and ethereally slender being, with an irregular-featured face perched upon a long, thin throat, a face all expression and colouring, illumined by a pair of startlingly bright and restless grey eyes and framed by a mass of crinkly hair, in tint the veritable Venetian gold. Her dress was no less effective than her eyes, her hair and her vivacious smile. In the early eighties, it would have been called aesthetic—long, clinging draperies of soft silk and rose velvet edged with brown fur and gathered at the waist by a golden girdle. Bastian Pacha, coming into the drawing-room, as in one of her restless movements she pulled out her voluminous skirt with the tips of her dainty fingers, made an admiring comment, at which she curtsied gaily.

"You put me in mind," he said, "of Nietzsche's 'Flame.'"

She was delighted at his appreciation of her costume.

"I made my dress myself, every bit of it!" she said. "Why, Mrs. Strange, it was not difficult—only to run together yards and yards of Liberty silk and send it to be accordion-pleated; then to fasten two strips of red velvet on each of my shoulders and to twist a girdle round me—and, here I am!"

She tossed her head like a child, and one of the loose coils of hair fell down her back.

"Mrs. Bray has promised me an artist's privilege," announced Mr. Vignolles. "I am going to see her hair in its natural state, unconfined."

"You'll be fearfully disappointed," returned she. "It has nothing but its colour to recommend it. My hair is dreadfully short, though it looks a great deal because it is fluffy!"

Uncle Gaston ventured gently to remove the hair-pins. Mrs. Bray's red-gold tresses now stood out round her fascinating face, the strands separating as though each hair were electrified. She ran her fingers through the mass.

"I'm like a cat. I give out sparks. My life is in my hair," she said.

Mr. Vignolles cast envious eyes at Uncle Gaston who ventured gently to lift one shining lock. "Cousin Oscar, I too claim an artist's privilege," he cried. "Mrs. Bray allows us both to admire."

"Oh, I don't mind," said Mrs. Bray. "How funny you all are! I was never asked before to put down my hair at a dinner-party. If I had only known, I would have made Louise wash it before I came. That brings the colour out and makes it look thicker."

Somebody commented upon the harmonious toning of red-gold hair, flame-coloured silk, and the deep red velvet upon her gown.

"Talk of Rossetti!" exclaimed Mr. Vignolles, enthusiastically. "There's a Rossetti before you—A blessed Damozel. A living picture. The dress, the eyes, the tinting of the face.—It is a perfect whole. We reverently adore."

"Gaston," said Aunt Felicia, "to-night you should study for a pose and to-morrow morning you must have a plate suitably and carefully prepared and photograph her, against the window—eh?—the head a little thrown back and the light shining through the wonderful hair."

"And I will get my sketching-block and paints and dash off an impression-now, to-night," said Oscar Vignolles.

Mrs. Bray smiled on them all whimsically. Bastian Pacha surveyed her somewhat in the manner of an Eastern potentate, between his halfclosed eyes. Mr. Vignolles went for his painting things. Uncle Gaston posed the model and then he too produced a sketching-block. The Hathaways, Mrs. Maunde, and the Indian man settled to whist. Aunt Felicia called for music and I sat down to the piano and played Grieg.

Bastian Pacha still surveyed the model. The two artists worked diligently.

"What an exquisite harmony!"—from one. "How it composes with that background of tapestry!"—from another.

Mr. Vignolles would get up at intervals to arrange a fold of the drapery, to adjust a tress of hair.

"Oscar is improving," mocked Bastian Pacha. "Gaston's old port has made him bold." And then he whispered to Aunt Felicia: "Should we have had the hair down if the husband had been here?"

"The modern husband likes to show off his possessions," said she.

"You remind me of my Lorelei picture," murmured Uncle Gaston to his model.

"I thought I had a little more on," derisively returned Mrs. Bray. "Good gracious!" she cried, "what does your butler think of me? Isn't he scandalised?"—as Aunt Felicia's sedate servant brought in the tray with spirit decanters and soda-water, and discreetly retired, carrying off a sleepy dachshund which yapped in his arms.

"Oh, he's used to this sort of thing. He's always being dressed up in hunting costume for me to experiment upon," said Oscar Vignolles, "when I'm doing illustrations for the American papers of English country life."

"Model, may I get you a lemon-squash? Poor Model! It shall be looked after; it shall take a rest. Does it like plenty of sugar in its squash?"

"Have I become 'It'?" cried Mrs. Bray, tragically. She left her seat and now posed herself before the fire, spreading out her flame-like draperies.

"Don't I make a good screen? What will you pay me for being an ornamental fire-screen?"

"A stuffed flamingo with outspread wings!" remarked Lady Hathaway, getting up from the whist-table.

"No—no, an Ophelia, a Saga Woman; a swan-eyed Daughter of the Bards; a Circe. Can't one think of some Homeric definition?" exclaimed the Virginian.

It was trivial chatter, losing its sparkle in repetition, but I let it stand, for looking back upon that evening and the interest centring round this gay, attractive creature, the sinister sense of contrast becomes, to me, dramatically sharpened.

Mrs. Bray laughed and caught up the ball of talk. Then presently noticing Miss Galbraith's drooping appearance she made a movement to retire.

"We ought to go to bed," she said. "I am sure that I have kept Mrs. Strange up later than usual and Lady Hathaway has said good-night. As for poor Eve, she's only a baby and can scarcely keep her eyes open. Besides, we've got a very fatiguing business before us to-morrow— looking over our new house. Did you know," she added, addressing

Aunt Felicia, "that we have really signed the lease of a delightful house in Elchester?—The quaintest place, with a dear old-world, walled garden. You must come and photograph me there, Mr. Strange."

"What is the name of your house?" Uncle Gaston asked quietly.

"Kingdon Lodge. Is it not like a suburban villa? I shall change the name. I should like to steal for it Henley's idea of 'the Castle of the Drowsy Doom.'"

"That is what my niece Ruth sometimes calls this old house," said Aunt Felicia. "But my dear Mrs. Bray"—she looked very grave—"do you mean to tell me that your husband has really signed the lease of Kingdon Lodge?"

"Most certainly. There's no getting out of it now—even if I wanted to—which I don't. Isn't it a nice house for us to take? Why do you look as if we had done something dreadful?"

"The house has some unfortunate associations," said Aunt Felicia, "but we won't talk of them now. Gaston, Lady Hathaway would like some lemonade," and she made a diversion towards the other end of the room.

Eve Galbraith and Mrs. Bray took their candles and we watched them as they went upstairs. Mrs. Bray turned half-way and pulled a petulant face.

"I'm so sorry to miss the run to-morrow," she said.

"It's too bad of you to be going away," said Uncle Gaston.

"I must."

"Oh, get out!" exclaimed Sir Thomas Hathaway, in his rough fashion.

"I *am* getting out," said she, mocking.

"No, no, keep in. . . . Why must you go?"

"Because my husband has made appointments with sanitary engineers and electricians and furniture people and gardeners and heaven knows who besides. He has set his heart upon our being settled in my Castle of the Drowsy Doom before a fortnight is over."

A sudden chill seemed to fall upon the company below. We looked at each other, the same meaning in the eyes of all of us. But Mrs. Bray had followed Eve Galbraith's drooped head and shadowy form which disappeared first in the darkness of the corridor and then the flame figure was swallowed up likewise.

"Felicia, can't you stop them from going into that place?" said Uncle Gaston, anxiously.

"I shall try," replied Aunt Felicia.

But Aunt Felicia's efforts met with no success. Poor little Eve Galbraith whitened at the tale, while Beatrix Bray became slightly hysterical over the horrors recounted, and left rather earlier than she had intended, on the plea that she must immediately consult with her husband and persuade him to give up the House of Ill Omen if there were any loophole for escape. Aunt Felicia did not gainsay her departure. Mrs. Maunde looked doubtful and apprehensive.

"I'm afraid that Henry Bray is not a man to be persuaded out of anything upon which he has set his heart," she said, "and least of all for any superstitious reason."

The result proved that she was right. In less than a fortnight, the Brays were established at Kingdon Lodge.

I did not see Mrs. Bray or her sister again during this particular visit to Castle Strange. Aunt Felicia wrote to me, however, that Colonel Bray had merely scoffed at his wife's entreaties, declaring that since he had taken at her desire a charming house which suited him exactly, he did not intend to sacrifice his money or his convenience because she was frightened at there having been two or three deaths in it. It was silly nonsense, he maintained, to say that the place had an evil influence about it. For his part he did not believe in influences or ghosts or anything of the kind, and nothing should induce him to pay heed to such twaddle. Thus had he delivered himself to Uncle Gaston, Aunt Felicia told me, one day when the Brays drove over to luncheon at Castle Strange after their installation in the ill-omened house. At that time Mrs. Bray was without her sister's companionship, Eve Galbraith having gone back to the aunt who had brought up both the motherless girls.

Then later, I heard that Mrs. Bray had been very ill. She had caught some kind of fever and had lost all her beautiful hair, which was a terrible grief to her. I remembered what she had said about her life being in her hair and thought of the adoring way in which Oscar Vignolles and Uncle Gaston had gazed at the red-gold masses of it that evening when she had worn her flamecoloured dress and had sat to them as a model while I played Grieg.

In late summer of the following year, I went on my customary holiday visit to Castle Strange. It was the time of garden-parties, and Aunt Felicia was very full of engagements in the near neighbourhood, so that I did not at first go to Elchester, which was a longish drive. Mrs. Bray was not to be seen at any of the garden-parties, but at one of them I made the acquaintance of Colonel Henry Bray. I found him a fine animal-handsome, fresh-coloured, devoted to out-of-door pursuits, strong-willed and stupid. Indeed, it was no surprise to me that fragile, intellectual Mrs. Maunde had disdained his suit.

He answered rather irritably when I inquired after his wife.

"Oh, she's all right again as far as health goes, but I can't get her out. She's full of whimsies; it's always one thing or the other with my wife," he went on. "When we first settled here, she wasn't happy unless she was in the saddle. Everything had to give way to hunting—she was worse than Lady Hathaway. Then she tired of it before the runs were nearly over and was all agog for balls, theatricals, skating—the Lord knows what, and I don't, except for the fact that she couldn't be still for a minute. I never saw anybody so restless as Beatrix until she fell ill at the end of the winter. Now she's well again, she has gone to the other extreme. She won't stir and I can't shake her out of the dumps. So she stops at home, and I come and play at tennis tournaments."

I hazarded the remark that perhaps Mrs. Bray found Kingdon Lodge depressing. A contemptuous yet angry look came over his florid face.

"I know what you're thinking of—that ghastly rot about the house being haunted. All I can say is that it would be a brave ghost who tackled *me*. Of course, there ain't any ghosts—how could there be? *I've* never seen anything, and nobody else has ever seen anything; and it's a first-rate house and suits me down to the ground. I'm not going to budge, until I take my trip to Algiers in the autumn."

"Is Mrs. Bray going to Algiers with you?" I asked.

"No, I'm going on business. I've got an interest in a vineyard up in the Kabyle country where it's rather rough and not fit for a lady. I'm hoping to get some shooting, though I don't suppose there's any chance now of bagging a lion. I shouldn't wonder if I made a dash into the desert."

"But you wouldn't leave Mrs. Bray alone at Kingdon Lodge?" I said.

"Why not? No harm could come to her. She's got the servants and plenty of friends to visit her. You'll be one of them—and Mrs. Strange?"

"Of course I will, if I stay so long, but I think she ought to have somebody in the house with her," I urged.

"Well, she can have Eve—her sister. Not but what Eve would be a bit depressing herself. She's been having an unlucky sort of love-affair—the man broke off the engagement and wouldn't tell her why. If he hadn't gone straight out of the country, I'd have given him a good horsewhipping!"

*   *   *   *   *

I took no particular interest in the love-affairs of Eve Galbraith, who had seemed to me a very colourless young woman, but I could not help thinking that the Galbraith family history, if revealed to an aspirant for Eve's hand, might well give the suitor pause. Equally, it occurred to my mind that if Colonel Bray had been fully informed upon the subject, he would have spoken a little less jauntily. However, this was none of my business. I did not wait for Aunt Felicia to find a spare afternoon, but drove into Elchester on my own account and called on Mrs. Bray. I found her alone and, as I had expected, very much changed. She looked pinched and haggard, the vivacious smile and pretty whimsical faces were gone, the grey eyes had a frightened, furtive expression; the irregular-featured, once brilliant face, retained but little of its former odd attractiveness. I attributed the alteration in a certain measure to the loss of her beautiful hair, which had seemed to impart to her its own peculiar vitality. Certainly, her face was still framed by a coiffure of so-called Venetian golden hue, the achievement of an expert hair-worker. But the crisp, artificial waves looked entirely different from the old natural undulations, and all the sheen of life was wanting. The whole effect was unmistakably meretricious and I felt very sorry for the poor woman shorn of her crowning glory.

She put her hands to her head, exclaiming plaintively—

"Oh, yes, I know! It's perfectly horrid. I hate to look at myself. And do you remember that night at Castle Strange—how they gloated over my hair?"

"But it will grow again," I said reassuringly.

"No, I don't think so. Anyhow, it could never be the same. . . . You know," she added, "I had a queer fancy about my hair—I've had it always—that so long as my hair kept thick and healthy no real harm would come to me. I had the idea that it was a kind of protection. And now," she concluded piteously, "it's gone—it's gone."

The pathos of her voice touched me deeply.

"My dear friend, what do you mean by saying it was a kind of protection? A protection against what?"

"Don't ask me!" She shuddered and turned away her face. "I can't tell you anything definite. I—I can't bear to think of it—" Her manner grew extremely agitated and she cast round that scared, apprehensive glance I had previously noticed. After a few moments, however, she seemed to recover herself somewhat and spoke, though with evident effort, in a conventional tone. "Tell me, do you like this house? Do you not think it quaint and comfortable?"

I agreed that it was certainly quaint and to all appearance comfortable. One could not have formed any other opinion. The room in which I sat and those I had passed through were very homelike and picturesque. The general effect was most agreeable—artistic furnishings, some fine pieces of Chippendale, old prints, a valuable collection of china, and, through the long Georgian easements at the back, glimpses of a delightful walled garden.

"The house is charming," I said.

"Henry likes it," she volunteered. "The stables are excellent, and of course, the position is very central for hunting. Nothing would induce him to give it up. . . . Oh I liked it too very much at first," she added, in reply to a vague question of mine.

"And don't you like it now?"

Again she gave that nervous backward glance, and her voice lowered as she asked a counter-question.

"Do you believe there's any truth in the things they say about the place?"

I inquired evasively: "What things?"

"Why, that it is haunted by an evil spirit which puts dreadful thoughts into the minds of people who live here?"

"I've never stayed in the house," I answered. "How can I tell?"

"It's the general idea," she went on, "that all those murders and suicides which have happened here were due to the promptings of that wicked spirit. Yet there was no real ghost. You couldn't say the house was haunted. I've asked people—servants, guests, tradesmen—everyone—and nobody has ever seen anything: nobody ever heard anything. So how is it possible for the house to be haunted?"

I tried to get her off the subject and began to talk county gossip, but she would hark back to the house and its evil influence.

"I haven't felt like myself since I came into it," she said. "That is why I should like to leave the place if only Henry would consent to give it up."

I could not, however, get from her any definite particulars as to the form her sufferings took.

"There is nothing definite—yet."

The way in which she pronounced that word "yet" alarmed me, but she only gave vague answers to my questions.

"I was so abominably restless after we came here, more so than ever in my life. I had to be out and about all day. The hunting was splendid for that: it took me out of myself. But I got frightened. I had one or two falls. I was always being driven to take impossible places. So I gave up hunting. But when I stayed at home it was worse. I couldn't occupy myself quietly because strange, dreadful thoughts would come into my mind. It was as if they were in the air around me—as if I took them in with my breath. I had to find some excitement outside in order to escape from them."

"But your husband told me that now he cannot persuade you to go out," I said.

"Oh, now it is different. Now, I don't want to go out. Because you see"—her voice lowered—"it wouldn't be of any use to try and fight against the things. I'm like Samson with my locks shorn. The strength has gone out of me."

She laughed wildly. In vain I begged her to describe the special "things" which distressed her. She shook her head. "I can't tell you. I mustn't. Besides, you'd think as Henry does, that I'm hysterical." And no more would she say upon the matter. We did our best, Aunt Felicia and I, to draw the poor thing out of her unwholesome seclusion. But Mrs. Bray refused all invitations, and several times when we took the long drive to Elchester hoping to see her, we were denied admittance. Colonel Bray had not yet started for Algiers, and therefore we did not agitate ourselves about her so much as we might otherwise have done, seeing that he was there to take care of his wife.

One day a little while later, I had driven over by myself and having been told at Kingdon Lodge that Mrs. Bray had gone out, that Colonel Bray had left, but that Miss Galbraith had arrived a few days before his departure, I went with a somewhat relieved heart to take a stroll in the town while the coachman baited the horses. Passing the cathedral which was open, I turned in and found the church empty, save for one woman who was kneeling in a side pew, her head buried in her hands, her body bent and shaking in the abandonment of devotion. At once I recognised Mrs. Bray and stole softly into the seat behind her. She was praying in an audible whisper broken by long-drawn sobs, and I caught some of the words of her petition, repeated over and over in a mechanical but wild fashion.

"O God, send him away. . . . O God, don't let me do it. O God, do make him go away." . . .

I waited until the paroxysm of emotion had passed. Then, gently attracting her attention, I made her come with me into the cloisters and there implored her to tell me what was the matter.

Her manner became odd and secretive and she seemed to resent my interference.

"Nothing is the matter. I was only saying my prayers. My husband has gone abroad. I was praying for his safe return."

"It sounded as though you were praying for somebody to be sent away," I answered.

She retorted angrily.

"You were listening—spying on me. I do not care for that sort of thing. You're like Eve who won't leave me alone for a minute. I had to run down a side street just to come in here and say my prayers. There she is now. I wish she wouldn't always come worrying after me."

As Mrs. Bray spoke, Miss Galbraith, looking anxious and upset, turned into the cloisters.

I saw that she too had changed since last year, and was certainly less crude and schoolgirlish. I could tell that the girl had passed through some painful experience which had matured and strengthened her, and remembered what her brother-in-law had told me about her unhappy love-affair.

She upbraided her sister for having left her, and afterwards said explanatorily to me—

"Henry gave me charge of Beatrix, when he went away, and I don't like her leaving me."

In Eve's presence Mrs. Bray appeared more like her normal self, and we chatted upon indifferent topics as the three of us walked back to Kingdon Lodge for tea. But every now and then, there would come a queer furtive gleam into Mrs. Bray's eyes which disturbed me. Going out to the carriage I had the chance of a few words apart with Eve Galbraith about the condition of her sister.

"Don't you think," I said, "that it would be a good thing to take her up to London for a short change, and, while she is there, get her to see a nerve specialist?" For Mrs. Bray had positively refused to consult any of the Elchester doctors.

"That is what we are going to do," Eve replied, "though it is only this morning that Beatrix consented to go. I am not easy at all about her; she is so odd and nervous and I feel that she ought to see a doctor," the girl went on. "She is so restless at nights, and, when I go to her room to see if she is sleeping, I find her walking about and muttering to herself in the strangest way as if she were frightened at something. But she has promised that to-night I may have a bed in her room, and I am hoping that I may be able to soothe her to sleep."

It is impossible to tell what really happened that night. The servants slept in another part of the building and heard nothing. When a maid took up hot water in the morning, she found the bedroom door locked and the silence of death seemed to reign within. From beneath the door there crept a thin sluggish and horrible stream of dark red, and on breaking the lock one glance showed that another tragedy, more terrible than any which had preceded it, had occurred in the House of Ill Omen.

A GHOST-CHILD

✦◆✦

Bernard Capes

In making this confession public, I am aware that I am giving a butterfly to be broken on a wheel. There is so much of delicacy in its subject, that the mere resolve to handle it at all might seem to imply a lack of the sensitiveness necessary to its understanding; and it is certain that the more reverent the touch, the more irresistible will figure its opportunity to the common scepticism which is bond-slave to its five senses. Moreover one cannot, in the reason of things, write to publish for Aristarchus alone; but the gauntlet of Grub Street must be run in any bid for truth and sincerity.

On the other hand, to withhold from evidence, in these days of what one may call a zetetic psychology, anything which may appear elucidatory, however exquisitely and rarely, of our spiritual relationships, must be pronounced, I think, a sin against the Holy Ghost.

All in all, therefore, I decide to give, with every passage to personal identification safeguarded, the story of a possession, or visitation, which is signified in the title to my narrative.

Tryphena was the sole orphaned representative of an obscure but gentle family which had lived for generations in the east of England. The spirit of the fens, of the long grey marshes, whose shores are the neutral ground of two elements, slumbered in her eyes. Looking into them, one seemed to see little beds of tiny green mosses luminous under water, or stirred by the movement of microscopic life in their midst. Secrets, one felt, were shadowed in their depths, too frail and sweet for understanding. The pretty love-fancy of babies seen in the eyes of maidens, was in hers to be interpreted into the very cosmic dust of sea-urchins, sparkling like chrysoberyls. Her son! looked out through them, as if they were the windows of a water-nursery.

She was always a child among children, in heart and knowledge most innocent, until Jason came and stood in her field of vision. Then, spirit of the neutral ground as she was, inclining to earth or water with the sway of the tides, she came wondering and dripping, as it were, to land, and took up her abode for final choice among the daughters of the earth. She knew her woman's estate, in fact, and the irresistible attraction of all completed perfections to the light that burns to destroy them.

Tryphena was not only an orphan, but an heiress. Her considerable estate was administered by her guardian, Jason's father, a widower, who was possessed of this single adored child. The fruits of parental infatuation had come early to ripen on the seedling. The boy was self-willed and perverse, the more so as he was naturally of a hot-hearted disposition. Violence and remorse would sway him in alternate moods, and be made, each in its turn, a self-indulgence. He took a delight in crossing his father's wishes, and no less in atoning for his gracelessness with moving demonstrations of affection.

Foremost of the old man's most cherished projects was, very naturally, a union between the two young people. He planned, manœuvred, spoke for it with all his heart of love and eloquence. And, indeed, it seemed at last as if his hopes were to be crowned. Jason, returning from a lengthy voyage (for his enterprising spirit had early decided for the sea, and he was a naval officer), saw, and was struck amazed before, the transformed vision of his old child-playfellow. She was an opened flower whom he had left a green bud—a thing so rare and flawless that it seemed a sacrilege for earthly passions to converse of her. Familiarity, however, and some sense of reciprocal attraction, quickly dethroned that eucharist. Tryphena could blush, could thrill, could solicit, in the sweet ways of innocent womanhood. She loved him dearly, wholly, it was plain—had found the realization of all her old formless dreams in this wondrous birth of a desire for one, in whose new-impassioned eyes she had known herself reflected hitherto only for the most patronized of small gossips. And, for her part, fearless as nature, she made no secret of her love. She was absorbed in, a captive to, Jason from that moment and for ever.

He responded. What man, however perverse, could have resisted, on first appeal, the attraction of such beauty, the flower of a radiant soul? The two were betrothed; the old man's cup of happiness was brimmed.

Then came clouds and a cold wind, chilling the garden of Hesperis. Jason was always one of those who, possessing classic noses, will cut them off, on easy provocation, to spite their faces. He was so proudly independent, to himself, that he resented the least assumption of proprietorship in him on the part of other people—even of those who had the best claim to his love and submission. This pride was an obsession. It stultified the real good in him, which was considerable. Apart from it, he was a good, warm-tempered fellow, hasty but affectionate. Under its dominion, he would have broken his own heart on an imaginary grievance.

He found one, it is to be supposed, in the privileges assumed by love; in its exacting claims upon him; perhaps in its little unreasoning jealousies. He distorted these into an implied conceit of authority over him on the part of an heiress who was condescending to his meaner fortunes. The suggestion was quite base and without warrant; but pride has no balance. No doubt, moreover, the rather childish self-deprecations of the old man, his father, in his attitude towards a match he had so fondly desired, helped to aggravate this feeling. The upshot was that, when within a few months of the date which was to make his union with Tryphena eternal, Jason broke away from a restraint which his pride pictured to him as intolerable, and went on a yachting expedition with a friend.

Then, at once, and with characteristic violence, came the reaction. He wrote, impetuously, frenziedly, from a distant port, claiming himself Tryphena's, and Tryphena his, for ever and ever and ever. They were man and wife before God. He had behaved like an insensate brute, and he was at that moment starting to speed to her side, to beg her forgiveness and the return of her love.

He had no need to play the suitor afresh. She had never doubted or questioned their mutual bondage, and would have died a maid for his sake. Something of sweet exultation only seemed to quicken and leap in her body, that her faith in her dear love was vindicated.

But the joy came near to upset the reason of the old man, already tottering to its dotage; and what followed destroyed it utterly.

The yacht, flying home, was lost at sea, and Jason was drowned.

I once saw Tryphena about this time. She lived with her near mindless charge, lonely, in an old grey house upon the borders of a salt mere, and had little but the unearthly cries of seabirds to answer to the questions of her widowed heart. She worked, sweet in charity, among the marsh folk, a beautiful unearthly presence; and was especially to be found where infants and the troubles of child-bearing women called for her help and sympathy. She was a wife herself, she would say quaintly; and some day perhaps, by grace of the good spirits of the sea, would be a mother. None thought to cross her statement, put with so sweet a sanity; and, indeed, I have often noticed that the neighbourhood of great waters breeds in souls a mysticism which is remote from the very understanding of land-dwellers.

How I saw her was thus:—

I was fishing, on a day of chill calm, in a dinghy off the flat coast. The stillness of the morning had tempted me some distance from the village where I was staying. Presently a sense of bad sport and healthy famine "plumped" in me, so to speak, for luncheon, and I looked about for a spot picturesque enough to add a zest to sandwiches, whisky, and tobacco. Close by, a little creek or estuary ran up into a mere, between which and the sea lay a cluster of low sand-hills; and thither I pulled. The spot, when I reached it, was calm, chill desolation manifest—lifeless water and lifeless sand, with no traffic between them but the dead interchange of salt. Low sedges, at first, and behind them low woods were mirrored in the water at a distance, with an interval between me and them of sheeted glass; and right across this shining pool ran a dim, half-drowned causeway—the sea-path, it appeared, to and from a lonely house which I could just distinguish squatting among trees. It was Tryphena's home.

Now, paddling dispiritedly, I turned a cold dune, and saw a mermaid before me. At least, that was my instant impression. The creature sat coiled on the strand, combing her hair—that was certain, for I saw the gold-green tresses of it whisked by her action into rainbow threads. It appeared as certain that her upper half was flesh and her lower fish; and it was only on my nearer approach that this latter resolved itself into a pale green skirt, roped, owing to her posture, about her limbs, and the hem fanned out at her feet into a tail fin. Thus also her bosom, which had appeared naked, became a bodice, as near to her flesh in colour and texture as a smock is to a lady's-smock, which some call a cuckoo-flower.

It was plain enough now; yet the illusion for the moment had quite startled me.

As I came near, she paused in her strange business to canvass me. It was Tryphena herself, as after-inquiry informed me. I have never seen so lovely a creature. Her eyes, as they regarded me passing, were something to haunt a dream: so great in tragedy—not fathomless, but all in motion near their surfaces, it seemed, with green and rooted sorrows. They were the eyes, I thought, of an Undine late-humanized, late awakened to the rapturous and troubled knowledge of the woman's burden. Her forehead was most fair, and the glistening thatch divided on it like a golden cloud revealing the face of a wondering angel.

I passed, and a sand-heap stole my vision foot by foot. The vision was gone when I returned. I have reason to believe it was vouchsafed me within a few months of the coming of the ghost-child.

On the morning succeeding the night of the day on which Jason and Tryphena were to have been married, the girl came down from her bedroom with an extraordinary expression of still rapture on her face. After breakfast she took the old man into her confidence. She was childish still; her manner quite youthfully thrilling; but now there was a new-born wonder in it that hovered on the pink of shame.

"Father! I have been under the deep waters and found him. He came to me last night in my dreams—so sobbing, so impassioned—to assure me that he had never really ceased to love me, though he had near broken his own heart pretending it. Poor boy! poor ghost! What could I do but take him to my arms? And all night he lay there, blest and forgiven, till in the morning he melted away with a sigh that woke me; and it seemed to me that I came up dripping from the sea."

"My boy! He has come back!" chuckled the old man. "What have you done with him, Tryphena?"

"I will hold him tighter the next time," she said.

But the spirit of Jason visited her dreams no more.

That was in March. In the Christmas following, when the mere was locked in stillness, and the wan reflection of snow mingled on the ceiling with the red dance of fire-light, one morning the old man came hurrying and panting to Tryphena's door.

"Tryphena! Come down quickly! My boy, my Jason, has come back! It was a lie that they told us about his being lost at sea!"

Her heart leapt like a candle-flame! What new delusion of the old man's was this? She hurried over her dressing and descended. A garrulous old voice mingled with a childish treble in the breakfast-room. Hardly breathing, she turned the handle of the door, and saw Jason before her.

But it was Jason, the prattling babe of her first knowledge; Jason, the flaxen-headed, apple-checked cherub of the nursery; Jason, the confiding, the merry, the loving, before pride had come to warp his innocence. She fell on her knees to the child, and with a burst of ecstasy caught him to her heart.

She asked no question of the old man as to when or whence this apparition had come, or why he was here. For some reason she dared not. She accepted him as some waif, whom an accidental likeness had made glorious to their hungering hearts. As for the father, he was utterly satisfied and content. He had heard a knock at the door, he said, and had opened it and found this. The child was naked, and his pink, wet body glazed with ice. Yet he seemed insensible to the killing cold. It was Jason—that was enough. There is no date nor time for imbecility. Its phantoms spring from the clash of ancient memories. This was just as actually his child as—more so, in fact, than—the grown young figure which, for all its manhood, had dissolved into the mist of waters. He was more familiar with, more confident of it, after all. It had come back to be unquestioningly dependent on him; and that was likest the real Jason, flesh of his flesh.

"Who are you, darling?" said Tryphena.

"I am Jason," answered the child.

She wept, and fondled him rapturously.

"And who am I?" she asked. "If you are Jason, you must know what to call me."

"I know," he said; "but I mustn't, unless you ask me."

"I won't," she answered, with a burst of weeping. "It is Christmas Day, dearest, when the miracle of a little child was wrought. I will ask you nothing but to stay and bless our desolate home."

He nodded, laughing.

"I will stay, until you ask me."

They found some little old robes of the baby Jason, put away in lavender, and dressed him in them. All day he laughed and prattled; yet it was strange that, talk as he might, he never once referred to matters familiar to the childhood of the lost sailor.

In the early afternoon he asked to be taken out—seawards, that was his wish. Tryphena clothed him warmly, and, taking his little hand, led him away. They left the old man sleeping peacefully. He was never to wake again.

As they crossed the narrow causeway, snow, thick and silent, began to fall. Tryphena was not afraid, for herself or the child. A rapture upheld her; a sense of some compelling happiness, which she knew before long must take shape on her lips.

They reached the seaward dunes—mere ghosts of foothold in that smoke of flakes. The lap of vast waters seemed all around them, hollow and mysterious. The sound flooded Tryphena's ears, drowning her senses. She cried out, and stopped.

"Before they go," she screamed—"before they go, tell me what you were to call me!"

The child sprang a little distance, and stood facing her. Already his lower limbs seemed dissolving in the mists.

"I was to call you 'mother'!" he cried, with a smile and toss of his hand.

Even as he spoke, his pretty features wavered and vanished. The snow broke into him, or he became part with it. Where he had been, a gleam of iridescent dust seemed to show one moment before it sank and was extinguished in the falling cloud. Then there was only the snow, heaping an eternal chaos with nothingness.

Tryphena made this confession, on a Christmas Eve night, to one who was a believer in dreams. The next morning she was seen to cross the causeway, and thereafter was never seen again. But she left the sweetest memory behind her, for human charity, and an elf-like gift of loveliness.

Honest John

J. Moffat

John Moffat founded the Nisbet Mills, at Milton, under the name of John Nisbet & Son, in 1787. He determined to be honest in all his dealings, and he kept his word. He certainly found that the proverb, "Honesty is the best policy," was a true one, for though he started with a small capital he died in 1812, at the age of sixty a rich man, and the owner of a small estate outside the town where he had first seen the light of day in a cottage.

A year or two before his death he built a mausoleum, and there he was laid to rest. His wife followed hint two years later.

He was a keen business man, a hard man, perhaps, but an honest man, and such was his reputation that for years before his death even the "bucks" of that day spoke of him with respect as "Honest John." But human nature can never be perfect, and the "Adam" in Nisbet showed itself in his conceit in his honesty. He delighted in his soubriquet, and as he lay dying he grasped his only son by the arm in a vice-like grip, and said to him in a voice hoarsened by approaching death:

"If ye do not deal honestly with men as I have done, I shall seek your answer from my grave."

Now this son William, so tradition has it, did not deal honestly with his brother men, nor with his patrimony. He ill-treated and under-paid his workpeople. His mother's death so soon after that of her husband was said to be a result of his behaviour. Moreover he mortgaged the estate to a money-lender, and he narrowly escaped the gallows for forgery.

One morning after a night of thunder and lightning, he was found dead just outside the burial-place of his father, and local gossip, embittered by a scoundrel's treatment, did not require the tinker's story of having seen "Honest John" walking that wild night, to state emphatically that William Nisbet had been made to answer his father for his misdeeds.

His son John Nisbet succeeded him. He might have been nicknamed "Prudent John," but he gained no such distinction. He was honest to all men. He set himself to undo the harm his father had done, and he succeeded. The estate was freed from debt. The mills prospered, and his aid was sought by the two political parties of the country.

He was, however, a reserved man, and he did not seek the publicity of politics. His ways were simple, but the neighbours were surprised one morning to learn that he had married his house-keeper. He was old when he married, but, like a certain patriarch, he was given a son in his old age. This son he named William Nisbet, and William Nisbet succeeded his father in his early twenties.

William had quite a lot of his great-grandfather in him. He was, however, ambitious. He loved money. He loved power. He invested judicially, became a director of many firms and a leading financier. Eventually, he became Sir William Nisbet and married a peer's daughter.

And so we find him, a widower, aged fifty-six, childless, sitting after dinner in a smoking-room of tire new mansion he had built on his great-grandfather's estate, on an August night about 11:30, the servants in their quarters, having been dismissed for the night—a lonely man.

There were heavy lines beneath Sir William's eyes, and a troubled look on his face, as he stared out across the fields that were his, lying white in the moonlight. Several times he clenched his hands, and sat alert in his chair, as if some sudden thought had opened a golden pathway leading away from his troubles. But his hands suddenly unclenched, and back he sank into his chair.

The crash was coming. He knew that. So did his friends. That was why he was alone in his mansion house. He smiled bitterly to himself when he thought of his friends, recalling the many words of flattery, the many house-parties he had given, the many he had attended, the many loans he had made, the valuable advice he had given.

He recalled his treatment at the hands of his friends these last months. There were the Castley brothers. He had helped them to wealth and a title for the elder brother. There was Lord Levald, whose estate he had saved from going into the market. There was Reubens, whose crazy schemes he had turned into money-making ones. Where were they now in his hour of need?

He laughed, and started at the sound of his laughter. It seemed to echo in the quiet room. He sprang up from his chair and hastily poured himself a glass of port, which he hurriedly drank, and then he sat down again, but he put the decanter within easy reach, and a minute or two later he gulped down another glass of port, and then another. In a short time he told himself that he was better. He was thinking more clearly, and the curious feeling in his temples was passing.

He would not give in. No, he was "Honest John's" great-grandson, "Honest John," the old fighter who had founded the family fortunes. No, he would find a way out, an honest one, surely, but a way out—he must find a way out.

He opened the windows just a little, for the room had become very warm. He noticed that the clouds had rolled up and obscured the moon, and that rain was falling, while in the distance there was a faint rumbling.

He paused in the act of lighting a cigar, a brand that Joyce had introduced to him. Curse Joyce, but for him and his infernal swindle he

(Sir William) would that night have been as he was these long years, respected, trusted, wealthy.

The cigar remained unlighted. Sir William's eyes narrowed and his hands clenched once more. He stepped back from the windows hurriedly as the lightning flashed across the sky as quick as a certain thought flashed across his brain.

The mills! Why had he not thought of the mills and their heavy insurance? He was glad he had kept them to himself, having refused all offers to turn them into a company. He had often been tempted, but he had felt bound to keep them in the family out of respect to his great-grandfather and his father. Now they must go. He had no heir. The insurance money would give him that financial backing he so desperately required.

It would be easy, too. He would take the short cut across the fields to the outskirts of the town where the mills stood. The watchman would have retired after his midnight tour of inspection. A few tins of petrol and the whole place would be ablaze, and the fire could be attributed to the storm. It was so simple.

He looked at his keys, and ran his fingers down one. It was the key that admitted him. to the newer portion of the building, where there was so much woodwork. Sir William smiled. He was saved.

His workpeople? The thought crossed his mind. What would they do? He would not rebuild—for a long time at least. He helped himself again to port. "A man's first duty is to himself," he muttered thickly, as he laid down the glass.

A water-proof over his dinner-suit and a cap pulled down over his eyes, he quietly let himself out of his house, as quietly as if he were a thief. He walked along the grass on his tiptoes, avoiding the gravel path, but stopped in his step as a brilliant flash of lightning lit up the landscape. He looked around for a minute or two, listening intently, but there was no sound, and then came the crash of thunder.

"I must hurry," he muttered, and he left the drive with its dark trees, and clumsily got over a wire fence. The storm was now at its height, and flash succeeded flash, while the night moaned.

He started to walk quickly across the field, and then he broke into a half-run, as a feeling that he was being pursued seized hold of him. He stopped once and tried to shake it off, but the blue forked tongue that split the sky unnerved him, and he sprang off again, his breath coming in heavy gasps.

"I must get it done quickly," he told himself, "very quickly."

Then a slip on the wet grass and down he crashed, all the breath knocked out of his body. For a minute or two he was dazed, but the lash of rain on his upturned face revived him, and he scrambled to his feet, and without taking note of his direction, so far as that was possible, he set off again. But this time the throbbing in his temples which had troubled him these last days returned more violently than ever.

Flash, and flicker and crash, and he was running—no, walking, no, running—making for somewhere. Ah, he was to fire the mills for money. Then he must get out of this dark field. He had no idea that this field was so large. He stopped suddenly. Where was he going? He asked himself again. Anywhere out of this accursed field. But this would never do. He was running blindly, and who or what was behind him, and who called his name?

He was a fool. He had a job to do. The mills must be fired. Would his heart never stop that awful beating? He was being hunted. It was foolishness. It could not be. He had done nothing—yet. Nobody knew. The mills

Flash, flicker and crash. Then the dark mass of masonry loomed out of the intermittent darkness on his right. He must get to the safety of one of the mill buildings for a minute or two to rest, and then the mills and money. Another twenty yards—

Flash and crash and blackness.

* * * * *

In the morning they found him lying beside the lightning-shattered mausoleum of his father. "Honest John's" coffin had been violently thrown from where it had so long rested. The old wood had given way, and one skeleton arm was lying, strangely enough, across the dead Sir William's body.

THE DÂK BUNGALOW AT DAKOR

B. M. Croker

> When shall these phantoms flicker away.
> Like the smoke of the guns on the wind-swept hill;
> Like the sounds and colours of yesterday,
> And the soul have rest, and the air be still?
>
> SIR A. LYALL

And so you two young women are going off on a three days' journey, all by yourselves, in a bullock tonga, to spend Christmas with your husbands in the jungle?"

The speaker was Mrs. Duff, the wife of our deputy commissioner, and the two enterprising young women were Mrs. Goodchild, the wife of the police officer of the district, and myself, wife of the forest officer. We were the only ladies in Karwassa, a little up-country station, more than a hundred miles from the line of rail. Karwassa was a pretty place, an oasis of civilization, amid leagues and leagues of surrounding forest and jungle; it boasted a post-office, public gardens (with tennis courts), a tiny church, a few well-kept shady roads, and half a dozen thatched bungalows, surrounded by luxuriant gardens. In the hot weather all the community were at home, under the shelter of their own roof-trees and punkahs, and within reach of ice—for we actually boasted an ice machine! During these hot months we had, so to speak, our "season." The deputy commissioner, forest officer, police officer, doctor, and engineer were all "in," and our gaieties took the form of tennis at daybreak, moonlight picnics, whist-parties, little dinners, and now and then a beat for tiger, on which occasions we ladies were safely roosted in trustworthy trees.

It is whispered that in small and isolated stations the fair sex are either mortal enemies or bosom-friends! I am proud to be in a position to state that we ladies of Karwassa came under the latter head. Mrs. Goodchild and I were especially intimate; we were nearly the same age, we were young, we had been married in the same year and tasted our first experiences of India together. We lent each other books, we read each other our home letters, helped to compose one another's dirzee-made costumes, and poured little confidences into one another's ears. We had made numerous joint excursions in the cold season, had been out in the same camp for a month at a time, and when our husbands were in a malarious or uncivilized district, had journeyed on horseback or in a bullock tonga and joined them at some accessible spot, in the regions of dâk bungalows and bazaar fowl.

Mrs. Duff, stout, elderly, and averse to locomotion, contented herself with her comfortable bungalow at Karwassa, her weekly budget of letters from her numerous olive-branches in England, and with adventures and thrilling experiences at secondhand.

"And so you are off to-morrow," she continued, addressing herself to Mrs. Goodchild. "I suppose you know *where* you are going?"

"Yes," returned my companion promptly, unfolding a piece of foolscap as she spoke; "I had a letter from Frank this morning, and he has enclosed a plan copied from the D.P.W. map. We go straight along the trunk road for two days, stopping at Korai bungalow the first night and Kular the second, you see; then we turn off to the left on the Old Jubbulpore Koad and make a march of twenty-five miles, halting at a place called Chanda. Frank and Mr. Loyd will meet us there on Christmas Day."

"Chanda—Chanda," repeated Mrs. Duff, with her hand to her head. "Isn't there some queer story about a bungalow near there—that is unhealthy—or haunted—or something?"

Julia Goodchild and I glanced at one another significantly. Mrs. Duff had set her face against our expedition all along; she wanted us to remain in the station and spend Christmas with her, instead of going this wild-goose chase into a part of the district we had never been in before. She assured us that we would be short of bullocks, and would probably have to walk miles; she had harangued us on the subject of fever and cholera and bad water, had warned us solemnly against dacoits, and now she was hinting at ghosts.

"Frank says that the travellers' bungalows after we leave the main road are not in very good repair—the road is so little used now that the new railway line comes within twenty miles; but he says that the one at Chanda is very decent, and we will push on there," returned Julia, firmly. Julia was nothing if not firm; she particularly prided herself on never swerving from any fixed resolution or plan. "We take my bullock tonga, and Mr. Loyd's peon Abdul, who is a treasure, as you know; he can cook, interpret, forage for provisions, and drive bullocks if the worst comes to the worst."

"And what about bullocks for three days' journey—a hundred miles if it's a yard?" inquired Mrs. Duff, sarcastically.

"Oh, the bazaar master has sent on a chuprassie and five natives, and we shall find a pair every five miles at the usual stages. As to food, we are taking tea, bread, plenty of tinned stores, and the plum-pudding. We shall have a capital outing, I assure you, and I only wish we could have persuaded you into coming with us."

"Thank you, my dear," said Mrs. Duff, with a patronizing smile. "I'm too old, and I *hope* too sensible to take a trip of a hundred miles in a bullock tonga, risking fever and dacoits and dâk bungalows full of bandicoots, just for the sentimental pleasure of eating a pudding with my husband. However, you are both young and hardy and full of spirits, and I wish you a happy Christmas, a speedy journey and safe return. Mind you take plenty of quinine—and a revolver"; and, with this cheerful parting suggestion, she conducted us into the front verandah and dismissed us each with a kiss, that was at once a remonstrance and a valediction.

Behold us the next morning, at sunrise, jogging off, behind a pair of big white bullocks, in the highest spirits. In the front seat of the tonga we had stowed a well-filled tiffin basket, two Gladstone bags, our blankets and pillows, a hamper of provisions, and last, not least, Abdul. Julia and I and Julia's dog "Boss" occupied the back seat, and as we rumbled past Mrs. Duff's bungalow, with its still silent compound and closed venetians, we mutually agreed that she was "a silly old thing," that she would have far more enjoyment of life if she was as enterprising as we were.

Our first day's journey went off without a hitch. Fresh and well-behaved cattle punctually awaited us at every stage. The country we passed through was picturesque and well wooded; doves, peacocks, and squirrels enlivened the roads; big black-faced monkeys peered at us from amid the crops that they were ravaging within a stone's throw of our route. The haunt of a well-known man-eating tiger was impressively pointed out to us by our cicerone Abdul—this beast resided in some dense jungle, that was unpleasantly close to human traffic. Morning and afternoon wore away speedily, and at sundown we found ourselves in front of the very neat travellers' bungalow at Korai. The interior was scrupulously clean, and contained the usual furniture: two beds, two tables, four chairs, lamps, baths, a motley collection of teacups and plates, and last, not least, the framed rules of the establishment and visitors' book. The khansamah cooked us an excellent dinner (for a travellers' bungalow), and, tired out, we soon went to bed and slept the sleep of the just. The second day was the same as the first—highly successful in every respect.

On the third morning we left the great highway and turned to the left, on to what was called the Old Jubbulpore Road, and here our troubles commenced! Bullocks were bad, lame, small, or un-broken; one of Mrs. Duff's dismal prophecies came to pass, for after enduring bullocks who lay down, who kicked and ran off the road into their owners' houses, or rushed violently down steep places, we arrived at one stage where there were no bullocks *at all*! It was four o'clock, and we were still sixteen miles from Chanda. After a short consultation, Julia and I agreed to walk on to the next stage or village, leaving Abdul to draw the neighbourhood for a pair of cattle and then to overtake us at express speed.

"No one coming much this road now, mem sahib," he explained apologetically; "village people never keeping tonga bullocks—only plough bullocks, and plenty bobbery."

"Bobbery or not, get them," said Julia with much decision; "no matter if you pay four times the usual fare. We shall expect you to overtake us in half an hour." And having issued this edict we walked on, leaving Abdul, a bullock-man, and two villagers all talking together and yelling at one another at the top of their voices.

Our road was dry and sandy, and lay through a perfectly flat country. It was lined here and there by rows of graceful trees, covered with wreaths of yellow flowers; now and then it was bordered by a rude thorn hedge, inside of which waved a golden field of ripe jawarri; in distant dips in the landscape we beheld noble topes of forest trees and a few red-roofed dwellings—the abodes of the tillers of the soil; but, on the whole, the country was silent and lonely; the few people we encountered driving their primitive little carts stared hard at us in utter stupefaction, as well they might—two mem sahibs trudging along, with no escort except a panting white dog. The insolent crows and lazy blue buffaloes all gazed at us in undisguised amazement as we wended our way through this monotonous and melancholy scene. One milestone was passed and then another, and yet another, and still no sign of Abdul, much less the tonga. At length we came in sight of a large village that stretched in a ragged way at either side of the road. There were the usual little mud hovels, shops displaying, say, two bunches of plantains and a few handfuls of grain, the usual collection of gaunt red pariah dogs, naked children, and unearthly-looking cats and poultry.

Julia and I halted afar off under a tree, preferring to wait for Abdul to chaperon us, ere we ran the gauntlet of the village streets. Time was getting on, the sun was setting; men were returning from the fields, driving bony bullocks before them; women were returning from the well, with water and the last bit of scandal; at last, to our great relief, we beheld Abdul approaching with the tonga, and our spirits rose, for we had begun to ask one another if we were to spend the night sitting on a stone under a tamarind tree without the village.

"No bullocks," was Abdul's explanation. The same tired pair had come on most reluctantly, and in this village of cats and cocks and hens it was the same story—"no bullocks." Abdul brought us this heavy and unexpected intelligence after a long and animated interview with the head man of the place.

"What is to be done?" we demanded in a breath.

"Stop here all night; going on to-morrow."

"Stop where?" we almost screamed.

"Over there," rejoined Abdul, pointing to a grove of trees at some little distance. "There is a travellers' bungalow; Chanda is twelve miles off."

A travellers' bungalow! Sure enough there was a building of some kind beyond the bamboos, and we lost no time in getting into the tonga and having ourselves driven in that direction. As we passed the village street, many came out and stared, and one old woman shook her hand in a warning manner, and called out something in a shrill cracked voice.

An avenue of feathery bamboos led to our destination, which proved to be the usual travellers' rest-house, with white walls, red roof, and roomy verandah; but when we came closer, we discovered that the drive was as grass-grown as a field; jungle grew up to the back of the house, heavy wooden shutters closed all the windows, and the door was locked. There was a forlorn, desolate, dismal appearance about the place; it looked as if it had not been visited for years. In answer to our shouts and calls no one appeared; but, as we were fully resolved to spend the night there, we had the tonga unloaded and our effects placed in the verandah, the bullocks untackled and turned out among the long rank grass. At length an old man in dirty ragged clothes, and with a villainous expression of countenance, appeared from some back cook-house, and seemed anything but pleased to see us. When Abdul told him of our intention of occupying the house, he would not hear of it. "The bungalow was out of repair; it had not been opened for years; it was full of rats; it was unhealthy; plenty fever coming. We must go on to Chanda."

Naturally we declined his hospitable suggestion. "Was he the khansamah—caretaker of the place?" we inquired imperiously.

"Yees," he admitted with a grunt.

"Drawing government pay, and refusing to open a government travellers' bungalow!" screamed Julia. "Let us have no more of this nonsense; open the house at once and get it ready for us, or I shall report you to the commissioner sahib."

The khansamah gave her an evil look, said "Missus please," shrugged his shoulders and hobbled away—as we hoped, to get the *key*; but after waiting ten minutes we sent Abdul to search for him, and found that he had departed—his lair was empty. There was nothing for it but to break the padlock on the door, which Abdul effected with a stone, and as soon as the door moved slowly back on its hinges Julia and I hurried in. What a dark, damp place! What a smell of earth, and what numbers of bats; they flew right in our faces as we stood in the doorway and tried to make out the interior. Abdul and the bullock-man quickly removed the shutters and let in the light, and then we beheld the usual dâk sitting-room—a table, chairs, and two charpoys (native beds), and an old pair of candlesticks; the table and chairs were covered with mould; cobwebs hung from the ceiling in dreadful festoons, and the walls were streaked with dreary green stains. I could not restrain an involuntary shudder as I looked about me rather blankly.

"I should think this *was* an unhealthy place!" I remarked to Julia. "It looks feverish; and see—the jungle comes right up to the back verandah; fever plants, castor-oil plants, young bamboos, all growing up to the very walls."

"It will do very well for to-night," she returned. "Come out and walk down the road whilst Abdul and the bullock-man clean out the rooms and get dinner. Abdul is a wonderful man—and we won't know the place in an hour's time; it's just the same as any other travellers' bungalow, only it has been neglected for years. I shall certainly report that old wretch! The *idea* of a dâk bungalow caretaker refusing admittance and running away with the key! What is the name of this place?" she asked, deliberately taking out her pocket-book; "did you hear?"

"Yes; I believe it is called Dakor."

"Ah, well! I shall not forget to tell Frank about the way we were treated at Dakor bungalow."

The red, red sun had set at last—gone down, as it were, abruptly behind the fiat horizon; the air began to feel chilly, and the owl and the jackal were commencing to make themselves heard, so we sauntered back to the bungalow, and found it indeed transformed: swept and garnished, and clean. The table was neatly laid for dinner, and one of our own fine hurricane lamps blazed upon it; our beds had been made up with our rugs and blankets, one at either end of the room; hot water and towels were prepared in a bath-room, and we saw a roaring fire in the cook-house in the jungle. Dinner, consisting of a sudden-death fowl, curry, bread, and *pâté de foie gras*, was, to our unjaded palates, an excellent meal. Our spirits rose to normal, the result of food and light, and we declared to one another that this old bungalow was a capital find, and that it was really both comfortable and cheerful, despite a slight *arrière pensée* of *earth* in the atmosphere!

Before going to bed we explored the next room, a smaller one than that we occupied, and empty save for a rickety camp table, which held some dilapidated crockery and a press. Need you ask if we opened this press? The press smelt strongly of mushrooms, and contained a man's topee, inch-deep with mould, a tiffin basket, and the bungalow visitors' book. We carried this away with us to read at leisure, for the visitors' book in dâk bungalows occasionally contains some rather amusing observations. There was nothing funny in this musty old volume! Merely a statement of who came, and how long they stayed, and what they paid, with a few remarks, not by any means complimentary to the khansamah: "A dirty, lazy rascal," said one; "A murderous-looking ruffian," said another; "An insolent, drunken hound," said a third—the last entry was dated seven years previously.

"Let us write our names," said Julia, taking out her pencil; "'Mrs. Goodchild and Mrs. Loyd, December 23rd. Bungalow deserted, and very dirty khansamah.' What shall we say?" she asked, glancing at me interrogatively.

"Why, there he is!" I returned with a little jump; and there he was sure enough, gazing in through the window. It was the face of some malicious animal, more than the face of a man, that glowered out beneath his filthy red turban. His eyes glared and rolled as if they would leave their sockets; his teeth were fangs, like dogs' teeth, and stood out almost perpendicularly from his hideous mouth. He surveyed us for a few seconds in savage silence, and then melted away into the surrounding darkness as suddenly as he appeared.

"He reminds me of the Cheshire cat in 'Alice in Wonderland,'" said Julia with would-be facetiousness, but I noticed that she looked rather pale.

"Let us have the shutters up at once," I replied, "and have them well barred and the doors bolted. That man looked as if he could cut our throats."

In a very short time the house was made fast. Abdul and the bullock-man spread their mats in the front verandah, and Julia and I retired for the night. Before going to bed we had a controversy about the lamp. I wished to keep it burning all night (I am a coward at heart), but Julia would not hear of this—impossible for her to sleep with a light in the room—and in the end I was compelled to be content with a candle and matches on a chair beside me. I fell asleep very soon. I fancy I must have slept long and soundly, when I was awoke by a bright light shining in my eyes. So, after the ridiculous fuss she had made, Julia *had* lit the candle after all! This was my first thought, but when I was fully awake I found I was mistaken, or dreaming. No, I was not dreaming, for I pinched my arm and rubbed my eyes. There was a man in the room, apparently another traveller, who appeared to be totally unaware of our vicinity, and to have made himself completely at home. A gun-case, a tiffin basket, a bundle of pillows and rugs—the usual Indian traveller's belongings—lay carelessly scattered about on the chairs and the floor. I leant up on my elbow and gazed at the intruder in profound amazement. He did not notice me, no more than if I had no existence; true, my charpoy was in a corner of the room and rather in the shade, so was Julia's. Julia was sound asleep and (low be it spoken) snoring. The stranger was writing a letter at the table facing me. Both candles were drawn up close to him, and threw a searching light upon his features. He was young and good-looking, but very, very pale; possibly he had just recovered from some long illness. I could not see his eyes, they were bent upon the paper before him; his hands, I noticed, were well shaped, white, and very thin. He wore a signet-ring on the third finger of the left hand, and was dressed with a care and finish not often met with in the jungle. He wore some kind of light Norfolk jacket and a blue bird's-eye tie. In front of him stood an open despatch-box, very shabby and scratched, and I could see that the upper tray contained a stout roundabout bag, presumably full of rupees, a thick roll of notes, and a gold watch. When I had deliberately taken in every item, the unutterable calmness of this stranger, thus establishing himself in our room, came home to me most forcibly, and clearing my throat I coughed—a clear decided cough of expostulation, to draw his attention to the enormity of the situation. It had no effect—he must be stone-deaf! He went on writing as indefatigably as ever. What he was writing was evidently a pleasant theme, possibly a love-letter, for he smiled as he scribbled. All at once I observed that the door was ajar. Two faces were peering in—a strange servant in a yellow turban, with cruel, greedy eyes, and *the khansamah*! Their gaze was riveted on the open despatch-box, the money, the roll of notes, and the watch. Presently the traveller's servant stole up behind his master noiselessly, and seemed to hold his breath; he drew a long knife from his sleeve. At this moment the stranger raised his eyes and looked at me. Oh, what a sad, strange look! a look of appeal. The next instant I saw the flash of the knife—it was buried in his back; he fell forward over his letter with a crash and a groan, and all was darkness. I tried to scream, but I could not. My tongue seemed paralyzed. I covered my head up in the clothes, and oh, how my heart beat! thump, thump, thump—surely *they* must hear it, and discover me. Half suffocated, at length I ventured to peer out for a second. All was still, black darkness. There was nothing to be seen, but much to be heard—the dragging of a heavy body, a *dead body*, across the room; then, after an appreciable pause, the sounds of digging outside the bungalow. Finally, the splashing of water—*some one washing the floor*. When I awoke the next morning, or came to myself—for I believe I had fainted—daylight was demanding admittance at every crevice in the shutters; night, its dark hours and its horrors, was past. The torture, the agony of fear, that had held me captive, had now released me, and, worn out, I fell fast asleep. It was actually nine o'clock when I opened my eyes. Julia was standing over me and shaking me vigorously, and saying, "Nellie, Nellie, wake; I've been up and out this two hours; I've seen the head man of the village."

"Have you?" I assented sleepily.

"Yes, and he says there are no bullocks to be had until to-morrow; we must pass another night here."

"Never!" I almost shrieked. "Never! Oh, Julia, I've had such a night. I've seen a murder!" And straightway I commenced, and told her of my awful experiences. "That khansamah murdered him. He is buried just outside the front step," I concluded tearfully. "Sooner than stay here another night I'll *walk* to Chanda."

"Ghosts! murders! walk to Chanda!" she echoed scornfully. "Why, you silly girl, did I not sleep here in this very room, and sleep as sound as a top? It was all the *pâté de foie gras.* You *know* it never agrees with you."

"I know nothing about *pâté de foie gras,*" I answered angrily; "but I know what I saw. Sooner than sleep another night in this room I'd *die.* I might as well—for such another night would kill me!"

Bath, breakfast, and Julia brought me round to a certain extent. I thought better of tearing off to Chanda alone and on foot, especially as we heard (per coolie) that our respective husbands would be with us the next morning—Christmas Day. We spent the day cooking, exploring the country, and writing for the English mail. As night fell, I became more and more nervous, and less amenable to Julia and Julia's jokes. I would sleep in the verandah; either there, or in the compound. In the bungalow again—*never.* An old witch of a native woman, who was helping Abdul to cook, agreed to place her mat in the same locality as my mattress, and Julia Goodchild valiantly occupied the big room within, alone. In the middle of the night I and my protector were awoke by the most piercing, frightful shrieks. We lit a candle and ran into the bungalow, and found

Julia lying on the floor in a dead faint. She did not come round for more than an hour, and when she opened her eyes she gazed about her with a shudder and displayed symptoms of going off again, so I instantly hunted up our flask and administered some raw brandy, and presently she found her tongue and attacked the old native woman quite viciously.

"Tell the truth about this place!" she said fiercely. "What is it that is here, in this room?"

"Devils," was the prompt and laconic reply.

"Nonsense! Murder has been done here; tell the truth."

"How I knowing?" she whined. "I only poor native woman."

"An English sahib was murdered here seven years ago; stabbed and dragged out, and buried under the steps."

"Ah, bah! ah, bah! How I telling? this not my country," she wailed most piteously.

"Tell all you know," persisted Julia. "You *do* know! My husband is coming to-day; he is a police officer. You bad better tell me than him."

After much whimpering and hand-wringing, we extracted the following information in jerks and quavers:—

The bungalow bad a bad name, no one ever entered it, and in spite of the wooden shutters there were *lights* in the windows every night up to twelve o'clock. One day (so the villagers said), many years ago, a young sahib came to this bungalow and stayed three days. He was alone. He was in the Forest Department. The last evening he sent his horses and servants on to Chanda, and said he would follow in the morning after having some shooting, he and his "boy"; but though his people waited two weeks, be never appeared—was never seen again. The khansamah declared that he and his servant bad left in the early morning, but no one met them. The khansamah became suddenly very rich; said he had found a treasure; also, be sold a fine gold watch in Jubbulpore, and took to drink. He had a bad name, and the bungalow had a bad name. No one would stay there more than one night, and no one had stayed there for many years till we came. The khansamah lived in the cook-house; he was *always* drunk. People said there were devils in the house, and no one would go near it after sundown. This was all she knew.

"Poor fellow, he was so good-looking!" sighed Julia when we were alone. "Poor fellow, and he was murdered and buried here!"

"So I told you," I replied, "and you would not believe me, but insisted on staying to see for yourself."

"I wish I had not—oh, I wish I had not! I shall never, never forget last night as long as I live."

"That must have been *his* topee and tiffin basket that we saw in the press," I exclaimed. "As soon as your husband comes, we will tell him everything, and set him on the track of the murderers."

Breakfast on Christmas morning was a very doleful meal; our nerves were completely shattered by our recent experiences, and we could only rouse ourselves up to offer a very melancholy sort of welcome to our two husbands, when they cantered briskly into the compound. In reply to their eager questions as to the cause of our lugubrious appearance, pale faces, and general air of mourning, we favoured them with a vivid description of our two nights in the bungalow. Of course, they were loudly, rudely incredulous, and, of course, we were very angry; vainly we re-stated our case, and displayed the old topee and tiffin basket; they merely laughed still more heartily and talked of "nightmare," and gave themselves such airs of offensive superiority, that Julia's soul flew to arms.

"Look here," she cried passionately, "*I* laughed at Nellie as you laugh at *us*. We will go out of this compound, whilst you two dig, or get people to dig, below the front verandah and in front of the steps, and if you don't find the skeleton of a murdered man, then you may laugh at us for ever."

With Julia impulse meant action, and before I could say three words I was out of the compound, with my arm wedged under hers; we went and sat on a little stone bridge within a stone's throw of the bungalow, glum and silent enough. What a Christmas Day! Half an hour's delay was as much as Julia's patience could brook. We then retraced our steps and discovered what seemed to be the whole village in the dâk bungalow compound. Frank came hurrying towards us, waving us frantically away. No need for questions; his face was enough. They had found it.

Frank Goodchild had known him—he was in his own department, a promising and most popular young fellow; his name was Gordon Forbes; he had been missed but never traced, and there was a report that he had been gored and killed in the jungle by a wild buffalo. In the same grave was found the battered despatch-box, by which the skeleton was identified. Mr. Goodchild and my husband re-interred the body under a tree, and read the Burial Service over it, Nellie and I and all the village patriarchs attending as mourners. The khansamah was eagerly searched for—alas! in vain. He disappeared from that part of the country, and was said to have been devoured by a tiger in the Jhanas jungles; but this is too good to be true. We left the hateful bungalow with all speed that same afternoon, and spent the remainder of the Christmas Day at Chanda; it was the least merry Christmas we ever remembered. The Goodchilds and ourselves have subscribed and placed a granite cross, with his name and the date of his death, over Gordon Forbes's lonely grave, and the news of the discovery of the skeleton was duly forwarded to the proper authorities, and also to the unfortunate young man's relations, and to these were sent the despatch-box, letters, and ring.

Mrs. Duff was full of curiosity concerning our trip. We informed her that we spent Christmas at Chanda, as we had originally intended, with our husbands, that they had provided an excellent dinner of black buck and jungle fowl, that the plum-pudding surpassed all expectations: but we never told her a word about our two nights' halt at Dakor bungalow.

THE HOUSEBOAT

———◆———

Richard Marsh

I

"I am sure of it!"

Inglis laid down his knife and fork. He stared round and round the small apartment in a manner which was distinctly strange. My wife caught him up. She laid down her knife and fork.

"You're sure of what?"

Inglis seemed disturbed. He appeared unwilling to give a direct answer. "Perhaps, after all, it's only a coincidence."

But Violet insisted. "What is a coincidence?"

Inglis addressed himself to me.

"The fact is, Millen, directly I came on board I thought I had seen this boat before."

"But I thought you said that you had never heard of the *Water Lily*."

"Nor have I. The truth is that when I knew it, it wasn't the *Water Lily*."

"I don't understand."

"They must have changed the name. Unless I am very much mistaken this—this used to be the *Sylph*."

"The *Sylph*?"

"You don't mean to say that you have never heard of the *Sylph*?"

Inglis asked this question in a tone of voice which was peculiar.

"My dear fellow, I'm not a riverain authority. I am not acquainted with every houseboat between Richmond and Oxford. It was only at your special recommendation that I took the *Water Lily*!"

"Excuse me, Millen, I advised a houseboat I didn't specify the *Water Lily*."

"But," asked my wife, "what was the matter with the *Sylph* that she should so mysteriously have become the *Water Lily*?"

Inglis fenced with this question in a manner which seemed to suggest a state of mental confusion.

"Of course, Millen, I know that that sort of thing would not have the slightest influence on you. It is only people of a very different sort who would allow it to have any effect on them. Then, after all, I may be wrong. And, in any case, I don't see that it matters."

"Mr. Inglis, are you suggesting that the *Sylph* was haunted?"

"Haunted!" Inglis started "I never dropped a hint about its being haunted. So far as I remember I never heard a word of anything of the kind." Violet placed her knife and fork together on her plate. She folded her hands upon her lap.

"Mr. Inglis, there is a mystery. Will you this mystery unfold?"

"Didn't you really ever hear about the *Sylph*—two years ago?"

"Two years ago we were out of England."

"So you were. Perhaps that explains it. You understand, this mayn't be the *Sylph*. I may be wrong—though I don't think I am." Inglis glanced uncomfortably at the chair on which he was sitting. "Why, I believe this is the very chair on which I sat! I remember noticing what a queer shape it was."

It was rather an odd-shaped chair. For that matter, all the things on board were odd.

"Then have you been on board this boat before?"

"Yes." Inglis positively shuddered. "I was, once; if it is the *Sylph*, that is." He thrust his hands into his trouser pockets. He leaned back in his chair. A curious look came into his face. "It is the *Sylph*, I'll swear to it. It all comes back to me. What an extraordinary coincidence! One might almost think there was something supernatural in the thing."

His manner fairly roused me.

"I wish you would stop speaking in riddles, and tell us what you are driving at."

He became preternaturally solemn.

"Millen, I'm afraid I have made rather an ass of myself; I ought to have held my tongue. But the coincidence is such a strange one that it took me unawares, and since I have said so much I suppose I may as well say more. After dinner I will tell you all there is to tell. I don't think it's a story which Mrs. Millen would like to listen to."

Violet's face was a study.

"I don't understand you, Mr. Inglis, because you are quite well aware it is a principle of mine that what is good for a husband to hear is good for a wife. Come, don't be silly. Let us hear what the fuss is about. I daresay it's about nothing after all."

"You think so? Well, Mrs. Millen, you shall hear." He carefully wiped his moustache. He began: "Two years ago there was a houseboat on the river called the *Sylph*. It belonged to a man named Hambro. He lent it to a lady and a gentleman. She was rather a pretty woman, with a lot of fluffy, golden hair. He was a quiet unassuming-looking man, who looked as though he had something to do with horses. I made their acquaintance on the river. One evening he asked me on board to dine. I sat, as I believe, on this very chair, at this very table. Three days afterwards they disappeared."

"Well?" I asked. Inglis had paused.

"So far as I know, he has never been seen or heard of since."

"And the lady?"

"Some of us were getting up a picnic. We wanted them to come with us. We couldn't quite make out their sudden disappearance. So, two days after we had missed them, I and another man tried to rout them out I looked through the window. I saw something lying on the floor. 'Jarvis,' I whispered, 'I believe that Mrs. Bush is lying on the floor dead drunk.' 'She can't have been drunk two days,' he said. He came to my side. 'Why, she's in her nightdress. This is very queer. Inglis, I wonder if the door is locked.' It wasn't. We opened it and went inside."

Inglis emptied his glass of wine.

"The woman we had known as Mrs. Bush lay in her nightdress, dead upon the floor. She had been stabbed to the heart. She was lying just about where Mrs. Millen is sitting now."

"Mr. Inglis!" Violet rose suddenly.

"There is reason to believe that, from one point of view, the woman was no better than she ought to have been. That is the story."

"But"—I confess it was not at all the story I had expected it was going to be; I did not altogether like it—"who killed her?"

"That is the question. There was no direct evidence to show. No weapon was discovered. The man we had known as Bush had vanished, as it seemed, off the face of the earth. He had not left so much as a pocket-handkerchief behind him. Everything both of his and hers had gone. It turned out that nobody knew anything at all about him. They had no servant. What meals they had on board were sent in from the hotel Hambro had advertised the *Sylph*. Bush had replied to the advertisement. He had paid the rent in advance, and Hambro had asked no questions."

"And what became of the *Sylph*?"

"She also vanished. She had become a little too notorious. One doesn't fancy living on board a houseboat on which a murder has been committed; one is at too close quarters. I suppose Hambro sold her for what he could get, and the purchaser painted her, and rechristened her the *Water Lily*!"

"But are you sure this is the *Sylph*?"

"As sure as that I am sitting here. It is impossible that I could be mistaken. I still seem to see that woman lying dead just about where Mrs. Millen is standing now."

"Mr. Inglis!"

Violet was standing up. She moved away—towards me. Inglis left soon afterwards. He did not seem to care to stop. He had scarcely eaten any dinner. In fact, that was the case with all of us. Mason had exerted herself to prepare a decent meal in her cramped little kitchen, and we had been so ungrateful as not even to reach the end of her bill of fare. When Inglis had gone she appeared in her bonnet and cloak. We supposed that, very naturally, she had taken umbrage.

"If you please, ma'am, I'm going."

"Mason! What do you mean?"

"I couldn't think of stopping in no place in which murder was committed, least of all a houseboat. Not to mention that last night I heard ghosts, if ever anyone heard them yet."

"Mason! Don't be absurd. I thought you had more sense."

"All I can say is, ma'am, that last night as I lay awake, listening to the splashing of the water, all at once I heard in here the sound of quarrelling. I couldn't make it out. I thought that you and the master was having words. Yet it didn't sound like your voices. Besides, you went on awful. Still, I didn't like to say nothing, because it might have been, and it wasn't my place to say that I had heard. But now I know that it was ghosts."

She went. She was not to be persuaded to stay any more than Inglis. She did not even stay to clear the table. I have seldom seen a woman in a greater hurry. As for wages, there was not a hint of them. Staid, elderly, self-possessed female though she was, she seemed to be in a perfect panic of fear. Nothing would satisfy her but that she should, with the greatest possible expedition, shake from her feet the dust of the *Water Lily*. When we were quit of her I looked at Violet and Violet looked at me. I laughed. I will not go so far as to say that I laughed genially; still, I laughed.

"We seem to be in for a pleasant river holiday."

"Eric, let us get outside."

We went on deck. The sun had already set. There was no moon, but there was a cloudless sky. The air was languorous and heavy. Boats were stealing over the waters. Someone in the distance was playing a banjo accompaniment while a clear girlish voice was singing "The Garden of Sleep." The other houseboats were radiant with Chinese lanterns. The *Water Lily* alone was still in shadow. We drew our deck-chairs close together. Violet's hand stole into mine.

"Eric, do you know that last night I, too, heard voices?"

"You!" I laughed again. "Violet!"

"I couldn't make it out at all. I was just going to wake you when they were still."

"You were dreaming, child. Inglis's story—confound him and his story!—has recalled your dream to mind. I hope you don't wish to follow Mason's example, and make a bolt of it. I have paid pretty stiffly for the honour of being the *Water Lily* tenant for a month, not to mention the fact of disarranging all our plans."

Violet paused before she answered.

"No; I don't think I want, as you say, to make a bolt of it. Indeed," she nestled closer to my side, "it is rather the other way. I should like to see it through. I have sometimes thought that I should like to be with someone I can trust in a situation such as this. Perhaps we may be able to fathom the mystery—who knows?"

This tickled me. "I thought you had done with romance."

"With one sort of romance I hope I shall never have done." She pressed my hand. She looked up archly into my face. I knew it, although we were in shadow. "With another sort of romance I may be only just beginning. I have never yet had dealings with a ghost."

II

At first I could not make out what it was that had roused me. Then I felt Violet's hand steal into mine. Her voice whispered in my ear, "Eric!" I turned over towards her on the pillow. "Be still. They're here." I did as she bade me. I was still. I heard no sound but the lazy rippling of the river.

"Who's here?" I asked, when, as I deemed, I had been silent long enough.

"S-sh!" I felt her finger pressed against my lips. I was still again. The silence was broken in rather a peculiar manner.

"I don't think you quite understand me."

The words were spoken in a man's voice, as it seemed to me, close behind my back. I was so startled by the unexpected presence of a third person that I made as if to spring up in bed. My wife caught me by the arm. Before I could remonstrate or shake off her grasp a woman's laughter rang through the little cabin. It was too metallic to be agreeable. And a woman's voice replied —

"I understand you well enough, don't you make any error!"

There was a momentary pause.

"You don't understand me, fool!"

The first four words were spoken with a deliberation which meant volumes, while the final epithet came with a sudden malignant ferocity which took me aback. The speaker, whoever he might be, meant mischief. I sprang up and out of bed.

"What are you doing here?" I cried.

I addressed the inquiry apparently to the vacant air. The moonlight flooded the little cabin. It showed clearly enough that it was empty. My wife sat up in bed.

"Now," she observed, "you've done it."

"Done what? Who was that speaking?"

"The voices."

"The voices! What voices? I'll voice them! Where the dickens have they gone?"

I moved towards the cabin door, with the intention of pursuing my inquiries further. Violet's voice arrested me.

"It is no use your going to look for them. They will not be found by searching. The speakers were Mr. and Mrs. Bush."

"Mr. and Mrs. Bush?"

Violet's voice dropped to an awful whisper. "The murderer and his victim."

I stared at her in the moonlight. Inglis's pleasant little story had momentarily escaped my memory. Suddenly roused from a dreamless slumber, I had not yet had time to recall such trivialities. Now it all came back in a flash.

"Violet," I exclaimed, "have you gone mad?"

"They are the voices which I heard last night. They are the voices which Mason heard. Now you have heard them. If you had kept still the mystery might have been unravelled. The crime might have been re-acted before our eyes, or at least within sound of our ears."

I sat down upon the ingenious piece of furniture which did duty as a bed. I seemed to have struck upon a novel phase in my wife's character. It was not altogether a pleasing novelty. She spoke with a degree of judicial calmness which, under all the circumstances, I did not altogether relish.

"Violet, I wish you wouldn't talk like that. It makes my blood run cold."

"Why should it? My dear Eric, I have heard you yourself say that in the presence of the seemingly mysterious our attitude should be one of passionless criticism. A mysterious crime has been committed in this very chamber." I shivered. "Surely it is our duty to avail ourselves of any opportunities which may offer, and which may enable us to probe it to the bottom."

I made no answer. I examined the doors. They were locked and bolted. There was no sign that anyone had tampered with the fastenings. I returned to bed. As I was arranging myself between the sheets Violet whispered in my ear. "Perhaps if we are perfectly quiet they may come back again."

I am not a man given to adjectives; but I felt adjectival then. I was about to explain, in language which would not have been wanting in force, that I had no desire that they should come back again, when—

"You had better give it to me."

The words were spoken in a woman's voice, as it seemed, within twelve inches of my back. The voice was not that of a lady. I should have said without hesitation, had I heard the voice under any other circumstances, that the speaker had been born within the sound of Bow Bells.

"Had I?"

It was a man's voice which put the question. There was something about the tone in which the speaker put it which reminded one of the line in the people's ballad, "It ain't exactly what 'e sez, it's the nasty way 'e sez it." The question was put in a very "nasty way" indeed.

"Yes, my boy, you had."

"Indeed?"

"Yes, you may say 'indeed,' but if you don't I tell you what I'll do—I'll spoil you."

"And what, my dear Gertie, am I to understand by the mystic threat of spoiling me?"

"I'll go straight to your wife, and I'll tell her everything."

"Oh, you will, will you?"

There was a movement of a chair. The male speaker was getting up.

"Yes, I will."

There was a slight pause. One·could fancy that the speakers were facing each other. One could picture the look of impudent defiance upon the woman's countenance, the suggestion of coming storm upon that of the man. It was the man's voice which broke the silence.

"It is odd, Gertrude, that you should have chosen this evening to threaten me, because I myself had chosen this evening, I won't say to threaten, but to make a communication to you."

"Give me a match." The request came from the woman.

"With pleasure. I will give you anything, my dear Gertrude, within reason." There was another pause. In the silence I seemed to hear my wife holding her breath—as I certainly was holding mine. All at once there came a sound of scratching, a flash of light. It came so unexpectedly, and such was the extreme tension of my nerves, that, with a stifled exclamation, I half rose in bed. My wife pressed her hand against my lips. She held me down. She spoke in so attenuated a whisper that it was only because all my senses were so keenly on the alert that I heard her.

"You goose! He's only striking a match."

He might have been, but who? She took things for granted. I wanted to know. The light continued flickering to and fro, as a match does flicker. I would have given much to know who held it, or even what was its position in the room. As luck had it, my face was turned the other way. My wife seemed to understand what was passing in my mind.

"There's no one there," she whispered.

No one, I presumed, but the match. I took it for granted that was there. Though I did not venture to inquire, I felt that I might not have such perfect control over my voice as my wife appeared to have.

While the light continued to flicker there came stealing into my nostrils—I sniffed, the thing was unmistakable!—the odour of tobacco. The woman was lighting a cigarette. I knew it was the woman because presently there came this request from the man, "After you with the light, my dear."

I presume that the match was passed. Immediately the smell of tobacco redoubled. The man had lit a cigarette as well. I confess that I resented—silently, but still strongly—the idea of two strangers, whether ghosts or anybody else, smoking, uninvited, in my cabin.

The match went out. The cigarettes were lit. The man continued speaking.

"The communication, my dear Gertrude, which I intended to make to you was this. The time has come for us to part."

He paused, possibly for an answer. None came.

"I need not enlarge on the reasons which necessitate our parting. They exist."

Pause again. Then the woman.

"What are you going to give me?"

"One of the reasons which necessitate our parting—a very strong reason, as you, I am sure, will be the first to admit—is that I have nothing left to give you."

"So you say."

"Precisely. So I say and so I mean."

"Do you mean that you are going to give me nothing?"

"I mean, my dear Gertrude, that I have nothing to give you. You have left me nothing."

"Bah!"

The sound which issued from the lady's lips was expressive of the most complete contempt.

"Look here, my boy, you give me a hundred sovereigns or I'll spoil you."

Pause again. Probably the gentleman was thinking over the lady's observation.

"What benefit do you think you will do yourself by what you call 'spoiling' me?"

"Never mind about that: I'll do it. You think I don't know all about you, but I do. Perhaps I'm not so soft as you think. Your wife's got some money if you haven't. Suppose you go back and ask her for some. You've treated me badly enough. I don't see why you shouldn't go and treat her the same. She wouldn't make things warm for you if she knew a few things I could tell her—not at all! You give me a hundred sovereigns or, I tell you straight, I'll go right to your house and I'll tell her all."

"Oh, no, you won't."

"Won't I? I say I will!"

"Oh, no, you won't."

"I say I will! I've warned you, that's all. I'm not going to stop here, talking stuff to you. I'm going to bed. You can go and hang yourself for all I care."

There was a sound, an indubitable sound—the sound of a pair of shoes being thrown upon the floor. There were other sounds, equally capable of explanation: sounds which suggested—I wish the printer would put it in small type—that the lady was undressing. Undressing, too, with scant regard to ceremony. Garments were thrown off and tossed higgledy-piggledy here and there. They appeared to be thrown, with sublime indifference, upon table, chairs, and floor. I even felt something alight upon the bed. Some feminine garment, perhaps, which, although it fell by no means heavily, made me conscious, as it fell, of the most curious sensation I had in all my life—till then—experienced. It seemed that the lady, while she unrobed, continued smoking. From her next words it appeared that the gentleman, also smoking, stood and stared at her.

"Don't stand staring at me like a gawk. I'm going to turn in."

"And I'm going to turn out. Not, as you suggested, to hang myself, but to finish this cigarette upon the roof. Perhaps, when I return, you will be in a more equable frame of mind."

"Don't you flatter yourself. What I say I mean. A hundred sovereigns, or I tell your wife."

He laughed very softly, as though he was determined not to be annoyed. Then we heard his footsteps as he crossed the floor. The door opened, then closed. We heard him ascend the steps. Then, with curious distinctness, his measured tramp, tramp, as he moved to and fro upon the roof. In the cabin for a moment there was silence. Then the woman said, with a curious faltering in her voice—

"I'll do it. I don't care what he says." There was a choking in her throat. "He don't care for me a bit."

Suddenly she flung herself upon her knees beside the bed. She pillowed her head and arms upon the coverlet. I lay near the outer edge of the bed, which was a small one, by the way. As I lay I felt the pressure of her limbs. My sensations, as I did, I am unable to describe. After a momentary interval there came the sound of sobbing. I could feel the woman quivering with the strength of her emotion. Violet and I were speechless. I do not think that, for the instant, we could have spoken even had we tried. The woman's presence was so evident, her grief so real. As she wept disjointed words came from her.

"I've given everything for him! If he only cared for me! If he only did."

All at once, with a rapid movement, she sprang up. The removal of the pressure was altogether unmistakable. I was conscious of her resting her hands upon the coverlet to assist her to her bed. I felt the little jerk; then the withdrawal of the hands. She choked back her sobs when she had gained her feet her tone was changed.

"What a fool I am to make a fuss. He don't care for me—not that." We heard her snap her fingers in the air. "He never did. Us women are always fools—we're all the same. I'll go to bed."

Violet clutched my arm. She whispered, in that attenuated fashion she seemed to have caught the trick of—

"She's getting into bed. We must get out."

It certainly was a fact, someone was getting into bed. The bed-clothes were moved; not our bed-clothes, but some phantom coverings. We heard them rustle, we were conscious of a current of air across our faces as someone caught them open. And then!—then someone stepped upon the bed.

"Let's get out!" gasped Violet.

III

She moved away from me. She squeezed herself against the side of the cabin. She withdrew her limbs from between the sheets. As for me, the person who had stepped upon the bed had actually stepped upon me, and that without seeming at all conscious of my presence. Someone sat down plump upon the sheet beside me. That was enough. I took advantage of my lying on the edge of the bed to slip out upon the floor. I might possess an unsuspected capacity for undergoing strange experiences, but I drew the line at sleeping with a ghost.

The moonlight streamed across the room. As I stood, in something very like a state of nature on the floor, I could clearly see Violet cowering on the further side of the bed. I could distinguish all her features.

But when I looked upon the bed itself—there was nothing there. The moon's rays fell upon the pillow. They revealed its snowy whiteness. There seemed nothing else it could reveal. It was untenanted. And yet, if one looked closely at it, it seemed to be indented, just as it might have been indented had a human head been lying there. But about one thing there could be no mistake whatever—my ears did not play me false, I heard it too distinctly—the sound made by a person who settles himself between the sheets, and then the measured respiration of one who composes himself to slumber.

I remained there silent. On her hands and knees Violet crept towards the foot of the bed. When she had gained the floor she stole on tiptoe to my side.

"I did not dare to step across her." I felt her, as she nestled to me, give me a little shiver. "I could not do it. Can you see her?"

"What a fool I am!" As Violet asked her question there came this observation from the person in the bed—whom, by the way, I could not see. There was a long-drawn sigh. "What fools all we women are! What fools!"

There was a sincerity of bitterness about the tone, which, coming as it did from an unseen speaker—one so near and yet so far—had on one a most uncomfortable effect. Violet pressed closer to my side. The woman in the bed turned over. Overhead there still continued the measured tramp, tramping of the man. We were conscious, in some subtle way, that the woman lay listening to the footsteps. They spoke more audibly to her ears even than to ours.

"Ollie! Ollie!" she repeated the name softly to herself, with a degree of tenderness which was in startling contrast to her previous bitterness.

"I wish you would come to bed."

She was silent. There was only the sound of her gentle breathing. Her bitter mood had been but transient. She was falling asleep with words of tenderness upon her lips. Above, the footsteps ceased. All was still. There was not even the murmur of the waters. The wife and I, side by side, stood looking down upon what seemed an empty bed.

"She is asleep," said Violet.

It seemed to me she was: although I could not see her, it seemed to me she was. I could hear her breathing as softly as a child Violet continued whispering—

"How strange! Eric, what can it mean?"

I muttered a reply—

"A problem for the Psychical Research Society."

"It seems just like a dream."

"I wish it were a dream."

"S-sh! There is someone coming down the stairs."

There was—at least, if we could trust our ears, there was. Apparently the man above had had enough of solitude. We heard him move across the roof, then pause just by the steps, then descend them one by one. It seemed to us that in this step there was something stealthy, that he was endeavouring not to arouse attention, to make as little noise as possible. Half-way down he paused; at the foot he paused again.

"He's listening outside the door." It almost seemed that he was. We stood and listened too. "Let's get away from the bed."

My wife drew me with her. At the opposite end of the cabin was a sort of little alcove, which was screened by a curtain, and behind which were hung one or two of our garments which we were not actually using. Violet drew me within the shadow of this alcove. I say drew me because, offering no resistance, I allowed myself to be completely passive in her hands. The alcove was not large enough to hold us. Still the curtain acted as a partial screen.

The silence endured for some moments. Then we heard without a hand softly turning the handle of the door. While I was wondering whether, after all, I was not the victim of an attack of indigestion, or whether I was about to witness an attempt at effecting a burglarious entry into a houseboat, a strange thing happened, the strangest thing that had happened yet.

As I have already mentioned, the moon's rays flooded the cabin. This was owing to the fact that a long narrow casement, which ran round the walls near the roof of the cabin, had been left open for the sake of admitting air and ventilation; but, save for the moonbeams, the cabin was unlighted. When, however, we heard the handle being softly turned, a singular change occurred. It was like the transformation scene in a theatre. The whole place, all at once, was brilliantly illuminated. The moonbeams disappeared. Instead, a large swinging lamp was hanging from the centre of the cabin. So strong was the light which it shed around that our eyes were dazzled. It was not our lamp; we used small hand-lamps, which stood upon the table. By its glare we saw that the whole cabin was changed. For an instant we failed to clearly realise in what the change consisted. Then we understood it was a question of decoration. The contents of the cabin, for the most part, were the same, though they looked newer, and the positions of the various articles were altered; but the panels of the cabin of the *Water Lily* were painted blue and white. The panels of this cabin were coloured chocolate and gold.

"Eric, it's the *Sylph*!"

The suggestion conveyed by my wife's whispered words, even as she spoke, occurred to me. I understood where, for Inglis, had lain the difficulty of recognition. The two cabins were the same, and yet were not. It was just as though someone had endeavoured, without spending much cash, to render one as much as possible unlike the other.

In this cabin there were many things which were not ours. In fact, so far as I can see, there was nothing which was ours. Strange articles of costume were scattered about; the table was covered with a curious litter; and on the ingenious article of furniture which did duty as a bed, and which stood where our bed stood, and which, indeed, seemed to be our bed, there was someone sleeping.

As my startled eyes travelled round this amazing transformation scene, at last they reached the door. There they stayed. Mechanically I shrank back nearer to the wall. I felt my wife tighten her grasp upon my hand.

The door was open some few inches. Through the aperture thus formed there peered a man. He seemed to be listening. It was so still that one could hear the gentle breathing of the woman sleeping in the bed. Apparently satisfied, he opened the door sufficiently wide to admit of his entering the cabin. My impression was that he could not fail to perceive us, yet to all appearances he remained entirely unconscious of our neighbourhood. He was a man certainly under five feet six in height. He was slight in build, very dark, with face clean shaven; his face was long and narrow. In dress and bearing he seemed a gentleman, yet there was that about him which immediately reminded me of what Inglis had said of the man Bush—"he looked as though he had something to do with horses."

He stood for some seconds in an attitude of listening, so close to me that I had only to stretch out my hand to take him by the throat. I did not do it. I don't know what restrained me; I think, more than anything, it was the feeling that these things which were passing before me must be passing in a dream. His face was turned away. He looked intently towards the sleeping woman.

After he had had enough of listening he moved towards the bed. His step was soft and cat-like; it was absolutely noiseless. Glancing down, I perceived that he was without boots or shoes. He was in his stockinged feet I had distinctly heard the tramp, tramping of a pair of shoes upon the cabin roof. I had heard them descend the steps. Possibly he had paused outside the door to take them off.

When he reached the bed he stood looking down upon the sleeper. He stooped over her, as if the better to catch her breathing. He whispered softly—

"Gerty!"

He paused for a moment, as if for an answer. None came. Standing up, he put his hand, as it seemed to me, into the bosom of his flannel shirt. He took out a leather sheath. From the sheath he drew a knife. It was a long, slender, glittering blade. Quite twelve inches in length, at no part was it broader than my little finger. With the empty sheath in his left hand, the knife behind his back in his right, he again leaned over the sleeper. Again he softly whispered, "Gerty!"

Again there was no answer. Again he stood upright, turning his back towards the bed, so that he looked towards us. His face was not an ugly one, though the expression was somewhat saturnine. On it, at the instant, there was a peculiar look, such a look as I could fancy upon the face of a jockey who, toward the close of a great race, settles himself in the saddle with the determination to "finish" well. The naked blade he placed upon the table, the empty sheath beside it. Then he moved towards us. My first thought was that now, at last, we were discovered; but something in the expression of his features told me that this was not so. He approached us with an indifference which was amazing. He passed so close to us that we were conscious of the slight disturbance of the air caused by his passage. There was a Gladstone bag on a chair within two feet of us. Picking it up, he bore it to the table. Opening it out, he commenced to pack it. All manner of things he placed within it, both masculine and feminine belongings, even the garments which the sleeper had taken off, and which lay scattered on the chair and on the floor, even her shoes and stockings! When the bag was filled he took a long brown ulster, which was thrown over the back of a chair. He stuffed the pockets with odds and ends. When he had completed his operations the cabin was stripped of everything except the actual furniture. He satisfied himself that this was so by overhauling every nook and corner, in the process passing and repassing Violet and me with a perfect unconcern which was more and more amazing. Being apparently at last clear in his mind upon that point, he put on the ulster and a dark cloth cap, and began to fasten the Gladstone bag.

While he was doing so, his back being turned to the bed, without the slighest warning, the woman in the bed sat up. The man's movements had been noiseless. He had made no sound which could have roused her. Possibly some sudden intuition had come to her in her sleep. However that might be, she all at once was wide awake. She stared round the apartment with wondering eyes. Her glance fell on the man, dressed as for a journey.

"Where are you going?"

The words fell from her lips as unawares. Then some sudden conception of his purpose seemed to have flown to her brain. She sprang out of bed with a bound.

"You shan't go," she screamed.

She rushed to him. He put his hand on the table. He turned to her. Something flashed in the lamplight. It was the knife. As she came he plunged it into her side right to the hilt. For an instant he held her spitted on the blade. He put his hand to her throat. He thrust her from him. With the other hand he extricated the blade. He let her fall upon the floor. She had uttered a sort of sigh as the weapon was being driven home. Beyond that she had not made a sound.

All was still. He remained for some seconds looking down at her as she lay. Then he turned away. We saw his face. It was, if possible, paler than before. A smile distorted his lips. He stood for a moment as if listening. Then he glanced round the cabin, as if to make sure that he was unobserved. His black eyes travelled over our startled features, in evident unconsciousness that we were there. Then he glanced at the blade in his hand. As he did so he perceptibly shuddered. The glittering steel was obscured with blood. As he perceived that this was so he gasped. He seemed to realise for the first time what it was that he had done. Taking an envelope from an inner pocket of his ulster he began to wipe the blood from off the blade. While doing so his wandering glance fell upon the woman lying on the floor. Some new aspect of the recumbent figure seemed to strike him with a sudden horror. He staggered backwards. I thought he would have fallen. He caught at the wall to help him stand—caught at the wall with the hand which held the blade. At that part of the cabin the wall was doubly panelled half-way to the roof. Between the outer and the inner panel there was evidently a cavity, because, when in his sudden alarm he clutched at the wall, the blade slipped from his relaxing grasp and fell between the panels. Such was his state of panic that he did not appear to perceive what had happened. And at that moment a cry rang out upon the river—possibly it was someone hailing the keeper of the lock— "Ahoy!"

The sound seemed to fill him with unreasoning terror. He rushed to the table. He closed the Gladstone with a hurried snap; he caught it up; he turned to flee. As he did so I stepped out of the alcove. I advanced right in front of him. I cannot say whether he saw me, or whether he didn't. But he seemed to see me. He started back. A look of the most awful terror came on his countenance. And at that same instant the whole scene vanished. I was standing in the cabin of the *Water Lily*. The moon was stealing through the little narrow casement. Violet was creeping to my side. She stole into my arms. I held her to me.

"Eric," she moaned.

For myself, I am not ashamed to own that, temporarily, I had lost the use of my tongue. When, in a measure, the faculty of speech returned to me—

"Was it a dream?" I whispered.

"It was a vision."

"A vision?" I shuddered. "Look!"

As I spoke she turned to look. There, in the moonbeams, we saw a woman in her nightdress, lying on the cabin floor. We saw that she had golden hair. It seemed to us that she was dead. We saw her but a moment—she was gone! It must have been imagination; we know that these things are not, but it belonged to that order of imagination which is stranger than reality.

My wife looked up at me.

"Eric, it is a vision which has been sent to us in order that we may expose in the light of day a crime which was hidden in the night."

I said nothing. I felt for a box of matches on the table. I lit a lamp. I looked round and round the cabin, holding the lamp above my head the better to assist my search. It was with a feeling of the most absurd relief that I perceived that everything was unchanged, that, so far as I could see, there was no one there but my wife and I.

"I think, Violet, if you don't mind, I'll have some whisky."

She offered no objection. She stood and watched me as I poured the stuff into a glass. I am bound to admit that the spirit did me good.

"And what," I asked, "do you make of the performance we have just now witnessed?" She was still. I took another drink. There can be no doubt that, under certain circumstances, whisky is a fluid which is not to be despised. "Have we both suddenly become insane, or do you attribute it to the cucumber we ate at lunch?"

"How strange that Mr. Inglis should have told us the story only this afternoon."

"I wish Mr. Inglis had kept the story to himself entirely."

"They were the voices which I heard last night. They were the voices Mason heard. It was all pre-destined. I understand it now."

"I wish that I could say the same."

"I see it all!"

She pressed her hands against her brow. Her eyes flashed fire.

"I see why it was sent to us, what it is we have to do. Eric, we have to find the knife."

I began to fear, from her frenzied manner, that her brain must in reality be softening.

"What knife?"

"The knife which he dropped between the panels. The boat has only been repainted. We know that in all essentials the *Sylph* and the *Water Lily* are one and the same. Mr. Inglis said that the weapon which did the deed was never found. No adequate search was ever made. It is waiting for us where he dropped it."

"My dear Violet, don't you think you had better have a little whisky? It will calm you."

"Have you a hammer and a chisel?"

"What do you want them for?"

"It was here that he was standing; it was here that he dropped the knife." She had taken up her position against the wall at the foot of the bed. Frankly, I did not like her manner at all. It was certainly where, in the latter portion of that nightmare, the fellow had been standing. "I will wrench this panel away." She rapped against a particular panel with her knuckles. "Behind it we shall find the knife."

"My dear Violet, this houseboat isn't mine. We cannot destroy another man's property in that wanton fashion. He will hardly accept as an adequate excuse the fact that at the time we were suffering from a severe attack of indigestion."

"This will do."

She took a large carving-knife out of the knife-basket which was on the shelf close by her. She thrust the blade between the panel and the woodwork. It could scarcely have been securely fastened. In a surprisingly short space of time she had forced it loose. Then, grasping it with both her hands, she hauled the panel bodily away.

"Eric, it is there!"

Something was there, resting on a little ledge which had checked its fall on to the floor beneath—something which was covered with paint, and dust, and cobwebs, and Violet all at once grew timid.

"You take it; I dare not touch the thing."

"It is very curious; something is there, and, by George, it is a knife!"

It was a knife—the knife which we had seen in the vision, the dream, the nightmare, call it what you will—the something which had seemed so real. There was no mistaking it, tarnished though it was—the long, slender blade which we had seen the man draw from the leather sheath. Stuck to it by what was afterwards shown to be coagulated blood was an envelope—the envelope which we had seen the fellow take from his pocket to wipe off the crimson stain. It had adhered to the blade. When the knife fell the envelope fell too.

"At least," I murmured as I stared at this grim relic, "this is a singular coincidence."

The blood upon the blade had dried. It required but little to cause the envelope to fall away. As a matter of fact, while I was still holding the weapon in my hand it fell to the floor. I picked it up. It was addressed in a woman's hand, "Francis Joynes, Esq., Fairleigh, Streatham."

I at once recognised the name as that of a well-known owner of racehorses and so-called "gentleman rider."

Not the least singular part of all that singular story was that the letter inside that envelope, which was afterwards opened and read by the proper authorities, was from Mr. Joynes's wife. It was a loving, tender letter, from a wife who was an invalid abroad to a husband whom she supposed was thinking of her at home.

Mr. Joynes was never arrested, and that for this sufficient reason: that when the agents of the law arrived at his residence Mr. Joynes was dead. He had committed suicide on the very night on which we saw that—call it vision—on board the *Water Lily*. I viewed the corpse against my will. I was not called in evidence. Had I been, I was prepared to swear, as was my wife, that Mr. Joynes was the man whom I had seen in a dream that night. It was shown at the inquest that he had suffered of late from horrid dreams—that he had scarcely dared to sleep. I wonder if, in that last and most awful of his dreams, he had seen my face—seen it as I saw his?

It was afterwards shown, from inquiries which were made, that Mr. Joynes and "Mr. Bush," tenant of the *Sylph*, were, beyond all doubt, one and the same person. On the singular circumstances which caused that discovery to be made I offer no comment.

THE WOMAN AT
SEVEN BROTHERS

Wilbur Daniel Steele

I tell you sir, I was innocent. I didn't know any more about the world at twenty-two than some do at twelve. My uncle and aunt in Duxbury brought me up strict; I studied hard in high school, I worked hard after hours, and I went to church twice on Sundays, and I can't see it's right to put me in a place like this, with crazy people. Oh yes, I know they're crazy—you can't tell *me*. As for what they said in court about finding her with her husband, that's the Inspector's lie, sir, because he's down on me, and wants to make it look like my fault.

No, sir, I can't say as I thought she was handsome—not at first. For one thing, her lips were too thin and white, and her color was bad. I'll tell you a fact, sir; that first day I came off to the Light I was sitting on my cot in the store-room (that's where the assistant keeper sleeps at the Seven Brothers), as lonesome as I could be, away from home for the first time and the water all around me, and, even though it was a calm day, pounding enough on the ledge to send a kind of a *woom-woom-woom* whining up through all that solid rock of the tower. And when old Fedderson poked his head down from the living-room with the sunshine above making a kind of bright frame around his hair and whiskers, to give me a cheery, "Make yourself to home, son!" I remember I said to myself: "*He's* all right. I'll get along with *him*. But his wife's enough to sour milk." That was queer, because she was so much under him in age—'long about twenty-eight or so, and him nearer fifty. But that's what I said, sir.

Of course that feeling wore off, same as any feeling will wear off sooner or later in a place like the Seven Brothers. Cooped up in a place like that you come to know folks so well that you forget what they *do* look like. There was a long time I never noticed her, any more than you'd notice the cat. We used to sit of an evening around the table, as if you were Fedderson there, and me here, and her somewhere back there, in the rocker, knitting. Fedderson would be working on his Jacob's-ladder, and I'd be reading. He'd been working on that Jacob's-ladder a year, I guess, and every time the Inspector came off with the tender he was so astonished to see how good that ladder was that the old man would go to work and make it better. That's all he lived for.

If I was reading, as I say, I daren't take my eyes off the book, or Fedderson had me. And then he'd begin—what the Inspector said about him. How surprised the member of the board had been, that time, to see everything so clean about the light. What the Inspector had said about Fedderson's being stuck here in a second-class light—best keeper on the coast. And so on and so on, till either he or I had to go aloft and have a look at the wicks.

He'd been there twenty-three years, all told, and he'd got used to the feeling that he was kept down unfair—so used to it, I guess, that he fed on it, and told himself how folks ashore would talk when he was dead and gone—best keeper on the coast—kept down unfair. Not that he said that to me. No, he was far too loyal and humble and respectful, doing his duty without complaint, as anybody could see.

And all that time, night after night, hardly ever a word out of the woman. As I remember it, she seemed more like a piece of furniture than anything else—not even a very good cook, nor over and above tidy. One day, when he and I were trimming the lamp, he passed the remark that his *first* wife used to dust the lens and take a pride in it. Not that he said a word against Anna, though. He never said a word against any living mortal; he was too upright.

I don't know how it came about; or, rather, I *do* know, but it was so sudden, and so far away from my thoughts, that it shocked me, like the world turned over. It was at prayers. That night I remember Fedderson was uncommon long-winded. We'd had a batch of newspapers out by the tender, and at such times the old man always made a long watch of it, getting the world straightened out. For one thing, the United States minister to Turkey was dead. Well, from him and his soul, Fedderson got on to Turkey and the Presbyterian college there, and from that to heathen in general. He rambled on and on, like the surf on the ledge, *woom-woom-woom*, never coming to an end.

You know how you'll be at prayers sometimes. My mind strayed. I counted the canes in the chair-seat where I was kneeling; I plaited a corner of the table-cloth between my fingers for a spell, and by and by my eyes went wandering up the back of the chair.

The woman, sir, was looking at me. Her chair was back to mine, close, and both our heads were down in the shadow under the edge of the table, with Fedderson clear over on the other side by the stove. And there were her two eyes hunting mine between the spindles in the shadow. You won't believe me, sir, but I tell you I felt like jumping to my feet and running out of the room—it was so queer.

I don't know what her husband was praying about after that. His voice didn't mean anything, no more than the seas on the ledge away down there. I went to work to count the canes in the seat again, but all my eyes were in the top of my head. It got so I couldn't stand it. We were at the Lord's prayer, saying it singsong together, when I had to look up again. And there her two eyes were, between the spindles, hunting mine. Just then all of us were saying, "Forgive us our trespasses—" I thought of it afterward.

When we got up she was turned the other way, but I couldn't help seeing her cheeks were red. It was terrible. I wondered if Fedderson would notice, though I might have known he wouldn't—not him. He was in too much of a hurry to get at his Jacob's-ladder, and then he had to tell me for the tenth time what the Inspector'd said that day about getting him another light—Kingdom Come, maybe, he said.

I made some excuse or other and got away. Once in the store-room, I sat down on my cot and stayed there a long time, feeling queerer than anything. I read a chapter in the Bible, I don't know why. After I'd got my boots off I sat with them in my hands for as much as an hour, I guess, staring at the oil-tank and its lopsided shadow on the wall. I tell you, sir, I was shocked. I was only twenty-two remember, and I was shocked and horrified.

And when I did turn in, finally, I didn't sleep at all well. Two or three times I came to, sitting straight up in bed. Once I got up and opened the outer door to have a look. The water was like glass, dim, without a breath of wind, and the moon just going down. Over on the black shore I made out two lights in a village, like a pair of eyes watching. Lonely? My, yes! Lonely and nervous. I had a horror of her, sir. The dinghy-boat hung on its davits just there in front of the door, and for a minute I had an awful hankering to climb into it, lower away, and row off, no matter where. It sounds foolish.

Well, it seemed foolish next morning, with the sun shining and everything as usual—Fedderson sucking his pen and wagging his head over his eternal "log," and his wife down in the rocker with her head in the newspaper, and her breakfast work still waiting. I guess that jarred it out of me more than anything else—sight of her slouched down there, with her stringy, yellow hair and her dusty apron and the pale back of her neck, reading the Society Notes. *Society Notes!* Think of it! For the first time since I came to Seven Brothers I wanted to laugh.

I guess I did laugh when I went aloft to clean the lamp and found everything so free and breezy, gulls flying high and little whitecaps making under a westerly. It was like feeling a big load dropped off your shoulders. Fedderson came up with his dust-rag and cocked his head at me.

"What's the matter, Ray?" said he.

"Nothing," said I. And then I couldn't help it. "Seems kind of out of place for society notes," said I, "out here at Seven Brothers."

He was the other side of the lens, and when he looked at me he had a thousand eyes, all sober. For a minute I thought he was going on dusting, but then he came out and sat down on a sill.

"Sometimes," said he, "I get to thinking it may be a mite dull for her out here. She's pretty young, Ray. Not much more'n a girl, hardly."

"Not much more'n a *girl*"! It gave me a turn, sir, as though I'd seen my aunt in short dresses.

"It's a good home for her, though," he went on slow. "I've seen a lot worse ashore, Ray. Of course if I could get a shore light—"

"Kingdom Come's a shore light."

He looked at me out of his deep-set eyes, and then he turned them around the light-room, where he'd been so long.

"No," said he, wagging his head. "It ain't for such as me."

I never saw so humble a man.

"But look here," he went on, more cheerful. "As I was telling her just now, a month from yesterday's our fourth anniversary, and I'm going to take her ashore for the day and give her a holiday—new hat and everything. A girl wants a mite of excitement now and then, Ray."

There it was again, that "girl." It gave me the fidgets, sir. I had to do something about it. It's close quarters for last names in a light, and I'd taken to calling him Uncle Matt soon after I came. Now, when I was at table that noon, I spoke over to where she was standing by the stove, getting him another help of chowder.

"I guess I'll have some, too, *Aunt* Anna," said I, matter of fact.

She never said a word nor gave a sign—just stood there kind of round-shouldered, dipping the chowder. And that night at prayers I hitched my chair around the table, with its back the other way.

You get awful lazy in a lighthouse, some ways. No matter how much tinkering you've got, there's still a lot of time and there's such a thing as too much reading. The changes in weather get monotonous, too, by and by; the light burns the same on a thick night as it does on a fair one. Of course there's the ships, north-bound, south-bound—wind-jammers, freighters, passenger-boats full of people. In the watches at night you can see their lights go by, and wonder what they are, how they're laden, where they'll fetch up, and all. I used to do that almost every evening when it was my first watch, sitting out on the walk-around up there with my legs hanging over the edge and my chin propped on the railing—lazy. The Boston boat was the prettiest to see, with her three tiers of port-holes lit, like a string of pearls wrapped round and round a woman's neck—well away, too, for the ledge must have made a couple of hundred fathoms off the Light, like a white dog-tooth of a breaker, even on the darkest night.

Well, I was lolling there one night, as I say, watching the Boston boat go by, not thinking of anything special, when I heard the door on the other side of the tower open and footsteps coming around to me.

By and by I nodded toward the boat and passed the remark that she was fetching in uncommon close to-night. No answer. I made nothing of that, for oftentimes Fedderson wouldn't answer, and after I'd watched the lights crawling on through the dark a spell, just to make conversation I said I guessed there'd be a bit of weather before long.

"I've noticed," said I, "when there's weather coming on, and the wind in the northeast, you can hear the orchestra playing aboard of her just over there. I make it out now. Do you?"

"Yes. Oh—yes! *I hear it all right!*"

You can imagine I started. It wasn't him, but *her*. And there was something in the way she said that speech, sir—something—well— unnatural. Like a hungry animal snapping at a person's hand.

I turned and looked at her sidewise. She was standing by the railing, leaning a little outward, the top of her from the waist picked out bright by the lens behind her. I didn't know what in the world to say, and yet I had a feeling I ought not to sit there mum.

"I wonder," said I, "what that captain's thinking of, fetching in so handy to-night. It's no way. I tell you, if 'twasn't for this light, she'd go to work and pile up on the ledge some thick night—"

She turned at that and stared straight into the lens. I didn't like the look of her face. Somehow, with its edges cut hard all around and its two eyes closed down to slits, like a cat's, it made a kind of mask.

"And then," I went on, uneasy enough—"and then where'd all their music be of a sudden, and their goings-on and their singing—"

"And dancing!" She clipped me off so quick it took my breath.

"D-d-dancing?" said I.

"That's dance-music," said she. She was looking at the boat again.

"How do you know?" I felt I had to keep on talking.

Well, sir—she laughed. I looked at her. She had on a shawl of some stuff or other that shined in the light; she had it pulled tight around her with her two hands in front at her breast, and I saw her shoulders swaying in tune.

"How do I *know*?" she cried. Then she laughed again, the same kind of a laugh. It was queer, sir, to see her, and to hear her. She turned, as quick as that, and leaned toward me. "Don't you know how to dance, Ray?" said she.

"N-no," I managed, and I was going to say *"Aunt Anna,"* but the thing choked in my throat. I tell you she was looking square at me all the time with her two eyes and moving with the music as if she didn't know it. By heavens, sir, it came over me of a sudden that she wasn't so bad-looking, after all. I guess I must have sounded like a fool.

"You—you see," said I, "she's cleared the rip there now, and the music's gone. You—you—hear?"

"Yes," said she, turning back slow. "That's where it stops every night—night after night—it stops just there—at the rip."

When she spoke again her voice was different. I never heard the like of it, thin and taut as a thread. It made me shiver, sir.

"I hate 'em!" That's what she said. "I hate 'em all. I'd like to see 'em dead. I'd love to see 'em torn apart on the rocks, night after night. I could bathe my hands in their blood, night after night."

And do you know, sir, I saw it with my own eyes, her hands moving in each other above the rail. But it was her voice, though. I didn't know what to do, or what to say, so I poked my head through the railing and looked down at the water. I don't think I'm a coward, sir, but it was like a cold—ice-cold—hand, taking hold of my beating heart.

When I looked up finally, she was gone. By and by I went in and had a look at the lamp, hardly knowing what I was about. Then, seeing by my watch it was time for the old man to come on duty, I started to go below. In the Seven Brothers, you understand, the stair goes down in a spiral through a well against the south wall, and first there's the door to the keeper's room, and then you come to another, and that's the living-room, and then down to the store-room. And at night, if you don't carry a lantern, it's as black as the pit.

Well, down I went, sliding my hand along the rail, and as usual I stopped to give a rap on the keeper's door, in case he was taking a nap after supper. Sometimes he did.

I stood there, blind as a bat, with my mind still up on the walk-around. There was no answer to my knock. I hadn't expected any. Just from habit, and with my right foot already hanging down for the next step, I reached out to give the door one more tap for luck.

Do you know, sir, my hand didn't fetch up on anything. The door had been there a second before, and now the door wasn't there. My hand just went on going through the dark, on and on, and I didn't seem to have sense or power enough to stop it. There didn't seem any air in the well to breathe, and my ears were drumming to the surf—that's how scared I was. And then my hand touched the flesh of a face, and something in the dark said, "Oh!" no louder than a sigh.

Next thing I knew, sir, I was down in the living-room, warm and yellow-lit, with Fedderson cocking his head at me across the table, where he was at that eternal Jacob's-ladder of his.

"What's the matter, Ray?" said he. "Lord's sake, Ray!"

"Nothing," said I. Then I think I told him I was sick. That night I wrote a letter to A. L. Peters, the grain-dealer in Duxbury, asking for a job—even though it wouldn't go ashore for a couple of weeks, just the writing of it made me feel better.

It's hard to tell you how those two weeks went by. I don't know why, but I felt like hiding in a corner all the time. I had to come to meals. But I didn't look at her, though, not once, unless it was by accident. Fedderson thought I was still ailing and nagged me to death with advice and so on. One thing I took care not to do, I can tell you, and that was to knock on his door till I'd made certain he wasn't below in the living-room—though I was tempted to.

Yes, sir; that's a queer thing, and I wouldn't tell you if I hadn't set out to give you the truth. Night after night, stopping there on the landing in that black pit, the air gone out of my lungs and the surf drumming in my ears and sweat standing cold on my neck—and one hand lifting up in the air—God forgive me, sir! Maybe I did wrong not to look at her more, drooping about her work in her gingham apron, with her hair stringing.

When the Inspector came off with the tender, that time, I told him I was through. That's when he took the dislike to me, I guess, for he looked at me kind of sneering and said, soft as I was, I'd have to put up with it till next relief. And then, said he, there'd be a whole house-cleaning at Seven Brothers, because he'd gotten Fedderson the berth at Kingdom Come. And with that he slapped the old man on the back.

I wish you could have seen Fedderson, sir. He sat down on my cot as if his knees had given 'way. Happy? You'd think he'd be happy, with all his dreams come true. Yes, he was happy, beaming all over—for a minute. Then, sir, he began to shrivel up. It was like seeing a man cut down in his prime before your eyes. He began to wag his head.

"No," said he. "No, no; it's not for such as me. I'm good enough for Seven Brothers, and that's all, Mr. Bayliss. That's all."

And for all the Inspector could say, that's what he stuck to. He'd figured himself a martyr so many years, nursed that injustice like a mother with her first-born, sir; and now in his old age, so to speak, they weren't to rob him of it. Fedderson was going to wear out his life in a second-class light, and folks would talk—that was his idea. I heard him hailing down as the tender was casting off:

"See you to-morrow, Mr. Bayliss. Yep. Coming ashore with the wife for a spree. Anniversary. Yep."

But he didn't sound much like a spree. They *had* robbed him, partly, after all. I wondered what *she* thought about it. I didn't know till night. She didn't show up to supper, which Fedderson and I got ourselves—had a headache, he said. It was my early watch. I went and lit up and came back to read a spell. He was finishing off the Jacob's-ladder, and thoughtful, like a man that's lost a treasure. Once or twice I caught him looking about the room on the sly. It was pathetic, sir.

Going up the second time, I stepped out on the walk-around to have a look at things. She was there on the seaward side, wrapped in that silky thing. A fair sea was running across the ledge and it was coming on a little thick—not too thick. Off to the right the Boston boat was blowing, *whroom-whroom!* Creeping up on us, quarter-speed. There was another fellow behind her, and a fisherman's conch farther offshore.

I don't know why, but I stopped beside her and leaned on the rail. She didn't appear to notice me, one way or another. We stood and we stood, listening to the whistles, and the longer we stood the more it got on my nerves, her not noticing me. I suppose she'd been too much on my mind lately. I began to be put out. I scraped my feet. I coughed. By and by I said out loud:

"Look here, I guess I better get out the foghorn and give those fellows a toot."

"Why?" said she, without moving her head—calm as that.

"Why?" It gave me a turn, sir. For a minute I stared at her. "Why? Because if she don't pick up this light before very many minutes she'll be too close in to wear—tide 'll have her on the rocks—that's why!"

I couldn't see her face, but I could see one of her silk shoulders lift a little, like a shrug. And there I kept on staring at her, a dumb one, sure enough. I know what brought me to was hearing the Boston boat's three sharp toots as she picked up the light—mad as anything—and swung her helm a-port. I turned away from her, sweat stringing down my face, and walked around to the door. It was just as well, too, for the feed-pipe was plugged in the lamp and the wicks were popping. She'd have been out in another five minutes, sir.

When I'd finished, I saw that woman standing in the doorway. Her eyes were bright. I had a horror of her, sir, a living horror.

"If only the light had been out," said she, low and sweet.

"God forgive you," said I. "You don't know what you're saying."

She went down the stair into the well, winding out of sight, and as long as I could see her, her eyes were watching mine. When I went, myself, after a few minutes, she was waiting for me on that first landing, standing still in the dark. She took hold of my hand, though I tried to get it away.

"Good-by," said she in my ear.

"Good-by?" said I. I didn't understand.

"You heard what he said to-day—about Kingdom Come? Be it so—on his own head. I'll never come back here. Once I set foot ashore—I've got friends in Brightonboro, Ray."

I got away from her and started on down. But I stopped. "Brightonboro?" I whispered back. "Why do you tell *me*?" My throat was raw to the words, like a sore.

"So you'd know," said she.

Well, sir, I saw them off next morning, down that new Jacob's-ladder into the dinghy-boat, her in a dress of blue velvet and him in his best cutaway and derby—rowing away, smaller and smaller, the two of them. And then I went back and sat on my cot, leaving the door open and the ladder still hanging down the wall, along with the boat-falls.

I don't know whether it was relief, or what. I suppose I must have been worked up even more than I'd thought those past weeks, for now it was all over I was like a rag. I got down on my knees, sir, and prayed to God for the salvation of my soul, and when I got up and climbed to the living-room it was half past twelve by the clock. There was rain on the windows and the sea was running blue-black under the sun. I'd sat there all that time not knowing there was a squall.

It was funny; the glass stood high, but those black squalls kept coming and going all afternoon, while I was at work up in the light-room. And I worked hard, to keep myself busy. First thing I knew it was five, and no sign of the boat yet. It began to get dim and kind of purplish-gray over the land. The sun was down. I lit up, made everything snug, and got out the night-glasses to have another look for that boat. He'd said he intended to get back before five. No sign. And then, standing there, it came over me that of course he wouldn't be coming off—he'd be hunting *her*, poor old fool. It looked like I had to stand two men's watches that night.

Never mind. I felt like myself again, even if I hadn't had any dinner or supper. Pride came to me that night on the walk-around, watching the boats go by—little boats, big boats, the Boston boat with all her pearls and her dance-music. They couldn't see me; they didn't know who I was; but to the last of them, they depended on *me*. They say a man must be born again. Well, I was born again. I breathed deep in the wind.

Dawn broke hard and red as a dying coal. I put out the light and started to go below. Born again; yes, sir. I felt so good I whistled in the well, and when I came to that first door on the stair I reached out in the dark to give it a rap for luck. And then, sir, the hair prickled all over my scalp, when I found my hand just going on and on through the air, the same as it had gone once before, and all of a sudden I wanted to yell, because I thought I was going to touch flesh. It's funny what their just forgetting to close their door did to me, isn't it?

Well, I reached for the latch and pulled it to with a bang and ran down as if a ghost was after me. I got up some coffee and bread and bacon for breakfast. I drank the coffee. But somehow I couldn't eat, all along of that open door. The light in the room was blood. I got to thinking. I thought how she'd talked about those men, women and children on the rocks, and how she'd made to bathe her hands over the rail. I almost jumped out of my chair then; it seemed for a wink she was there beside the stove watching me with that queer half-smile—really, I seemed to see her for a flash across the red table-cloth in the red light of dawn.

"Look here!" said I to myself, sharp enough; and then I gave myself a good laugh and went below. There I took a look out of the door, which was still open, with the ladder hanging down. I made sure to see the poor old fool come pulling around the point before very long now.

My boots were hurting a little, and, taking them off, I lay down on the cot to rest, and somehow I went to sleep. I had horrible dreams. I saw her again standing in that blood-red kitchen, and she seemed to be washing her hands, and the surf on the ledge was whining up the tower, louder and louder all the time, and what it whined was, "Night after night—night after night." What woke me was cold water in my face.

The store-room was in gloom. That scared me at first; I thought night had come, and remembered the light. But then I saw the gloom was of a storm. The floor was shining wet, and the water in my face was spray, flung up through the open door. When I ran to close it it almost made me dizzy to see the gray-and-white breakers marching past. The land was gone; the sky shut down heavy overhead; there was a piece of wreckage on the back of a swell, and the Jacob's-ladder was carried clean away. How that sea had picked up so quick I can't think. I looked at my watch and it wasn't four in the afternoon yet.

When I closed the door, sir, it was almost dark in the store-room. I'd never been in the Light before in a gale of wind. I wondered why I was shivering so, till I found it was the floor below me shivering, and the walls and stair. Horrible crunchings and grindings ran away up the tower, and now and then there was a great thud somewhere, like a cannon-shot in a cave. I tell you, sir, I was alone, and I was in a mortal fright for a minute or so. And yet I had to get myself together. There was the light up there not tended to, and an early dark coming on and a heavy night and all, and I had to go. And I had to pass that door.

You'll say it's foolish, sir, and maybe it *was* foolish. Maybe it was because I hadn't eaten. But I began thinking of that door up there the minute I set foot on the stair, and all the way up through that howling dark well I dreaded to pass it. I told myself I wouldn't stop. I didn't stop.

I felt the landing underfoot and I went on, four steps, five—and then I couldn't. I turned and went back. I put out my hand and it went on into nothing. That door, sir, was open again.

I left it be; I went on up to the light-room and set to work. It was Bedlam there, sir, screeching Bedlam, but I took no notice. I kept my eyes down. I trimmed those seven wicks, sir, as neat as ever they were trimmed; I polished the brass till it shone, and I dusted the lens. It wasn't till that was done that I let myself look back to see who it was standing there, half out of sight in the well. It was her, sir.

"Where'd you come from?" I asked. I remember my voice was sharp.

"Up Jacob's-ladder," said she, and hers was like the syrup of flowers.

I shook my head. I was savage, sir. "The ladder's carried away."

"I cast it off," said she, with a smile.

"Then," said I, "you must have come while I was asleep." Another thought came on me heavy as a ton of lead. "And where's *he*?" said I. "Where's the boat?"

"He's drowned," said she, as easy as that. "And I let the boat go adrift. You wouldn't hear me when I called."

"But look here," said I. "If you came through the store-room, why didn't you wake me up? Tell me that!" It sounds foolish enough, me standing like a lawyer in court, trying to prove she *couldn't* be there.

She didn't answer for a moment. I guess she sighed, though I couldn't hear for the gale, and her eyes grew soft, sir, so soft.

"I couldn't," said she. "You looked so peaceful—dear one."

My cheeks and neck went hot, sir, as if a warm iron was laid on them. I didn't know what to say. I began to stammer, "What do you mean—" but she was going back down the stair, out of sight. My God! sir, and I used not to think she was good-looking!

I started to follow her. I wanted to know what she meant. Then I said to myself, "If I don't go—if I wait here—she'll come back." And I went to the weather side and stood looking out of the window. Not that there was much to see. It was growing dark, and the Seven Brothers looked like the mane of a running horse, a great, vast, white horse running into the wind. The air was a-welter with it. I caught one peep of a fisherman, lying down flat trying to weather the ledge, and I said, "God help them all tonight," and then I went hot at sound of that "God."

I was right about her, though. She was back again. I wanted her to speak first, before I turned, but she wouldn't. I didn't hear her go out; I didn't know what she was up to till I saw her coming outside on the walk-around, drenched wet already. I pounded on the glass for her to come in and not be a fool; if she heard she gave no sign of it.

There she stood, and there I stood watching her. Lord, sir—was it just that I'd never had eyes to see? Or are there women who bloom? Her clothes were shining on her, like a carving, and her hair was let down like a golden curtain tossing and streaming in the gale, and there she stood with her lips half open, drinking, and her eyes half closed, gazing straight away over the Seven Brothers, and her shoulders swaying, as if in tune with the wind and water and all the ruin. And when I looked at her hands over the rail, sir, they were moving in each other as if they bathed, and then I remembered, sir.

A cold horror took me. I knew now why she had come back again. She wasn't a woman—she was a devil. I turned my back on her. I said to myself: "It's time to light up. You've got to light up"—like that, over and over, out loud. My hand was shivering so I could hardly find a match; and when I scratched it, it only flared a second and then went out in the back draught from the open door. She was standing in the doorway, looking at me. It's queer, sir, but I felt like a child caught in mischief.

"I—I—was going to light up," I managed to say, finally.

"Why?" said she. No, I can't say it as she did.

"*Why?*" said I. "*My God!*"

She came nearer, laughing, as if with pity, low, you know. "Your God? And who is your God? What is God? What is anything on a night like this?"

I drew back from her. All I could say anything about was the light.

"Why not the dark?" said she. "Dark is softer than light—tenderer—dearer than light. From the dark up here, away up here in the wind and storm, we can watch the ships go by, you and I. And you love me so. You've loved me so long, Ray."

"I never have!" I struck out at her. "I don't! I don't!"

Her voice was lower than ever, but there was the same laughing pity in it. "Oh yes, you have." And she was near me again.

"I have?" I yelled. "I'll show you! I'll show you if I have!"

I got another match, sir, and scratched it on the brass. I gave it to the first wick, the little wick that's inside all the others. It bloomed like a yellow flower. "I *have*?" I yelled, and gave it to the next.

Then there was a shadow, and I saw she was leaning beside me, her two elbows on the brass, her two arms stretched out above the wicks, her bare forearms and wrists and hands. I gave a gasp:

"Take care! You'll burn them! For God's sake—"

She didn't move or speak. The match burned my fingers and went out, and all I could do was stare at those arms of hers, helpless. I'd never noticed her arms before. They were rounded and graceful and covered with a soft down, like a breath of gold. Then I heard her speaking, close to my ear:

"Pretty arms," she said. "Pretty arms!"

I turned. Her eyes were fixed on mine. They seemed heavy, as if with sleep, and yet between their lids they were two wells, deep and deep, and as if they held all the things I'd ever thought or dreamed in them. I looked away from them, at her lips. Her lips were red as poppies, heavy with redness. They moved, and I heard them speaking:

"Poor boy, you love me so, and you want to kiss me—don't you?"

"No," said I. But I couldn't turn around. I looked at her hair. I'd always thought it was stringy hair. Some hair curls naturally with damp, they say, and perhaps that was it, for there were pearls of wet on it, and it was thick and shimmering around her face, making soft shadows by the temples. There was green in it, queer strands of green like braids.

"What is it?" said I.

"Nothing but weed," said she, with that slow, sleepy smile.

Somehow or other I felt calmer than I had any time. "Look here," said I. "I'm going to light this lamp." I took out a match, scratched it, and touched the third wick. The flame ran around, bigger than the other two together. But still her arms hung there. I bit my lip. "By God, I will!" said I to myself, and I lit the fourth.

It was fierce, sir, fierce! And yet those arms never trembled. I had to look around at her. Her eyes were still looking into mine, so deep and deep, and her red lips were still smiling with that queer sleepy droop; the only thing was that tears were raining down her cheeks—big, glowing round, jewel tears. It wasn't human, sir. It was like a dream.

"Pretty arms," she sighed, and then, as if those words had broken something in her heart, there came a great sob bursting from her lips. To hear it drove me mad. I reached to drag her away, but she was too quick, sir; she cringed from me and slipped out from between my hands. It was like she faded away, sir, and went down in a bundle, nursing her poor arms and mourning over them with those terrible, broken sobs.

The sound of them took the manhood out of me—you'd have been the same, sir. I knelt down beside her on the floor and covered my face.

"Please," I moaned. "Please! Please!" That's all I could say. I wanted her to forgive me. I reached out a hand, blind, for forgiveness, and I couldn't find her anywhere. I had hurt her so, and she was afraid of me, of *me*, sir, who loved her so deep it drove me crazy.

I could see her down the stair, though it was dim and my eyes were filled with tears. I stumbled after her, crying, "Please! Please!" The little wicks I'd lit were blowing in the wind from the door and smoking the glass beside them black. One went out. I pleaded with them, the same as I would plead with a human being. I said I'd be back in a second. I promised. And I went on down the stair, crying like a baby because I'd hurt her, and she was afraid of me—of *me*, sir.

She had gone into her room. The door was closed against me and I could hear her sobbing beyond it, broken-hearted. My heart was broken too. I beat on the door with my palms. I begged her to forgive me. I told her I loved her. And all the answer was that sobbing in the dark.

And then I lifted the latch and went in, groping, pleading. "Dearest— please! Because I love you!"

I heard her speak down near the floor. There wasn't any anger in her voice; nothing but sadness and despair.

"No," said she. "You don't love me, Ray. You never have."

"I do! I have!"

"No, no," said she, as if she was tired out.

"Where are you?" I was groping for her. I thought, and lit a match. She had got to the door and was standing there as if ready to fly. I went toward her, and she made me stop. She took my breath away. "I hurt your arms," said I, in a dream.

"No," said she, hardly moving her lips. She held them out to the match's light for me to look, and there was never a scar on them—not even that soft, golden down was singed, sir. "You can't hurt my body," said she, sad as anything. "Only my heart, Ray; my poor heart."

I tell you again, she took my breath away. I lit another match. "How can you be so beautiful?" I wondered. She answered in riddles—but oh, the sadness of her, sir.

"Because," said she, "I've always so wanted to be."

"How come your eyes so heavy?" said I.

"Because I've seen so many things I never dreamed of," said she.

"How come your hair so thick?"

"It's the seaweed makes it thick," said she smiling queer, queer.

"How come seaweed there?"

"Out of the bottom of the sea."

She talked in riddles, but it was like poetry to hear her, or a song.

"How come your lips so red?" said I.

"Because they've wanted so long to be kissed."

Fire was on me, sir. I reached out to catch her, but she was gone, out of the door and down the stair. I followed, stumbling. I must have tripped on the turn, for I remember going through the air and fetching up with a crash, and I didn't know anything for a spell—how long I can't say. When I came to, she was there, somewhere, bending over me, crooning, "My love—my love—" under her breath like, a song.

But then when I got up, she was not where my arms went; she was down the stair again, just ahead of me. I followed her. I was tottering and dizzy and full of pain. I tried to catch up with her in the dark of the store-room, but she was too quick for me, sir, always a little too quick for me. Oh, she was cruel to me, sir. I kept bumping against things, hurting myself still worse, and it was cold and wet and a horrible noise all the while, sir; and then, sir, I found the door was open, and a sea had parted the hinges.

I don't know how it all went, sir. I'd tell you if I could, but it's all so blurred—sometimes it seems more like a dream. I couldn't find her any more; I couldn't hear her; I went all over, everywhere. Once, I remember, I found myself hanging out of that door between the davits, looking down into those big black seas and crying like a baby. It's all riddles and blur. I can't seem to tell you much, sir. It was all—all—I don't know.

I was talking to somebody else—not her. It was the Inspector. I hardly knew it was the Inspector. His face was as gray as a blanket, and his eyes were bloodshot, and his lips were twisted. His left wrist hung down, awkward. It was broken coming aboard the Light in that sea. Yes, we were in the living-room. Yes, sir, it was daylight—gray daylight. I tell you, sir, the man looked crazy to me. He was waving his good arm toward the weather windows, and what he was saying, over and over, was this:

"Look what you done, damn you! Look what you done!"

And what I was saying was this:

"I've lost her!"

I didn't pay any attention to him, nor him to me. By and by he did, though. He stopped his talking all of a sudden, and his eyes looked like the devil's eyes. He put them up close to mine. He grabbed my arm with his good hand, and I cried, I was so weak.

"Johnson," said he, "is that it? By the living God—if you got a woman out here, Johnson!"

"No," said I. "I've lost her."

"What do you mean—lost her?"

"It was dark," said I—and it's funny how my head was clearing up—"and the door was open—the store-room door—and I was after her—and I guess she stumbled, maybe—and I lost her."

"Johnson," said he, "what do you mean? You sound crazy—downright crazy. Who?"

"Her," said I. "Fedderson's wife."

"Who?"

"Her," said I. And with that he gave my arm another jerk.

"Listen," said he, like a tiger. "Don't try that on me. It won't do any good—that kind of lies—not where *you're* going to. Fedderson and his wife, too—the both of 'em's drowned deader 'n a door-nail."

"I know," said I, nodding my head. I was so calm it made him wild.

"You're crazy! Crazy as a loon, Johnson!" And he was chewing his lip red. "I know, because it was me that found the old man laying on Back

Water Flats yesterday morning—*me*! And she'd been with him in the boat, too, because he had a piece of her jacket tore off, tangled in his arm."

"I know," said I, nodding again, like that.

"You know *what*, you *crazy, murdering fool*?" Those were his words to me, sir.

"I know," said I, "what I know."

"And *I* know," said he, "what *I* know."

And there you are, sir. He's Inspector. I'm—nobody.

FORCE MAJEURE

———◆———

J. D. Beresford

As a midge before an elephant, so is man when opposed to Fate. The elephant breathes or lies down, and the high shrill of the midge is done. The midge believes passionately that the looming monster which shuts out his whole world has come across the earth with this one awful purpose of destroying his little life. But the elephant knows less of the midge than the midge knows of the elephant. . . .

George Coleman was not a figure that one would associate with the blunderings of outrageous destiny. He was of the type that seems born to move easily and contentedly through life; neither success nor failure; a tall, thin, fair man, reasonably intelligent, placidly thirty-five, and neither too diligent nor noticeably lazy. He was one of the many who had failed to find briefs; and one of the few who had, nevertheless, succeeded in earning a decent income. He had obtained, through special influence, a post as legal secretary and adviser to a great firm of financiers in the City. The post was almost a sinecure and the salary £800 a year. Added to that, he had another £300 of his own. He spent his holidays in Switzerland or Italy or Norway.

Any suburb would have made him a church-warden, but he preferred to go on living in his chambers, in Old Buildings, Lincoln's Inn. He was used to the inconveniences, and the place satisfied his feeble feeling for romance.

His friend Morley Price, the architect, told him that there was a sinister influence about those chambers. They were on the fifth floor, and boasted a dormer window that might have been done by Sime, in a mood of final recklessness. The dormer was in the sitting-room, and looked out on to the court. Price loved to lie back in his chair and stare at it, attempting vainly to account by archaeology and building construction for the twists and contortions of the jambs and soffit.

"It's a filthy freak, Coleman," was his usual conclusion; "not the work of a decent human mind, but a horrid, sinister growth that comes from within. One day it will put out another tentacle and crush you." After that he would fit his pipe into the gap in his front teeth and return to another attempt at formulating a theory of causation. He had always refused to consider any artificial substitute for those lost teeth. He said that the hole was the natural place for his pipe. Also, that the disfigurement was distinguished and brought him business.

If it had been Morley Price, now. . . . However, it was the absurdly commonplace George Coleman.

The beginning of it all was ordinary enough. He fell in love with a young woman who lived in Surbiton. She was pretty, dark, svelte, and looked perfectly fascinating with a pole at the stern of a punt, while her fox-terrier, Mickie, barked at swallows from the bow.

Coleman was quite acceptable. He punted even better than she did, and he was devoted to dogs, and more especially to Mickie. Nothing could have been more satisfactory and altogether delightful before the elephant came a vast, ubiquitous, imperturbable beast that the doctors called typhoid.

After Muriel died, Coleman took Mickie home to his chambers in Old Buildings, Lincoln's Inn. Mickie was more than a legacy; he was a sacred trust. Coleman had sworn to cherish him when his lovely mistress had been called away to join the headquarters of that angelic host to which she had hitherto belonged as a planetary member. She had appeared to be more concerned about Mickie than about George, at the last. She had not known George so long.

But it was George who cherished her memory. Mickie settled down at once. Within a week Muriel might never have existed, so far as he was concerned. If there was no longer a punt for him, there was a dormer window with a broad, flat seat that served equally well; and in place of migrant swallows there were perennial sparrows.

Coleman was not more sentimental than the average Englishman. At first he was "terribly cut up," as he might have phrased it; but six weeks after Muriel's death the cuts, in normal conditions, would doubtless have cicatrized.

Unhappily, the conditions were anything but normal. The vast bulk of the elephant was between him and any possible road of escape. In this second instance Fate assumed the form of certain mannerisms in Mickie.

He was quite an ordinary fox-terrier, with prick-ears that had spoiled him for show purposes, but he had lived with Muriel from puppyhood, and all his reactions showed her influence. He had, in fact, all the mannerisms of a spoilt lap-dog. He craved attention he could not bark at the sparrows without turning every few seconds to Coleman for praise and encouragement; he was fussy and restless, on Coleman's lap one minute and up at the window the next; he was noisy and mischievous, and had no sense of shame; when he was reprimanded he jumped up joyfully and tried to lick Coleman's face.

And every one of his foolish tricks was inextricably associated in Coleman's mind with Muriel. . . .

At the end of six weeks Coleman was conscious that he had mourned long enough. He began to feel that it was not healthy for a man of thirty-five to continue in grief for one girl when there were so many others. He decided that the time had come when his awful gloom might melt into resigned sadness. Moreover, a sympathetic young woman he knew, who had a fine figure and tender eyes, had quite noticeably ceased to insist upon the fact that she was sorry for him. In other circumstances Coleman would have changed his unrelieved tie for one with a faint, white stripe.

But Mickie, cheerful beast as he was, stood between Coleman and half-mourning. Mickie was an awful reminder. Muriel had died, but her personality lived on. Every time Mickie barked Coleman could hear Muriel's clear, happy voice say: "Oh, Mickie, *darling*, shut up; you'll simply *deafen* mummy if you bark like that!"

Mickie began to get on Coleman's nerves. Sometimes when he was alone with him in the evening he regarded him with a heart full of evil desires; thoughts of losing him in the country, of selling him to a dog-fancier in Soho, of sending him to live with a married sister in Yorkshire. But that was just the breaking-point with Coleman. He was a shade too sentimental to shirk a sacred trust. Muriel, almost with her "dying breath," had confided Mickie to his keeping; bright, beautiful, happy Muriel who had loved and trusted him. Coleman would have regarded himself as a damned soul if he had been false to that trust.

Then he tried to train Mickie. He might as well have tried to train the dormer window. Mickie was four years old, and long past any possibility of alteration by the methods of Coleman. For he simply could not beat the dog; it would have been too sickeningly like beating Muriel.

His gloom deepened, and the young woman with the tender eyes lost sight of him for days at a time. She had no idea of the true state of the case; she merely thought that he was rather silly to go on making himself miserable about a little feather-brained thing like Muriel Hepworth.

The awful thing happened nearly ten weeks after Muriel's death. For many days Coleman had met no one outside his office routine. Most afternoons and every evening he had been shut up with the wraith of a happy voice which laughingly reproved the unchangeable Mickie. He had begun to imagine foolish things; to try experiments; he had kept away from any sight of those tender eyes for nearly a fortnight, hoping to lay the ghost of that insistent, inaudible voice.

It was a hot July evening, and Mickie was on and off the window-sill every moment, divided between furious contempt for the sparrows and the urgent desire for his master's co-operation and approval.

The voice of Muriel filled the room.

Coleman heaved himself out of his chair with a deep groan and went to the window. Below the sill a few feet of sloping tiles pitched steeply down to a narrow eaves-gutter; below the eaves- gutter was a sheer fall of fifty feet on to a paved court.

Mickie had his fore-feet on the sill; he was barking delightedly now that he had an audience.

The fantastic contortions of the dormer seemed to bend over man and dog; and the evil thing that had come to stay with Coleman crept into his brain and paralysed his will.

He stretched out his hand and gave Mickie a strong push.

Mickie slithered down the tiles, yelped, turned clean round, missed the gutter with his hind feet, but caught it at the last moment with both front paws, and so hung, shrieking desperately, struggling to lift himself back to safety while his whole body hung over the abyss.

For a moment man and dog stared into each other's eyes.

Then the virtue returned to Coleman. He was temporarily heroic. "Hold on, old man, hold on," he said tenderly, and began to work his shoulders down the short length of tiles, while he felt about inside the room with his feet trying to maintain some sort of hook on jamb or window board.

He was a long, thin man, and the feat was not a difficult one; the trouble was that he was too slow over it. For as he gingerly lifted one hand from the tiles to grasp Mickie's neck, the dog gave one last terrified yelp and let go.

Coleman heard the thud of his fall into the court.

He could not summon up courage to go down and gather up the mangled heap he so vividly pictured in his imagination.

That night he believed he was going mad, but he slept well and awoke with a strange sense of relief. He awoke much later than usual; a new and beautiful peace reigned that morning.

Strangely enough, neither his bedmaker nor the porter made any reference to Mickie; and while Coleman wondered at their failure to comment on so remarkable a tragedy, he could not bring himself to ask a question.

All through the day, as he worked at his office, a delicious sense of lightness and freedom exhilarated him. He dined at the Cock in Fleet Street, and when he returned to the exquisite stillness of his chambers he sat down to write to the girl with tender eyes. . . .

He thought he had closed the outer door.

He was enormously startled when he heard a strangely familiar patter of feet behind him.

He did not turn his head; he sat cold and rigid, and his ringers began to pick at the blotting-paper. He sat incredibly still and waited for the next sign.

It came with excruciating suddenness: a shrill, joyful, agonising bark, followed with a new distinctness by the echo of a voice that said: "Oh! Mickie, darling, you'll simply *deafen* mummy if you bark like that."

He did not move his body, but slowly and reluctantly first his eyes and then his head turned awfully to the window. . . .

The porter told Morley Price that he had not seen Mr. Coleman fall. He thought he heard a dog bark, he said, just like the little terrier as

Mr. Coleman'd been so fond of; and he was surprised because the pore little feller 'ad fallen out o' the self-same winder the night afore, and he 'adn't cared to speak of it to Mr. Coleman knowin' 'ow terrible cut-up 'e'd be about it. . . .

The chambers have remained unlet ever since.

Morley Price went up there once on a still July evening, and rushed out again with his hands to his ears.

THE SECRET OF
MACARGER'S GULCH

Ambrose Bierce

Northwestwardly from Indian Hill, about nine miles as the crow flies, is Macarger's Gulch. It is not much of a gulch—a mere depression between two wooded ridges of inconsiderable height. From its mouth up to its head—for gulches, like rivers, have an anatomy of their own—the distance does not exceed two miles, and the width at bottom is at only one place more than a dozen yards; for most of the distance on either side of the little brook which drains it in winter, and goes dry in the early spring, there is no level ground at all: the steep slopes of the hills, covered with an almost impenetrable growth of manzanita and chemisal, are divided by nothing but the width of the water course. No one but an occasional enterprising hunter of the vicinity ever goes into Macarger's Gulch, and five miles away it is unknown, even by name. Within that distance in any direction are far more conspicuous topographical features without names, and one might try a long time in vain to ascertain by local inquiry the origin of the name of this one.

About midway between the head and the mouth of Macarger's Gulch, the hill on the right as you ascend is cloven by another gulch, a short dry one, and at the junction of the two is a level space of two or three acres, and there, a few years ago, stood an old board house containing one small room. How the component parts of the house, few and simple as they were, had been assembled at that almost inaccessible point is a problem, in the solution of which there would be greater satisfaction than advantage. Possibly, the creek bed is a reformed road. It is certain that the gulch was at one time pretty thoroughly prospected by miners, who must have had some means of getting in with at least pack animals carrying tools and supplies; their profits, apparently, were not such as would have justified any considerable outlay to connect Macarger's Gulch with any center of civilization enjoying the distinction of a sawmill. The house, however, was there, most of it. It lacked a door and a window frame, and the chimney of mud and stones had fallen into an unlovely heap, overgrown with rank weeds. Such humble furniture as there may once have been, and much of the lower weatherboarding, had served as fuel in the camp fires of hunters; as had also, probably, the curbing of an old well, which at the time I write of existed in the form of a rather wide but not very deep depression near by.

One afternoon in the summer of 1874, I passed up Macarger's Gulch from the narrow valley into which it opens, by following the dry bed of the brook. I was quail-shooting and had made a bag of about a dozen birds by the time I had reached the house described, of whose existence I was until then unaware. After rather carelessly inspecting the ruin, I resumed my sport, and having fairly good success prolonged it until nearly sunset, when it occurred to me that I was a long way from any human habitation—too far to reach one by nightfall. But in my game bag was food, and the old house would afford shelter, if shelter were needed on a warm and dewless night in the foothills of the Sierra Nevada, where one may sleep in comfort on the pine needles, without covering. I am fond of solitude and love the night, so my resolution to "camp out" was soon taken, and by the time that it was dark I had made my bed of boughs and grasses in a corner of the room and was roasting a quail at a fire which I had kindled on the hearth. The smoke escaped out of the ruined chimney, the light illuminated the room with a kindly glow, and as I ate my simple meal of plain bird and drank the remains of a bottle of red wine which had served me all the afternoon in place of the water, which the region did not afford, I experienced a sense of comfort which better fare and accommodations do not always give.

Nevertheless, there was something lacking. I had a sense of comfort, but not of security. I detected myself staring more frequently at the open doorway and blank window than I could find warrant for doing. Outside these apertures all was black, and I was unable to repress a certain feeling of apprehension as my fancy pictured the outer world and filled it with unfriendly existences, natural and supernatural—chief among which, in their respective classes, were the grizzly bear, which I knew was occasionally still seen in that region, and the ghost, which I had reason to think was not. Unfortunately, our feelings do not always respect the law of probabilities, and to me that evening, the possible and the impossible were equally disquieting.

Everyone who has had experience in the matter must have observed that one confronts the actual and imaginary perils of the night with far less apprehension in the open air than in a house with an open doorway. I felt this now as I lay on my leafy couch in a corner of the room next to the chimney and permitted my fire to die out. So strong became my sense of the presence of something malign and menacing in the place, that I found myself almost unable to withdraw my eyes from the opening, as in the deepening darkness it became more and more distinct. And when the last little flame flickered and went out I grasped the shotgun which I had laid at my side and actually turned the muzzle in the direction of the now invisible entrance, my thumb on one of the hammers, ready to cock the piece, my breath suspended, my muscles rigid and tense. But later I laid down the weapon with a sense of shame and mortification. What did I fear, and why?—I to whom the night had been

> a more familiar face
> Than that of man—

I, in whom that element of hereditary superstition from which none of us is altogether free had but given to solitude and darkness and silence a more alluring interest and charm! I was unable to comprehend my folly, and losing in the conjecture the thing conjectured of, I fell asleep. And then I dreamed.

I was in a great city in a foreign land—a city whose people were of my own race, with minor differences of speech and costume; yet precisely what these were I could not say; my sense of them was indistinct. The city was dominated by a great castle upon an overlooking height whose name I knew, but could not speak. I walked through many streets, some broad and straight with high modern buildings, some narrow, gloomy, and tortuous, between the gables of quaint old houses whose overhanging stories, elaborately ornamented with carvings in wood and stone, almost met above my head.

I sought someone whom I had never seen, yet knew that I should recognize when found. My quest was not aimless and fortuitous; it had a definite method. I turned from one street into another without hesitation and threaded a maze of intricate passages, devoid of the fear of losing my way.

Presently I stopped before a low door in a plain stone house which might have been the dwelling of an artisan of the better sort, and without announcing myself, entered. The room, rather sparely furnished, and lighted by a single window with small diamond-shaped panes, had but two occupants: a man and a woman. They took no notice of my intrusion, a circumstance which, in the manner of dreams, appeared entirely natural. They were not conversing; they sat apart, unoccupied and sullen.

The woman was young and rather stout, with fine large eyes and a certain grave beauty; my memory of her expression is exceedingly vivid, but in dreams one does not observe the details of faces. About her shoulders was a plaid shawl. The man was older, dark, with an evil face made more forbidding by a long scar extending from near the left temple diagonally downward into the black mustache; though in my dreams it seemed rather to haunt the face as a thing apart—I can express it no otherwise—than to belong to it. The moment that I found the man and woman I knew them to be husband and wife.

What followed, I remember indistinctly; it was confused and inconsistent—made so, I think, by gleams of consciousness. It was as if two pictures, the scene of my dream, and my actual surroundings, had been blended, one overlying the other, until the former, gradually fading, disappeared, and I was broad awake in the deserted cabin, entirely and tranquilly conscious of my situation.

My foolish fear was gone and, opening my eyes, I saw that my fire, not altogether burned out, had revived by the falling of a stick and was again lighting the room. I had probably slept but a few minutes, but my commonplace dream had somehow so strongly impressed me, that I was no longer drowsy, but after a little while rose, pushed the embers of my fire together, and lighting my pipe, proceeded in a rather ludicrously methodical way to meditate upon my vision.

It would have puzzled me then to say in what respect it was worth attention. In the first moment of serious thought that I gave to the matter, I recognized the city of my dream as Edinburgh, where I had never been; so if the dream was a memory, it was a memory of pictures and description. The recognition somehow deeply impressed me; it was as if something in my mind insisted rebelliously against will and reason on the importance of all this. And that faculty, whatever it was, asserted also a control of my speech. "Surely," I said aloud, quite involuntarily, "the MacGregors must have come here from Edinburgh."

At the moment, neither the substance of this remark nor the fact of my making it, surprised me in the least; it seemed entirely natural that I should know the name of my dreamfolk and something of their history. But the absurdity of it all soon dawned upon me: I laughed audibly, knocked the ashes from my pipe, and again stretched myself upon my bed of boughs and grass, where I lay staring absently into my failing fire, with no further thought of either my dream or my surroundings. Suddenly the single remaining flame crouched for a moment, then, springing upward, lifted itself clear of its embers and expired in air. The darkness seemed absolute.

At that instant—almost, it seemed, before the gleam of the blaze had faded from my eyes—there was a dull, dead sound, as of some heavy body falling upon the floor, which shook beneath me as I lay. I sprang to a sitting posture and groped at my side for my gun; my notion was that some wild beast had leaped in through the open window. While the flimsy structure was still shaking from the impact, I heard the sound of blows, the scuffling of feet upon the floor, and then—it seemed to come from almost within reach of my hand, the sharp shrieking of a woman in mortal agony. So horrible a cry I had never heard nor conceived; it utterly unnerved me; I was conscious for a moment of nothing but my own terror! Fortunately my hand now found the weapon of which it was in search, and the familiar touch somewhat restored me. I leaped to my feet, straining my eyes to pierce the darkness. The violent sounds had ceased, but more terrible than these, I heard, at what seemed long intervals, the faint intermittent gasping of some living thing!

As my eyes grew accustomed to the dim light of the coals in the fireplace, I saw first the shapes of the door and window, looking blacker than the black of the walls. Next, the distinction between wall and floor became discernible, and at last I was sensible to the form and full expanse of the latter from end to end and side to side. Nothing was visible and the silence was unbroken.

With a hand that shook a little, the other still grasping my gun, I restored my fire, and made a critical examination of the place. There was nowhere any sign that the cabin had been entered. My own tracks were visible in the dust covering the floor, but there were no others. I relit my pipe, provided fresh fuel by ripping a thin board or two from the inside of the house—I did not care to go into the darkness out of doors—and passed the rest of the night smoking and thinking, and feeding my fire; not for a hundred added years of life would I have permitted that little flame to expire again.

Some years afterward, I met in Sacramento a man named Morgan, to whom I had a note of introduction from a friend in San Francisco. Dining with him one evening at his home, I observed various "trophies" upon the wall, indicating that he was fond of shooting. It turned out that he was, and in relating some of his feats, he mentioned having been in the region of my own adventure.

"Mr. Morgan," I asked abruptly, "do you know a place up there called Macarger's Gulch?"

"I have good reason to," he replied; "it was I who gave to the newspapers, last year, the accounts of the finding of the skeleton there."

I had not heard of it; the accounts had been published, it appeared, while I was absent in the East.

"By the way," said Morgan, "the name of the gulch is a corruption; it should have been called 'MacGregor's.' My dear," he added, speaking to his wife, "Mr. Elderson has upset his wine."

That was hardly accurate—I had simply dropped it, glass and all.

"There was an old shanty once in the gulch," Morgan resumed when the ruin wrought by my awkwardness had been repaired, "but just previously to my visit it had been blown down, or rather blown away, for its *débris* was scattered all about, the very floor being parted, plank from plank. Between two of the sleepers still in position, I and my companion observed the remnant of an old plaid shawl, and examining it, found that it was wrapped about the shoulders of the body of a woman, of which but little remained beside the bones, partly covered with fragments of clothing, and brown dry skin—but we will spare Mrs. Morgan," he added, with a smile. The lady had indeed exhibited signs of disgust rather than sympathy.

"It is necessary to say, however," he went on, "that the skull was fractured in several places, as by blows of some blunt instrument; and that instrument itself—a pick handle, still stained with blood—lay under the boards near by."

Mr. Morgan turned to his wife. "Pardon me, my dear," he said with affected solemnity, "for mentioning these disagreeable particulars, the natural though regrettable incidents of a conjugal quarrel resulting, doubtless, from the wife's insubordination."

"I ought to be able to overlook it," the lady replied with composure; "you have so many times asked me to in those very words."

I thought he seemed rather glad to go on with his story.

"From these and other circumstances," he said, "the coroner's jury found that the deceased, Janet MacGregor, came to her death from blows inflicted by some person to the jury unknown; but it was added that the evidence pointed strongly to her husband, Thomas MacGregor, as the guilty person. But Thomas MacGregor has never been found nor heard of. It was learned that the couple came from Edinburgh, but not—my dear, do you not observe that Mr. Elderson's bone plate has water in it?"

I had deposited a chicken bone in my finger bowl.

"In a little cupboard I found a photograph of MacGregor, but it did not lead to his capture."

"Will you let me see it?" I said.

The picture showed a dark man with an evil face made more forbidding by a long scar extending from near the temple diagonally downward into the black mustache.

"By the way, Mr. Elderson," said my affable host, "may I know why you asked about 'Macarger's Gulch'?"

"I lost a mule near there once," I replied, "and the mischance has—has quite—upset me."

"My dear," said Mr. Morgan, with the mechanical intonation of an interpreter translating, "the loss of Mr. Elderson's mule has peppered his coffee."

THE EMPTY HOUSE

Algernon Blackwood

Certain houses, like certain persons, manage somehow to proclaim at once their character for evil. In the case of the latter, no particular feature need betray them; they may boast an open countenance and an ingenuous smile; and yet a little of their company leaves the unalterable conviction that there is something radically amiss with their being: that they are evil. Willy nilly, they seem to communicate an atmosphere of secret and wicked thoughts which makes those in their immediate neighbourhood shrink from them as from a thing diseased.

And, perhaps, with houses the same principle is operative, and it is the aroma of evil deeds committed under a particular roof, long after the actual doers have passed away, that makes the gooseflesh come and the hair rise. Something of the original passion of the evil-doer, and of the horror felt by his victim, enters the heart of the innocent watcher, and he becomes suddenly conscious of tingling nerves, creeping skin, and a chilling of the blood. He is terror-stricken without apparent cause.

There was manifestly nothing in the external appearance of this particular house to bear out the tales of the horror that was said to reign within. It was neither lonely nor unkempt. It stood, crowded into a corner of the square, and looked exactly like the houses on either side of it. It had the same number of windows as its neighbours; the same balcony overlooking the gardens; the same white steps leading up to the heavy black front door; and, in the rear, there was the same narrow strip of green, with neat box borders, running up to the wall that divided it from the backs of the adjoining houses. Apparently, too, the number of chimney pots on the roof was the same; the breadth and angle of the eaves; and even the height of the dirty area railings.

And yet this house in the square, that seemed precisely similar to its fifty ugly neighbours, was as a matter of fact entirely different—horribly different.

Wherein lay this marked, invisible difference is impossible to say. It cannot be ascribed wholly to the imagination, because persons who had spent some time in the house, knowing nothing of the facts, had declared positively that certain rooms were so disagreeable they would rather die than enter them again, and that the atmosphere of the whole house produced in them symptoms of a genuine terror; while the series of innocent tenants who had tried to live in it and been forced to decamp at the shortest possible notice, was indeed little less than a scandal in the town.

When Shorthouse arrived to pay a "week-end" visit to his Aunt Julia in her little house on the sea-front at the other end of the town, he found her charged to the brim with mystery and excitement. He had only received her telegram that morning, and he had come anticipating boredom; but the moment he touched her hand and kissed her apple-skin wrinkled cheek, he caught the first wave of her electrical condition. The impression deepened when he learned that there were to be no other visitors, and that he had been telegraphed for with a very special object.

Something was in the wind, and the "something" would doubtless bear fruit; for this elderly spinster aunt, with a mania for psychical research, had brains as well as will power, and by hook or by crook she usually managed to accomplish her ends. The revelation was made soon after tea, when she sidled close up to him as they paced slowly along the sea-front in the dusk.

"I've got the keys," she announced in a delighted, yet half awesome voice. "Got them till Monday!"

"The keys of the bathing-machine, or—?" he asked innocently, looking from the sea to the town. Nothing brought her so quickly to the point as feigning stupidity.

"Neither," she whispered. "I've got the keys of the haunted house in the square—and I'm going there to-night."

Shorthouse was conscious of the slightest possible tremor down his back. He dropped his teasing tone. Something in her voice and manner thrilled him. She was in earnest.

"But you can't go alone—" he began.

"That's why I wired for you," she said with decision.

He turned to look at her. The ugly, lined, enigmatical face was alive with excitement. There was the glow of genuine enthusiasm round it like a halo. The eyes shone. He caught another wave of her excitement, and a second tremor, more marked than the first, accompanied it.

"Thanks, Aunt Julia," he said politely; "thanks awfully."

"I should not dare to go quite alone," she went on, raising her voice; "but with you I should enjoy it immensely. You're afraid of nothing, I know."

"Thanks *so* much," he said again. "Er—is anything likely to happen?"

"A great deal *has* happened," she whispered, "though it's been most cleverly hushed up. Three tenants have come and gone in the last few months, and the house is said to be empty for good now."

In spite of himself Shorthouse became interested. His aunt was so very much in earnest.

"The house is very old indeed," she went on, "and the story—an unpleasant one—dates a long way back. It has to do with a murder committed by a jealous stableman who had some affair with a servant in the house. One night he managed to secrete himself in the cellar, and when everyone was asleep, he crept upstairs to the servants' quarters, chased the girl down to the next landing, and before anyone could come to the rescue threw her bodily over the banisters into the hall below."

"And the stableman—?"

"Was caught, I believe, and hanged for murder; but it all happened a century ago, and I've not been able to get more details of the story."

Shorthouse now felt his interest thoroughly aroused; but, though he was not particularly nervous for himself, he hesitated a little on his aunt's account.

"On one condition," he said at length.

"Nothing will prevent my going," she said firmly; "but I may as well hear your condition."

"That you guarantee your power of self-control if anything really horrible happens. I mean—that you are sure you won't get too frightened."

"Jim," she said scornfully, "I'm not young, I know, nor are my nerves; but *with you* I should be afraid of nothing in the world!"

This, of course, settled it, for Shorthouse had no pretensions to being other than a very ordinary young man, and an appeal to his vanity was irresistible. He agreed to go.

Instinctively, by a sort of sub-conscious preparation, he kept himself and his forces well in hand the whole evening, compelling an accumulative reserve of control by that nameless inward process of gradually putting all the emotions away and turning the key upon them—a process difficult to describe, but wonderfully effective, as all men who have lived through severe trials of the inner man well understand. Later, it stood him in good stead.

But it was not until half-past ten, when they stood in the hall, well in the glare of friendly lamps and still surrounded by comforting human influences, that he had to make the first call upon this store of collected strength. For, once the door was closed, and he saw the deserted silent street stretching away white in the moonlight before them, it came to him clearly that the real test that night would be in dealing with *two fears* instead of one. He would have to carry his aunt's fear as well as his own. And, as he glanced down at her sphinx-like countenance and realised that it might assume no pleasant aspect in a rush of real terror, he felt satisfied with only one thing in the whole adventure—that he had confidence in his own will and power to stand against any shock that might come.

Slowly they walked along the empty streets of the town; a bright autumn moon silvered the roofs, casting deep shadows; there was no breath of wind; and the trees in the formal gardens by the sea-front watched them silently as they passed along. To his aunt's occasional remarks Shorthouse made no reply, realising that she was simply sur-rounding herself with mental buffers—saying ordinary things to pre-vent herself thinking of extra-ordinary things. Few windows showed lights, and from scarcely a single chimney came smoke or sparks. Shorthouse had already begun to notice everything, even the smallest details. Presently they stopped at the street corner and looked up at the name on the side of the house full in the moonlight, and with one accord, but without remark, turned into the square and crossed over to the side of it that lay in shadow.

"The number of the house is thirteen," whispered a voice at his side; and neither of them made the obvious reference, but passed across the broad sheet of moonlight and began to march up the pave-ment in silence.

It was about half-way up the square that Shorthouse felt an arm slipped quietly but significantly into his own, and knew then that their adventure had begun in earnest, and that his companion was already yielding imperceptibly to the influences against them. She needed support.

A few minutes later they stopped before a tall, narrow house that rose before them into the night, ugly in shape and painted a dingy white. Shutterless windows, without blinds, stared down upon them, shining here and there in the moonlight. There were weather streaks in the wall and cracks in the paint, and the balcony bulged out from the first floor a little unnaturally. But, beyond this generally forlorn appearance of an unoccupied house, there was nothing at first sight to single out this particular mansion for the evil character it had most certainly acquired.

Taking a look over their shoulders to make sure they had not been followed, they went boldly up the steps and stood against the huge black door that fronted them forbiddingly. But the first wave of nervousness was now upon them, and Shorthouse fumbled a long time with the key before he could fit it into the lock at all. For a moment, if truth were told, they both hoped it would not open, for they were a prey to various unpleasant emotions as they stood there on the threshold of their ghostly adventure. Shorthouse, shuffling with the key and hampered by the steady weight on his arm, certainly felt the solemnity of the moment. It was as if the whole world—for all experience seemed at that instant concentrated in his own consciousness—were listening to the grating noise of that key. A stray puff of wind wandering down the empty street woke a momentary rustling in the trees behind them, but otherwise this rattling of the key was the only sound audible; and at last it turned in the lock and the heavy door swung open and revealed a yawning gulf of darkness beyond.

With a last glance at the moonlit square, they passed quickly in, and the door slammed behind them with a roar that echoed prodigiously through empty halls and passages. But, instantly, with the echoes, another sound made itself heard, and Aunt Julia leaned suddenly so heavily upon him that he had to take a step backwards to save himself from falling.

A man had coughed close beside them—so close that it seemed they must have been actually by his side in the darkness.

With the possibility of practical jokes in his mind, Shorthouse at once swung his heavy stick in the direction of the sound; but it met nothing more solid than air. He heard his aunt give a little gasp beside him.

"There's someone here," she whispered; "I heard him."

"Be quiet!" he said sternly. "It was nothing but the noise of the front door."

"Oh! get a light—quick!" she added, as her nephew, fumbling with a box of matches, opened it upside down and let them all fall with a rattle on to the stone floor.

The sound, however, was not repeated; and there was no evidence of retreating footsteps. In another minute they had a candle burning, using an empty end of a cigar case as a holder; and when the first flare had died down he held the impromptu lamp aloft and surveyed the scene. And it was dreary enough in all conscience, for there is nothing more desolate in all the abodes of men than an unfurnished house dimly lit, silent, and forsaken, and yet tenanted by rumour with the memories of evil and violent histories.

They were standing in a wide hall-way; on their left was the open door of a spacious dining-room, and in front the hall ran, ever narrowing, into a long, dark passage that led apparently to the top of the kitchen stairs. The broad uncarpeted staircase rose in a sweep before them, everywhere draped in shadows, except for a single spot about half-way up where the moonlight came in through the window and fell on a bright patch on the boards. This shaft of light shed a faint radiance above and below it, lending to the objects within its reach a misty outline that was infinitely more suggestive and ghostly than complete darkness. Filtered moonlight always seems to paint faces on the surrounding gloom, and as Shorthouse peered up into the well of darkness and thought of the countless empty rooms and passages in the upper part of the old house, he caught himself longing again for the safety of the moonlit square, or the cosy, bright drawing-room they had left an hour before. Then realising that these thoughts were dangerous, he thrust them away again and summoned all his energy for concentration on the present.

"Aunt Julia," he said aloud, severely, "we must now go through the house from top to bottom and make a thorough search."

The echoes of his voice died away slowly all over the building, and in the intense silence that followed he turned to look at her. In the candle-light he saw that her face was already ghastly pale; but she dropped his arm for a moment and said in a whisper, stepping close in front of him—

"I agree. We must be sure there's no one hiding. That's the first thing."

She spoke with evident effort, and he looked at her with admiration.

"You feel quite sure of yourself? It's not too late—"

"I think so," she whispered, her eyes shifting nervously toward the shadows behind. "Quite sure, only one thing—"

"What's that?"

"You must never leave me alone for an instant."

"As long as you understand that any sound or appearance must be investigated at once, for to hesitate means to admit fear. That is fatal."

"Agreed," she said, a little shakily, after a moment's hesitation. "I'll try—"

Arm in arm, Shorthouse holding the dripping candle and the stick, while his aunt carried the cloak over her shoulders, figures of utter comedy to all but themselves, they began a systematic search.

Stealthily, walking on tip-toe and shading the candle lest it should betray their presence through the shutterless windows, they went first into the big dining-room. There was not a stick of furniture to be seen.

Bare walls, ugly mantel-pieces and empty grates stared at them. Every-thing, they felt, resented their intrusion, watching them, as it were, with veiled eyes; whispers followed them; shadows flitted noiselessly to right and left; something seemed ever at their back, watching, waiting an opportunity to do them injury. There was the inevitable sense that operations which went on when the room was empty had been tempo-rarily suspended till they were well out of the way again. The whole dark interior of the old building seemed to become a malignant Pres-ence that rose up, warning them to desist and mind their own business; every moment the strain on the nerves increased.

Out of the gloomy dining-room they passed through large folding doors into a sort of library or smoking-room, wrapt equally in silence, darkness, and dust; and from this they regained the hall near the top of the back stairs.

Here a pitch black tunnel opened before them into the lower regions, and—it must be confessed—they hesitated. But only for a minute. With the worst of the night still to come it was essential to turn from nothing. Aunt Julia stumbled at the top step of the dark descent, ill lit by the flickering candle, and even Shorthouse felt at least half the decision go out of his legs.

"Come on!" he said peremptorily, and his voice ran on and lost itself in the dark, empty spaces below.

"I'm coming," she faltered, catching his arm with unnecessary violence.

They went a little unsteadily down the stone steps, a cold, damp air meeting them in the face, close and mal-odorous. The kitchen, into which the stairs led along a narrow passage, was large, with a lofty ceil-ing. Several doors opened out of it—some into cupboards with empty jars still standing on the shelves, and others into horrible little ghostly back offices, each colder and less inviting than the last. Black beetles scurried over the floor, and once, when they knocked against a deal table standing in a corner, something about the size of a cat jumped down with a rush and fled, scampering across the stone floor into the darkness. Everywhere there was a sense of recent occupation, an impression of sadness and gloom.

Leaving the main kitchen, they next went towards the scullery. The door was standing ajar, and as they pushed it open to its full extent Aunt Julia uttered a piercing scream, which she instantly tried to stifle by placing her hand over her mouth. For a second Shorthouse stood stock-still, catching his breath. He felt as if his spine had suddenly become hollow and someone had filled it with particles of ice.

Facing them, directly in their way between the doorposts, stood the figure of a woman. She had dishevelled hair and wildly staring eyes, and her face was terrified and white as death.

She stood there motionless for the space of a single second. Then the candle flickered and she was gone—gone utterly—and the door framed nothing but empty darkness.

"Only the beastly jumping candle-light," he said quickly, in a voice that sounded like someone else's and was only half under control. "Come on, aunt. There's nothing there."

He dragged her forward. With a clattering of feet and a great appearance of boldness they went on, but over his body the skin moved as if crawling ants covered it, and he knew by the weight on his arm that he was supplying the force of locomotion for two. The scullery was cold, bare, and empty; more like a large prison cell than anything else. They went round it, tried the door into the yard, and the windows, but found them all fastened securely. His aunt moved beside him like a person in a dream. Her eyes were tightly shut, and she seemed merely to follow the pressure of his arm. Her courage filled him with amazement. At the same time he noticed that a certain odd change had come over her face, a change which somehow evaded his power of analysis.

"There's nothing here, aunty," he repeated aloud quickly. "Let's go upstairs and see the rest of the house. Then we'll choose a room to wait up in."

She followed him obediently, keeping close to his side, and they locked the kitchen door behind them. It was a relief to get up again. In the hall there was more light than before, for the moon had travelled a little further down the stairs. Cautiously they began to go up into the dark vault of the upper house, the boards creaking under their weight.

On the first floor they found the large double drawing-rooms, a search of which revealed nothing. Here also was no sign of furniture or recent occupancy; nothing but dust and neglect and shadows. They opened the big folding doors between front and back drawing-rooms and then came out again to the landing and went on upstairs.

They had not gone up more than a dozen steps when they both simultaneously stopped to listen, looking into each other's eyes with a new apprehension across the flickering candle flame. From the room they had left hardly ten seconds before came the sound of doors quietly closing. It was beyond all question; they heard the booming noise that accompanies the shutting of heavy doors, followed by the sharp catching of the latch.

"We must go back and see," said Shorthouse briefly, in a low tone, and turning to go downstairs again.

Somehow she managed to drag after him, her feet catching in her dress, her face livid.

When they entered the front drawing-room it was plain that the folding doors had been closed—half a minute before. Without hesitation Shorthouse opened them. He almost expected to see someone facing him in the back room; but only darkness and cold air met him.

They went through both rooms, finding nothing unusual. They tried in every way to make the doors close of themselves, but there was not wind enough even to set the candle flame flickering. The doors would not move without strong pressure. All was silent as the grave. Undeniably the rooms were utterly empty, and the house utterly still.

"It's beginning," whispered a voice at his elbow which he hardly recognised as his aunt's.

He nodded acquiescence, taking out his watch to note the time. It was fifteen minutes before midnight; he made the entry of exactly what had occurred in his notebook, setting the candle in its case upon the floor in order to do so. It took a moment or two to balance it safely against the wall.

Aunt Julia always declared that at this moment she was not actually watching him, but had turned her head towards the inner room, where she fancied she heard something moving; but, at any rate, both positively agreed that there came a sound of rushing feet, heavy and very swift—and the next instant the candle was out!

But to Shorthouse himself had come more than this, and he has always thanked his fortunate stars that it came to him alone and not to his aunt too. For, as he rose from the stooping position of balancing the candle, and before it was actually extinguished, a face thrust itself forward so close to his own that he could almost have touched it with his lips. It was a face working with passion; a man's face, dark, with thick features, and angry, savage eyes. It belonged to a common man, and it was evil in its ordinary normal expression, no doubt, but as he saw it, alive with intense, aggressive emotion, it was a malignant and terrible human countenance.

There was no movement of the air; nothing but the sound of rushing feet—stockinged or muffled feet; the apparition of the face; and the almost simultaneous extinguishing of the candle.

In spite of himself, Shorthouse uttered a little cry, nearly losing his balance as his aunt clung to him with her whole weight in one moment of real, uncontrollable terror. She made no sound, but simply seized him bodily. Fortunately, however, she had seen nothing, but had only heard the rushing feet, for her control returned almost at once, and he was able to disentangle himself and strike a match.

The shadows ran away on all sides before the glare, and his aunt stooped down and groped for the cigar case with the precious candle. Then they discovered that the candle had not been *blown* out at all; it had been *crushed* out. The wick was pressed down into the wax, which was flattened as if by some smooth, heavy instrument.

How his companion so quickly overcame her terror, Shorthouse never properly understood; but his admiration for her self-control increased tenfold, and at the same time served to feed his own dying flame—for which he was undeniably grateful. Equally inexplicable to him was the evidence of physical force they had just witnessed. He at once suppressed the memory of stories he had heard of "physical mediums" and their dangerous phenomena; for if these were true, and either his aunt or himself was unwittingly a physical medium, it meant that they were simply aiding to focus the forces of a haunted house already charged to the brim. It was like walking with unprotected lamps among uncovered stores of gun-powder.

So, with as little reflection as possible, he simply relit the candle and went up to the next floor. The arm in his trembled, it is true, and his own tread was often uncertain, but they went on with thoroughness, and after a search revealing nothing they climbed the last flight of stairs to the top floor of all.

Here they found a perfect nest of small servants' rooms, with broken pieces of furniture, dirty cane-bottomed chairs, chests of drawers, cracked mirrors, and decrepit bedsteads. The rooms had low sloping ceilings already hung here and there with cobwebs, small windows, and badly plastered walls—a depressing and dismal region which they were glad to leave behind.

It was on the stroke of midnight when they entered a small room on the third floor, close to the top of the stairs, and arranged to make themselves comfortable for the remainder of their adventure. It was absolutely bare, and was said to be the room—then used as a clothes closet—into which the infuriated groom had chased his victim and finally caught her. Outside, across the narrow landing, began the stairs leading up to the floor above, and the servants' quarters where they had just searched.

In spite of the chilliness of the night there was something in the air of this room that cried for an open window. But there was more than this. Shorthouse could only describe it by saying that he felt less master of himself here than in any other part of the house. There was something that acted directly on the nerves, tiring the resolution, enfeebling the will. He was conscious of this result before he had been in the room five minutes, and it was in the short time they stayed there that he suffered the wholesale depletion of his vital forces, which was, for himself, the chief horror of the whole experience.

They put the candle on the floor of the cupboard, leaving the door a few inches ajar, so that there was no glare to confuse the eyes, and no shadow to shift about on walls and ceiling. Then they spread the cloak on the floor and sat down to wait, with their backs against the wall.

Shorthouse was within two feet of the door on to the landing; his position commanded a good view of the main staircase leading down into the darkness, and also of the beginning of the servants' stairs going to the floor above; the heavy stick lay beside him within easy reach.

The moon was now high above the house. Through the open window they could see the comforting stars like friendly eyes watching in the sky. One by one the clocks of the town struck midnight, and when the sounds died away the deep silence of a windless night fell again over everything. Only the boom of the sea, far away and lugubrious, filled the air with hollow murmurs.

Inside the house the silence became awful; awful, he thought, because any minute now it might be broken by sounds portending terror. The strain of waiting told more and more severely on the nerves; they talked in whispers when they talked at all, for their voices aloud sounded queer and unnatural. A chilliness, not altogether due to the night air, invaded the room, and made them cold. The influences against them, whatever these might be, were slowly robbing them of self-confidence, and the power of decisive action; their forces were on the wane, and the possibility of real fear took on a new and terrible meaning. He began to tremble for the elderly woman by his side, whose pluck could hardly save her beyond a certain extent.

He heard the blood singing in his veins. It sometimes seemed so loud that he fancied it prevented his hearing properly certain other sounds that were beginning very faintly to make themselves audible in the depths of the house. Every time he fastened his attention on these sounds, they instantly ceased. They certainly came no nearer. Yet he could not rid himself of the idea that movement was going on somewhere in the lower regions of the house. The drawing-room floor, where the doors had been so strangely closed, seemed too near; the sounds were further off than that. He thought of the great kitchen, with the scurrying black-beetles, and of the dismal little scullery; but, somehow or other, they did not seem to come from there either. Surely they were not *outside* the house!

Then, suddenly, the truth flashed into his mind, and for the space of a minute he felt as if his blood had stopped flowing and turned to ice.

The sounds were not downstairs at all; they were *upstairs*—upstairs, somewhere among those horrid gloomy little servants' rooms with their bits of broken furniture, low ceilings, and cramped windows—upstairs where the victim had first been disturbed and stalked to her death.

And the moment he discovered where the sounds were, he began to hear them more clearly. It was the sound of feet, moving stealthily along the passage overhead, in and out among the rooms, and past the furniture.

He turned quickly to steal a glance at the motionless figure seated beside him, to note whether she had shared his discovery. The faint candle-light coming through the crack in the cupboard door, threw her strongly-marked face into vivid relief against the white of the wall. But it was something else that made him catch his breath and stare again. An extraordinary something had come into her face and seemed to spread over her features like a mask; it smoothed out the deep lines and drew the skin everywhere a little tighter so that the wrinkles disappeared; it brought into the face—with the sole exception of the old eyes—an appearance of youth and almost of childhood.

He stared in speechless amazement—amazement that was dangerously near to horror. It was his aunt's face indeed, but it was her face of forty years ago, the vacant innocent face of a girl. He had heard stories of that strange effect of terror which could wipe a human countenance clean of other emotions, obliterating all previous expressions; but he had never realised that it could be literally true, or could mean anything so simply horrible as what he now saw. For the dreadful signature of overmastering fear was written plainly in that utter vacancy of the girlish face beside him; and when, feeling his intense gaze, she turned to look at him, he instinctively closed his eyes tightly to shut out the sight.

Yet, when he turned a minute later, his feelings well in hand, he saw to his intense relief another expression; his aunt was smiling, and though the face was deathly white, the awful veil had lifted and the normal look was returning.

"Anything wrong?" was all he could think of to say at the moment. And the answer was eloquent, coming from such a woman.

"I feel cold—and a little frightened," she whispered.

He offered to close the window, but she seized hold of him and begged him not to leave her side even for an instant.

"It's upstairs, I know," she whispered, with an odd half laugh; "but I can't possibly go up."

But Shorthouse thought otherwise, knowing that in action lay their best hope of self-control.

He took the brandy flask and poured out a glass of neat spirit, stiff enough to help anybody over anything. She swallowed it with a little shiver. His only idea now was to get out of the house before her collapse became inevitable; but this could not safely be done by turning tail and running from the enemy. Inaction was no longer possible; every minute he was growing less master of himself, and desperate, aggressive measures were imperative without further delay. Moreover, the action must be taken *towards* the enemy, not away from it; the climax, if necessary and unavoidable, would have to be faced boldly. He could do it now; but in ten minutes he might not have the force left to act for himself, much less for both!

Upstairs, the sounds were meanwhile becoming louder and closer, accompanied by occasional creaking of the boards. Someone was moving stealthily about, stumbling now and then awkwardly against the furniture.

Waiting a few moments to allow the tremendous dose of spirits to produce its effect, and knowing this would last but a short time under the circumstances, Shorthouse then quietly got on his feet, saying in a determined voice—

"Now, Aunt Julia, we'll go upstairs and find out what all this noise is about. You must come too. It's what we agreed."

He picked up his stick and went to the cupboard for the candle. A limp form rose shakily beside him breathing hard, and he heard a voice say very faintly something about being "ready to come." The woman's courage amazed him; it was so much greater than his own; and, as they advanced, holding aloft the dripping candle, some subtle force exhaled from this trembling, white-faced old woman at his side that was the true source of his inspiration. It held something really great that shamed him and gave him the support without which he would have proved far less equal to the occasion.

They crossed the dark landing, avoiding with their eyes the deep black space over the banisters. Then they began to mount the narrow staircase to meet the sounds which, minute by minute, grew louder and nearer. About half-way up the stairs Aunt Julia stumbled and Shorthouse turned to catch her by the arm, and just at that moment there came a terrific crash in the servants' corridor overhead. It was instantly followed by a shrill, agonised scream that was a cry of terror and a cry for help melted into one.

Before they could move aside, or go down a single step, someone came rushing along the passage overhead, blundering horribly, racing madly, at full speed, three steps at a time, down the very staircase where they stood. The steps were light and uncertain; but close behind them sounded the heavier tread of another person, and the staircase seemed to shake.

Shorthouse and his companion just had time to flatten themselves against the wall when the jumble of flying steps was upon them, and two persons, with the slightest possible interval between them, dashed past at full speed. It was a perfect whirlwind of sound breaking in upon the midnight silence of the empty building.

The two runners, pursuer and pursued, had passed clean through them where they stood, and already with a thud the boards below had received first one, then the other. Yet they had seen absolutely nothing—not a hand, or arm, or face, or even a shred of flying clothing.

There came a second's pause. Then the first one, the lighter of the two, obviously the pursued one, ran with uncertain footsteps into the little room which Shorthouse and his aunt had just left. The heavier one followed. There was a sound of scuffling, gasping, and smothered screaming; and then out on to the landing came the step—of a single person *treading weightily.*

A dead silence followed for the space of half a minute, and then was heard a rushing sound through the air. It was followed by a dull, crashing thud in the depths of the house below—on the stone floor of the hall.

Utter silence reigned after. Nothing moved. The flame of the candle was steady. It had been steady the whole time, and the air had been undisturbed by any movement whatsoever. Palsied with terror, Aunt Julia, without waiting for her companion, began fumbling her way downstairs; she was crying gently to herself, and when Shorthouse put his arm round her and half carried her he felt that she was trembling like a leaf. He went into the little room and picked up the cloak from the floor, and, arm in arm, walking very slowly, without speaking a word or looking once behind them, they marched down the three flights into the hall.

In the hall they saw nothing, but the whole way down the stairs they were conscious that someone followed them; step by step; when they went faster IT was left behind, and when they went more slowly IT caught them up. But never once did they look behind to see; and at each turning of the staircase they lowered their eyes for fear of the following horror they might see upon the stairs above.

With trembling hands Shorthouse opened the front door, and they walked out into the moonlight and drew a deep breath of the cool night air blowing in from the sea.

A Night of Horror

Dick Donovan

Bleak Hill Castle

My dear old Chum,—

Before you leave England for the East I claim the redemption of a promise you made to me some time ago that you would give me the pleasure of a week or two of your company. Besides, as you may have already guessed, I have given up the folly of my bachelor days, and have taken unto myself the sweetest, dearest little woman that ever walked the face of the earth. We have been married just six months, and are as happy as the day is long. And then, this place is entirely after your own heart. It will excite all your artistic faculties, and appeal with irresistible force to your romantic nature. To call the building a castle is somewhat pretentious, but I believe it has been known as the Castle ever since it was built, more than two hundred years ago. Hester—need I say that Hester is my better half!—is just delighted with it, and if either of us was in the least degree superstitious, we might see or hear ghosts every hour of the day. Of course, as becomes a castle, we have a haunted room, though my own impression is that it is haunted by nothing more fearsome than rats. Anyway, it is such a picturesque, curious sort of chamber that if it hasn't a ghost it ought to have. But I have no doubt, old chap, that you will make one of us, for, as I remember, you have always had a love for the eerie and creepy, and you cannot forget how angry you used to get with me sometimes for chaffing you about your avowed belief in the occult and supernatural, and what you were pleased to term the "unexplainable phenomena of psychomancy." However, it is possible you have got over some of the errors of your youth; but whether or not, come down, dear boy, and rest assured that you will meet with the heartiest of welcomes.

Your old pal,

DICK DIRCKMAN

The above letter was from my old friend and college chum, who, having inherited a substantial fortune, and being passionately fond of the country and country pursuits, had thus the means of gratifying his tastes to their fullest bent. Although Dick and I were very differently constituted, we had always been greatly attached to each other. In the best sense of the term he was what is generally called a hard-headed, practical man. He was fond of saying he never believed in anything he couldn't see, and even that which he could see he was not prepared to accept as truth without due investigation. In short, Dick was neither romantic, poetical, nor, I am afraid, artistic, in the literal sense. He preferred facts to fancies, and was possessed of what the world generally calls "an unimpressionable nature." For nearly four years I had lost sight of my friend, as I had been wandering about Europe as tutor and companion to a delicate young nobleman. His death had set me free; but I had no sooner returned to England than I was offered and accepted a lucrative appointment in the service of his High-ness the Nyzam of Chundlepore, in Northern India, and there was every probability of my being absent for a number of years.

On returning home I had written to Dick to the chambers he had formerly occupied, telling him of my appointment, and expressing a fear that unless we could snatch a day or two in town I might not be able to see him, as I had so many things to do. It was true I had promised that when opportunity occurred I should do myself the pleasure of accepting his oft-proffered hospitality, which I knew to be lavish and generous. I had not heard of his marriage; his letter gave me the first intimation of that fact, and I confess that when I got his missive I experienced some curiosity to know the kind of lady he had succeeded in captivating. I had always had an idea that Dick was cut out for a bachelor, for there was nothing of the ladies' man about him, and he used at one time to speak of the gentler sex with a certain levity and brusqueness of manner that by no means found favour with the majority of his friends. And now Dick was actually mar-ried, and living in a remote region, where most town-bred people would die of ennui.

It will be gathered from the foregoing remarks that I did not hesitate about accepting Dick's cordial invitation. I determined to spare a few days at least of my somewhat limited time, and duly notified Dick to that effect, giving him the date of my departure from London, and the hour at which I should arrive at the station nearest to his residence.

Bleak Hill Castle was situated in one of the most picturesque parts of Wales; consequently, on the day appointed I found myself comfortably ensconsed in a smoking carriage of a London and North-Western train. And towards the close of the day—the time of the year was May—I was the sole passenger to alight at the wayside station, where Dick awaited me with a smart dog-cart. His greeting was hearty and robust, and when his man had packed in my traps he gave the handsome little mare that drew the cart the reins, and we spanked along the country roads in rare style. Dick always prided himself on his knowledge of horseflesh, and with a sense of keen satisfaction he drew my attention to the points of the skittish little mare which bowled along as if we had been merely featherweights.

A drive of eight miles through the bracing Welsh air so sharpened our appetites that the smell of dinner was peculiarly welcome; and telling me to make a hurried toilet, as his cook would not risk her reputation by keeping a dinner waiting, Dick handed me over to the guidance of a natty chambermaid. As it was dark when we arrived I had no opportunity of observing the external characteristics of Bleak Hill Castle; but there was nothing in the interior that suggested bleakness. Warmth, comfort, light, held forth promise of carnal delights.

Following my guide up a broad flight of stairs, and along a lofty and echoing corridor, I found myself in a large and comfortably-furnished bedroom. A bright wood fire burned upon the hearthstone, for although it was May the temperature was still very low on the Welsh hills. Hastily changing my clothes, I made my way to the dining-room, where Mrs. Dirckman emphasised the welcome her husband had already given me. She was an exceedingly pretty and rather delicate-looking little woman, in striking contrast to her great, bluff, burly husband. A few neighbours had been gathered together to meet me, and we sat down, a dozen all told, to a dinner that from a gastronomic point of view left nothing to be desired. The viands were appetising, the wines perfect, and all the appointments were in perfect consonance with the good things that were placed before us.

It was perhaps natural, when the coffee and cigar stage had arrived, that conversation should turn upon our host's residence, by way of affording me—a stranger to the district—some information. Of course, the information was conveyed to me in a scrappy way, but I gathered in substance that Bleak Hill Castle had originally belonged to a Welsh family, which was chiefly distinguished by the extravagance and gambling propensities of its male members. It had gone through some exciting times, and numerous strange and startling stories had come to centre round it. There were stories of wrong, and shame, and death, and more than a suggestion of dark crimes. One of these stories turned upon the mysterious disappearance of the wife and daughter of a young scion of the house, whose career had been somewhat shady. His wife was considerably older than he, and it was generally supposed that he had married her for money. His daughter, a girl of about twelve, was an epileptic patient, while the husband and father was a gloomy, disappointed man. Suddenly the wife and daughter disappeared. At first no surprise was felt; but, then, some curiosity was expressed to know where they had gone to; and curiosity led to wonderment, and wonderment to rumour—for people will gossip, especially in a country district. Of course, Mr. Greeta Jones, the husband, had to submit to much questioning as to where his wife and child were staying. But being sullen and morose of temperament he contented himself by brusquely and tersely saying, "They had gone to London." But as no one had seen them go, and no one had heard of their going, the statement was accepted as a perversion of fact. Nevertheless, incredible as it may seem, no one thought it worth his while to insist upon an investigation, and a few weeks later Mr. Greeta Jones himself went away—and to London, as was placed beyond doubt. For a long time Bleak Hill Castle was shut up, and throughout the country side it began to be whispered that sights and sounds had been seen and heard at the castle which were suggestive of things unnatural, and soon it became a crystallised belief in men's minds that the place was haunted.

On the principle of giving a dog a bad name you have only to couple ghosts with the name of an old country residence like this castle for it to fall into disfavour, and to be generally shunned. As might have been expected in such a region the castle *was* shunned; no tenant could be found for it. It was allowed to go to ruin, and for a long time was the haunt of smugglers. They were cleared out in the process of time, and at last hard-headed, practical Dick Dirckman heard of the place through a London agent, went down to see it, took a fancy to it, bought it for an old song, and, having taste and money, he soon converted the half-ruined building into a country gentleman's home, and thither he carried his bride.

Such was the history of Bleak Hill Castle as I gathered it in outline during the post-prandial chat on that memorable evening.

On the following day I found the place all that my host had described it in his letter to me. Its situation was windows that didn't command a magnificent view of landscape and sea. He and I rambled about the house, he evinced a keen delight in showing me every nook and corner, in expatiating on the beauties of the locality generally, and of the advantages of his dwelling-place in particular. Why he reserved taking me to the so-called haunted chamber until the last I never have known; but so it was; and as he threw open the heavy door and ushered me into the apartment he smiled ironically and remarked:

"Well, old man, this is the ghost's den; and as I consider that a country mansion of this kind should, in the interests of all tradition and of fiction writers, who, under the guise of truth, lie like Ananias, have its haunted room, I have let this place go untouched, except that I have made it a sort of lumber closet for some antique and mouldering old furniture which I picked up a bargain in Wardour Street, London. But I needn't tell you that I regard the ghost stories as rot."

I did not reply to my friend at once, for the room absorbed my attention. It was unquestionably the largest of the bedrooms in the house, and, while in keeping with the rest of the house, had characteristics of its own. The walls were panelled with dark oak, the floor was oak, polished. There was a deep V-shaped bay, formed by an angle of the castle, and in each side of the bay was a diamond-paned window, and under each window an oak seat, which was also a chest with an ancient iron lock. A large wooden bedstead with massive hangings stood in one corner, and the rest of the furniture was of a very nondescript character, and calls for no special mention. In a word, the room was picturesque, and to me it at once suggested the *mise-en-scène* for all sorts of dramatic situations of a weird and eerie character. I ought to add that there was a very large fireplace with a most capacious hearthstone, on which stood a pair of ponderous and rusty steel dogs. Finally, the window commanded superb views, and altogether my fancy was pleased, and my artistic susceptibilities appealed to in an irresistible manner, so that I replied to my friend thus:

"I like this room, Dick, awfully. Let me occupy it, will you?"

He laughed.

"Well, upon my word, you are an eccentric fellow to want to give up the comfortable den which I have assigned to you for this mouldy, draughty, dingy old lumber room. However"—here he shrugged his shoulders—"there is no accounting for tastes, and as this is liberty hall, my friends do as they like; so I'll tell the servants to put the bed in order, light a fire, and cart your traps from the other room."

I was glad I had carried my point, for I frankly confess to having romantic tendencies. I was fond of old things, old stories and legends, old furniture, and anything that was removed above the dull level of commonplaceness. This room, in a certain sense, was unique, and I was charmed with it.

When pretty little Mrs. Dirckman heard of the arrangements she said, with a laugh that did not conceal a certain nervousness, "I am sorry you are going to sleep in that wretched room. It always makes me shudder, for it seems so uncomfortable. Besides, you know, although Dick laughs at me and calls me a little goose, I am inclined to believe there may be some foundation for the current stories. Anyway, I wouldn't sleep in the room for a crown of gold. I do hope you will be comfortable, and not be frightened to death or into insanity by gruesome apparitions."

I hastened to assure my hostess that I should be comfortable enough, while as for apparitions, I was not likely to be frightened by them.

The rest of the day was spent in exploring the country round about, and after a *recherché* dinner Dick and I played billiards until one o'clock, and then, having drained a final "peg," I retired to rest. When I reached the haunted chamber I found that much had been done to give an air of cheerfulness and comfort to the place. Some rugs had been laid about the floor, a modern chair or two introduced, a wood fire blazed on the earth. On a little "occasional table" that stood near the fire was a silver jug, filled with hot water, and an antique decanter containing spirits, together with lemon and sugar, in case I wanted a final brew. I could not but feel grateful for my host and hostess's thoughtfulness, and, having donned my dressing-gown and slippers, I drew a chair within the radius of the wood fire's glow, and proceeded to fill my pipe for a few whiffs previous to tumbling into bed. This was a habit of mine—a habit of years and years of growth, and, while perhaps an objectionable one in some respects, it afforded me solace and conduced to restful sleep. So I lit my pipe, and fell to pondering and trying to see if I could draw any suggestiveness as to my future from the glowing embers. Suddenly a remarkable thing happened. My pipe was drawn gently from my lips and laid upon the table, and at the same moment I heard what seemed to me to be a sigh. For a moment or two I felt confused, and wondered whether I was awake or dreaming. But there was the pipe on the table, and I could have taken the most solemn oath that to the best of my belief it had been placed there by unseen hands.

My feelings, as may be imagined, were peculiar. It was the first time in my life that I had ever been the subject of a phenomenon which was capable of being attributed to supernatural agency. After a little reflection, and some reasoning with myself, however, I tried to believe that my own senses had made a fool of me, and that in a half-somnolent and dreamy condition I had removed the pipe myself, and placed it on the table. Having come to this conclusion I divested myself of my clothing, extinguished the two tall candles, and jumped into bed. Although usually a good sleeper, I did not go to sleep at once, as was my wont, but lay thinking of many things, and mingling with my changing thoughts was a low, monotonous undertone—nature's symphony—of booming sea on the distant beach, and a bass piping-rising occasionally to a shrill and weird upper note—of the wind. From its situation the house was exposed to every wind that blew, hence its name "Bleak Hill Castle," and probably a southeast gale would have made itself felt to an uncomfortable degree in this room, which was in the south-east angle of the building. But now the booming sea and wind had a lullaby effect, and my nerves sinking into restful repose I fell asleep. How long I slept I do not know, and never shall know; but I awoke suddenly, and with a start, for it seemed as if a stream of ice-cold water was pouring over my face. With an impulse of indefinable alarm I sprang up in bed, and then a strange, awful, ghastly sight met my view.

I don't know that I could be described as a nervous man in any sense of the word. Indeed, I think I may claim to be freer from nerves than the average man, nor would my worst enemy, if he had a regard for truth, accuse me of lacking courage. And yet I confess here, frankly, that the sight I gazed upon appalled me. Yet was I fascinated with a horrible fascination, that rendered it impossible for me to turn my eyes away. I seemed bound by some strange weird spell. My limbs appeared to have grown rigid; there was a sense of burning in my eyes; my mouth was parched and dry; my tongue swollen, so it seemed. Of course, these were mere sensations, but they were sensations I never wish to experience again. They were sensations that tested my sanity. And the sight that held me in the thrall was truly calculated to test the nerves of the strongest.

There, in mid-air, between floor and ceiling, surrounded or made visible by a trembling, nebulous light, that was weird beyond the power of any words to describe, was the head and bust of a woman. The face was paralysed into an unutterably awful expression of stony horror; the long black hair was tangled and dishevelled, and the eyes appeared to be bulging from the head. But this was not all. Two ghostly hands were visible. The fingers of one were twined savagely in the black hair, and the other grasped a long-bladed knife, and with it hacked, and gashed, and tore, and stabbed at the bare white throat of the woman, and the blood gushed forth from the jagged wounds, reddening the spectre hand and flowing in one continuous stream to the oak floor, where I heard it drip, drip, drip until my brain seemed as if it would burst, and I felt as if I was going raving mad. Then I saw with my strained eyes the unmistakable sign of death pass over the woman's face; and next, the devilish hands flung the mangled remnants away, and I *heard* a low chuckle of satisfaction— heard, I say, and swear it, as plainly as I have ever heard anything in this world. The light had faded; the vision of crime and death had gone, and yet the spell held me. Although the night was cold, I believe I was bathed in perspiration. I think I tried to cry out—nay, I am sure I did—but no sound came from my burning, parched lips; my tongue refused utterance; it clove to the roof of my mouth. Could I have moved so much as a joint of my little finger, I could have broken the spell; at least, such was the idea that occupied my half-stunned brain. It was a nightmare of waking horror, and I shudder now, and shrink within myself as I recall it all. But the revelation—for revelation it was—had not yet reached its final stage. Out of the darkness was once more evolved a faint, phosphorescent glow, and in the midst of it appeared the dead body of a beautiful girl with the throat all gashed and bleeding, the red blood flowing in a crimson flood over her night-robe, which only partially concealed her young limbs; and the cruel, spectral hands, dyed with her blood, appeared again, and grasped her, and lifted her, and bore her along. Then that vision faded, and a third appeared. This time I seemed to be looking into a gloomy, damp, arched cave or cellar, and the horror that froze me was intensified as I saw the hands busy preparing a hole in the wall at one end of the cave; and presently they lifted two bodies—the body of the woman, and the body of the young girl—all gory and besmirched; and the hands crushed them into the hole in the wall, and then proceeded to brick them up.

All these things I saw as I have described them, and this I solemnly swear to be the truth as I hope for mercy at the Supreme Judgment.

It was a vision of crime; a vision of merciless, pitiless, damnable murder. How long it all lasted I don't know. Science has told us that dreams which seem to embrace a long series of years, last but seconds; and in the few moments of consciousness that remain to the drowning man his life's scroll is unrolled before his eyes. This vision of mine, therefore, may only have lasted seconds, but it seemed to me hours, years, nay, an eternity. With that final stage in the ghostly drama of blood and death, the spell was broken, and flinging my arms wildly about, I know that I uttered a great cry as I sprang up in bed.

"Have I been in the throes of a ghastly nightmare?" I asked myself.

Every detail of the horrific vision I recalled, and yet somehow it seemed to me that I had been the victim of a hideous nightmare. I felt ill; strangely ill. I was wet and clammy with perspiration, and nervous to a degree that I had never before experienced in my existence. Nevertheless, I noted everything distinctly. On the hearthstone there was still a mass of glowing red embers. I heard the distant booming of the sea, and round the house the wind moaned with a peculiar, eerie, creepy sound.

Suddenly I sprang from the bed, impelled thereto by an impulse I was bound to obey, and by the same impulse I was drawn towards the door. I laid my hand on the handle. I turned it, opened the door, and gazed into the long dark corridor. A sigh fell upon my ears. An unmistakable human sigh, in which was expressed an intensity of suffering and sorrow that thrilled me to the heart. I shrank back, and was about to close the door,

when out of the darkness was evolved the glowing figure of a woman
clad in blood-stained garments and with dishevelled hair. She turned her
white corpse-like face towards me, and her eyes pleaded with a pleading
that was irresistible, while she pointed the index finger of her left hand
downwards, and then beckoned me. Then I followed whither she led. I
could no more resist than the unrestrained needle can resist the attracting magnet. Clad only in my night apparel, and with bare feet and legs,
I followed the spectre along the corridor, down the broad oak stairs,
traversing another passage to the rear of the building until I found myself
standing before a heavy barred door. At that moment the spectre vanished, and I retraced my steps like one who walked in a dream. I got back
to my bedroom, but how I don't quite know; nor have I any recollection
of getting into bed. Hours afterwards I awoke. It was broad daylight. The
horror of the night came back to me with overwhelming force, and made
me faint and ill. I managed, however, to struggle through with my toilet,
and hurried from that haunted room. It was a beautifully fine morning.
The sun was shining brightly, and the birds carolled blithely in every tree
and bush. I strolled out on to the lawn, and paced up and down. I was
strangely agitated, and asked myself over and over again if what I had
seen or dreamed about had any significance.

Presently my host came out. He visibly started as he saw me.

"Hullo, old chap. What's the matter with you?" he exclaimed. "You
look jolly queer; as though you had been having a bad night of it."

"I have had a bad night."

His manner became more serious and grave.

"What—seen anything?"

"Yes."

"The deuce! You don't mean it, really!"

"Indeed I do. I have gone through a night of horror such as I could
not live through again. But let us have breakfast first, and then I will

try and make you understand what I have suffered, and you shall judge for yourself whether any significance is to be attached to my dream, or whatever you like to call it."

We walked, without speaking, into the breakfast room, where my charming hostess greeted me cordially; but she, like her husband, noticed my changed appearance, and expressed alarm and anxiety. I reassured her by saying I had had a rather restless night, and didn't feel particularly well, but that it was a mere passing ailment. I was unable to partake of much breakfast, and both my good friend and his wife again showed some anxiety, and pressed me to state the cause of my distress. As I could not see any good cause that was to be gained by concealment, and even at the risk of being laughed at by my host, I recounted the experience I had gone through during the night of terror.

So far from my host showing any disposition to ridicule me, as I quite expected he would have done, he became unusually thoughtful, and presently said:

"Either this is a wild phantasy of your own brain, or there is something in it. The door that the ghost of the woman led you to is situated on the top of a flight of stone steps, leading to a vault below the building, which I have never used, and have never even had the curiosity to enter, though I did once go to the bottom of the steps; but the place was so exceedingly suggestive of a tomb that I mentally exclaimed, 'I've no use for this dungeon,' and so I shut it up, bolted and barred the door, and have never opened it since."

I answered that the time had come when he must once more descend into that cellar or vault, whatever it was. He asked me if I would accompany him, and, of course, I said I would. So he summoned his head gardener, and after much searching about, the key of the door was found; but even then the door was only opened with difficulty, as lock and key alike were foul with rust.

As we descended the slimy, slippery stone steps, each of us carrying a candle, a rank, mouldy smell greeted us, and a cold noisome atmosphere pervaded the place. The steps led into a huge vault, that apparently extended under the greater part of the building. The roof was arched, and was supported by brick pillars. The floor was the natural earth, and was soft and oozy. The miasma was almost overpowering, notwithstanding that there were ventilating slits in the wall in various places.

We proceeded to explore this vast cellar, and found that there was an air shaft which apparently communicated with the roof of the house; but it was choked with rubbish, old boxes, and the like. The gardener cleared this away, and then, looking up, we could see the blue sky overhead.

Continuing our exploration, we noted that in a recess formed by the angle of the walls was a quantity of bricks and mortar. Under other circumstances this would not, perhaps, have aroused our curiosity or suspicions. But in this instance it did; and we examined the wall thereabouts with painful interest, until the conviction was forced upon us that a space of over a yard in width, and extending from floor to roof, had recently been filled in. I was drawn towards the new brickwork by some subtle magic, some weird fascination. I examined it with an eager, critical, curious interest, and the thoughts that passed through my brain were reflected in the faces of my companions. We looked at each other, and each knew by some unexplainable instinct what was passing in his fellow's mind.

"It seems to me we are face to face with some mystery," remarked Dick, solemnly. Indeed, throughout all the years I had known him I had never before seen him so serious. Usually his expression was that of good-humoured cynicism, but now he might have been a judge about to pronounce the doom of death on a red-handed sinner.

"Yes," I answered, "there is a mystery, unless I have been tricked by my own fancy."

"Umph! it is strange," muttered Dick to himself.

"Well, sir," chimed in the gardener, "you know there have been some precious queer stories going about for a long time. And before you come and took the place plenty of folks round about used to say they'd seen some uncanny sights. I never had no faith in them stories myself; but, after all, maybe there's truth in 'em."

Dick picked up half a brick and began to tap the wall with it where the new work was, and the taps gave forth a hollow sound, quite different from the sound produced when the other parts of the wall were struck.

"I say, old chap," exclaimed my host, with a sorry attempt at a smile, "upon my word, I begin to experience a sort of uncanny kind of feeling. I'll be hanged if I am not getting as superstitious as you are."

"You may call me superstitious if you like, but either I have seen what I have seen, or my senses have played the fool with me. Anyway, let us put it to the test."

"How?"

"By breaking away some of that new brickwork."

Dick laughed a laugh that wasn't a laugh, as he asked:

"What do you expect to find?" I hesitated what to say, and he added the answer himself—"Mouldering bones, if your ghostly visitor hasn't deceived you."

"Mouldering bones!" I echoed involuntarily.

"Gardener, have you got a crowbar amongst your tools?" Dick asked.

"Yes, sir."

"Go up and get it."

The man obeyed the command.

"This is a strange sort of business altogether," Dick continued, after glancing round the vast and gloomy cellar. "But, upon my word, to tell you the truth, I'm half ashamed of myself for yielding to anything like superstition. It strikes me that you'll find you are the victim of a trick of the imagination, and that these bogey fancies of yours have placed us in rather a ridiculous position."

In answer to this I could not possibly resist reminding Dick that even scientists admitted that there were certain phenomena—they called them "natural phenomena"—that could not be accounted for by ordinary laws.

Dick shrugged his shoulders and remarked with assumed indifference:

"Perhaps—perhaps it is so." He proceeded to fill his pipe with tobacco, and having lit it he smoked with a nervous energy quite unusual with him.

The gardener was only away about ten minutes, but it seemed infinitely longer. He brought both a pickaxe and a crowbar with him, and in obedience to his master's orders he commenced to hack at the wall. A brick was soon dislodged. Then the crowbar was inserted in the hole, and a mass prized out. From the opening came forth a sickening odour, so that we all drew back instinctively, and I am sure we all shuddered, and I saw the pipe fall from Dick's lips; but he snatched it up quickly and puffed at it vigorously until a cloud of smoke hung in the foetid and stagnant air. Then, picking up a candle from the ground, where it had been placed, he approached the hole, holding the candle in such a position that its rays were thrown into the opening. In a few moments he started back with an exclamation:

"My God! the ghost hasn't lied," he said, and I noticed that his face paled. I peered into the hole and so did the gardener, and we both drew back with a start, for sure enough in that recess were decaying human remains.

"This awful business must be investigated," said Dick. "Come, let us go."

We needed no second bidding. We were only too glad to quit that place of horror, and get into the fresh air and bright sunlight. We verily felt that we had come up out of a tomb, and we knew that once more the adage, "Murder will out," had proved true.

Half an hour later Dick and I were driving to the nearest town to lay information of the awful discovery we had made, and the subsequent search carried out by the police brought two skeletons to light. Critical medical examination left not the shadow of a doubt that they were the remains of a woman and a girl, and each had been brutally murdered. Of course it became necessary to hold an inquest, and the police set to work to collect evidence as to the identity of the bodies hidden in the recess in the wall.

Naturally all the stories which had been current for so many years throughout the country were revived, and the gossips were busy in retailing all they had heard, with many additions of their own, of course. But the chief topic was that of the strange disappearance of the wife and daughter of the once owner of the castle, Greeta Jones. This story had been touched upon the previous night, during the after-dinner chat in my host's smoking room. Morgan, as was remembered, had gambled his fortune away, and married a lady much older than himself, who bore him a daughter who was subject to epileptic fits. When this girl was about twelve she and her mother disappeared from the neighbourhood, and, according to the husband's account, they had gone to London.

Then he left, and people troubled themselves no more about him and his belongings.

A quarter of a century had passed since that period, and Bleak Hill Castle had gone through many vicissitudes until it fell into the hands of my friend Dick Dirckman. The more the history of Greeta Jones was gone into the more it was made clear that the remains which had been bricked up in the cellar were those of his wife and daughter. That the unfortunate girl and woman had been brutally and barbarously murdered there wasn't a doubt. The question was, who murdered them? After leaving Wales Greeta

Jones—as was brought to light—led a wild life in London. One night, while in a state of intoxication, he was knocked down by a cab, and so seriously injured that he died while being carried to the hospital; and with him his secret, for could there be any reasonable doubt that, even if he was not the actual murderer, he had connived at the crime. But there was reason to believe that he killed his wife and child with his own hand, and that with the aid of a navvy, whose services he bought, he bricked the bodies up in the cellar. It was remembered that a navvy named Howell Williams had been in the habit of going to the castle frequently, and that suddenly he became possessed of what was, for him, a considerable sum of money. For several weeks he drank hard; then, being a single man, he packed up his few belongings and gave out that he was going to California, and all efforts to trace him failed.

So much for this ghastly crime. As to the circumstances that led to its discovery, it was curious that I should have been selected as the medium for bringing it to light. Why it should have been so I cannot and do not pretend to explain. I have recorded facts as they occurred; I leave others to solve the mystery.

It was not a matter for surprise that Mrs. Dirckman should have been deeply affected by the terrible discovery, and she declared to her husband that if she were to remain at the castle she would either go mad or die. And so poor Dick, who was devoted to his charming little wife, got out as soon as he could, and once more Bleak Hill Castle fell into neglect and ultimate ruin, until at last it was razed to the ground and modern buildings reared on its site. As for myself, that night of horror I endured under Dick's roof affected me to such an extent that my hair became prematurely grey, and even now, when I think of the agony I endured, I shudder with an indefinable sense of fear.

THE FOOTSTEPS IN THE DUST

Alice Perrin

Here and there, mysteriously, in India exist Englishmen who seem to have been left behind on the strenuous march of British administration; who, from instability, misfortune, or wickedness, have sunk down, not entirely to the level of the loafer, but to a stage where they remain rooted in exile, apparently without home connections, correspondents, or interests, and who live and die in apathetic obscurity, while their histories, curious, pitiful, or unworthy, remain unrecorded and forgotten.

Captain Bogle was one of these derelicts. Being the oldest European inhabitant of Mynapur, he was accepted by the ever-changing officials of the district, who played cards and billiards with him in the little club, and whose wives occasionally asked him to dinner. He was an elderly man, and lived in a miserable little two-roomed bungalow opposite the great white stuccoed mansion owned by Gunga Pershad, the rich Hindoo "buniah," or merchant; but no one could say how long he had lived there, who he was, whence came his means of living, what had been his regiment, or why he voluntarily buried himself in a small civil station in Northern India. There had been rumours; of course: he had eloped with his Colonel's wife and been ruined over the damages; he had been dismissed from the army for embezzling mess funds; he was a Russian spy, a suspected murderer, the rightful heir to a great title, etc. etc. But nothing was ever proved, and Captain Bogle saw Collector, Joint Magistrate, Civil Surgeon, Police Officer, and Engineer, come and go, while his bungalow, and that of Gunga Pershad, remained the only dwellings in the station that still held their original occupants.

Captain Bogle and the buniah were apparently close friends, that is to say, the Englishman had the use of the native's horses, baskets of vegetables and fruit from the rambling garden, and they occasionally attended a race meeting down country together, when it was popularly supposed that if Captain Bogle lost, Gunga Pershad paid up—but not *vice versa*. In the evenings the couple were frequently to be seen driving in Gunga Pershad's roomy old-fashioned landau drawn by a pair of big Australian horses, with a fat coachman in purple livery, and a tatterdemalion outrider clattering behind on a white stallion. Gunga Pershad, clad in a plum-coloured satin coat, with a yellow turban, his loose lips stained red with betel-nut juice, would loll in his seat deep in conversation with his companion whose appearance resembled that of a decayed Mephistopheles.

"It's a queer alliance," said the Civil Surgeon, who had lately been transferred to Mynapur, and had not yet assimilated the accepted customs of the place. "And it's my belief that Bogle gets far more out of Gunga Pershad than meets the naked eye."

"I have sometimes thought so myself lately," replied Petersham, the police officer, with whom the doctor had been dining, and the two were now seated in the veranda smoking their Bahadur cheroots. "And yet the fellow lives on like a half-caste in that little pig-sty of a bungalow, and his clothes would disgrace a rag-and-bone shop."

"You see he drinks," said the doctor.

"I've never seen him drunk, and I've been here six months—worse luck!"

"No, and I don't suppose you ever would. That chap's pickled with spirit from head to foot. He can stand any amount, I should say; but it must come to an end sooner or later, It's my belief that he's taught Gunga Pershad the same game—half brandy, half champagne is probably their usual drink. A native does that kind of thing pretty thoroughly when he once takes to it."

The police officer grew thoughtful. "I was here some years ago as assistant," he said recollectively, "and now I come to think of it, Gunga Pershad was then a very different being from what he is at present. He was a smart, healthy-looking fellow, always riding about, and ready for a chat whenever one met him, and now he's fat and bloated and never stirs out except in that old shandridan of his; and he can't look one in the face or answer civilly when he's spoken to. I see a great change in him for the worse."

"Natives go down hill fast when they start, and I fancy our friend the Captain gave him the first shove and keeps him going. My bearer declares that the pair of them sit up till four o'clock every morning drinking and gambling in Gunga Pershad's bungalow."

Then, since the hour was late, and he had to be up early on duty, the doctor said good-night, and started home on foot, carrying his own lantern, for all the bungalows in Mynapur were fairly close together. His route led him past the large untidy compound, in the centre of which stood Gunga Pershad's mansion with the deep verandas, pucca roof, and imposing porch. The long doors, reaching almost from ceiling to floor, stood wide open, for the night was hot and airless, and the lofty room facing the road was brightly illuminated with rows of wall lamps, while a great white punkah waved to and fro. Under the punkah stood a card table, and at it sat Gunga Pershad and the Captain, absorbed in their game, with long tumblers full of liquid at their elbows.

The doctor, fascinated by the curious picture, stood and gazed, and presently the native threw down his cards, and stood up gesticulating wildly. Captain Bogle leaned back in his chair, and proceeded to light a cheroot. Then the voice of Gunga Pershad rose in angry remonstrance, though to the watcher outside the words were not distinguishable; but they sounded threatening, beseeching, despairing by turns. The man dragged off his turban, tore his clothes, and beat his breast; he knelt in front of the Englishman, and laid his forehead on the stone floor, and throughout this piteous scene the Captain sat apparently unmoved, blowing clouds of smoke through his nostrils. The doctor turned away in disgust. The sight sickened him, it was sordid and revolting, and made him ashamed of his countryman. What did it all mean? That Bogle had been compassing the ruin of Gunga Pershad for some years past he felt convinced, and it now seemed as though a crisis had arrived. Something was going to happen.

And next morning came the news that Gunga Pershad had committed suicide by taking poison; moreover, it eventually transpired that the once rich merchant had died penniless, and that the big bungalow, the landau and horses, the mirrors, chandeliers, marble-topped tables, and all the rest of the garish possessions so dear to the heart of a native, together with savings, and investments, and valuable house property in the bazaar, had all been gambled away to Captain Bogle.

The question most discussed in the station was what the man would do with his evilly won fortune? That he was legally entitled to it all there was no disputing, but public opinion rose high against him, and though curiosity raged in every breast, Captain Bogle found himself ignored when he entered the little club, and apparently invisible when he met any one on the road.

This treatment at last caused him to avoid the club and his English neighbours, but he remained on in the shabby bungalow, and only took long solitary drives in the landau so lately the property of his victim. People wondered why he did not occupy the big white house now it was his own, or why he stayed on in Mynapur instead of going home, and old gossip and conjectures concerning him revived with additions and improvements.

Still he continued his curious existence, driving out in the evenings along the hard, dusty roads; and the doctor who met him often on his way back from the Government dispensary, expressed his opinion that the man was on the verge of delirium tremens.

"I saw him yesterday afternoon," he said to Petersham, "driving along jabbering like a monkey, just for all the world as if he had some one beside him! He seemed to be arguing and explaining till I felt quite uncanny. I could have sworn that old Gunga Pershad was sitting next him if I hadn't seen for myself that the seat was empty!"

"He was going on anyhow last night too," said Petersham. "I heard him when I was coming home from dining with the Dunnes. You know how close that little hovel of his is to the road; he was standing outside waving his hands and shouting in Hindustani. I pulled up and asked him what was the matter, and he solemnly implored me to go over and tell Gunga Pershad to stop calling him, because nothing would induce him to go over to the bungalow and give the native his revenge at cards. I said, 'My dear chap, Gunga Pershad's dead, how *can* he call you, or play cards, or do anything else?' But he only looked at me like a screwed owl and said he knew Gunga Pershad was dead, well enough, and that was just why he didn't want to go over and play cards with him! We shall have trouble with that fellow, sooner or later."

"I think I'd better go and look him up to-day," said the doctor, who was a kind-hearted individual. But, owing to an unexpected press of work, it was not until after a late and hurried tiffin at a patient's house that he found himself free to visit Captain Bogle.

The little bungalow looked deserted when he drove up to the veranda, and it was some minutes before his shouts attracted the attention of the servants. He could hear them laughing, coughing, gossiping in the cook-house. At length a disreputable creature appeared who pronounced himself to be the Captain-sahib's bearer, as he hastily wound a dirty turban about his greasy black head.

"Where is the sahib?" inquired the doctor.

"Huzoor! He commanded the carriage but two hours since, and drove forth to eat the air. Whither he went thy slave knoweth not."

Rather relieved than otherwise the doctor turned his trap round; but as he drove down the road past the opposite compound he caught sight of the well-known landau standing under the porch of the big bungalow, and he drove in through the white gate-posts and up the ill-kept drive. The place had not been touched since Gunga Pershad's death, and the house had stood unlived in and neglected.

When he reached the porch he found the pair of horses standing in easy attitudes with drooping heads, while the coachman and groom were seated on the ground sharing a hookah and conversing in low tones. They had the patient apathetic air of natives, to whom time is no object, and one spot quite as satisfactory as another in which to smoke and discuss the price of food. They rose when they saw the doctor, and the fat coachman explained that the Captain-sahib was within the bungalow, and had been there for nearly two hours.

"It be the first time he hath entered the building since the death of Gunga Pershad," he added, as though to account for the length of the visit.

The utter silence of the neglected house struck the doctor with an odd sense of uneasiness. He descended from his trap and looked into the entrance hall. The dust lay thick on the matting, and in the dust, sharply imprinted, were the marks of Captain Bogle's boots. The doctor followed the footsteps, and they led him into the principal room where the dust covered everything. It soiled the satin upholstered chairs and couches, dimmed the mirrors, clung to the dingy punkah frill, and was deep on the floor. In the middle of the vast room was a little green-covered card table with two chairs, one of which had been pushed aside as though the occupant had risen abruptly. Cards were scattered over the table and a few lay on the floor with the remains of a broken tumbler. Evidently, thought the doctor, the room had never been touched since Gunga Pershad had played his last disastrous game.

He followed the fresh footmarks up to the table, noticed that the Captain must have first sat down in the chair that was turned aside, for it had been pushed back quite recently, and the footmarks about it were a little confused. He was vaguely conscious of something unnatural, and then realised suddenly that though the steps had led up to the table they were neither continued nor retraced. The dust lay undisturbed everywhere else—the fine grey Indian dust that gathers thickly even in a few hours if unopposed; and yet Captain Bogle was not present.

The doctor stood completely puzzled, gazing with attention at the tracks that were unmistakably in one direction only. Then he lifted up his voice and called the Captain by name again and again. His voice echoed through the lofty rooms; but there was no reply, except the scream of a frightened starling that had built its nest in a ventilator in the ceiling. He picked his way carefully back, stepping as far as possible in his own footmarks, and looked into the other rooms that led from the entrance hall. There was nothing but silence, emptiness, undisturbed dust.

Captain Bogle was not in the bungalow, and with a feeling of resentful bewilderment the doctor drove off to fetch Petersham, after giving the waiting servants orders that no one was to enter the house until his return. He brought the police officer back with him, and together they surveyed the single line of footsteps terminating at the table, the chair's position, the evidence of its occupant having sat down and risen hurriedly.

"The other chair hasn't been sat in," said Petersham, peering at it closely; "it's covered with dust, but those cards have only lately been dropped on the floor. Bogle came in here right enough, but how the devil did he get out again—unless he flew!"

Together the two men went over every room and every corner. They searched the roof, the garden, the stables, the outhouses; but Captain Bogle was nowhere to be found. He had disappeared completely and unaccountably, and the very last traces of him ever discovered were the footsteps in the dust that led up to the card table in the middle of the big room of Gunga Pershad's bungalow—and no farther.

THE CRIMSON BLIND

Mrs. H. D. Everett

I

Ronald McEwan, aged sixteen, was invited to spend a vacation fortnight at his uncle's rectory. Possibly some qualms of conscience
had tardily spurred the Rev. Sylvanus Applegarth to offer this hospitality,
aware that he had in the past neglected his dead sister's son. Also, with a
view to the future, it might be well for Ronald to make acquaintance with
his own two lads, now holidaying from English public schools.

Mr. Applegarth was a gentleman and a scholar, one who loved above
all things leisure and a quiet house: he retained a curate at his own
expense to run matters parochial in Swanmere, and buried himself among
his books. The holidays were seasons of trial to him on each of the three
yearly occasions, and it would not be much worse, so he reflected, to have
three hobbledehoy lads ramping about the place, and clumping up and
down stairs with heavy boots, when it was inevitable he must have two.

The young Applegarths were not ill-natured lads, but they were somewhat disposed to make a butt of the shy Scottish cousin, who was midway
between them in age, and had had a different upbringing and schooling
from themselves. Ronald found it advisable to listen much and say little,
not airing his own opinions unless they were directly challenged. But in

one direction he had been outspoken, afterwards wishing devoutly he had held his tongue. Spooks were under discussion, and it was discovered—a source of fiendish glee to the allied brothers—that Ronald believed in ghosts, as he preferred more respectfully to term them, and also in such marvels as death-warnings, wraiths, and second-sight.

"That comes of being a Highlander," said Jack the elder. "Superstition is a taint that gets into the blood, and so is born with you. But I'll wager anything you have no valid reason for believing. The best evidence is only second-hand; most of it third or fourth hand, if as near. You have never seen a ghost yourself?"

"No," acknowledged Ronald somewhat sourly, for he had been more than sufficiently badgered. "But I've spoken with those that have."

"Would you like to see one? Now give a straight answer for once,"— and Jack winked at his brother.

"I wouldn't mind." Then, more stoutly, "Yes, I would like—if I'd the chance."

"I think we can give you a chance of seeing something, if not exactly a ghost. We've got no Highland castles to trot out, but there's a house here in Swanmere that is said to be haunted. Just the thing for you to investigate, now you are on the spot. Will you take it on?"

It would have been fatal to say no, and give these cousins the opening to post him as a coward. Ronald gave again the grudging admission that he "wouldn't mind." And then, being Sunday morning, the lads said they would take him round that way after church, and he should have a look at the window which had earned a bad repute. Then they might find out who had the keys in charge, if he felt inclined to pass a night within.

"I suppose, as neither of you believe, you would not be afraid to sleep there?" said Ronald, addressing the two.

"Certainly we would not be *afraid*." Jack was speech-valiant at least. "As we believe there is nothing in it but a sham, like all the other tales."

Alfred, the younger boy, did not contradict his brother, but it might have been noticed that he kept silence.

"Then I'll do what you do." This was Ronald's ultimatum. "If you two choose to sleep in the haunted house, I'll sleep there too."

But, as the event fell out, the Applegarths did not push matters to the point of borrowing keys from the house-agent and camping out rolled in blankets on the bare floors—an attractive picture Jack went on to draw of the venture to which Ronald stood committed. After the morning service, the three lads walked some half mile beyond the village in the direction of the sea shore. Here the houses were few and far between, but two or three villas were in course of building, and other plots beyond them were placarded as for sale. Swanmere was "rising"—in other words, in process of being spoiled. Niched in between two of these plots was an empty house to let, well placed in being set some way back from the high road, within the privacy of thick shrubberies, and screened at the back by a belt of forest trees.

A desirable residence, one would have said at a first glance, but closer acquaintance was apt to induce a change of mind. The iron gates of the drive were fastened with padlock and chain, but the young Applegarths effected an entrance by faulting over the palings at the side. Everywhere was to be seen the encroachment and overgrowth of long neglect: weeds knee high, and branches pushing themselves across the side-paths, though the carriage approach had been kept clear. The main entrance was at the side, and in front bowed windows, on two floors, were closely shuttered within, and grimed with dirt without.

The boys pushed their way round to the back, where the kitchen offices were enclosed by a yard. But midway between the better and the inferior part of the house, a large flat window on the first floor overlooked the flower-garden and shrubbery. This window was not shuttered, but was completely screened by a wide blind of faded red, drawn down to meet the sill. Jack pointed to it.

"That is where the ghost shows—not every night, but sometimes. Maybe you'll have to watch for a whole week before there is anything to see. But, if rumour says true, you will be repaid in the end. Whatever the appearance may be."

Ronald thought he saw a wink pass between the brothers. He was to be hoaxed in some way; of that he felt assured.

"I'll go, if we three go together, you and Alfred and I. If there is a real ghost to be seen, you shall see it too. What is it said to be like?"

"A light comes behind the red blind, and some people see a figure, or the shadow of a figure, in the room. Perhaps it is according to the open eye, some less and some more. You may see more still, being Highland born and bred. Very well, as you make it a condition, we will go together."

"To-night?"

"Better not to-night. There's evening church and supper, and the governor plight not like it, being Sunday. We will go to-morrow. That will serve as well for you."

The fake, whatever it might be, could not be prepared in time for that first evening, Ronald reflected. He was quite unbelieving about the red blind and the light, but firm in his resolve. If he was to be trotted out to see a ghost, the Applegarth cousins should go too. It was a matter of indifference to him which night was chosen for the expedition, so Monday was agreed upon, the trio to set out at midnight, when all respectable inhabitants of Swanmere should be in their beds.

When Monday night came, the sky was clear and starlit, but it was the dark of the moon. One of the lads possessed an electric torch, which Jack put in his pocket. And when it came to the point, it appeared that only Jack was going with him. Alfred, according to his brother, had developed a sore-throat, and Mrs. Dawson the house-keeper, was putting him on a poultice which had to be applied in bed.

So it was the younger Applegarth who had been chosen to play the ghost, Ronald instantly concluded: he had no faith at all in the poultice, or in Mrs. Dawson's application of it, though he remembered Alfred had complained of the soreness of his throat more than once during the day.

There was little interchange of words between the two lads as they went. Ronald was inwardly resentful, and Jack seemed to have some private thoughts which amused him, for he smiled to himself in the darkness. Arrived at the Portsmouth road, they got over the fence at the same place as before; and now Jack's torch was of use, as they pushed their way through the tangled garden to the spot determined on as likely to afford the best view of the window with the crimson blind. Neither blind nor window could now be distinguished; the house reared itself before them a silhouette of blacker darkness, against that other darkness of the night.

"We can sit on this bench while we wait," and young Applegarth flashed his torch on a rustic structure, set beneath overshadowing trees. "I propose to time ourselves and give an hour to the watch. Then, if you have seen nothing, we can come away and return another night. For myself, sceptic as I am, I don't expect to see."

He could hardly be more sceptical than Ronald felt at the moment. Certain that a trick was about to be played on him, all his senses had been on the alert from the moment they left the road, and he felt sure that as they plunged through the wilderness of shrubbery, he had heard another footstep following. He did not refuse to seat himself on the bench, but he took care to have the bole of the tree immediately at his back, as some protection from assault in the rear.

Some five or six minutes went by, and he was paying little attention to the house, but much to certain rustling noises in the shrubbery behind them, when Jack Applegarth exclaimed in an altered voice: "By Jove, there *is* a light there after all!" and he became aware that the broad parallelo-gram of the window was now faintly illuminated behind the crimson blind, sufficiently to show its shape and size, and also the colour of the screen. Could young Alfred have found some means of entrance, and set up a lighted candle in the room?—but somehow he doubted whether, without his brother to back him, the boy would have ventured into the ghostly house alone. The fake he anticipated was of a different sort to this.

As the boys watched, the light grew stronger, glowing through the blind; the lamp within that room must have been a strong one of many candle-power. Then a shadow became visible, as if cast by some person moving to and fro in front of the light; this was faint at first, but gradually it increased in intensity, and presently came close to the window, pulling the blind aside to look out.

This was so ordinary an action that it did not suggest the supernatural. A moment later, however, the whole framework of the window seemed to give way and fall outwards with a crash of breaking glass. The figure now showed clearly defined, standing outside on the sill with the red illumina-tion behind; but its pause there was one only of seconds before it leaped to the ground and came rushing towards them; a figure so far in ghostly likeness that it appeared to be clad in white. Following the crash of glass came other sounds, a pistol-shot and a scream, but the rush of the flying figure was unaccompanied by noise. It passed close to the bench where they were seated, and young Applegarth grasped Ronald's arm in a terror well-acted if unreal.

"Come away," he said thickly. "I've had enough of this. Come away."

The light behind the blind was dying out, and presently the window was again in darkness, but these spectators did not stay to see. Jack Applegarth dragged Ronald back towards the road, and the younger lad broke from the bushes and followed them, sobbing in what seemed to be real affright, and with a white bundle hugged in his arms. They climbed the palings and went pelting home, and not till the distance was half accomplished did any one of them speak. Then Ronald had the first word.

"Why Alfred, I thought you were in bed. I hope your throat will not suffer through coming out to trick me with a sham ghost. I made sure all along that was what you and Jack would do."

Alfred hugged tighter the bundle he was carrying: did he fear it would be snatched off him and displayed?—it looked exceedingly like a white sheet.

"I had nothing to do with *that thing*," he blurted out between chattering teeth. "I don't know what it was, or where it came from. But I swear I'll never go near the blamed place again, either by night or by day!"

II

Whether there was any natural explanation of what they had seen, Ronald never knew. His visit to his Applegarth relatives was drawing to a close, and, shortly after, the old Rector died suddenly during the service in church. The home was broken up, the two schoolboy cousins had their way to make in the world, and, whether ill or well made, this history knows them no more. And between the just concluded chapter, and this which is now begun, must be set an interval of twenty years.

Ronald had done well for himself in the meantime. He had become an alert hard-headed business man, a good deal detached from the softer side of life, for which, he told himself, there would be time and to spare by-and-bye. But now, at thirty-six, there began to be a different telling. He could afford to keep a wife in comfort, and it seemed to him that the time for choice had come.

This does not pretend to be a love-story, so it will only briefly chronicle that it was the business of wife-selection which took Ronald again to Swanmere. He happened to act as best man at his friend Parkinson's wedding, and one of the bridesmaids seemed to him an unusually attractive girl, happy herself, and likely to make others happy, which is better than mere beauty. Probably he let fall a wish that he might see Lilian again; any way, some time later, he was invited to run down and pay a week-end visit to the newly-married pair, when Lilian was at the same time expected to stay. And, as it happened, the Peregrine Parkinsons had settled at Swanmere.

"Do you know this place at all?" queried Mrs. Parkinson, who was meeting him at the station with the small pony-carriage, of which, and of her skill as a whip, she was inordinately proud.

"I was here once before, many years ago," was Ronald's answer. "I was only a school-boy in those days, visiting an old uncle, who then was rector of the parish. Swanmere seems to have grown a good deal bigger than I remember it, or else my recollection is at fault."

"Oh yes, it has grown; places do grow, don't they? There was a great deal of new building before the war; villas you know, and that style; but 1914 stopped everything. Peregrine and I were fortunate in meeting with an older house, in a quite delightful well-grown garden. Oh no, not old enough to be inconvenient, and it has been brought up-to-date for us. We were lucky to get it, I can assure you: it is so difficult in these days to find anything moderate-sized. They are snapped up directly they are vacant, the demand is so much in excess of the supply."

Ronald did not recognise the direction taken, even when the pony willingly turned in at an open pair of iron gates, which he had last seen chained and padlocked—or if not these gates, their predecessors, as gates have a way of, perishing in untended years. All was trim within, pruned and swept and gravelled, and the garden a riot of colour with its summer flowers. But the front of the house, with double bows carried up to the first floor, did strike a chord of association. "I wonder!" he said to himself, and then the wonder was negatived. "No, it isn't possible; it would be too odd a coincidence." And upon this he dismissed the thought from mind.

It did not return during the evening, not even when he went up—in a hurry, and at the last moment—to dress for dinner in the bed-room allotted to him; a spacious and well-appointed one, where his portmanteau had been unpacked and habiliments laid out. After dinner there was the diversion of some food music; Mrs. Parkinson played and Lilian sang. The Swanmere experience of twenty years ago was quite out of mind when he retired for the night; pleasanter thoughts had pushed it into the background and held the stage. But the recollection was vaguely renewed last thing, when he drew aside the curtains and opened the window, noting its unusual square shape, divided into three uprights, two of which opened casement fashion.

It was the only window in the room, but so wide that it nearly filled the outer wall. Certainly its shape recalled the window of twenty years ago which was screened by a crimson blind, and his watch in the garden with Jack Applegarth. He was never likely to forget that night, though he was far from sure whether the ghost was ghost indeed, or a sham faked by the Applegarth boys for his discomfiture. Probably these suburban villas were built all upon one plan, and an older foundation had set the note of fashion for those that followed. He never knew the name or number of the haunted house, or locality, except that it was entered from the Portsmouth road so in that way he could not identify it. And again he dismissed the idea, and addressed himself to sleep.

Neither this recollection nor the dawning love-interest was potent to keep him awake. He slept well the early part of the night, and did not wake till morning was brightening in the east. Then, as he opened his eyes and turned to face the light, he saw, and was astonished seeing, that the window was covered with a crimson blind, drawn down from top to sill.

He could have declared that nothing of the sort was in place there over night. The drawn-back curtains had revealed a quite ordinary green Venetian, which he had raised till it clicked into stoppage at its height. To all outward seeming this was a material blind, swaying in the air of the open casement, and with no light behind it but that of the summer dawn. And yet, for all that, he lay staring at it with nerves on edge, and hammering pulses which beat thickly in his ears and throat: something within him recognised the nature of the appearance and responded with agitation, despite the scepticism of the outward man. That was a bird's song vocal outside, wheels went by in the road, the ordinary world was astir. He would rise and assure himself that the blind was a mundane affair, palpable to touch; it had of course slipped down in the night owing to a loosened cord, and was hung within the other.

And then he discovered that his limbs were powerless: it was as if invisible hands restrained him. He writhed against them in vain, and in the end, despite those rapid pulses of the affrighted heart, he fell suddenly into trance or sleep.

He had had a seizure of nightmare, he concluded when he awoke later, with the servant knocking at the door to bring in tea and shaving-water, and the open window cheerful and unscreened, letting in the summer air.

His first act was to examine the window-frame, but—of course, as he told himself—there was no crimson blind, nothing but the green Venetian, and the curtains drawing on their rod. He had dreamt the whole thing, on the suggestion of that memory of a school-boy visit long ago.

He was well assured of the folly of it all, and yet he had again and again to reason the thing out, and repeat that it was folly—himself in colloquy with himself. This was still more necessary when in the course of the morning he strolled out into the garden and round the shrubbery paths. Though the wild growth of long ago had been pruned back and certain changes made, he had no difficulty in finding the spot—what he thought the spot—where he and Jack Applegarth had watched. There was still a rustic seat under the trees, full in view of the square window of his room where the red blind no longer was displayed. He sat down to light a cigarette, and presently his host appeared, pipe in mouth, and joined him on the bench in the shade.

"You have a nice place here," Ronald said, by way of opening conversation.

"Yes," Parkinson agreed. "I like it, and Cecilia likes it, and in every way it suits us well. Convenient for business you know, and not too pretentious for young beginners. We both fell in love with it at first sight. But I heard something the other day" (poking with his knife at a pipe which declined to draw) "something that rather disturbed me. Not that I believe it, you know; I'm not that sort. I only hope and trust that no busybody will consider it his, or her, duty to inform Cecilia."

"What did you hear?"

"Why, some fools were saying the house used to be haunted, and that was the reason why it stood long unlet, and fell into bad repair. Stories of that sort are always put about when a place happens to be nobody's fancy, whether the real drawback is rats or drains, or somebody wanting to keep it vacant for interests of their own. As you know. In this case I should say it was the latter. Because the man told me lights were seen when the place was shut up and empty. A thieves' dumping ground, no doubt. Or possibly coiners."

This in pauses, between whiffs of the pipe. Parkinson ended:

"I don't want Cecilia to know. She is fond of the place, and I wouldn't like her to be nervous or upset."

"Couldn't you warn the man?"

"I did that. But there are other men who know. And, what is worse, women. You know what women's tongues are. Especially when they think they have got hold of something spicey. Or what will annoy somebody else!"

"Why not tell your wife yourself, and trust to her good sense not to mind. Better for her to learn it so, than by chance whispers from a stranger. She won't like it if she thinks you were aware, and kept it up your sleeve."

But Parkinson shook his head. Fond as he was of his Cecilia, perhaps his opinion of her good sense had not been heightened by the experience of four or five months of marriage. And Ronald checked his own impulse to communicate the history of that former episode, together with the odd dream—if it was a dream—which visited him the night before. But he had found out one thing: now it was beyond doubt. This smartly done-up villa with its modern improvements, was identical with the closed and neglected house of long ago.

That day was Saturday. He had been invited to stay over the week-end, so there were two more nights that he was bound to spend at the villa. He did not enjoy the anticipation of those nights, though some slight uneasiness would cheaply purchase the intermediate day to be spent with Lilian. And what harm could any ghost do him, and what did it matter whether the window was covered with a crimson blind, or a white or a green!

It mattered little when regarded in the day, but during the watches of the night such affairs take on a different complexion, though Ronald McEwan was no coward. He woke earlier on this second night: woke to be aware of a faint illumination in the room, and of—he thought after, though it was hardly realised at the time—the instantaneous glimpse of a figure crossing from wall to wall. One thing he did distinctly see: over the window there hung again—the crimson blind! Then in the space of half a dozen heart-beats, the faint light faded out, and the room was left in darkness.

This time the paralysis of the night before did not recur. He had been careful to place within reach at the bedside the means of striking a light, and presently his candle showed the window unscreened and open, and the door locked as he left it over night. He did not extinguish that candle, but let it burn down in the socket; and he was not again disturbed.

During Sunday he debated with himself the question to speak or not to speak. That spare room might next be occupied by some one to whom the terror of such a visitation would be harmful; and yet, he supposed, all turned on whether or not the occupier was gifted (or shall we say cursed?) with the open eye. He felt thankful he had been quartered there and not Lilian. Finally he resolved that Parkinson must be warned, but not till he himself was on the point of leaving—not till he had passed a third night in the haunted room, disturbed or not disturbed. And, after all, what had he to allege against it in this later time? Could a room be haunted by the apparition of a crimson blind?

Saturday had been brilliantly fine throughout, but Sunday dawned upon unsettled weather, and a wet gale rushing over from the not distant sea. He went to rest that night resolved to keep a light burning through the dark hours, but found it necessary to shut the window on account of the driven storm. He strove to reason himself into indifference and so prepare for sleep, which visited him sooner than he expected, and for a while was profound. It was somewhere between two and three o'clock when he started up, broad awake on the instant, with the consciousness of something wrong.

It was not the moderate light of his candle which now illuminated the room, but the fierce glow of mounting flames, though he could not see whence they proceeded. The red blind hung again over the window, but that was a negligible matter: some carelessness of his had set the Parkinsons' house on fire, and he must give the alarm. He struggled up in bed, only to find he was not alone. There at the bed-foot stood gazing at him a man, a stranger, plainly seen in the glare of light. A man haggard of countenance, with the look of a soul that despaired; clad in white or light-coloured garments; possibly a sleeping-suit.

Ronald believed he made an attempt to speak to this creature, to ask who he was and what doing there, but whether he really achieved articulate words he does not know. For the space of perhaps a minute the two stared at each other, the man in the flesh and he who was flesh no more; then the latter sprang to the window, standing on the low sill, and tore aside the crimson blind. There was a great crash of glass like that other crash he remembered, a cry from below in the garden, and a report like a pistol-shot; the figure had disappeared, leaping through the broken gap. Then all was still and the room in darkness; those fierce flames were suddenly extinguished, and his own candle had gone out.

He groped for the matches and struck a light. The red blind had disappeared from the window, there was no broken glass and no fire, and everything remained as he had left it over night.

No one else appeared to have heard that shot and cry in the dead middle of the night. After breakfast he took Parkinson into confidence, who heard the story gloomily enough, plainly discomforted though unwilling to believe.

"You have been right to tell me, my dear fellow, and I am sure you think you experienced all these impossible things. But look at probability. Those Applegarth boys hoaxed you years ago, the impression dwelt on your mind, and was revived by discovering this house to be the same. Such was the simple cause of your visions; any doctor would tell you so. As for my own action, I don't see clear. It is a horribly awkward affair, and we have been to no end of expense settling in. Cecilia likes the place, and it suits her. So long as she does not know—!"

"Look here, Parkinson. There is one thing I think I may ask—suggest, at least. You have another spare bedroom. Don't put any other guest where I have been sleeping. Couldn't you make it a storeroom—box-room— anything that is not used at night?"

Parkinson still was doubtful: he shook his head.

"Not without an explanation to Cecilia. She happens to be particularly *gone* on that room on account of the big window. It was just a toss-up that she didn't put Lilian there, and you in the other. And—if in time to come a nursery should be needed, that is the room on which she has her eye. She would never consent to give it up for a glory-hole or a store-room without a strong reason. A very strong reason indeed."

Ronald could do no more: his friend was warned, the responsibility was no longer his. It was some comfort to know that Lilian was leaving two days later, going on to another visit, and the fatal house did not seem to have affected her up to now.

After this, a couple of months went by, during which the Parkinsons made no sign, and he for his part kept his lips entirely sealed about his experiences at Swanmere. It might be, as Jack Applegarth said long before, his Highland blood which rendered him vulnerable to uncanny influences, and the Parkinsons and their Southron friends might remain entirely immune. But at the end of two months he received the following letter:

> Dear Old Chum,—
>
> It is all up with us here, and I think you will wish to know how it came about. I am trying to sub-let Ashcroft, and hope to find somebody fool enough to take it. I haven't a fault to find with the place, neither of us have seen or heard a thing, and really it seems absurd. The servants picked up some gossip about the haunting, and then one of them was scared—by her own shadow, I expect, and promptly had hysterics. After that, all three of them went to Cecilia in a body, and said they were willing to forfeit their wages, and sorry to cause us inconvenience, but nothing would induce them to stop on in a haunted house—not if we paid them hundreds—and they must leave at once. Then I had to have it out with Cecilia, and she was not pleased to have been kept in the dark. She says I hoodwinked her—but if I did, it was for her own good; and when

we took the place, I had not the least idea. Of course she could not stay when the servants cleared out—and nor could I; so she has gone to her mother's, and I am at the hotel—with every one asking questions, which I can assure you is not pleasant. I shall take very good care not to be trapped a second time into a place where ghosts are on the loose.

There is one thing that may interest you, as it seems to throw light on your experience. The house was built by a doctor who took in lunatic patients—harmless ones they were supposed to be, and he was properly certificated and all that: there was no humbug about it that I know. One man who was thought quite a mild case suddenly became violent. He locked himself into his room and set it on fire, and then smashed a window—I believe it was *that* window—and jumped out. It was only from the first floor, but he was so badly injured that he died: a good riddance of bad rubbish, I. should say. I don't know anything about a red blind or a pistol-shot: those matters seem to have been embroidered on. But the coincidence is an odd one, I allow.

We were pleased to hear of your engagement to Lilian, and I send you both congratulations and good wishes, in which Cecilia would join if here. I suppose you will soon be Benedick the married man.

Yours ever,

PEREGRINE PARKINSON

THE WELL

W. W. Jacobs

I

Two men stood in the billiard-room of an old country house, talking. Play, which had been of a half-hearted nature, was over, and they sat at the open window, looking out over the park stretching away beneath them, conversing idly.

"Your time's nearly up, Jem," said one at length, "this time six weeks you'll be yawning out the honeymoon and cursing the man—woman I mean—who invented them."

Jem Benson stretched his long limbs in the chair and grunted in dissent.

"I've never understood it," continued Wilfred Carr, yawning. "It's not in my line at all; I never had enough money for my own wants, let alone for two. Perhaps if I were as rich as you or Crœsus I might regard it differently."

There was just sufficient meaning in the latter part of the remark for his cousin to forbear to reply to it. He continued to gaze out of the window and to smoke slowly.

"Not being as rich as Crœsus—or you," resumed Carr, regarding him from beneath lowered lids, "I paddle my own canoe down the stream of Time, and, tying it to my friends' door-posts, go in to eat their dinners."

"Quite Venetian," said Jem Benson, still looking out of the window. "It's not a bad thing for you, Wilfred, that you have the doorposts and dinners—and friends."

Carr grunted in his turn. "Seriously though, Jem," he said, slowly, "you're a lucky fellow, a very lucky fellow. If there is a better girl above ground than Olive, I should like to see her."

"Yes," said the other, quietly.

"She's such an exceptional girl," continued Carr, staring out of the window. "She's so good and gentle. She thinks you are a bundle of all the virtues."

He laughed frankly and joyously, but the other man did not join him. "Strong sense—of right and wrong, though," continued Carr, musingly. "Do you know, I believe that if she found out that you were not—"

"Not what?" demanded Benson, turning upon him fiercely, "Not what?"

"Everything that you are," returned his cousin, with a grin that belied his words, "I believe she'd drop you."

"Talk about something else," said Benson, slowly; "your pleasantries are not always in the best taste."

Wilfred Carr rose and taking a cue from the rack, bent over the board and practiced one or two favourite shots. "The only other subject I can talk about just at present is my own financial affairs," he said slowly, as he walked round the table.

"Talk about something else," said Benson again, bluntly.

"And the two things are connected," said Carr, and dropping his cue he half sat on the table and eyed his cousin.

There was a long silence. Benson pitched the end of his cigar out of the window, and leaning back closed his eyes.

"Do you follow me?" inquired Carr at length.

Benson opened his eyes and nodded at the window.

"Do you want to follow my cigar?" he demanded.

"I should prefer to depart by the usual way for your sake," returned the other, unabashed. "If I left by the window all sorts of questions would be asked, and you know what a talkative chap I am."

"So long as you don't talk about my affairs," returned the other, restraining himself by an obvious effort, "you can talk yourself hoarse."

"I'm in a mess," said Carr, slowly, "a devil of a mess. If I don't raise fifteen hundred by this day fortnight, I may be getting my board and lodging free."

"Would that be any change?" questioned Benson.

"The quality would," retorted the other. "The address also would not be good. Seriously, Jem, will you let me have the fifteen hundred?"

"No," said the other, simply.

Carr went white. "It's to save me from ruin," he said, thickly.

"I've helped you till I'm tired," said Benson, turning and regarding him, "and it is all to no good. If you've got into a mess, get out of it. You should not be so fond of giving autographs away."

"It's foolish, I admit," said Carr, deliberately. "I won't do so any more. By the way, I've got some to sell. You needn't sneer. They're not my own."

"Whose are they?" inquired the other.

"Yours."

Benson got up from his chair and crossed over to him. "What is this?" he asked, quietly. "Blackmail?"

"Call it what you like," said Carr. "I've got some letters for sale, price fifteen hundred. And I know a man who would buy them at that price for the mere chance of getting Olive from you. I'll give you first offer."

"If you have got any letters bearing my signature, you will be good enough to give them to me," said Benson, very slowly.

"They're mine," said Carr, lightly; "given to me by the lady you wrote them to. I must say that they are not all in the best possible taste."

His cousin reached forward suddenly, and catching him by the collar of his coat pinned him down on the table.

"Give me those letters," he breathed, sticking his face close to Carr's.

"They're not here," said Carr, struggling. "I'm not a fool. Let me go, or I'll raise the price."

The other man raised him from the table in his powerful hands, apparently with the intention of dashing his head against it. Then suddenly his hold relaxed as an astonished-looking maid-servant entered the room with letters. Carr sat up hastily.

"That's how it was done," said Benson, for the girl's benefit as he took the letters.

"I don't wonder at the other man making him pay for it, then," said Carr, blandly.

"You will give me those letters?" said Benson, suggestively, as the girl left the room.

"At the price I mentioned, yes," said Carr; "but so sure as I am a living man, if you lay your clumsy hands on me again, I'll double it. Now, I'll leave you for a time while you think it over."

He took a cigar from the box and lighting it carefully quitted the room. His cousin waited until the door had closed behind him, and then turning to the window sat there in a fit of fury as silent as it was terrible.

The air was fresh and sweet from the park, heavy with the scent of new-mown grass. The fragrance of a cigar was now added to it, and glancing out he saw his cousin pacing slowly by. He rose and went to the door, and then, apparently altering his mind, he returned to the window and watched the figure of his cousin as it moved slowly away into the moonlight. Then he rose again, and, for a long time, the room was empty.

It was empty when Mrs. Benson came in some time later to say good-night to her son on her way to bed. She walked slowly round the table, and pausing at the window gazed from it in idle thought, until she saw the figure of her son advancing with rapid strides toward the house. He looked up at the window.

"Good-night," said she.

"Good-night," said Benson, in a deep voice.

"Where is Wilfred?"

"Oh, he has gone," said Benson.

"Gone?"

"We had a few words; he was wanting money again, and I gave him a piece of my mind. I don't think we shall see him again."

"Poor Wilfred!" sighed Mrs. Benson. "He is always in trouble of some sort. I hope that you were not too hard upon him."

"No more than he deserved," said her son, sternly. "Good-night."

II

The well, which had long ago fallen into disuse, was almost hidden by the thick tangle of undergrowth which ran riot at that corner of the old park. It was partly covered by the shrunken half of a lid, above which a rusty windlass creaked in company with the music of the pines when the wind blew strongly. The full light of the sun never reached it, and the ground surrounding it was moist and green when other parts of the park were gaping with the heat.

Two people walking slowly round the park in the fragrant stillness of a summer evening strayed in the direction of the well.

"No use going through this wilderness, Olive," said Benson, pausing on the outskirts of the pines and eyeing with some disfavour the gloom beyond.

"Best part of the park," said the girl briskly; "you know it's my favourite spot."

"I know you're very fond of sitting on the coping," said the man slowly, "and I wish you wouldn't. One day you will lean back too far and fall in."

"And make the acquaintance of Truth," said Olive lightly. "Come along."

She ran from him and was lost in the shadow of the pines, the bracken crackling beneath her feet as she ran. Her companion followed slowly, and emerging from the gloom saw her poised daintily on the edge of the well with her feet hidden in the rank grass and nettles which surrounded it. She motioned her companion to take a seat by her side, and smiled softly as she felt a strong arm passed about her waist.

"I like this place," said she, breaking a long silence, "it is so dismal—so uncanny. Do you know I wouldn't dare to sit here alone, Jem. I should imagine that all sorts of dreadful things were hidden behind the bushes and trees, waiting to spring out on me. Ugh!"

"You'd better let me take you in," said her companion tenderly; "the well isn't always wholesome, especially in the hot weather.

"Let's make a move."

The girl gave an obstinate little shake, and settled herself more securely on her seat.

"Smoke your cigar in peace," she said quietly. "I am settled here for a quiet talk. Has anything been heard of Wilfred yet?"

"Nothing."

"Quite a dramatic disappearance, isn't it?" she continued. "Another scrape, I suppose, and another letter for you in the same old strain; 'Dear Jem, help me out.'"

Jem Benson blew a cloud of fragrant smoke into the air, and holding his cigar between his teeth brushed away the ash from his coat-sleeves.

"I wonder what he would have done without you," said the girl, pressing his arm affectionately. "Gone under long ago, I suppose. When we are married, Jem, I shall presume upon the relationship to lecture him. He is very wild, but he has his good points, poor fellow."

"I never saw them," said Benson, with startling bitterness. "God knows I never saw them."

"He is nobody's enemy but his own," said the girl, startled by this outburst.

"You don't know much about him," said the other, sharply. "He was not above blackmail; not above ruining the life of a friend to do himself a benefit. A loafer, a cur, and a liar!"

The girl looked up at him soberly but timidly and took his arm without a word, and they both sat silent while evening deepened into night and the beams of the moon, filtering through the branches, surrounded them with a silver network. Her head sank upon his shoulder, till suddenly with a sharp cry she sprang to her feet.

"What was that?" she cried breathlessly.

"What was what?" demanded Benson, springing up and clutching her fast by the arm.

She caught her breath and tried to laugh.

"You're hurting me, Jem."

His hold relaxed.

"What is the matter?" he asked gently.

"What was it startled you?"

"I was startled," she said, slowly, putting her hands on his shoulder. "I suppose the words I used just now are ringing in my ears, but I fancied that somebody behind us whispered '*Jem, help me out.*'"

"Fancy," repeated Benson, and his voice shook; "but these fancies are not good for you. You—are frightened—at the dark and the gloom of these trees. Let me take you back to the house."

"No, I'm not frightened," said the girl, reseating herself. "I should never be really frightened of anything when you were with me, Jem. I'm surprised at myself for being so silly."

The man made no reply but stood, a strong, dark figure, a yard or two from the well, as though waiting for her to join him.

"Come and sit down, sir," cried Olive, patting the brickwork with her small, white hand, "one would think that you did not like your company."

He obeyed slowly and took a seat by her side, drawing so hard at his cigar that the light of it shone upon his fare at every breath. He passed his arm, firm and rigid as steel, behind her, with his hand resting on the brickwork beyond.

"Are you warm enough?" he asked tenderly, as she made a little movement.

"Pretty fair," she shivered; "one oughtn't to be cold at this time of the year, but there's a cold, damp air comes up from the well."

As she spoke a faint splash sounded from the depths below, and for the second time that evening, she sprang from the well with a little cry of dismay.

"What is it now?" he asked in a fearful voice. He stood by her side and gazed at the well, as though half expecting to see the cause of her alarm emerge from it.

"Oh, my bracelet," she cried in distress, "my poor mother's bracelet. I've dropped it down the well."

"Your bracelet!" repeated Benson, dully. "Your bracelet? The diamond one?"

"The one that was my mother's," said Olive. "Oh, we can get it back surely. We must have the water drained off."

"Your bracelet!" repeated Benson, stupidly.

"Jem," said the girl in terrified tones, "dear Jem, what is the matter?"

For the man she loved was standing regarding her with horror. The moon which touched it was not responsible for all the whiteness of the distorted face, and she shrank back in fear to the edge of the well. He saw her fear and by a mighty effort regained his composure and took her hand.

"Poor little girl," he murmured, "you frightened me. I was not looking when you cried, and I thought that you were slipping from my arms, down—down—"

His voice broke, and the girl throwing herself into his arms clung to him convulsively.

"There, there," said Benson, fondly, "don't cry, don't cry."

"To-morrow," said Olive, half-laughing, half-crying, "we will all come round the well with hook and line and fish for it. It will be quite a new sport."

"No, we must try some other way," said Benson. "You shall have it back."

"How?" asked the girl.

"You shall see," said Benson. "To-morrow morning at latest you shall have it back. Till then promise me that you will not mention your loss to anyone. Promise."

"I promise," said Olive, wonderingly. "But why not?"

"It is of great value, for one thing, and— But there—there are many reasons. For one thing it is my duty to get it for you."

"Wouldn't you like to jump down for it?" she asked mischievously. "Listen."

She stooped for a stone and dropped it down.

"Fancy being where that is now," she said, peering into the blackness; "fancy going round and round like a mouse in a pail, clutching at the slimy sides, with the water filling your mouth, and looking up to the little patch of sky above."

"You had better come in," said Benson, very quietly. "You are developing a taste for the morbid and horrible."

The girl turned, and taking his arm walked slowly in the direction of the house; Mrs. Benson, who was sitting in the porch, rose to receive them.

"You shouldn't have kept her out so long," she said chidingly. "Where have you been?"

"Sitting on the well," said Olive, smiling, "discussing our future."

"I don't believe that place is healthy," said Mrs. Benson, emphatically. "I really think it might be filled in, Jem."

"All right," said her son, slowly. "Pity it wasn't filled in long ago."

He took the chair vacated by his mother as she entered the house with Olive, and with his hands hanging limply over the sides sat in deep thought. After a time he rose, and going upstairs to a room which was set apart for sporting requisites selected a sea fishing line and some hooks and stole softly downstairs again. He walked swiftly across the park in the direction of the well, turning before he entered the shadow of the trees to look back at the lighted windows of the house. Then having arranged his line he sat on the edge of the well and cautiously lowered it.

He sat with his lips compressed, occasionally looking about him in a startled fashion, as though he half expected to see something peering at him from the belt of trees. Time after time he lowered his line until at length in pulling it up he heard a little metallic tinkle against the side of the well.

He held his breath then, and forgetting his fears drew the line in inch by inch, so as not to lose its precious burden. His pulse beat rapidly, and his eyes were bright. As the line came slowly in he saw the catch hanging to the hook, and with a steady hand drew the last few feet in. Then he saw that instead of the bracelet he had hooked a bunch of keys.

With a faint cry he shook them from the hook into the water below, and stood breathing heavily. Not a sound broke the stillness of the night. He walked up and down a bit and stretched his great muscles; then he came back to the well and resumed his task.

For an hour or more the line was lowered without result. In his eagerness he forgot his fears, and with eyes bent down the well fished slowly and carefully. Twice the hook became entangled in something, and was with difficulty released. It caught a third time, and all his efforts failed to free it. Then he dropped the line down the well, and with head bent walked toward the house.

He went first to the stables at the rear, and then retiring to his room for some time paced restlessly up and down. Then without removing his clothes he flung himself upon the bed and fell into a troubled sleep.

III

Long before anybody else was astir he arose and stole softly downstairs. The sunlight was stealing in at every crevice, and flashing in long streaks across the darkened rooms. The dining-room into which he looked struck chill and cheerless in the dark yellow light which came through the lowered blinds. He remembered that it had the same appearance when his father lay dead in the house; now, as then, everything seemed ghastly and unreal; the very chairs standing as their occupants had left them the night before seemed to be indulging in some dark communication of ideas.

Slowly and noiselessly he opened the hall door and passed into the fragrant air beyond. The sun was shining on the drenched grass and trees, and a slowly vanishing white mist rolled like smoke about the grounds. For a moment he stood, breathing deeply the sweet air of the morning, and then walked slowly in the direction of the stables.

The rusty creaking of a pump-handle and a spatter of water upon the red-tiled courtyard showed that somebody else was astir, and a few steps farther he beheld a brawny, sandy-haired man gasping wildly under severe self-infliction at the pump.

"Everything ready, George?" he asked quietly.

"Yes, sir," said the man, straightening up suddenly and touching his forehead. "Bob's just finishing the arrangements inside. It's a lovely morning for a dip. The water in that well must be just icy."

"Be as quick as you can," said Benson, impatiently.

"Very good, sir," said George, burnishing his face harshly with a very small towel which had been hanging over the top of the pump. "Hurry up, Bob."

In answer to his summons a man appeared at the door of the stable with a coil of stout rope over his arm and a large metal candlestick in his hand.

"Just to try the air, sir," said George, following his master's glance, "a well gets rather foul sometimes, but if a candle can live down it, a man can."

His master nodded, and the man, hastily pulling up the neck of his shirt and thrusting his arms into his coat, followed him as he led the way slowly to the well.

"Beg pardon, sir," said George, drawing up to his side, "but you are not looking over and above well this morning. If you'll let me go down I'd enjoy the bath."

"No, no," said Benson, peremptorily.

"You ain't fit to go down, sir," persisted his follower. "I've never seen you look so before. Now if—"

"Mind your business," said his master curtly.

George became silent and the three walked with swinging strides through the long wet grass to the well. Bob flung the rope on the ground and at a sign from his master handed him the candlestick.

"Here's the line for it, sir," said Bob, fumbling in his pockets.

Benson took it from him and slowly tied it to the candlestick. Then he placed it on the edge of the well, and striking a match, lit the candle and began slowly to lower it.

"Hold hard, sir," said George, quickly, laying his hand on his arm, "you must tilt it or the string'll burn through."

Even as he spoke the string parted and the candlestick fell into the water below.

Benson swore quietly.

"I'll soon get another," said George, starting up.

"Never mind, the well's all right," said Benson.

"It won't take a moment, sir," said the other over his shoulder.

"Are you master here, or am I?" said Benson hoarsely.

George came back slowly, a glance at his master's face stopping the protest upon his tongue, and he stood by watching him sulkily as he sat on the well and removed his outer garments. Both men watched him curiously, as having completed his preparations he stood grim and silent with his hands by his sides.

"I wish you'd let me go, sir," said George, plucking up courage to address him. "You ain't fit to go, you've got a chill or something. I shouldn't wonder it's the typhoid. They've got it in the village bad."

For a moment Benson looked at him angrily, then his gaze softened. "Not this time, George," he said, quietly. He took the looped end of the rope and placed it under his arms, and sitting down threw one leg over the side of the well.

"How are you going about it, sir?" queried George, laying hold of the rope and signing to Bob to do the same.

"I'll call out when I reach the water," said Benson; "then pay out three yards more quickly so that I can get to the bottom."

"Very good, sir," answered both.

Their master threw the other leg over the coping and sat motionless. His back was turned toward the men as he sat with head bent, looking down the shaft. He sat for so long that George became uneasy.

"All right, sir?" he inquired.

"Yes," said Benson, slowly. "If I tug at the rope, George, pull up at once. Lower away."

The rope passed steadily through their hands until a hollow cry from the darkness below and a faint splashing warned them that he had reached the water. They gave him three yards more and stood with relaxed grasp and strained ears, waiting.

"He's gone under," said Bob in a low voice.

The other nodded, and moistening his huge palms took a firmer grip of the rope.

Fully a minute passed, and the men began to exchange uneasy glances. Then a sudden tremendous jerk followed by a series of feebler ones nearly tore the rope from their grasp.

"Pull!" shouted George, placing one foot on the side and hauling desperately. "Pull! pull! He's stuck fast; he's not coming; P—U—LL!"

In response to their terrific exertions the rope came slowly in, inch by inch, until at length a violent splashing was heard, and at the same moment a scream of unutterable horror came echoing up the shaft.

"What a weight he is!" panted Bob. "He's stuck fast or something. Keep still, sir; for heaven's sake, keep still."

For the taut rope was being jerked violently by the struggles of the weight at the end of it. Both men with grunts and sighs hauled it in foot by foot.

"All right, sir," cried George, cheerfully.

He had one foot against the well, and was pulling manfully; the burden was nearing the top. A long pull and a strong pull, and the face of a dead man with mud in the eyes and nostrils came peering over the edge. Behind it was the ghastly face of his master; but this he saw too late, for with a great cry he let go his hold of the rope and stepped back. The suddenness overthrew his assistant, and the rope tore through his hands. There was a frightful splash.

"You fool!" stammered Bob, and ran to the well helplessly.

"Run!" cried George. "Run for another line."

He bent over the coping and called eagerly down as his assistant sped back to the stables shouting wildly. His voice re-echoed down the shaft, but all else was silence.

OVER AN ABSINTHE BOTTLE

W. C. Morrow

Arthur Kimberlin, a young man of very high spirit, found himself a total stranger in San Francisco one rainy evening, at a time when his heart was breaking; for his hunger was of that most poignant kind in which physical suffering is forced to the highest point without impairment of the mental functions. There remained in his possession not a thing that he might have pawned for a morsel to eat; and even as it was, he had stripped his body of all articles of clothing except those which a remaining sense of decency compelled him to retain. Hence it was that cold assailed him and conspired with hunger to complete his misery. Having been brought into the world and reared a gentleman, he lacked the courage to beg and the skill to steal. Had not an extraordinary thing occurred to him, he either would have drowned himself in the bay within twenty-four hours or died of pneumonia in the street. He had been seventy hours without food, and his mental desperation had driven him far in its race with his physical needs to consume the strength within him; so that now, pale, weak, and tottering, he took what comfort he could find in the savory odors which came steaming up from the basement kitchens of the restaurants in Market Street, caring more to gain them than to avoid the rain. His teeth chattered; he shambled, stooped, and gasped. He was too desperate to curse his fate—he could only long for food. He could not reason; he could not understand that ten thousand hands might gladly have fed him; he could think only of the hunger which consumed him, and of food that could give him warmth and happiness.

When he had arrived at Mason Street, he saw a restaurant a little way up that thoroughfare, and for that he headed, crossing the street diagonally. He stopped before the window and ogled the steaks, thick and lined with fat; big oysters lying on ice; slices of ham as large as his hat; whole roasted chickens, brown and juicy. He ground his teeth, groaned, and staggered on.

A few steps beyond was a drinking-saloon, which had a private door at one side, with the words "Family Entrance" painted thereon. In the recess of the door (which was closed) stood a man. In spite of his agony, Kimberlin saw something in the man's face that appalled and fascinated him. Night was on and the light in the vicinity was dim; but it was apparent that the stranger had an appearance of whose character he himself must have been ignorant. Perhaps it was the unspeakable anguish of it that struck through Kimberlin's sympathies. The young man came to an uncertain halt and stared at the stranger. At first he was unseen, for the stranger looked straight out into the street with singular fixity, and the death-like pallor of his face added a weirdness to the immobility of his gaze. Then he took notice of the young man.

"Ah," he said, slowly and with peculiar distinctness, "the rain has caught you, too, without overcoat or umbrella! Stand in this doorway— there is room for two."

The voice was not unkind, though it had an alarming hardness. It was the first word that had been addressed to the sufferer since hunger had seized him, and to be spoken to at all, and his comfort regarded in the slightest way, gave him cheer. He entered the embrasure and stood beside the stranger, who at once relapsed into his fixed gaze at nothing across the street. But presently the stranger stirred himself again.

"It may rain a long time," said he; "I am cold, and I observe that you tremble. Let us step inside and get a drink."

He opened the door and Kimberlin followed, hope beginning to lay a warm hand upon his heart. The pale stranger led the way into one of the little private booths with which the place was furnished. Before sitting down he put his hand into his pocket and drew forth a roll of bank-bills.

"You are younger than I," he said; "won't you go to the bar and buy a bottle of absinthe, and bring a pitcher of water and some glasses? I don't like for the waiters to come around. Here is a twenty-dollar bill."

Kimberlin took the bill and stared down through the corridor towards the bar. He clutched the money tightly in his palm; it felt warm and comfortable, and sent a delicious thrill through his arm. How many glorious hot meals did that represent? He clutched it tighter and hesitated. He thought he smelled a broiled steak, with fat little mushrooms and melted butter in the steaming dish. He stopped and looked back towards the door of the booth. He saw that the stranger had closed it. He could pass it, slip out the door, and buy something to eat. He turned and started, but the coward in him (there are other names for this) tripped his resolution; so he went straight to the bar and made the purchase. This was so unusual that the man who served him looked sharply at him.

"Ain't goin' to drink all o' that, are you?" he asked.

"I have friends in the box," replied Kimberlin, "and we want to drink quietly and without interruption. We are in Number 7."

"Oh, beg pardon. That's all right," said the man.

Kimberlin's step was very much stronger and steadier as he returned with the liquor. He opened the door of the booth. The stranger sat at the side of the little table, staring at the opposite wall just as he had stared across the street. He wore a wide-brimmed, slouch hat, drawn well down. It was only after Kimberlin had set the bottle, pitcher, and glasses on the table, and seated himself opposite the stranger and within his range of vision, that the pale man noticed him.

"Oh! you have brought it? How kind of you! Now please lock the door." Kimberlin had slipped the change into his pocket, and was in the act of bringing it out when the stranger said—

"Keep the change. You will need it, for I am going to get it back in a way that may interest you. First, let us drink, and then I will explain."

The pale man mixed two drinks of absinthe and water, and the two drank. Kimberlin, unsophisticated, had never tasted the liquor before, and he found it harsh and offensive; but no sooner had it reached his stomach than it began to warm him, and sent the most delicious thrill through his frame.

"It will do us good," said the stranger; "presently we shall have more. Meanwhile, do you know how to throw dice?"

Kimberlin weakly confessed that he did not.

"I thought not. Well, please go to the bar and bring a dice-box. I would ring for it, but I don't want the waiters to be coming in."

Kimberlin fetched the box, again locked the door, and the game began. It was not one of the simple old games, but had complications, in which judgment, as well as chance, played a part. After a game or two without stakes, the stranger said—

"You now seem to understand it. Very well—I will show you that you do not. We will now throw for a dollar a game, and in that way I shall win the money that you received in change. Otherwise I should be robbing you, and I imagine you cannot afford to lose. I mean no offence. I am a plain-spoken man, but I believe in honesty before politeness. I merely want a little diversion, and you are so kind-natured that I am sure you will not object."

"On the contrary," replied Kimberlin, "I shall enjoy it."

"Very well; but let us have another drink before we start. I believe I am growing colder." They drank again, and this time the starving man took his liquor with relish—at least, it was something in his stomach, and it warmed and delighted him.

The stake was a dollar a side. Kimberlin won. The pale stranger smiled grimly, and opened another game. Again Kimberlin won. Then the stranger pushed back his hat and fixed that still gaze upon his opponent, smiling yet. With this full view of the pale stranger's face, Kimberlin was more appalled than ever. He had begun to acquire a certain self-possession and ease, and his marvelling at the singular character of the adventure had begun to weaken, when this new incident threw him back into confusion. It was the extraordinary expression of the stranger's face that alarmed him. Never upon the face of a living being had he seen a pallor so death-like and chilling. The face was more than pale; it was white. Kimberlin's observing faculty had been sharpened by the absinthe, and, after having detected the stranger in an absentminded effort two or three times to stroke a beard which had no existence, he reflected that some of the whiteness of the face might be due to the recent removal of a full beard. Besides the pallor, there were deep and sharp lines upon the face, which the electric light brought out very distinctly. With the exception of the steady glance of the eyes and an occasional hard smile, that seemed out of place on such a face, the expression was that of stone artistically cut. The eyes were black, but of heavy expression; the lower lip was purple; the hands were fine, white, and thin, and dark veins bulged out upon them. The stranger pulled down his hat.

"You are lucky," he said. "Suppose we try another drink. There is nothing like absinthe to sharpen one's wits, and I see that you and I are going to have a delightful game."

After the drink the game proceeded. Kimberlin won from the very first, rarely losing a game. He became greatly excited. His eyes shone; color came to his cheeks. The stranger, having exhausted the roll of bills which he first produced, drew forth another, much larger and of higher denominations. There were several thousand dollars in the roll. At Kimberlin's right hand were his winnings—something like two hundred dollars. The stakes were raised, and the game went rapidly on. Another drink was taken. Then fortune turned the stranger's way, and he won easily. It went back to Kimberlin, for he was now playing with all the judgment and skill he could command. Once only did it occur to him to wonder what he should do with the money if he should quit winner; but a sense of honor decided him that it would belong to the stranger.

By this time the absinthe had so sharpened Kimberlin's faculties that, the temporary satisfaction which it had brought to his hunger having passed, his physical suffering returned with increased aggressiveness. Could he not order a supper with his earnings? No; that was out of the question, and the stranger said nothing about eating. Kimberlin continued to play, while the manifestations of hunger took the form of sharp pains, which darted through him viciously, causing him to writhe and grind his teeth. The stranger paid no attention, for he was now wholly absorbed in the game. He seemed puzzled and disconcerted. He played with great care, studying each throw minutely. No conversation passed between them now. They drank occasionally, the dice continued to rattle, the money kept piling up in Kimberlin's hand.

The pale young man began to behave strangely. At times he would start and throw back his head, as though he were listening. For a moment his eyes would sharpen and flash, and then sink into heaviness again. More than once Kimberlin, who had now begun to suspect that his antagonist was some kind of monster, saw a frightfully ghastly expression sweep over his face, and his features would become fixed for a very short time in a peculiar grimace. It was noticeable, however, that he was steadily sinking deeper and deeper into a condition of apathy. Occasionally he would raise his eyes to Kimberlin's face after the young man had made an astonishingly lucky throw, and keep them fixed there with a steadiness that made the young man quail.

The stranger produced another roll of bills when the second was gone, and this had a value many times as great as the others together. The stakes were raised to a thousand dollars a game, and still Kimberlin won. At last the time came when the stranger braced himself for a final effort. With speech somewhat thick, but very deliberate and quiet, he said—

"You have won seventy-four thousand dollars, which is exactly the amount I have remaining. We have been playing for several hours. I am tired and I suppose you are. Let us finish the game. Each will now stake his all and throw a final game for it."

Without hesitation, Kimberlin agreed. The bills made a considerable pile on the table. Kimberlin threw, and the box held but one combination that could possibly beat him, this combination might be thrown once in ten thousand times. The starving man's heart beat violently as the stranger picked up the box with exasperating deliberation. It was a long time before he threw. He made his combinations and ended by defeating his opponent. He sat looking at the dice a long time, and then slowly leaned back in his chair, settled himself comfortably, raised his eyes to Kimberlin's, and fixed that unearthly stare upon him. He said not a word; his face contained not a trace of emotion or intelligence. He simply looked. One cannot keep one's eyes open very long without winking, but the stranger did. He sat so motionless that Kimberlin began to be tortured.

"I will go now," he said to the stranger—said that when he had not a cent and was starving. The stranger made no reply, but did not relax his gaze; and under the gaze the young man shrank back in his own chair, terrified. He became aware that two men were cautiously talking in the adjoining booth. As there was now a deathly silence of his own. He listened, and this is what he heard:

"Yes; he was seen to turn into this street about three hours ago."

"And he had shaved?"

"He must have done so; and to remove a full beard would naturally make a great change in a man."

"But it may not have been he."

"True enough; but this extreme pallor attracted attention. You know that he has been troubled with heart-disease lately, and it has affected him seriously."

"Yes, but his old skill remains. Why, this is the most daring bank-robbery we ever had here. A hundred and forty-eight thousand dollars—think of it! How long has it been since he was let out of Joliet?"

"Eight years. In that time he has grown a beard, and lived by dice-throwing with men who thought they could detect him if he should swindle them; but that is impossible. No human being can come winner out of a game with him. He is evidently not here; let us look farther."

Then the two men clinked glasses and passed out.

The dice-players—the pale one and the starving one—sat gazing at each other, with a hundred and forty-eight thousand dollars piled up between them. The winner made no move to take in the money; he merely sat and stared at Kimberlin, wholly unmoved by the conversation in the adjoining room. His imperturbability was amazing, his absolute stillness terrifying.

Kimberlin began to shake with an ague. The cold, steady gaze of the stranger sent ice into his marrow. Unable to bear longer this unwavering look, Kimberlin moved to one side, and then he was amazed to discover that the eyes of the pale man, instead of following him, remained fixed upon the spot where he had sat, or, rather, upon the wall behind it. A great dread beset the young man. He feared to make the slightest sound. Voices of men in the barroom were audible, and the sufferer imagined that he heard others whispering and tiptoeing in the passage outside his booth. He poured out some absinthe, watching his strange companion all the while, and drank alone and unnoticed. He took a heavy drink, and it had a peculiar effect upon him: he felt his heart bounding with an alarming force and rapidity, and breathing was difficult. Still his hunger remained, and that and the absinthe gave him an idea that the gastric acids were destroying him by digesting his stomach. He leaned forward and whispered to the stranger, but was given no attention. One of the man's hands lay upon the table; Kimberlin placed his upon it, and then drew back in terror—the hand was as cold as a stone.

The money must not lie there exposed. Kimberlin arranged it into neat parcels, looking furtively every moment at his immovable companion, *and in mortal fear that he would stir!* Then he sat back and waited. A deadly fascination impelled him to move back into his former position, so as to bring his face directly before the gaze of the stranger. And so the two sat and stared at each other.

Kimberlin felt his breath coming heavier and his heart-beats growing weaker, but these conditions gave him comfort by reducing his anxiety and softening the pangs of hunger. He was growing more and more comfortable and yawned. If he had dared he might have gone to sleep.

Suddenly a fierce light flooded his vision and sent him with a bound to his feet. Had he been struck upon the head or stabbed to the heart? No; he was sound and alive. The pale stranger still sat there staring at nothing and immovable; but Kimberlin was no longer afraid of him. On the contrary, an extraordinary buoyancy of spirit and elasticity of body made him feel reckless and daring. His former timidity and scruples vanished, and he felt equal to any adventure. Without hesitation he gathered up the money and bestowed it in his several pockets.

"I am a fool to starve," he said to himself, "with all this money ready to my hand."

As cautiously as a thief he unlocked the door, stepped out, reclosed it, and boldly and with head erect stalked out upon the street. Much to his astonishment, he found the city in the bustle of the early evening, yet the sky was clear. It was evident to him that he had not been in the saloon as long as he had supposed. He walked along the street with the utmost concern of the dangers that beset him, and laughed softly but gleefully. Would he not eat now—ah, would he not? Why, he could buy a dozen restaurants! Not only that, but he would hunt the city up and down for hungry men and feed them with the fattest steaks, the juiciest roasts, and the biggest oysters that the town could supply. As for himself, he must eat first, after that he would set up a great establishment for feeding other hungry mortals without charge. Yes, he would eat first; if he pleased, he would eat till he should burst. In what single place could he find sufficient to satisfy his hunger? Could he live sufficiently long to have an ox killed and roasted whole for his supper? Besides an ox he would order two dozen broiled chickens, fifty dozen oysters, a dozen crabs, ten dozen eggs, ten hams, eight young pigs, twenty wild ducks, fifteen fish of four different kinds, eight salads, four dozen bottles each of claret, burgundy, and champagne; for pastry, eight plum-puddings, and for dessert, bushels of nuts, ices, and confections. It would require time to prepare such a meal, and if he could only live until it could be made ready it would be infinitely better than to spoil his appetite with a dozen or two meals of ordinary size. He thought he could live that long, for he felt amazingly strong and bright. Never in his life before had he walked with so great ease and lightness; his feet hardly touched the ground—he ran and leaped. It did him good to tantalize his hunger, for that would make his relish of the feast all the keener. Oh, but how they would stare when he would give his order, and how comically they would hang back, and how amazed they would be when he would throw a few thousands of dollars on the counter and tell them to take their money out of it and keep the change! Really, it was worth while to be so hungry as that, for then eating became an unspeakable luxury. And one must not be in too great a hurry to eat when one is so hungry—that is beastly. How much of the joy of living do rich people miss from eating before they are hungry—before they have gone three days and nights without food! And how manly it is, and how great self-control it shows, to dally with starvation when one has a dazzling fortune in one's pocket and every restaurant has an open door! To be hungry without money—that is despair; to be starving with a bursting pocket—that is sublime! Surely the one true heaven is that in which one famishes in the presence of abundant food, which he might have for the taking, and then a gorged stomach and a long sleep.

The starving wretch, speculating thus, still kept from food. He felt himself growing in stature, and the people whom he met became pygmies. The streets widened, the stars became suns and dimmed the electric lights, and the most intoxicating odors and the sweetest music filled the air. Shouting, laughing, and singing, Kimberlin joined in a great chorus that swept over the city, and then—

The two detectives who had traced the famous bank-robber to the saloon in Mason Street, where Kimberlin had encountered the stranger of the pallid face, left the saloon; but, unable to pursue the trail farther, had finally returned. They found the door of booth No. 7 locked. After rapping and calling and receiving no answer, they burst open the door, and there they saw two men—one of middle age and the other very young—sitting perfectly still, and in the strangest manner imaginable staring at each other across the table. Between them was a great pile of money arranged neatly in parcels. Near at hand were an empty absinthe bottle, a water-pitcher, glasses, and a dice-box, with the dice lying before the elder man as he had thrown them last. One of the detectives covered the elder man with a revolver and commanded—

"Throw up your hands!"

But the dice-thrower paid no attention. The detectives exchanged startled glances. They looked closer into the faces of the two men, and then they discovered that both were dead.

A Ghost's Revenge

Lettice Galbraith

It was a dismal evening. Heavy clouds covered the sky. The air was full of a raw dampness, which hung like a veil over the flat marshy district through which the London train was winding its way, like some huge fiery serpent, now pausing in its sinuous course, now darting forward with a writhe and a shriek, to vanish under a lurid cloud of steam.

"Mallowby," shouted the hoarse voice of the porter, "Mallowby." The door of a first-class smoking carriage was reluctantly opened, and a solitary passenger alighted.

"What a beast of a night!" he muttered, hastily buttoning up his fur-lined overcoat, "and what a beast of a place!" peering discontentedly across the low white railing at the monotonous stretch of snow-powdered fallow and pasture. "What on earth has induced Forster to bury himself in such a desolate hole?"

"Any luggage, sir? Two portmanteaus and a gun-case—very good, sir. Where for—the Rectory? The cart is just outside, through the gate on the left."

With another malediction on the rawness of the atmosphere, the passenger from town picked his way across the sloppy platform and climbed into the dogcart which was in waiting for him. He was cold, hungry, and, if the truth must be told, considerably out of temper; and, as he splashed down the mile of muddy road which lay between the station and the village, Gerald Harrison was half inclined to repent his promise of spending a couple of days with his old college chum on his way to Scotland.

A hearty welcome, a sherry and bitters, a roaring fire, and a hot bath went a long way towards dispelling his ill-humour. The Reverend Richard Forster, now acting as *locum tenens* for the absent rector of Mallowby, thoroughly understood the art of making his guests comfortable.

"You will not have too much time, old fellow," he said, when he had conducted Harrison to his room. "I am sorry to hurry you, but dinner is at half-past seven, and I cannot well put it back because I have asked another man. His name is Granville. He has lately come to the old Hall, and we are going to shoot over one of his farms to-morrow."

Twenty minutes later, when Gerald (with temperature and temper alike restored to their normal condition) descended to the library, he found his host in earnest confabulation with the visitor—a slight dark man, with an anxious, rather worried expression, and a trick of glancing nervously over his shoulder.

"I give you my word, Forster," he was saying, "that it is going on worse than ever. I can't get a servant to sleep in the front of the house, and if I were not ashamed of acknowledging myself a fool, I would cut the place to-morrow and go back to town."

The opening of the door put an end to the discussion. Forster changed the subject by introducing his guests, and as dinner was almost immediately announced, the conversation fell into general channels—such as the Irish question, pheasant-rearing, and the chances of an open season. It struck Harrison that Mr. Granville had all the appearance of a man who has received some severe mental shock. Though he talked intelligently and even well, it was evident that his attention was never wholly given to the subject in hand. He seemed to be constantly listening for some expected sound, and once, when footsteps were audible on the gravel without, he started violently and turned as white as a sheet.

"It is only Kenwell bringing back the keys of the church," remarked Forster. "He has been taking the choir practice for me this evening. There is the bell."

A servant answered the door, and the footsteps died away again, accompanied by the distant clash of the iron gate. Granville sank back in his chair with a long breath of relief. He had let his cigar out, and now looked round for a light. Harrison offered him a match, and, as the elder man took it, he could feel that his hand was cold and shaking.

The evening passed in pleasant desultory chat. At eleven o'clock Granville rose. "Will you order my cart?" he said. Then, in answer to his host's demur, he answered nervously, "Don't tempt me to stay, Forster; it only makes matters worse. Yes, I know it is quite early and all that; but they will take ten minutes to put the horse in, and," with a ghastly attempt at a smile, "I am like Cinderella, I must be indoors before midnight. You will come up early to-morrow, and of course you both lunch with me. I would ask you to dine as well, only—only I am not good company in my own house now."

Forster's hand was on the bell. He paused, and looked keenly into his friend's face.

"Don't go back, Granville," he said, earnestly. "Let me tell your man that you will stay the night here. I can easily put you up."

"No, thanks; no," with the nervous haste of one who fears that his resolution may fail him, "I cannot do that. After all I have said, I dare not show the white feather to the servants. They would think me a fool; but, my God! they don't hear it as I do. Tell them to bring the cart round, Forster. For pity's sake, man, don't waste time! It is ten minutes past eleven already."

The order was given. As the minutes wore on, Granville became increasingly uneasy. He could not restrain his restless anxiety to be off, and it was a relief to every one when the grating of wheels outside announced that the trap was in readiness. Forster accompanied him to the door, whither Harrison presently followed.

"It is not much of a night," he commented, peering out into the chill darkness. "Your friend will have a coolish drive."

Forster was standing on the step.

"Hush!" he said, holding up his hand. "Listen! He is galloping."

From the old grey tower on their left chimed the half-hour, and, as the notes died away, they could hear the receding rattle of a cart being driven at a furious pace along the road below.

"He must be cracked to drive at that rate in the dark," cried Gerald, as the clatter of hoofs grew fainter and finally died away. "It will be more by luck than management if he doesn't upset at the first corner. What is the matter with him, Dick—does he drink, or is he off his head?"

"Neither at present. He thinks his house is haunted, and it is getting on his nerves."

"Oh, he must be cracked, then," with easy decision.

"No one but a lunatic believes in ghosts in these days. Accept the possibilities of terrestrial elementaries and left-hand magic if you like; but the common or garden ghost, never."

"There is something queer about the old Hall, though," persisted Forster. "I do not believe that any consideration you could offer would induce a Mallowby man to sleep there alone. The place has a bad name. It stood empty for years before Granville bought it. He spent no end of money in repairs and furniture too, which makes it additionally hard on him to be driven out by—"

"A ghost," concluded Harrison, with a shout of laughter. "My dear Dick, it is too absurd. Let us exorcise the place. I will back my six-shooter at thirty feet against any combination of goblins and blue fire. We will arrange a match to-morrow. Fifty pounds a side, to be paid in material currency only. Come, admit now that the thing is a huge joke."

"It is a good deal more like death to Granville," returned Forster, seriously. "His nerves are regularly gone to pieces. He is not like the same fellow who came down in the autumn."

"Have the ghosts been trying to evict him ever since?"

"Sounds weak, I dare say," Dick answered, "but I am inclined to believe, Gerald, that there is more in it than meets the eye. Last October Granville was every bit as sceptical as you are. If he heard anything he treated it with contempt. When the servants complained of mysterious noises, he laughed them to scorn. You saw for yourself that he does not laugh at it now. He told me this evening that these—these—manifestations are of nightly occurrence. I am afraid it is taking serious effect upon his health. I wish I had kept him here to-night."

"Oh, he will be all right," said Harrison, lightly. "Funk is a deuced unpleasant complaint, but it don't often kill. Twelve o'clock; I think I'll be turning in. This time to-morrow, I suppose, we shall be wishing each other a happy new year."

But the glad new year was destined to be ushered in by no hearty shaking of hands, no joyous congratulations at Mallowby Rectory. In the grey dawn of the December morning Harrison was awakened by the flashing of a candle before his eyes. Forster was standing beside the bed, with a pale and horror-stricken face.

"Gerald," he said hurriedly, "will you get up at once? I want you to come with me to the Hall. Something terrible has happened. Poor Granville is dead."

"Dead!" repeated the other blankly, "dead! Why, he only left here at eleven."

"I know that. Seven hours ago he was here, only seven hours ago, and now they are carrying his body up from the pond where it was found. Why did I not keep him?" he cried, pacing the room in deep agitation. "Why did I let him go back to that accursed house? I knew his mind was unhinged by what he had heard there. Poor fellow! poor Granville! and now it is too late."

Harrison was already out of bed.

"I will be downstairs in five minutes," he said. "Of course, I know no particulars, but has any one thought of sending for a doctor?"

Forster caught eagerly at the implied hope.

"Some one shall go for Mr. Tilling at once," he said, hurrying out of the room.

It was a relief to be able to do something, but long before the surgeon arrived they knew that his services would be useless. Death had sealed the master of Ravenshill for his own. The cold and rigid limbs refused to respond to the revivifying influences of hot blankets and artificial respiration.

Harrison was of opinion, as he assisted in his friend's frantic endeavours to restore some semblance of life, that poor Granville had been dead for several hours.

It was a painful task. In vain Forster tried to close the dull, lack-lustre eyes, fixed in a wide stare of indescribable horror. The tense features would not relax. Never had human being passed away from life leaving behind him so terrible an impression of fear. At seven o'clock the surgeon for whom Forster had sent appeared on the scene. One glance at the body was sufficient for him.

"He's dead," said the plain-spoken country practitioner. "Dead as a door-nail. How did it happen?"

Ah! how indeed? That was a mystery. A secret known only to the dead man and to those unspeakable powers who work behind the veil.

In the early morning of the last day of the year the household at the Hall had been startled from their slumbers by a wild, agonised cry, followed by shriek upon shriek of demoniacal laughter. The horrible sounds lasted only for a minute. Before the terrified servants were fairly aroused and crow ding together into the corridor, to learn the meaning of this strange alarm, the house was wrapped in its customary silence. For a few moments they had been too scared to do more than wonder at their master remaining undisturbed; then some one, bolder than the rest, suggested that it would be as well to waken him. They knocked at his door and received no answer. They called, but no voice replied. At last the butler ventured into the room. It was empty. The night lamp, which Granville had lately used, was burning brightly, the fire was nearly out. The bed had not been occupied. Thoroughly alarmed now, a search party was formed, and, armed with lights and a brace of revolvers, the men descended to the ground floor. In the library the lamp was also burning. The odour of tobacco still hung in the air; a few embers glowed in the grate; the spirit decanters and an empty soda-water bottle lay on the table beside an open book. There was no trace of any disturbance, and there was no sign of Granville.

The servants looked at each other in silence. No one dared to put into words the fear that lay chill at his heart. Suddenly the butler uttered an exclamation. His eyes had fallen on one of the windows. The long curtains were swaying gently backward and forward in the current of cold air from without.

The shutters were thrown back, and the casement stood wide open. They crowded round. "Steady, keep back a bit," protested one man, more astute than his fellows, "there is snow enough to hold footmarks. It's a pity to tread it about till we've got a lantern and struck the trail."

In a few minutes a covered light had been procured, and the threshold of the window was examined. There could be no doubt as to the way in which Granville had quitted the room. Straight from the sill the footprints were distinctly traced in the light snow. Along the path they tracked the marks, round the corner of the house, across the lawn to the edge of the pond. And there, beneath the willows, half-hidden by the drooping frost-browned ferns, they found the body of their master, still in evening dress, with clenched fingers, and features transfixed in an expression of ghastly dread.

The quiet little village was shaken to its core. All day long the people gathered in knots to discuss the awful tragedy which had been enacted in their midst. Horror was in the air. Old superstition reasserted its sway with renewed strength. Old stories were repeated with bated breath; for once again the curse of the Deverels had fallen, and the truth of the half-forgotten legend was triumphantly vindicated.

By nightfall every human being had quitted the precincts of the fateful Hall. The scared domestics absolutely refused to remain on the premises, and the big house was deserted, save for the silent form lying so still beneath the white sheet on one of the sofas in the library, in which room the body of Philip Granville had been laid to await the coroner's inquest.

To Forster this desertion of the helpless corpse seemed terrible. He would have spent the night in watching beside the poor fellow who had so lately been his guest, and was only dissuaded from his purpose by the earnest solicitations of his churchwarden, a stalwart farmer, on whose grey head seventy odd years sat lighter than most men's fifty.

"Parson," said the old man, solemnly, "theer's noa good a flyin' in the faace o' Providence. Noa body thinks as you're a coward, but what sort o' use be theer in flingin' good loives a'ter bad uns? Yon poor lad tried it, and see how they've served him. Thirty year back Lord Broadborough's agent died in saame way. My feyther used to tell how, when he were a little lad, one of the Dawbenys caam doon hissen' and boasted as how he'd better the Deverels. It was i' the summer toime, and all went well enow. But as soon as winter caame on, 'they' were at work ag'in, and t' ould squoire, he began to grow graave and stern-like. He would na gi' in, till, on New Year's Eve, the house were fetched up by a fearful cry, and next mornin' they found his body in the pond theer, with a look on t' faace as, God forbid, should iver be sean on yours or rnoine. Mony an' mony a good mon has met that death, sin' the noight that Katharine Deverel stood in yon winder and cursed the mon who had robbed her of her husband's naame, an' theer lad of his lawful inheritance. 'You hev ta'an it by fraud,' she croid; 'but the Lord will avenge me. Noa good shall it bring thee. You shall neyther live in it yoursen, nor shall another receive it at your hands. Though I lose my immortal soul,' she says, 'I'll hev revenge. You may tak' my choild's birthright, you may slur ma fair naame, but noa mon—be he young or auld, good or evil, so that he does na' bear th' naame o' Deverel—shall live to see a new year dawn wi'in these walls. I'll die on Deverel land,' says she; 'and he who braves ma curse shall die even as I hev died.' Then she called on the God of the feytherless to hear her words and turned awa', and next mornin' they found her body stiff an' stark in yonder pond, with the dead baby still clasped in her arms. You'll bear in moind, sir, what the Lord did to the mon who built up the walls o' Jericho. It's His will, an' you bein' a parson, should knaw better than to goa agin' Him. What harm can taake von poor bit o' clay now? But you hev a wark to do i' the warld, and you ain't got no reet to chuck you loife a'ter his'n."

"Mr. Dawson is right, Dick," urged Harrison; "you can't do the poor fellow any good. Your nerves are shaken, and I am free to confess, ghost or no ghost, to spend the night in that dismal house with a dead man is more than I should care about."

Very unwillingly Forster at last agreed to yield.

Three days later the local jury brought in a verdict of "Died by the visitation of God," and once again the spirit of Katharine Deverel had triumphed and the home of her ancestors stood empty.

Five years had come and gone, bringing with them many changes. Dick Forster, now Bishop of Honduras, was doing good work for God and man in his far-off colonial diocese. His place in Harrison's daily life had been filled by another friend of his schoolboy days, who was also shortly to become his brother-in-law. Jack Chamberlayne was a handsome, genial young fellow, blessed with a fine constitution, a sweet temper, and a very considerable fortune, and the match between his favourite sister and his special chum was a source of unmixed satisfaction to Gerald. The two men were constantly together until a matter of business obliged Harrison to visit the South of Europe. The transaction occupied him for some months, and it was not till the end of December that he found himself once more on English soil. He reached Dover at noon on the last day of the year, and went straight to the "Lord Warden." A packet of letters was awaiting him. They had been forwarded from San Carrémo after his departure, and among them was an envelope addressed in Chamberlayne's characteristic handwriting.

"Dear old boy," ran the letter, "what do you mean by spending Christmas in a dirty Italian village, instead of returning to the bosom of your family like a respectable Englishman? I don't believe a word about the vineyards. Tell your agent to go to the devil, and come to us for the new year, or neither Elaine nor I will have anything more to do with you. The Hunt Ball is on the 5th, the Cardwell's on the following evening. On the 7th Mrs. Verelst is giving some theatricals in which we are going to distinguish ourselves, and there are three or four other minor events which you ought not to miss. Also I want your valuable advice as to the wisdom of buying a place in Creamshire. I only heard of it last week, and have already made up my mind to purchase, so your counsel must tend in that direction if you wish me to profit by it. It is a jolly old house, with capital stabling, and nice gardens. There is a ripping tennis-lawn (room for two courts, if I fill up a pond at the end), and a lot of old oak indoors. I forgot to say the house is furnished. It is in the best part of the Broadborough country, and within reach of the outside meets of Lord Cremorne's and the Turton. Plenty of shooting, and the whole thing going for a mere song. I believe there is even a family ghost thrown in. I am running down on Friday for a week to see how I like it; but of course you will put up at my place as you come through town whether I am there or not—"

Harrison waited to hear no more. In a moment the letter was crushed into his pocket, and he was out in the street, and, hurrying to the nearest telegraph-office, without a second's delay he wrote the message and handed it in to the clerk—

Chamberlayne, 112 Piccadilly
    On no account go to Ravenshill Hall till you have seen me. Shall be in town this afternoon and will explain.
                                                —GERALD

Then he hastened back to the hotel and ordered some luncheon. While he was eating he looked out the trains for town. The next was due in twenty minutes. His portmanteaus had not been unstrapped. Harrison sent for a cab, paid his bill, and in less than an hour was well on his way to London. From the moment of reading Chamberlayne's description of his projected purchase, he had decided on the course he must pursue. Though the name of the place was not mentioned he knew, by a sudden swift intuition, that it was Ravenshill Hall. Back to his mind, with the freshness of yesterday, swept the memory of that terrible night five years ago, and he shuddered as he recalled the words of the old farmer.

"No man—be he young or old, good or evil, so that he does not bear the name of Deverel—shall live to see the new year break within these walls. I will die on Deverel land, and he who braves my curse shall die even as I have died."

"Many and many a good man has met that death since." Was another victim destined to be added to the long roll-call of that terrible vengeance, and that victim his old playmate, his friend, his almost brother? No, thank God; there was yet time to avert the stroke of fate. Jack must have received his wire by now. He would be waiting for the promised explanation. The slow hours wore on; the train rattled and ground its way through the wintry landscape. The sky was leaden and dull. On the horizon lay dense masses of clouds, black and heavy with snow. By the time they ran into Charing Cross, large flakes were floating lazily down to join their crushed and mud-stained comrades on the dirty pavement. Evidently there had been a considerable fall earlier in the day, for the roofs down the Strand were gleaming white, and great heaps of snow had been scraped up from the roadway and piled behind the pillars of the station gates. Harrison got his luggage on to a hansom and drove straight to his friend's chambers. As he glanced up at the windows, it struck him as odd that no lights were to be seen.

The housekeeper answered his ring.

"Oh, is it you, Mr. Harrison? Very glad to see you back, sir. There is a letter for you upstairs and three telegrams. The first came on Wednesday, sir. The note Mr. Chamberlayne left for you; he expected you would be here on Wednesday."

"Left for me," repeated Gerald, anxiously. "He has not gone, surely? Did he not get my wire?"

"I sent it on with the other letters this morning, sir. Mr, Chamberlayne has been gone a week—him and Mr. Curtis. He is staying at Creamshire, at Ravenshill Hall, Mallowby."

Harrison's brain reeled. He saw it all now. That letter had been a week in travelling to Italy and back again to England. He had cried, "Peace, peace," when there was no peace; when all the time he was too late, and Jack had gone to that accursed house, and—this was New Year's Eve.

"Fetch the letters, Mrs. Williams; or, stay, I will get them myself."

He tore upstairs, two steps at a time, snatched the envelopes from the mantelpiece and was back to the cab before the astounded house-keeper could utter a syllable.

"King's Cross!" he shouted to the driver; "and a double fare if I catch the 7.5 for the north. It is a matter of life and death."

"I'll do my best, sir," said the man, dubiously; "but it's darned bad going."

Never had the way seemed so long; never did time go faster and horse more slowly. To Harrison's over-wrought fancy they crept along, and again and again he raised the trap and implored the man to whip up. The agony and anxiety in his white drawn face moved the cabby's heart to pity, and he generously refrained from swearing at his impetuous fare.

"A cove is that onreasonable when 'e's in trouble," he growled to himself aloft. "Does 'e want me to let the mare down and make sure of losing 'is blooming train?"

At last they turned into the Euston Road. The snow was coming down in good earnest now, and Gerald could hardly see the hands of the clock for the blinding flakes. It wanted eight minutes to seven.

"Thank God!" he murmured, as the hansom turned into the yard of the Great Northern. Before the man had time to pull up, he was out on the ground.

"Mallowby," he called to the porter, "can I do it?"

"Four minutes," was the response.

Gerald flung half a sovereign to the driver, and rushed into the booking-office. The bell was ringing when he got on to the platform.

The porter had put his portmanteaus into a carriage and was holding open the door. He threw himself into a seat with a sense of gratitude that he was to have the compartment to himself.

To maintain an appearance of indifferent calm at this moment would, he felt, have been impossible. He was enduring a martyrdom of suspense. If his friend's life had not already paid the forfeit for another's sin, every second that ticked its course was bringing him nearer to its end. He conjured up with horrible distinctness the dark library, the deep recesses on either side of the fireplace lined with books, the massive oak furniture. He could hear the weird murmur of voices, without, the ghostly steps on the drive; then the heavy velvet curtains trembled, parted, and a woman's figure stood framed in the long window—a woman with dripping garments and a white set face, lighted by strange, lurid eyes—eyes which were dead, and yet alive in their fierce hatred and unquenchable thirst for revenge. How they glittered! They were close to him now, looking in through the carriage window, and Harrison, who had once laughed contemptuously at the mere notion of supernatural manifestations, was perilously near raising a ghost for himself from the intensity of his nervous excitement. Fortunately, at this juncture he remembered that Jack's letter and the telegrams were still unopened in his pocket, and the break in the sequence of thought gave him time to pull himself together.

With a half-laugh at his own weakness, he drew the curtains across the windows, and, lighting a cigar, tore open the yellow envelopes.

All three messages had been handed in at Mallowby Station

The first was dated December 29, and said:

Come down as soon as possible. Dull and seedy. Want cheering up.

—CHAMBERLAYNE

"He is getting nervous," Gerald said to himself "and did not like to acknowledge it."

The second telegram was more urgent, and enclosed a reply form.

> Must see you to-day. Important. Wire what train. Don't
> fail me.
>
> —JACK

The third was signed by Chamberlayne's valet.

> Something seriously wrong here. Please come at once,
> very anxious about master.

Harrison's face grew very grave. Something must indeed have been wrong before the punctilious Curtis would take upon himself to send a wire like that. His fears returned with renewed force. It was torture to think of Jack sending message after message only to meet with blank silence. There was a piteous reproach in the last appeal, "Don't fail me."

"As if I were likely to do that so long as I am above ground," thought Gerald. "Poor old Jack, he might have known I should have answered if I'd ever got the things."

At Peterborough he went to the refreshment-room and swallowed a sandwich and a few mouthfuls of soup while his flask was replenished with brandy. Very few passengers joined the train, and no one came into Harrison's carriage. As the hours dragged out their weary length he grew more and more restless and nervous. He paced the six feet of floor like a caged animal. He let down the window. A cloud of fine snow blew in through the opening. All around hedges, fields, and trees were wrapped in a dense white mantle. It was bitterly cold. Despite his fur-lined coat, hot tin, and a couple of rugs, his teeth were chattering and his hands were like ice.

He looked at his watch. It was half-past nine. In thirty minutes the train was due at Mallowby, and they had not passed Grantham yet. Surely, too, they were slackening speed. Half doubting the evidence of his senses, he again opened the window. The train was unmistakably at a standstill, but there was not the slightest sign of a station. The wind had risen, and whistled through the telegraph-wires overhead. Between the gusts he could hear the murmur of voices. Presently a man passed along the foot-board. It was the guard. Harrison inquired the cause of the delay.

"Line blocked, I'm afraid, sir," was the reply, "but I will let you know as I come back."

With an exclamation, which was almost a groan, Gerald flung himself back in his seat. Were the fates league against him, that now, when every moment might seal Jack Chamberlayne's death-warrant, he must perforce sit idle, bound hand and foot by the victory of the forces of nature over the inventions of man? Five minutes passed, ten, twenty, thirty. Then the guard put his head in at the door.

"All right, sir, line is clear; we shall go on directly."

At one minute past eleven the London train, more than an hour behind its time, set down a single passenger at Mallowby. Harrison at once addressed himself to the station master, and inquired how he could get to the old Hall. The man had been on the coroner's jury five years before, and remembered his face.

"Going to the Hall to-night, sir? Why, were not you here when poor Mr. Granville was drowned? You don't want to see it a second time, surely!"

"God forbid!" answered Gerald, quickly, "but I want to prevent it. A dear friend of mine is at that devilish house to-night. He does not know his danger, and I mean to save him."

"You can't do it," returned the man, bluntly. "Best keep clear of the black work that will be going forward up there. There is no baulking the

Deverel curse. It will have its victim God help him I say, and all those who sleep under that roof on New Year's Eve. You can do nothing for them."

"I mean to try," answered Harrison, with set teeth. "I have no time to waste. Where can I get a trap?"

"Nowhere nearer than the village. It will take you as long as walking the whole way. The roads are awful."

"Then I must walk. Can you find me a lantern? For Heaven's sake be quick. Every minute may mean his life now. What do I care about the danger? Man, I tell you he is my friend. He is to marry my sister in a fortnight, and I will either save him or die with him."

The stationmaster hesitated a moment.

"Look here, sir," he said, hurriedly, "you're a brave man, and I'll do what I can to help you. That was my last train till 1:30. I'll come with you as far as the gates. It will save you losing the way, and perhaps a bit of time getting through the drifts beside."

Gerald thanked him heartily, and side by side they turned their backs to the lights of the little station, and struck into the lonely road which lay between the railway and the haunted house. It had ceased snowing now. A few stars gleamed out between the rifts in the cloudy sky. From time to time a pale moon showed her face, now flooding the white landscape with a cold grey light, now hiding herself in a veil of fleecy vapour, as though she feared to see those things which should be done on the earth. By the help of the stationmaster's lantern the two men managed to keep to the narrow cart tract. The road was desperately bad. In places the snow was fully two feet deep. With the rising moon a keen wind had got up, which came sweeping over the level fields right in their faces, and cut like a knife. At the turning into the village where the land sloped a little, the drifts were almost impassable. At every step they sank above the knee. Harrison could hear his companion's breath coming thick and short. He was evidently getting done. For himself he was impervious

to all outward discomfort. Cold, fatigue, hunger; he was vaguely conscious that he should know them all, if he were not past feeling now.
His whole mind, will, nerve, aye, his very being, were centred in the one
intense determination to save his friend. At length they gained the main
street of the village. Here the snow was trodden down, and the going
comparatively easy. Hardly a light was to be seen in any of the cottages.
Involuntarily Gerald's eyes turned towards the rectory. It was wrapped
in shadow and silence; but from the old grey tower, looming up behind,
gleamed a small point of yellow light. Slowly it crept from window to
window, steadily rising, rising. A cold shudder ran through the man who
watched it. He knew what it meant; that the last sands were falling from
the hour-glass of time; that the life of the old year must now be measured
by minutes. The ringers were going up to the belfry.

"Oh, God!" he groaned inwardly, "give me strength, give me time."

"Have you got a drop of brandy about you, sir?" suggested the practical Miles. "It would help to keep the spirit in us a bit."

Without slackening his pace, Gerald held out his flask.

"A'ter you, sir, a'ter you."

"I don't want any, thanks." His ears were strained for the first stroke
of that ominous bell.

"Oh, come now, sir, fair do's. You will need your strength more than
me, and I say a'ter you."

To save discussion, Harrison put the flask to his lips. The spirit sent a
warm glow through his sluggish veins. At the same moment the stillness
of the night was broken by the solemn tolling of the passing bell. With a
cry of horror he thrust the brandy into his companion's hands, and began
to run as if for his life. Immediately before him the road curved sharply
to the left, and far ahead through the skeleton branches of the leafless
elms gleamed half a dozen irregular patches of light. They shone from
the windows of the Hall.

Slowly, mournfully pealed the muffled notes from the belfry. The knell of the old year, dying hard in the chill winter night; the knell of a human soul, who might even now be passing from life and love to the horror of unknown darkness, through the gate of a fearful death. The thought was torture. How he lived through those moments of suspense Harrison never knew. He could not have told how he covered the ground, or when he passed the gates which led up to the house. His brain burned like molten iron, on which the slow, monotonous clang of the bell fell like the strokes of a heavy hammer. He forgot the station-master, plodding along in the rear—forgot everything but that his goal was reached, if only he had not come too late.

The lower windows were closed, but from the chinks in the shutters stole the warm glow of fire and lamp, and as he reached the corner of the house he could catch the sound of approaching voices. Voices, yes!—but what sort of voices? Nearer they came, now swelling louder, now sinking to a whisper, but ever drawing nearer, till he could hear the words repeated in every shade of tone, from malignant exultation to concentrated passion of resolve.

"We shall have him to-night!" they said, with ghastly reiteration. "We shall have him to-night!"

Like a wave of ice-cold air, the horrible sounds passed by him, receded, and died away with an echo of fiendish laughter.

Despite, an inexpressible thrill of fear, that sent a shudder through his whole frame and nearly raised the hair on his head, Harrison was conscious of a faint hope that all was not over yet. Slowly and more slowly came the tolling of the bell. It was on the verge of midnight.

Suddenly from within the closed windows of the library issued a wild awful cry. The shutters were flung back, as if by magic the casement was thrown open, and the dark shadow of a man crossed the sill.

The moon emerging suddenly from behind a bank of clouds poured down a flood of silvery light on the stone wall, the snow-covered path, and on the figure of Jack Chamberlayne, who, with hands clenched as if in mortal pain, his eyes fixed with an expression of nameless horror on some object, invisible to all but him, was slowly following the ghostly vision along the drive, across the lawn, to—

With a supreme effort Harrison threw off the paralysing numbness which was creeping over him. Instinctively he dashed across the grass and stood between Chamberlayne and the fatal pond. Twelve paces from him his friend was advancing, slowly, unswervingly, like one who walks in his sleep.

"Jack," he shouted, "Jack, it is I, Gerald. Don't you know me?"

There was not a quiver of the tense eyeballs, not a sign that his voice had reached those ears, deaf now to all earthly sounds, but from the open window of the library a man rushed towards them, crying wildly, "Stop him, for God's sake, stop him before it is too late."

Gathering all his strength, Gerald flung himself upon the approaching figure. A frantic struggle ensued, for Chamberlayne was the taller by a head, and was at this moment, moreover, endowed with abnormal strength. It was then that his knowledge of wrestling, acquired during a "long" spent in the Cumberland dales, stood Harrison in right good stead. He closed with his antagonist, and by a sudden dexterous manœuvre threw him heavily to the ground, while overhead across the snowy fields the bells rang out their joyous welcome to the glad new year.

"Is he—dead?"

The valet on his knees beside his master's prostrate form had torn open Chamberlayne's vest and shirt, and was feeling for the faint pulsation which tells that the spirit has not yet quitted its earthly tenement.

"Fainted, I think; I can feel his heart beat."

"Thank God, sir, you came when you did. I should have been too late. Can you help me to carry him, Mr. Harrison? No, not to that d——d place!" as Gerald glanced involuntarily towards the lighted windows. "They are all up at the gardener's cottage. I wanted Mr. Chamberlayne to sleep there to-night; but you know what he is—told me to go myself if I was frightened. I had not been out of the room five minutes when I heard that awful cry, and—Holy Virgin! What is that?"

Harrison turned instinctively towards the library window. From the open sash a long tongue of yellow flame leaped out, curling round the edge of the curtain and licking up the thick silk cording as though it were a mere thread. Then another, and another. Fanned by the fresh breeze from without, the yellow glare broadened and deepened till the whole room was filled with a fierce lurid glow, succeeded by dense clouds of smoke and an ominous crackling sound.

"The place is on fire!" cried Gerald. "There is not a moment to lose. We must get your master into shelter and give the alarm!"

"Holy St. Patrick, defend us!" murmured Curtis, hastily crossing himself, as he stooped to raise the helpless form of poor Chamberlayne. Then, as best they could, the two men carried their burden across the lawn, along the drive, and up the side path leading to the fruit-gardens.

"Who is in the house?" gasped Harrison, as, staggering and breathless, they reached the door of the cottage. "Are any servants there?"

"Not a soul. Mrs. Bamfield here came in the day. She left directly dinner was served. There is no one in the place to burn but the devil's spawn as lighted it."

The valet's resonant knocks soon brought the gardener to the door, and while his wife was helping Curtis to restore his master to consciousness, Bamfield hurried Gerald off to the village to obtain assistance.

Just outside the gates they encountered the station-master, who was hanging about in great distress of mind, too anxious on Harrison's account to return to Mallowby, yet not daring to adventure himself within the fatal precincts of the Hall. His relief and joy at finding Gerald still alive knew no bounds, and he readily undertook to see a messenger despatched for the nearest doctor on his way back to the station. Meanwhile an alarm had been raised, and the sleeping village was raised by the hoarse cries of "Fire!" The ringers had been the first to see the red glare through the trees; but before long some forty men had turned out to join the little crowd already assembled before the burning house. Under Harrison's direction a body of labourers, headed by the gardener and bailiff, made an attempt to check the progress of the flames. But their efforts were scarcely perceptible. With a sharp wind blowing, and no better appliances at command than a line of buckets and a couple of garden-hose, it was evident from the first that the Hall was practically doomed. The old oak, of which the interior was chiefly built, burned like tinder. Within twenty minutes of the first outbreak the flames had spread to the upper story. Window after window lent its aid to that weird illumination. The great carved bedsteads, the massive presses and cabinets glowed and crackled in the fierce heat. Deverel after Deverel, clothed in dainty satin or shining armour, shrivelled and cracked away from their frames, to go down calm and unflinching as became true knights and brave gentlewomen into that burning fiery furnace. Still the fire-fiend raged on, vast clouds of black smoke mingling with the glare, while from time to time could be heard the heavy crash of falling beams and flooring. As the clock of the old church chimed the first hour of the new year, with a sound like the roll of distant artillery, swelling gradually into a deafening roar, the roof fell in and there shot up to heaven one mighty sheet of flame, which turned the sky into a crimson pall, and lighted up the snow-clad country for miles around. Was it a trick of over-heated imagination, a play of superstitious fancy, or did those who stood by at that moment really hear that hideous peal of shrill triumphant laughter, which made the stoutest heart among them quail, and forced each man to edge involuntarily nearer his neighbour? It lasted but for an instant, then nothing was audible but the continuous roar of the flames. Before the pale dawn had warmed into the red flush of sunrise, Ravenshill Hall was a heap of smouldering ashes enclosed in four grim, smoke-blackened walls. From attic to cellar not a corner had been spared. The fire had done its work thoroughly, and of the original structure nothing remained save the bare tottering shell.

"It wer' th' Lord's will," said old Dawson, who had come down to inspect the scene of the late catastrophe, "that Katharine Deverel should hev her reets; and now as He's proved as mon caan't go agin' Him, He's maade awa' wi' th' dommed ould plaace, an' a good riddance too. The Lord avenges the widder and the feytherless, though He keeps 'un waitin' a bit first soom-toimes, and it seams to me," concluded the farmer, thoughtfully, "as soom o' they poor bodies in Oireland should be hevin' theer turn afore long."

"It will be a bad look-out for the Moonlighters when they do," answered Harrison, with a quiet smile.

He was a little oppressed by the situation in which he found himself; for the events of that New Year's Eve were the talk of the country-side, and Gerald the hero of the hour. A man who, single-handed, had braved the Deverel ghosts and baulked them of their prey ranked, by the Mallowby standard, above Gordon, and only a little lower than Nelson. The worthy Miles was never tired of recounting the incidents of that midnight walk, and drew upon his imagination for certain effective touches to that part of the adventure to which he had not been an eye-witness.

The rustic mind is slow to receive a new impression; but when it does get a sensation, it makes the most of it. The people would listen to the story twenty times a day. They repeated it to each other; they turned it inside and out and discussed it threadbare, beginning it over again for the benefit of every fresh comer. To Gerald, who was heartily sick of the place and the subject, this lionising was inexpressibly irritating, and he was thankful when the doctor at last gave permission for Chamberlayne to be removed.

Thanks to his splendid constitution, backed up by the devoted nursing of Curtis and his friend, Jack escaped brain fever; but he had received a terrible shock, and his nerves were sorely shaken. It was not till the snow-wreaths had melted on the Creamshire Wolds, and crocuses were showing their gold and purple heads above the dark earth in suburban gardens, that Harrison was called upon to officiate as best man at a very pretty wedding in a certain fashionable London church, after which ceremony Mr. and Mrs. Jack Chamberlayne went off to the Riviera, where it was hoped that southern sunshine and a little judicious excitement at Monte Carlo would efface from the bridegroom's memory the experiences of that terrible New Year's Eve.

Of what he had actually seen and heard in the awful interval between his servant's departure and his subsequent return to consciousness Chamberlayne never speaks.

"I used to wonder," he once said to Gerald, "why Lazarus and those other fellows who were raised from the dead never told what they did and how they felt. I think I understand now. It was too terrible. They could not put it into words, and that is how I feel about that night—as if I had been brought back from the dead."

FAR TOO CONVENTIONAL

Frank Clements

The stranger laughed. "I suppose you are all trying to pull my leg," he said.

"You can think that if you like, sir," muttered the landlord, and the others in the bar murmured assent.

"But really the whole thing is so . . . so conventional. It's a stock property story: a house that has been empty for years, sudden deaths, some local legend, and then a mysterious creature whose touch is fatal. Come on, now. You ought to be able to invent a better ghost than that. It's hopelessly old-fashioned."

"So are ghosts," remarked the old gentleman, who, till then, had taken no part in the conversation.

The stranger turned. "Do you really believe this as well, sir?" he asked, a slightly mocking glint in his eyes.

"I don't disbelieve it, just because it has all the conventional ingredients of a ghost story. After all, how did such things become conventional?"

"Because they are so obviously frightening, I suppose."

"Rather because they are the circumstances in which ghosts have always been seen. The description of a man dying with a bullet in his brain would be conventional, wouldn't it? Because men shot in the head die quite conventionally. In the same way, ghosts generally appear in the same surroundings."

"But have there really been deaths in that old house?"

"Since I retired and settled here—twenty years ago—there have been two. Tramps, both of them. It was a long time before their bodies were discovered, and no longer possible to state the exact cause of death."

"A long time before their bodies were discovered?"

"No one in the village visits the house. It was the dogs which drew attention to them."

"That's right," interrupted the landlord. "And there may be a corpse there, for all we know. No one wants to look."

Involuntarily, the stranger shuddered:

"Brr, what a horrible idea!"

"It's a horrible house," sighed the old gentleman.

The stranger drained his glass and nodded to the landlord as a sign that he should take the company's orders.

"Well, what's the ghost supposed to be like? Rattling bones and all that?"

The gentleman shook his head gravely. "No one has described it, for the simple reason that the only two who may have seen it recently— the tramps—both died."

"Isn't there some sort of traditional description?"

"As the landlord said, there is the old legend of some . . . hairy bestial presence."

"Just as I thought—so vague that it's obviously imagined."

Again the old gentleman disagreed:

"On the contrary, when people imagine things, they usually invent detailed descriptions."

The stranger pursed his lips and shrugged:

"All the same, I'm afraid it all seems ridiculous."

"Would you like to go there, sir?" asked the landlord jokingly, as he placed full glasses on the table before them.

The stranger looked round the bar with its taciturn country occupants, while his lips curled with the townsman's contempt for the yokel:

"Yes, I would. I'll go now, if there's one of you not afraid to show me the way."

The old gentleman raised his hand:

"Now, please, don't do anything foolish."

"I'm not foolish," declared the stranger, a little flushed with the unusually strong beer, and conscious that he was the centre of attraction. "But all this talk is. Who's going to show me the way?"

There was silence in the bar.

He laughed again, this time unpleasantly and with a jeering joke:

"Well, they say some things about you country bumpkins in town, but this is the limit. I'll have a fine story to tell when I get back."

At this there was a mutter, and a scowling young labourer stepped forward.

"All right, mister. If you wants to be smart, I'll show 'ee the way."

"Brave fellow," sneered the stranger, rising from the table. "We won't waste any time. I'll stay till twelve—that's the fatal hour, isn't it? I'd spend the night, there, only I must be moving on to-morrow and want a good sleep."

He buttoned on his coat and drew a flask from his pocket.

"Fill this up, please, landlord. It'll be cold there, I expect."

"Aye, very cold," confirmed a voice.

The old gentleman protested once more:

"If nothing happens while you're there, it also proves nothing. These stories are not made or unmade in one night. Whereas if . . ."

"There you are, sir," chuckled the stranger. "'If nothing happens.' You know that nothing will."

He took the flask from the landlord:

"Do you want me to pay the reckoning before I go?" he asked tauntingly.

The landlord hesitated a moment, and then replied:

"I do, sir."

His face was grim and unsmiling, so that the stranger felt vaguely disturbed in spite of himself. But he drew out a note and slapped it on to the counter:

"Good, leave the change. I'll be back for it."

With a challenging glance around him, he followed the labourer outside. The old gentleman rose and hurried after them.

"So you insist on going? Very well, you know what I think. We pass my cottage on your way. I'll give you a lantern."

"Thank you, sir," said the stranger, genuinely grateful, for the evening air had already chilled some of his zest.

"And I'd like you to take my dog. He'll be company for you, and not only that, animals have a very keen sense of the supernatural. Watch him closely. If he shows any alarm, leave the house at once. You'll promise me that?"

The stranger promised while the labourer grunted. They waited outside the cottage, which was on the fringe of the village, while the old gentleman went inside.

"Why don't you come with me?" asked the stranger. "You'd have a fine laugh over the others afterwards."

"Not me," refused the labourer shortly, and turned away.

After a few minutes, the old gentleman returned with an old lantern and a shaggy Airedale, who sniffed at the stranger with friendly curiosity.

"His name's Robber," said the old gentleman. "Don't forget what you promised me."

When they reached the entrance to the short gravel drive that led between two rows of elms to the house, the labourer halted.

"This is as far as I come. Please yourself what you do."

With a wave of his hand, the stranger walked briskly up the drive. Standing beneath the porch, he hesitated before he pushed open the door. The village seemed far away, for its lights were hidden by the trees, and he felt very lonely.

At that moment it would have been very easy to retrace his steps, but the thought of the grins on the broad country faces restrained him. Then the dog pushed his wet nose gently against his hand, as if the beast also cherished the awareness of another living presence.

The touch gave him confidence and he fondled the dog's ear, before, with an unconsciously defiant swagger, he flung open the door. Little was revealed by the faint rays of the lantern.

He suddenly remembered the landlord's words:

"And there may be a corpse there now, for all we know."

Indeed, there might be anything outside the small circle of life within the glimmering light cast by the lamp on to the dusty floor and murky walls of an abandoned corridor. The dog yawned with a forced creaking sound which set his skin tingling, so that he muttered anxiously:

"Quiet Robber, quiet!"

He left the front door wide open behind him. In three paces he could be outside in the open air, so different from the musty chill in the house. Immediately on his left, there was a room. He entered, leaving this door also open.

Some while passed before he made any effort to explore the room, but as his imagination set to work, the need to do so in order to quieten his nerves overcame his repugnance. He moved slowly, holding the lantern first high above his head and then close to the floor before he shifted position.

In circling the room he encountered no obstacles or furniture. He sat on the window seat. Outside the trees hovered in the gloom, but there came no sound of their rustling.

He strove in vain to control his thoughts, to direct them to calm or amusing matters. But whenever he recalled any humorous story, it would fade unwittingly from his mind, and some horrible one would come forward persistently to demand his attention. One story grew particularly vivid in his fancy. It told of a crouching monster with yellow eyes, which sprang upon its victims through closed windows.

Looking nervously over his shoulder, he saw the branches of the trees swaying as with a life of their own, and they took on threatening shapes as he watched them. Soon, the influence of the story became so strong that he was afraid to look through the window, yet also terrified to turn his back on it, for fear of what might approach from behind. He sat awkwardly in profile, till the strained position drove him to leap up suddenly and rush across the room.

Here, he could hear the rustling of the trees, and that fixed his attention while his ears strained for any break in the normal rhythm of sound. He heard the deep breathing of the dog, who had fallen asleep, his nose buried between his paws. A sharp pressure on his hip recalled the presence of the flask. Gratefully, he withdrew it from his pocket.

The whisky brought him confidence and his old bravado. The dog slept so peacefully and unalarmed that he resolved to explore the house. He did not take the lantern with him. Ever since his childhood he had trained himself to see in the dark, also his fear of the dark had been lessened if he had a lit room to make for; that had always been of more importance than carrying a light himself.

His stumbles were frequent, mainly because his mood led him to advance with a deliberately blundering recklessness, for the sounds of his own progress reassured his latently tense nerves. He came upon nothing of interest, and was about to return to the room below, when he heard rapid pattering footsteps along the corridor. Obviously, the noise had disturbed the dog.

He whispered: "Robber, Robber!" and the gentle patter approached to his side. It was too dark for him to make out the Airedale's form, but he stroked the beast, whose ragged coat was quite dank, revealing to him how unhealthy was the atmosphere of the house. He felt sorry for Robber and caressed him soothingly.

Although it was not yet twelve, he resolved to put an end to the nonsense and return to the inn. He heard the scratching and pattering follow him downstairs; the animal was faithfully at his heels, giving warmth and comfort by his presence.

But when he reached the room, he halted, and his mouth opened for the cry he could not utter. It was as if his heart stopped with the sudden shock, and his body tingled with horror. There, in the light of the lantern, still sleeping soundly, lay the dog. . . .

A Terrible Vengeance

Charlotte Riddell

I. Very Strange

Round Dockett Point and over Dumsey Deep the water-lilies were blooming as luxuriantly as though the silver Thames had been the blue Mummel Lake.

It was time for them. The hawthorn had long ceased to scent the air; the wild roses had shed their delicate leaves; the buttercups and cardamoms and dog-daisies that had dotted the meadows were garnered into hay. The world in early August needed a fresh and special beauty, and here it was floating in it matchless green bark on the bosom of the waters.

If those fair flowers, like their German sisters, ever at nightfall assumed mortal form, who was there to tell of such vagaries? Even when the moon is at her full there are few who care to cross Chertsey Mead, or face the lonely Stabbery.

Hard would it be indeed, so near life, railways, civilization, and London to find a more lonely stretch of country, when twilight visits the landscape and darkness comes brooding down over the Surrey and Middlesex shores, then the path which winds along the river from Shepperton Lock to Chertsey Bridge. At high noon for months together it is desolate beyond description—silent, save for the rippling and sobbing of

the currents, the wash of the stream, the swaying of the osiers, the trembling of an aspen, the rustle of the withies, or the noise made by a bird,
or rat, or stoat, startled by the sound of unwonted footsteps. In the warm
summer nights also, when tired holiday-makers are sleeping soundly,
when men stretched on the green sward outside their white tents are
smoking, and talking, and planning excursions for the morrow; when in
country houses young people are playing and singing, dancing or walking
up and down terraces over-looking well-kept lawns, where the evening air
is laden with delicious perfumes—there falls on that almost uninhabited
mile or two of riverside stillness which may be felt, which the belated
traveller is lot to disturb even by the dip of his oars as he drifts down with
the current past objects that seem to him unreal as fragments of a dream.

It had been a wet summer—a bad summer for the hotels. There had
been some fine days, but not many together. The weather could not be
depended upon. It was not a season in which young ladies were to be met
about the reaches of the Upper Thames, disporting themselves in marvellous dresses and more marvellous headgear, unfurling brilliant parasols,
canoeing in appropriate attire, giving life and colour to the streets of old-
world villages, and causing many of their inhabitants to consider what
a strange sort of town it must be in which such extraordinarily-robed
persons habitually reside.

Nothing of the sort was to be seen that summer, even as high as
Hampton. Excursions were limited to one day; there were few tents, few
people camping-out, not many staying at the hotels; yet it was, perhaps
for that reason, an enjoyable summer to those who were not afraid of a
little, or rather a great deal, of rain, who liked a village in all the better
for not being crowded, and who were not heart-broken because their
women-folk for once found it impossible to accompany them.

Unless a man boldly decides to outrage the proprieties and decen-
cies of life, and go off by himself to take his pleasure selfishly alone,

there is in a fine summer no door of escape open to him. There was a time—a happy time—when a husband was not expected to sign away his holidays in the marriage articles. But what boots it to talk of that remote past now? Everything is against the father of a family at present. Unless the weather help him, what friend has he? and the weather does not often in these latter days prove a friend.

In that summer, however, with which this story deals, the stars in their courses fought for many an oppressed paterfamilias. Any curious inquirer might then have walked ankle-deep in mud from Penton Hook to East Molesey, and not met a man, harnessed like a beast of burden, towing all of his belongings up stream, or beheld him rowing against wind and tide as though he were a galley-slave chained to the oar, striving all the while to look as though enjoying the fun.

Materfamilias found it too wet to patronize the Thames. Her dear little children were conspicuous by their absence. Charming young ladies were rarely to be seen—indeed, the skies were so treacherous that it would have been a mere tempting of Providence to risk a pretty dress on the water; for which sufficient reasons furnished houses remained unlet, and lodgings were left empty; taverns and hotels welcomed visitors instead of treating them scurvily; and the river, with its green banks and its leafy aits, its white swans, its water-lilies, its purple loosestrife, its reeds, its rushes, it weeping willows, its quiet backwaters, was delightful.

One evening two men stood just outside the door of the Ship, Lower Halliford, looking idly at the water, as it flowed more rapidly than is usually the case in August. Both were dressed in suits of serviceable dark grey tweed; both wore round hats; both evidently belonged to that class which resembles the flowers of the field but in the one respect that it toils not, neither does it spin; both looked intensely bored; both were of rather good appearance.

The elder, who was about thirty, had dark hair, sleepy brown eyes, and a straight capable nose; a heavy moustache almost concealed his mouth, but his chin was firm and well cut. About him there was an indescribable something calculated to excite attention, but nothing in his expression to attract or repel. No one looking at him could have said offhand, "I think that is a pleasant fellow," or "I am sure that man could make him confoundedly disagreeable."

His face revealed as little as the covers of a book. It might contain interesting matter, or there might be nothing underneath save the merest commonplace. So far as it conveyed an idea at all, it was that of indolence. Every movement of his body suggested laziness; but it would have been extremely hard to say how far that laziness went. Mental energy and physical inactivity walk oftener hand in hand than the world suspects, and mental energy canon occasion make an indolent man active, while mere brute strength can never confer intellect on one who lacks brains.

In every respect the younger stranger was the opposite of his companion. Fair, blue-eyed, light-haired, with soft moustache and tenderly cared-for whiskers, he looked exactly what he was—a very shallow, kindly, good fellow, who did not trouble himself with searching into the depths of things, who took the world as it was, who did not go out to meet trouble, who loved his species, women included, in an honest way; who liked amusement, athletic sports of all sorts—dancing, riding, rowing, shooting; who had not one regret, save that hours in a Government office were so confoundedly long, "eating the best part out of a day, by Jove"; no cause for discontent, save that he had very little money, and into whose mind it had on the afternoon in question been forcibly borne that his friend was a trifle heavy—"carries too many guns," he considered—and not exactly the man to enjoy a modest dinner at Lower Halliford.

For which cause, perhaps, he felt rather relieved when his friend refused to partake of any meal.

"I wish you could have stayed," said the younger, with that earnest and not quite insincere hospitality people always assume when they feel a departing guest is not to be overpersuaded to stay.

"So do I," replied the other. "I should have liked to stop with you, and I should have liked to stay here. There is a sleepy dullness about the place which exactly suits my present mood, but I must get back to town. I promised Travers to look in at his chambers this evening, and to-morrow as I told you, I'm due in Norfolk."

"What will you do, then, till train-time? There is nothing up from here till nearly seven. Come on the river for an hour with me."

"Thank you, no. I will walk over to Staines."

"Staines! Why Staines in heaven's name."

"Because I am in the humour for a walk—a long, lonely walk; because a demon has taken possession of me I wish to exorcise; because there are plenty of trains from Staines; because I am weary of the Thames Valley line, and any other reason you like. I can give you none better than I have done."

"At least let me row you part of the way."

"Again thank you, no. The eccentricities of the Thames are not new to me. With the best intentions, you would land me at Laleham when I should be on my (rail) way to London. My dear Dick, step into that boat your soul has been hankering after for the past half-hour, and leave me to return to town according to my own fancy."

"I don't half like this," said genial Dick. "Ah! here comes a pretty girl—look."

Thus entreated, the elder man turned his head and saw a young girl accompanied by a young man, coming along the road, which leads from Walton to Shepperton.

She was very pretty, of the sparkling order of beauty, with dark eyes, rather heavy eye-brows, dark, thick hair, a ravishing fringe, a delicious hat, a coquettish dress, and shoes which by pretty gestures she seemed to be explaining to her companion were many—very many—sizes too large for her. Spite of her beauty, spite of her dress, spite of her shoes so much too large for her, it needed but a glance from one conversant with subtle social distinctions to tell that she was not quite her "young man's" equal.

For, in the parlance of Betsy Jane, as her "young man" she evidently regarded him, and as her young man he regarded himself. There could be no doubt about the matter. He was over head and ears in love with her; he was ready to quarrel—indeed, had quarrelled with father, mother, sister, brother on her account. He loved her unreasonably—he loved her miserably, distractedly; except at odd intervals, he was not in the least happy with her. She flouted, she tormented, she madden him; but then, after having nearly driven him to the verge of distraction, she would repent sweetly, and make up for all previous shortcomings by a few brief minutes of tender affection. If quarrelling be really renewal of love, theirs had been renewed once a day at all events, and frequently much oftener.

Yes, she was a pretty girl, a bewitching girl, and arrant flirt, a scarcely well-behaved coquette; for as she pleased the two friends she threw a glance at them, one arch, piquant, inviting glance, of which many would instantly have availed themselves, venturing the consequences certain to be dealt out by her companion, who, catching the look, drew closer to her side, not too well pleased, apparently. Spite of a little opposition, he drew her hand through his arm, and walked on with an air of possession infinitely amusing to onlookers, and plainly distasteful to his lady-love.

"A clear case of spoons," remarked the younger of the two visitors, looking after the pair.

"Poor devil!" said the other compassionately.

His friend laughed, and observed mockingly paraphrasing a very different speech,—

"But for the grace of God, there goes Paul Murray."

"You may strike out the 'but,'" replied the person so addressed, "for that is the very road Paul Murray is going, and soon."

"You are not serious!" asked the other doubtfully.

"Am I not? I am though, though not with such a vixen as I dare swear that little baggage is. I told you I was due to-morrow in Norfolk. But see, they are turning back; let us go inside."

"All right," agreed the other, following his companion into the hall. "This is a great surprise to me, Murray; I never imagined you were engaged."

"I am not engaged yet, though no doubt I shall soon be," answered the reluctant lover. "My grandmother and the lady's father have arranged the math. The lady does not object, I believe, and who am I, Savill, that I should refuse good looks, a good fortune, and a good temper?"

"You do not speak as though you like the proposed bride, nevertheless," Mr. Savill said dubiously.

"I do not dislike her, I only have having to marry her. Can't you understand that a man wants to pick a wife for himself—that the one girl he fancies seems worth ten thousand of a girl anybody else fancies? But I am so situated— Hang it, Dick! what are you staring at the dark-eyed witch for?"

"Because it is so funny. She is making him take a boat at the steps, and he does not want to do it. Kindly observe his face."

"What is his face to me?" retorted Mr. Murray savagely.

"Not much, I daresay, but it is a good deal to him. It is black as thunder, and hers is not much lighter. What a neat ankle, and how you like to show it, my dear. Well, there is no harm in a pretty ankle or a pretty foot either, and you have both. One would not wish one's wife to have a hoof like an elephant. What sort of feet has your destined maiden, Paul?"

"I never noticed."

"That looks deucedly bad," said the younger man, shaking his head.

"I know, however, she has a pure, sweet face," observed Mr. Murray, gloomily.

"No one could truthfully make the same statement about our young friend's little lady," remarked Mr. Savill, still gazing at the girl, who was seating herself in the stern. "A termagant, I'll be bound, if ever there was one. Wishes to go up stream, no doubt because he wishes to go down. Any caprice about the Norfolk 'fair'?"

"Not much, I think. She is good, Dick—too good for me," replied the other, sauntering out again.

"This is what we always say about the things we do not know. And so your grandmother has made up the match?"

"Yes: there is money, and the old lady loves money. She says she wants to see me settled—talks of buying me an estate. She will have to do something, because I am sure the stern parent on the other side would not allow his daughter to marry on expectations. The one drop of comfort in the arrangement is that my aged relative will have to come down, and pretty smartly too. I would wed Hecate, to end this state of bondage, which I have not courage to flee from myself. Dick, how I envy you who have no dead person's shoes to wait for!"

"You need not envy me," returned Dick, with conviction, "a poor unlucky devil chained to a desk. There is scarce a day of my life I fail to curse the service, the office, and Fate—"

"Curse no more, then," said the other; "rather go down on your knees and thank Heaven you have, without merit of your own, a provision for life. I wish Fate or anybody had coached me into the Civil

Service—apprenticed me to a trade—sent me to sea—made me enlist, instead of leaving me at the mercy of an old lady who knows neither justice nor reason—who won't let me do anything for myself, and won't do anything for me—who ought to have been dead long ago, but who never means to die—"

"And who often gives you in one cheque as much as the whole of my annual salary," added the other quietly.

"But you know you will have your yearly salary as long as you live. I never know whether I will have another cheque."

"It won't do, my friend," answered Dick Savill; "you feel quite certain you can get money when you want it."

"I feel certain of no such thing," was the reply. "If I once offended her—" he stopped, and then went on: "And perhaps when I have spent twenty years in trying to humour such caprices as surely woman never had before, I shall wake one morning to find she has left every penny to the Asylum for the Idiots."

"Why do you not pluck up courage, and strike out some line for yourself?"

"Too late, Dick, too late. Ten years ago I might have tried to make a fortune for myself, but I can't do that now. As I have waited so long, I must wait a little longer. At thirty a man can't take pick in hand and try to clear a road to fortune."

"Then you had better marry the Norfolk young lady."

"I am steadily determined to do so. I am going down with the firm intention of asking her."

"And do you think she will have you?"

"I think so. I feel sure she will. And she is a nice girl—the sort I would like for a wife, if she had not been thrust upon me."

Mr. Savill stood silent for a moment, with his hands plunged deep in his pockets.

"Then when I see you next?" he said tentatively.

"I shall be engaged, most likely—possibly even married," finished the other, with as much hurry as his manner was capable of. "And now jump into your boat, and I will go on my way to—Staines—"

"I wish you would change your mind, and have some dinner."

"I can't; it is impossible. You see I have so many things to do and to think of. Good-bye, Dick. Don't upset yourself. Go down stream, and don't get into mischief with those dark eyes you admired so much just now."

"Make your mind easy about that," returned the other, colouring, however, a little as he spoke. "Good-bye, Murray. I wish you well through the campaign." And so, after a hearty hand-shake, they parted, one to walk away from Halliford, and past Shepperton Church, and across Shepperton Range, and the other, of course, to row up stream, through Shepperton Lock, and on past Dockett Point.

In the grey of the summer's dawn, Mr. Murray awoke next morning from a terrible dream. He had kept his appointment with Mr. Travers and a select party, played heavily, drank deeply, and reached home between one and two, not much the better for his trip to Lower Halliford, his walk, and his carouse.

Champagne, followed by neat brandy, is not perhaps the best thing to insure a quiet night's rest; but Mr. Murray had often enjoyed sound repose after similar libations; and it was, therefore, all the more unpleasant that in the grey dawn he should wake suddenly from a dream, in which he thought some one was trying to crush his head with a heavy weight.

Even when he had struggled from sleep, it seemed to him that a wet dead hand lay across his eyes, and pressed them so hard he could not move the lids. Under the weight he lay powerless, while a damp, ice-cold hand felt burning into his brain, if such a contradictory expression may be permitted.

The perspiration was pouring from him; he felt the drops falling on his throat, and trickling down his neck; he might have been lying in a bath, instead of on his own bed, and it was with a cry of horror he at last flung the hand aside, and, sitting up, looked around the room, into which the twilight of morning was mysteriously stealing.

Then, trembling in every limb, he lay down again, and fell into another sleep, from which he did not awake till aroused by broad daylight and his valet.

"You told me to call you in good time, sir," said the man.

"Ah, yes, so I did," yawned Mr. Murray. "What a bore! I will get up directly. You can go, Davis. I will ring if I want you."

Davis was standing, as his master spoke, looking down at the floor. "Yes, sir," he answered, after the fashion of a man who has something on his mind,—and went.

He had not however, got to the bottom of the first flight when peal after peal summoned him back.

Mr. Murray was out of bed, and in the middle of the room, the ghastly pallor of his face brought into full prominence by the crimson dressing-gown he had thrown around him on rising.

"What is that?" he asked. "What in the world is that, Davis?" and he pointed to the carpet, which was covered, Mrs. Murray being an old-fashioned lady, with strips of white drugget.

"I am sure I don't know, sir," answered Davis. "I noticed it the moment I came into the room. Looks as if someone with wet feet had been walking round and round the bed."

It certainly did. Round and round, to and fro, backwards and forwards, the feet seemed to have gone and come, leaving a distinct mark where they pressed.

"The print is that of a rare small foot, too," observed Davis, who really seemed half stupefied with astonishment.

"But who would have dared—" began Mr. Murray.

"No one in this house," declared Davis stoutly. "It is not the mark of a boy or woman inside these doors"; and then the master and the man looked at each other for an instant with grave suspicion.

But for that second they kept their eyes thus occupied; then, as by commonest consent, they dropped their glances to the floor. "My God!" exclaimed Davis. "Where have the footprints gone?"

He might well ask. The drugget, but a moment before wet and stained by the passage and repassage of those small restless feet, was now smooth and white, as when first sent forth from the bleach-green. On its polished surface there could not be discerned a speck or mark.

II. WHERE IS LUCY?

In the valley of the Thames early hours are the rule. There the days have an unaccountable way of lengthening themselves out which makes it prudent, as well as pleasant, to utilize all the night in preparing for a longer morrow.

For this reason, when eleven o'clock P.M. strikes, it usually finds Church Street, Walton, as quiet as its adjacent graveyard, which lies still and solemn under the shadow of the old grey tower hard by that ancient vicarage which contains so beautiful a staircase.

About the time when Mr. Travers' friends were beginning their evening, when talk had abated and play was suggested, the silence of Church Street was broken and many a sleeper aroused by a continuous knocking at the door of a house as venerable as any in that part of Walton. Rap—rap—rap—rap awoke the echoes of the old-world village street, and at length brought to the window a young man, who, flinging up the sash, inquired,—

"Who is there?"

"Where is Lucy? What have you done with my girl?" answered a strained woman's voice from out the darkness of that summer night.

"Lucy?" repeated the young man; "Is she not at home?"

"No; I have never set eyes on her since you went out together."

"Why, we parted hours ago. Wait a moment, Mrs. Heath; I will be down directly."

No need to tell the poor woman to "wait." She stood on the step, crying softly and wringing her hands till the door opened, and the same young fellow who with the pretty girl had taken boat opposite the Ship Hotel bade her "Come in."

Awakened from some pleasant dream, spite of all the trouble and hurry of that unexpected summons, there still shone the light of a reflected sunshine in his eyes and the flush of happy sleep on his cheek. He scarcely understood yet what had happened, but when he saw Mrs. Heath's tear-stained face, comprehension came to him, and he said abruptly,—

"Do you mean she has never returned home?"

"Never!"

There were in the parlour by this time, and looking at each other by the light of one poor candle which she had set down on the table.

"Why, I left her," he said, "I left her long before seven."

"Where?"

"Just beyond Dockett Point. She would not let me row her back. I do not know what was the matter with her, but nothing I did seemed right."

"Had you any quarrel?" asked Mrs. Heath anxiously.

"Yes, we had; we were quarrelling all the time—at least she was with me; and at last she made me put her ashore, which I did sorely against my will."

"What had you done to my girl, then?"

"I prayed of her to marry me—no great insult, surely, but she took it as one. I would rather not talk of what she answered. Where can she be? Do you think she can have gone to her aunt's?"

"If so, she will be back by the last train. Let us get home as fast as possible. I never thought of that. Poor child! she will go out of her mind if she finds nobody to let her in. You will come with me. O, if she is not there, what shall I do—what ever shall I do?"

The young man had taken his hat, and was holding the door open for Mrs. Heath to pass out.

"You must try not to fret yourself," he said gently, yet with a strange repression in his voice. "Very likely she may stay at her aunt's all night."

"And leave me in misery, not knowing where she is? Oh, Mr. Grantley, I could never believe that."

Mr. Grantley's heart was very hot within him; but he could not tell the poor mother he believed that when Lucy's temper was up she would think of no other human being but herself.

"Won't you take my arm, Mrs. Heath?" he asked with tender pity. After all, though everything was over between him and Lucy, her mother could be held accountable for their quarrel; and he had loved the girl with all the romantic fervour of love's young dream.

"I can walk faster without it, thank you," Mrs. Heath answered. "But Mr. Grantley, whatever you and Lucy fell out over, you'll forget it, won't you? It isn't in you to be hard on anybody, and she's only spoiled child. I never had but the one, and I humoured her too much; and if she is wayward, t is all my own fault—all my own."

"In case she does not return by this train," said the young man, wisely ignoring Mrs. Heath's inquiry, "had I not better telegraph to her aunt directly the office opens?"

"I will be on my way to London long before that," was the reply. "But what makes you think she won't come? Surely you don't imagine she has done anything rash?"

"What do you mean by rash?" he asked evasively.

"Made away with herself."

"*That!*" he exclaimed. "No, I feel very sure she has done nothing of the sort."

"But she might have felt sorry when you left her—vexed for having angered you—heartbroken when she saw you leave her."

"Believe me, she was not vexed or sorry or heartbroken; she was only glad to know she had done with me," he answered bitterly.

"What has come to you, Mr. Grantley?" said Mr. Heath, in wonder. "I never heard you speak the same before."

"Perhaps not; I never felt the same before. It is best to be plain with you," he went on. "All is at an end between us; and that is what your daughter has long been trying for."

"How can you say that, and she so fond of you?"

"She has not been fond of me for many a day. The man she wants to marry is not a poor fellow like myself, but one who can give her carriages and horses, and a fine house, and as much dress as she cares to buy."

"But where could she ever find a husband able to do that?"

"I do not know, Mrs. Heath all I do know is that she considers I am no match for her; and now my eyes are opened, I see she was not a wife for me. We should never have known a day's happiness."

It was too dark to see his face, but his changed voice and words and manner told Lucy's mother the kindly lad, who a couple of years before came courting her pretty daughter, and offended all his friends for her sake, was gone away for ever. It was a man who walked by her side—who had eaten f the fruit of the tree, and had learned to be as a god, knowing good from evil.

"Well, well," she said brokenly, "you are the best judge, I suppose; but O, my child, my child!"

She was so blinded with tears she stumbled, and must have fallen had he not caught and prevented her. Then he drew her arm within his hand, and said,—

"I am so grieved for you. I never received anything but kindness from you."

"And indeed," she sobbed, "you never were anything except good to me. I always knew we couldn't be considered your equals. And I was so proud and happy, and fond of you—I was indeed; and I used to consider how, when you came down, I could have some little thing you fancied. But that's all over now. And I don't blame you; only my heart is sore and troubled about my foolish girl."

They were on Walton Bridge by this time, and the night air blew cold and raw down the river, and made Mrs. Heath shiver.

"I wonder where Lucy is," she murmured, "and what she'd think if she knew her mother walking through the night in an agony about her? Where was it you said you left her?"

"Between Dockett Point and Chertsey. I shouldn't have left her had she not insisted on my doing so."

"Is that the train?" asked Mrs. Heath, stopping suddenly short and listening intently.

"Yes; it is just leaving Sunbury Station. Do not hurry; we have plenty of time."

They had: they were at Lucy's home, one of the small houses situated between Battlecreese Hill and the Red Lion in Lower Haliford before a single passenger came along The Green, or out of Nannygoat Lane.

"My heart misgives me that she has not come down," said Mrs. Heath.

"Shall I go up to meet her?" asked the young man; and almost before the mother feverishly assented, he was striding through the summer night to Shepperton Station, where he found the lights extinguished and every door closed.

III. Poor Mrs. Heath

By noon the next day every one in Shepperton and Lower Halliford knew Lucy Heath was "missing."

Her mother had been up to Putney, but Lucy was not with her aunt, who lived not very far from the Bridge on the Fulham side, and who, having married a fruiterer and worked up a very good business, was inclined to take such bustling and practical views of life and its concerns as rather dismayed her sister-in-law, who had spent so many years in the remote country, and then so many other years in quiet Shepperton, that Mrs. Pointer's talk flurried her almost as much as the noise of London, which often maddens middle-aged and elderly folk happily unaccustomed to its roar.

Girt about with a checked apron which loving enfolded a goodly portion of her comfortable figure, Mrs. Pointer received her early visitor with a sportive remark, "Why, it's never Martha Heath! Come along in; a sight of you is good for sore eyes."

But Mrs. Heath repelled all such humorous observations, and chilled those suggestions of hospitality the Pointers were never backward in making by asking in a low choked voice,—

"Is Lucy here?"

"Lor! whatever put such a funny notion into your head?"

"Ah! I see she is," trying to smile. "After all, she spent the night with you."

"Did what?" exclaimed Mrs. Pointer. "Spent the night—was that what you said? No, nor the day, either, for this year nearly. Why, for the last four months she hasn't set foot across the doorstep, unless it might be to buy some cherries, or pears, or apples, or grapes, or such-like, and then she came with more air than any lady; and after paying her money and getting her goods went out again, just as if I had been her father's sister and Point my husband. But there! for any sake, woman, don't look like that! Come into the parlour and tell me what is wrong. You never mean she has gone away and left you?"

Poor Mrs. Heath was perfectly incapable at that moment of saying what she did mean. Seated on a stool, and holding fast by the edge of the counter for fear of falling, the shop and its contents, the early busses, the people going along the pavement, the tradesman's carts, the private carriages, were, as in some terrible nightmare, gyrating before her eyes. She could not think, she could scarcely think, until that wild whirligig came to a stand. For a minute or two even Mrs. Pointer seemed multiplied by fifty; while her checked apron, the bananas suspended from hooks, the baskets of fruit, the pine-apples, the melons, the tomatoes, and the cob-nuts appeared disappeared, only to reappear and disappear like the riders in a maddening giddy-go-round.

"Give me a drop of water," she said at last; and when the water was brought she drank little and poured some on her handkerchief and dabbed her face, and finally suffered herself to be escorted into the parlour, where she told her tale, interrupted by many sobs. It would have been unchristian in Mrs. Pointer to exult; but it was only human to remember she had remarked to Pointer, in that terrible spirit of prophecy bestowed for some inscrutable reason on dear friends and close relations, she knew some such trouble must befall her sister-in-law.

"You made an idol of that girl, Martha," she went on, "and now it is coming home to you. I am sure it was only last August as ever was that Pointer— But here he is, and he will talk to you himself."

Which Mr. Pointer did, being very fond of the sound of his own foolish voice. He stated how bad a thing it was for people to be above their station or to bring children up above the rank of life in which it had pleased God to place them. He quoted many pleasing saws uttered by his father and grandfather; remarked that as folks sowed they were bound to reap; reminded Mrs. Heath they had the word of Scripture for the fact—than, which, parenthetically, no fact could be truer, as he knew—that a man might not gather grapes from thorns or even figs from thistles. Further he went on to observe generally—the observation having a particular reference to Lucy—that it did not do to judge things by their looks. Over and over again salesmen had tried to "shove off a lot of foreign fruit on him, but he wasn't a young bird to be taken in by that chaff." No; what he looked to was quality; it was what his customers expected from him, and what he could honestly declare his customers got. He was a plain man, and he thought honesty was the best policy. So as Mrs. Heath had seen fit to come to them in her trouble he would tell her what he thought, without beating about the bush. He believed Lucy had "gone off."

"But where?" asked poor Mrs. Heath.

"That I am not wise enough to say; but you'll find she's gone off. Girls in her station don't sport chains and bracelets and brooches for nothing—"

"But they did not cost many shillings," interposed the mother.

"She might tell you that," observed Mrs. Pointer, with a world of meaning.

"To say nothing," went on Mr. Pointer, "of grey gloves she could not bear to be touched. One day she walked in when I was behind the counter, and, not knowing she had been raised to the peerage, I shook hands with her as a matter of course; but when I saw the young lady look at her glove as if I had dirtied it, I said, 'O, I beg your pardon, miss'—jocularly, you know. 'They soil so easily,' she lisped."

"I haven't patience with such ways!" interpolated Mrs. Pointer, without any lisp at all. "Yes, it's hard for you, Martha, but you may depend Pointer's right. Indeed, I expected how it would be long ago. Young women who are walking in the straight road don't dress as Lucy dressed, or dare their innocent little cousins to call them by their Christian names in the street. Since the Spring, and long before, Pointer and me has been sure Lucy was up to no good."

"And you held your tongues and never said a word to me!" retorted Mrs. Heath, goaded and driven to desperation.

"Much use it would have been saying any word to you," answered Mrs. Pointer. "When you told me about young Grantley, and I bid you be careful, how did you take my advice? Why, you blared out at me, went on as if I knew nothing and had never been anywhere. What I told you then, though, I tell you now: young Grantleys, the sons of rectors and the grandsons of colonels, don't come after farmer's daughters with any honest purpose."

"Yet young Grantley asked her last evening to fix a day for their marriage," said Mrs. Heath, with a little triumph.

"O, I daresay!" scoffed Mrs. Pointer.

"Talk is cheap," observed Mr. Pointer.

"Some folks have more of it than money," supplemented his wife.

"They have been, as I understand, keeping company for some time now," said the fruiterer, with what he deemed a telling and judicial calmness. "So if he asked her to name the day, why did she not name it?"

"I do not know. I have never seen her since."

"O, then you had only his word bout the matter," summed up Mrs. Pointer. "Just as I thought—just as I thought."

"What did you think?" inquired the poor troubled mother.

"Why, that she has gone off with this poor Mr. Grantley."

"Ah, you don't know Mr. Grantley, or you wouldn't say such a thing."

"It is true," observed Mr. Pointer, "that I do not know the gentleman, and, I may add, I do not want to know him; but speaking as a person acquainted with the world—"

"I'll be getting home," interrupted Mrs. Heath. "Most likely my girl is there waiting for me, and a fine laugh she will have against her poor old mother for being in such a taking. Yes, Lucy will have the breakfast ready. No, thank you; I'll not wait to take anything. There will be a train back presently; and besides, to tell you the truth, food will choke me till I sit down again with my girl, and then I won't be able to eat for joy."

Husband and wife looked at each other as Mr. Heath spoke, and for the moment a deep pity pierced the hard crust of their worldly egotism.

"Wait a minute," cried Mrs. Pointer, "and I'll put my bonnet on and go with you."

"No," interrupted Mr. Pointer, instantly seizing his wife's idea, and appropriating it as his own. "I am the proper person to see this affair out. There is not much doing, and if there were, I would leave everything to obtain justice for your niece. After all, however wrong she may have gone, she is your niece, Maria."

With which exceedingly nasty remark, which held a whole volume of unpleasant meaning as to what Mrs. Pointer might expect from that relationship in the future, Mr. Pointer took Mrs. Heath by the arm, and piloted her out into the street, and finally to Lower Halliford, where the missing Lucy was not, and where no tidings of her had come.

IV. Mr. Gage on Portents

About the time when poor distraught Mrs. Heath, having managed to elude the vigilance of that cleverest of men, Maria Pointer's husband, had run out of her small house, and was enlisting the sympathies of gossip-loving Shepperton in Lucy's disappearance, Mr. Paul Murray arrived at Liverpool Street Station, where his luggage and valet awaited him.

"Get tickets, Davis," he said; "I have run it rather close"; and he walked towards Smith's stall, while the man went into the booking-office.

As he was about to descend the stairs, Davis became aware of a very singular fact. Looking down the steps, he saw precisely the same marks that had amazed him so short a time previously, being printed hurriedly off by a pair of invisible feet, which ran to the bottom and then flew as if in the wildest haste to the spot where Mr. Murray stood.

"I am not dreaming, am I?" thought the man; and he shut his eyes and opened them gain,

The footprints were all gone!

At that moment his master turned from the bookstall and proceeded towards the train. A porter opened the door of a smoking carriage, but Murray shook his head and passed on. Mr. Davis, once more looking to the ground, saw that those feet belonging to no body were still following. There were not many passengers, and it was quite plain to him that wherever his master went, the quick, wet prints went too. Even on the step of the compartment Mr. Murray eventually selected the man beheld a mark, as though some one had sprung in after him. He secured the door, and then walked away, to find a place for himself, marvelling in the dazed state of mind what it all meant; indeed, he felt so much dazed that, after he had found a seat to his mind, he did not immediately notice an old acquaintance in the opposite corner, who affably inquired,—

"And how is Mr. Davis?"

Thus addressed, Mr. Davis started from his reverie, and exclaimed, "Why, bless my soul, Gage, who'd have thought of seeing you here?" after which exchange of courtesies the pair shook hands gravely and settled down to converse.

Mr. Davis explained that he was going down with his governor to Norwich; and Mr. Gage stated that he and the old general had been staying at Thorpe, and were on their way to Lowestoft. Mr. Gage and his old general had also just returned from paying a round of visit in the West of England. "Pleasant enough, but slow," finished the gentleman's gentleman. "After all, in the season or out of it, there is no place like London."

With this opinion Mr. Davis quite agreed, and said he only wished he had never to leave it, adding,—

"We have not been away before for a long time; and we should not be going where we are now bound if we had not to humour some fancy of our grandmother's."

"Deuced rough on a man having to humour a grandmother's fancy," remarked Mr. Gage.

"No female ought to be left the control of money," said Mr. Davis with conviction. "See what the consequences have been in this case— Mrs. Murray outlived her son, who had to ask for every shilling he wanted, and she is so tough she may see the last of her grandson."

"That is very likely," agreed the other. "He looks awfully bad."

"You saw him just now, I suppose?"

"No; but I saw him last night at Chertsey Station, and I could but notice the change in his appearance."

For a minute Mr. Davis remained silent. "Chertsey Station!" What could his master have been doing at Chertsey? That was a question he would have to put to himself again, and answer for himself at some convenient time; meanwhile he only answered,—

"Yes, I observe an alteration in him myself. Anything fresh in the paper?"

"No," answered Mr. Gage, handing his friend over the *Daily News*— the print he affected; "everything is as dull as ditchwater."

For many a mile Davis read or affected to read; then he laid the paper aside, and after passing his case, well filled with a tithe levied on Mr. Murray's finest cigars, to Gage, began solemnly,—

"I am going to ask you a curious question, Robert, as from man to man."

"Ask on," said Mr. Gage, striking a match.

"Do you believe in warnings?"

The old General's gentleman burst out laughing. He was so tickled that he let his match drop from his fingers unapplied.

"I am afraid most of us have to believe in them, whether we like it or not," he answered, when he could speak. "Has there been some little difference between you and your governor, then?"

"You mistake," was the reply. "I did not mean warnings in the sense of notice, but warnings as warnings, you understand."

"Bother me if I do. Yes, now I take you. Do I believe in 'coming events cast shadows before,' as some one puts it. Has any shadow of a coming event been cast across you?"

"No, nor across anybody, so far as I know; but I've been thinking the matter over lately, and wondering if there can be any truth in such notions."

"What notions?"

"Why, that there are signs and suchlike sent when trouble is coming to any one."

"You may depend it is right enough that signs and tokens are sent. Almost every good family has its special warning: one has its mouse, another its black dog, a third its white bird, a fourth its drummer-boy, and so on. There is no getting over facts, even if you don't understand them."

"Well, it I hard to believe."

"There wouldn't be much merit in believing if everything were as plain as a pikestaff. You know what the Scotch minister said to his boy:

'The very devils believe and tremble.' You wouldn't be worse than a devil, would you?"

"Has any sign ever appeared to you?" asked Davis.

"Not exactly; but lots of people have told me they have to them; for instance, Old Seal, who drove the Dowager Countess of Ongar till the day of her death, used to make our hair stand on end talking about phantom carriages that drove away one after another from the door of Hainault House, and wakened every soul on the premises, night after night till the old Earl died. It took twelve clergymen to lay the spirit."

"I wonder one wasn't enough!" ejaculated Davis.

"There may have been twelve spirits, for all I know," returned Gage, rather puzzled by this view of the question; "but anyhow, there were twelve clergymen, with the bishop in his lawn sleeves chief among them. And I once lived with a young lady's-maid, who told me when she was a girl she made her home with her father's parents. On a winter's night, after everybody else had gone to bed, she sat up to make some girdle-bread—that is a sort of bread the people in Ireland, where she came from, bake over the fire on a round iron plate; with plenty of butter it is not bad eating. Well, as I was saying, she was quite alone; she had taken all the bread off, and was setting it up on edge to cool, supporting one piece against the other, two and two, when she saw one drop of blood fall, and then another, and then another, like the beginning of a shower.

"She looked to the ceiling, but could see nothing, and still the drops kept on falling slowly, slowly; and then she knew something had gone wrong with one dear to her; and she put a shawl over her head, and without saying a word to anybody, went through the loneliness and darkness of night all by herself to her father's."

"She must have been a courageous girl," remarked Mr. Davis.

"She was, and I liked her well. But to the point. When she reached her destination she found her youngest brother dead. Now what do you make of that?"

"It's strange, but I suppose he would have died all the same if she had not seen the blood-drops, and I can't see any good seeing them did her. If she had reached her father's in time to bid brother good-bye, there would have been some sense in such a sign. As it is, it seems to me a lot trouble thrown away."

Mr. Gage shook his head.

"What a skeptic you are, Davis. But there! London makes sceptics of the best of us. If you had spent a dinner, as I did once, in the Highlands of Scotland, or heard the Banshee wailing for the General's nephew in the county of Mayo, you wouldn't have asked what was the use of second sight or Banshees. You would have just stood and trembled as I did many a time."

"I might," said Davis doubtfully, wondering what his friend would have thought of those wet little footprints. "Hillo, here's Peterborough! Hadn't we better stretch our legs? And a glass of something would be acceptable."

Of that glass, however, Mr. Davis was not destined to partake.

"If one of you is Murray's man," said the guard as they jumped out, "he wants you."

"I'll be back in a minute," observed Mr. Murray's man to his friend, and hastened off.

But he was not back in a minute; on the contrary, he never returned at all.

V. KISS ME

The first glance in his master's face filled Davis with a vague alarm. Gage's talk had produced an effect quite out of proportion to its merit, and a cold terror struck to the valet's heart as he thought there might, spite of his lofty skepticism, be something after all in the mouse, and the bird, and the drummer-boy, in the black dog, and the phantom carriages, and the spirits it required the united exertions of twelve clergymen (with bishop in lawn sleeves among them) to lay; in Highland second sight and Irish Banshees; and in little feet paddling round and about a man's bed and following wherever he went. What awful disaster could those footprints portend? Would the train be smashed up? Did any river lie before them? and if so, was the sign vouchsafed as a warning that they were likely to die by drowning? All these thoughts, and many more, passed through Davis' mind as he stood looking at his master's pallid face and waiting for him to speak.

"I wish you to come in here," said Mr. Murray after a pause, and with a manifest effort. "I am not quite well."

"Can I get you anything, sir?" asked the valet. "Will you not wait and go by another train?"

"No; I shall be better presently; only I do not like being alone."

Davis opened the door and entered the compartment. As he did so, he could not refrain from glancing at the floor, to see if those strange footsteps had been running races there.

"What are you looking for?" asked Mr. Murray irritably. "Have you dropped anything?"

"No, sir; O, no! I was only considering where I should be most out of the way."

"There," answered his master, indicating a seat next the window, and at the same time moving to one on the further side of the carriage.

"Let no one get in; say I am ill—mad; that I have scarlet fever—the plague—what you please." And with this wide permission Mr. Murray laid his legs across the opposite cushion, wrapped one rug around his shoulders and another round his body, turned his head aside, and went to sleep or seemed to do so.

"If he is going to die, I hope it will be considered in my wages, but I am afraid it won't. Perhaps it is the old lady; but that would be too good fortune," reflected Davis; and then he fell "a-thinkynge, a-thinkynge," principally of Gage's many suggestions and those mysterious footprints, for which he kept at intervals furtively looking. But they did not appear; and at last the valet, worn out with vain conjections, dropped into pleasant doze, from which he did not awake until they were near Norwich.

"We will got to an hotel till I find out what Mrs.Murray's plans are," said that lady's grandson when he found himself on the platform; and as if they had been only waiting this piece of information, two small invisible feet instantly skipped out of the compartment they had just vacated, and walked after Mr. Murray, leaving visible marks at every step.

"Great heavens! what is the meaning of this?" mentally asked Davis, surprised by fright after twenty prayerless and scheming years into an exclamation which almost did duty for a prayer. For a moment he felt sick with terror; then clutching his courage with the energy of desperation, he remembered that though wet footprints might mean death and destruction to the Murrays, his own ancestral annals held no record of such a portent.

Neither did the Murrays', so far as he was aware, but then he was aware of very little about that family. If the Irish girl Gage spoke of was informed by drops of blood that her brother lay dead, why should not Mr. Murray be made aware, through the token of these pattering footsteps, that he would very soon succeed to a large fortune?

Then any little extra attention Mr. Davis showed his master now would be remembered in his wages.

It was certainly unpleasant to know these damp feet had come down from London, and were going to the hotel with them; but "needs must" with a certain driver, and if portents and signs and warnings were made worth his while, Mr. Davis conceived there might be advantages connected with them.

Accordingly, when addressing Mr. Murray, his valet's voice assumed a more deferential tone than ever, and his manner became so respectfully tender, that onlookers rashly imagined the ideal master and the faithful servant of fiction had at last come in the flesh to Norwich. Davis' conduct was, indeed, perfect: devoted without being intrusive, he smoothed away all obstacles which could be smoothed, and even, by dint of a judicious two minutes alone with the doctor for whom he sent, managed the introduction of a useful sedative in some medicine, which the label stated was to be taken every four hours.

He saw to Mr. Murray's rooms and Mr. Murray's light repast, and then he waited on Mr. Murray's grandmother, and managed that lady so adroitly, she at length forgave the offender for having caught a chill.

"Your master is always doing foolish things," she said. "It would have been much better had he remained even for a day or two in London rather than risk being laid up. However, you must nurse him carefully, and try to get him well enough to dine at Losdale Court on Monday. Fortunately to-morrow is Sunday, and he can take complete rest. Now Davis, remember I trust to you."

"I will do my best, ma'am," Davis said humbly, and went back to tell his master the interview had gone off without any disaster.

Then, after partaking of some mild refreshment, he repaired to bed in a dressing-room opening off Mr. Murray's apartment, so that he might be within call and close at hand to administer those doses which were to be taken at intervals of four hours.

"I feel better to-night," said Mr. Murray, last thing.

"It is this beautiful air, sir," answered Davis, who knew it was the sedative. "I hope you will be quite well in the morning."

But spite of the air, in the grey dawn Mr. Murray again had a dreadful dream—a worse dream than which laid its heavy hand on him in London. He thought he was on the riverside beyond Dockett Point—beyond where the water-lilies grow. To his right was a grove of old and twisted willows guarding a dell strewed in dry seasons with the leaves of many autumns, but, in his dream, wet and sodden by reason of heavy rain. There in June wild roses bloomed; there in winter hips and haws shown ruddy against the snow. To his left flowed a turbid river—turbid with floods that had troubled its peace. On the other bank lay a stagnant length of Surrey, while close at hand the Middlesex portion of Chesney Mead stretched in a hopeless flat on the bridge, just visible in the early twilight of a summer's evening that had followed after a dull lowering day.

From out of the gathering gloom there advanced walking perilously near to Dumsey Deep, a solitary female figure who, when they met, said, "So you've come at last"; after which night seemed to close around him, silence for a space to lay its hands upon him.

About the same time Davis was seeing visions also. He had lain long awake, trying to evolve order out of the day's chaos, but in vain. The stillness fretted him; the idea that even then those mysterious feet might in the darkness be printing their impress about his master's bed irritated his brain. Twice he got up to give that medicine ordered to be taken every four hours, but finding on each occasion Mr. Murray sleeping quietly, he forebore to rouse him.

He heard hour after hour chime, and it was not till the first hint of dawn that he fell into a deep slumber. Then he dreamt about the subject nearest his heart—a public house.

He thought he had saved or gained enough to buy a roadside inn on which he had long cast eyes of affectionate regard—not in London, but not too far out: a delightful inn, where holiday-makers always stopped for refreshment, and sometimes for the day; an inn with a pretty old-fashioned garden filled with fruit trees and vegetables, with a grass-plot around which were erected little arbours, where people could have tea or stronger stimulants; a skittle-ground where men could soon make themselves very thirsty; and many other advantages tedious to mention. He had the purchase-money in his pocket, and, having paid a deposit, was proceeding to settle the affair, merely diverging from his way to call on a young widow he meant to make Mr. Davis—a charming woman, who, having stood behind a bar before, seemed the very person to make the Wheatsheaf a triumphant success. He was talking to her sensibly, when suddenly she amazed him by saying, in a sharp, hurried voice, "Kiss me, kiss me, kiss me," three times over.

The request seemed so strange that he stood astounded, and then awoke to hear the same words repeated.

"Kiss me, kiss me, kiss me!" some one said distinctly in Mr. Murray's room, the door of which stood open, and then all was quiet.

Only half awake, Davis sprang from his bed and walked across the floor, conceiving, so far as his brain was in a state to conceive anything, that his senses were playing him some trick.

"You won't?" said the voice again, in a tone which rooted him to the spot where he stood; "and yet, as we were never to meet again, you might *Kiss me once*," the voice added caressingly, "*only once more.*"

"Who the deuce has he got with him now?" thought Davis; but almost before the question was shaped in his mind there came a choked, gasping cry of "Unloose me, tigress, devil!" followed by a sound of desperate wrestling for life.

In a second, Davis was in the room. Though the white blinds light enough penetrated to show Mr. Murray in the grip apparently of some invisible antagonist, who seemed to be strangling him.

To and fro from side to side the man and the unseen phantom went swaying in that awful struggle. Short and fast came Mr. Murray's breath, while, making one supreme effort, he flung his opponent from him and sank back across the bed exhausted.

Wiping the moisture from his forehead, Davis, trembling in every limb, advanced to where his master lay, and found *he was fast asleep*!

Mr. Murray's eyes were wide open, and he did not stir hand or foot while the man covered him up as well as he was able, and then looked timidly around, dreading to see the second actor in the scene just ended.

"I can't stand much more of this," Davis exclaimed, and the sound of his own voice made him start.

There was brandy in the room which had been left over-night, and the man poured himself out and swallowed a glass of the liquor. He ventured to lift the blind and look at the floor, which was wet, as though buckets of water had been thrown over it, while the prints of little feet were everywhere.

Mr. Davis took another glass of brandy. *That* had not been watered.

"Well, this is a start!" he said in his own simple phraseology. "I wonder what the governor has been up to?"

For it was now borne upon the valet's understanding that this warning was no shadow of any event to come, but the tell-tale ghost of some tragedy which could never be undone.

VI. Found Drowned

After such a dreadful experience it might have been imagined that Mr. Murray would be very ill indeed; but what we expect rarely comes to pass, and though during the whole of Sunday and Monday Davis felt, as he expressed the matter, "awfully shaky," his master appeared well and in fair spirits.

He went to the Cathedral, and no attendant footsteps dogged him. On Monday he accompanied his grandmother to Losdale Court, where he behaved so admirably as to please even the lady on whose favour his income depended. He removed to a furnished house Mrs. Murray had taken, and prepared to carry out her wishes. Day succeeded day and night to night, but neither by day nor night did Davis hear the sound of any ghostly voices or trace the print of any phantom foot.

Could it be that nothing more was to come of it—that the mystery was never to be elucidated but fade away as the marks of dainty feet had vanished from floor, pavement, steps, and platform?

The valet did not believe it; behind those signs made by nothing human lay some secret well worth knowing, but it had never been possible to know much about Mr. Murray.

"He was so little of a gentleman" that he had no pleasant, careless ways. He did not leave his letters lying loose for all the world to read. He did not tear up papers, and toss them into a waste-paper basket. He had the nastiest practice of locking up and burning; and though it was Mr. Davis's commendable custom to collect and preserve unconsidered odds and ends as his master occasionally left in his pockets, these, after all, were trifles light as air.

Nevertheless, as a straw shows how the wind blows, so that chance remark anent Chertsey Station made by Gage promised to provide a string on which to thread various little beads in Davis' possession.

The man took them out and looked at them: a woman's fall—white tulle, with black spots, smelling strongly of tobacco-smoke and musk; a receipt for a bracelet, purchased from an obscure jeweller; a Chertsey Lock ticket; and the return half of a first-class ticket from Shepperton to Waterloo, stamped with the date of the day before they left London.

At these treasures Davis looked long and earnestly.

"We shall see," he remarked as he put them up again; "there I think the scent lies hot."

It could not escape the notice of so astute a servant that his master was unduly anxious for a sight of the London papers, and that he glanced through them eagerly for something he apparently failed to find-more, that he always laid the print aside with a sigh of relief. Politics did not seem to trouble him, or any public burning question. "He has some burning question of his own," thought the valet, though he mentally phrased his notion in different words.

Matters went on thus for a whole week. The doctor came and went and wrote prescriptions, for Mr. Murray either was still ailing or chose to appear so. Davis caught a word or two which had reference to the patient's heart, and some shock. Then he considered that awful night, and wondered how he, who "was in his sober senses, and wide awake, and staring," had lived through it.

"My heart, and a good many other things, will have to be considered," he said to himself. "No wages could pay for what has been put upon me this week past. I wonder whether I ought to speak to Mr. Murray now?"

Undecided on this point, he was still considering it when he called his master on the following Sunday morning. The first glance at the stained and polish floor decided him. Literally it was interlaced with footprints. The man's hand shook as he drew up the blind, but he kept his eyes turned on Mr. Murray while he waited for orders, and walked out of the room when dismissed as though such marks had been matters of customary occurrence in a nineteenth century bedroom.

No bell summoned him back on this occasion. Instead of asking for information, Mr. Murray dropped into a chair and nerved himself to defy the inevitable.

Once again there came a pause. For three days nothing occurred; hut on the fourth a newspaper and a letter arrived, both of which Davis inspected curiously. They were addressed in Mr. Savill's handwriting, and they bore the postmark "SHEPPERTON."

The newspaper was enclosed in an ungummed wrapper, tied round with a piece of string. After a moment's reflection Davis cut that string, spread out the print, and beheld a column marked at top with three blue crosses, containing the account of an inquest held at the King's Head on a body found on the previous Sunday morning, close by the "Tumbling Bay."

It was that of a young lady who had been missing since the previous Friday week, and could only be identified by the clothes.

Her mother, who, in giving evidence, frequently broke down, told how her daughter on the evening in question went out for a walk and never returned. She did not wish to go, because her boots were being mended, and her shoes were too large. No doubt they had dropped off. She had very small feet, and it was not always possible to get shoes to fit them. She was engaged to be married to the gentleman with whom she went out. He told her they bad quarrelled. She did not believe he could have anything to do with her child's death; but she did not know what to think. It had been said her girl was keeping company with somebody else, but that could not be true. Her girl was a good girl.

Yes; she had found a bracelet hidden away among her girl's clothes, and she could not say bow she got the seven golden sovereigns that were in the purse, or the locket taken off the body; but her girl was a good girl, and she did not know whatever she would do without her, for Lucy was all she had.

Walter Grantley was next examined, after being warned that anything he said might be used against him.

Though evidently much affected, he gave his evidence in a clear and straightforward manner. He was a clerk in the War Office. He had, against the wishes of all his friends, engaged himself to the deceased, who, after having so.me time professed much affection, had latterly treated him with great coldness. On the evening in question she reluctantly came out with him for a walk; but after they passed the Ship she insisted he should take a boat. They turned and got into a boat. He wanted to go down the river, because there was no lock before Sunbury. She declared if he would not row her up the river, she would go home.

They went up the river, quarrelling all the way. There had been so much of this sort of thing that after they passed through Shepperton Lock he tried to bring matters to a conclusion, and asked her to name a day for their marriage. She scoffed at him and asked if he thought she meant to marry a man on such a trumpery salary. Then she insisted he should land her; and after a good deal of argument he did land her; and rowed back alone to Halliford. He knew no more.

Richard Savill deposed he took a boat at Lower Halliford directly after the last witness, with whom he was not acquainted, and rowed up towards Chertsey, passing Mr. Grantley and Miss Heath, who were evidently quarrelling. He went as far as Dumsey Deep, where, finding the stream most heavily against him, he turned, and on his way back saw the young lady walking slowly along the bank. At Shepperton Lock he and Mr. Grantley exchanged a few words, and rowed down to Halliford almost side by side. They bade each other good-evening, and Mr. Grantley walked off in the direction of Walton where it was proved by other witnesses he arrived at eight o'clock, and did not go out again till ten, when he went to bed.

All efforts to trace what had become of the unfortunate girl proved unavailing, till a young man named Lemson discovered the body on the previous Sunday morning close by the Tumbling Bay. The coroner wished to adjourn the inquest, in hopes some further light might be thrown on such a mysterious occurrence; but the jury protested so strongly against any proceeding of the sort, that they were directed to return an open verdict.

No one could dispute that the girl had been "found drowned," or that there was "no evidence to explain how she came to he drowned."

At the close of the proceedings, said the local paper, an affecting incident occurred. The mother wished the seven pounds to be given to the man "who brought her child home," but the man refused to accept a penny. The mother said she would never touch it, when a relation stepped forward and offered to take charge of it for her.

The local paper contained also a leader on the tragedy, in the course of which it remarked how exceedingly fortunate it was that Mr. Savill chanced to be staying at the Ship Hotel, so well known to boating-men, and that he happened to go up the river and see the poor young lady after Mr. Grantley left her, as otherwise the latter gentleman might have found himself in a most unpleasant position. He was much to be pitied, and the leader-writer felt confident that every one who read the evidence would sympathize with him. It was evident the inquiry had failed to solve the mystery connected with Miss Heath's untimely fate, but it was still competent to pursue the matter if any fresh facts transpired.

"I must get to know more about all this," thought Davis as he refolded and tied up the paper.

VII. DAVIS SPEAKS

If there be any truth in old saws, Mr. Murray's wooing was a very happy one. Certainly it was very speedy. By the end of October he and Miss Ketterick were engaged, and before Christmas the family lawyers had their hands full drawing settlements and preparing deeds. Mrs. Murray disliked letting any money slip out of her own control, but she had gone too far to recede, and Mr. Ketterick was not a man who would have tolerated any proceeding of the sort.

Perfectly straightforward himself, he compelled straightforwardness in others, and Mrs. Murray was obliged to adhere to the terms proposed when nothing seemed to her less probable than that the marriage she wished ever would take place. As for the bridegroom, he won golden opinions from Mr. Ketterick. Beyond the income to be insured to his wife and himself, he asked for nothing. Further he objected to nothing. Never before, surely, had a man been so easily satisfied.

"All I have ever wanted," he said, "was some settled income, so that I might not feel completely dependent on my grandmother. That will now be secured, and I am quite satisfied."

He deferred to Mr. Ketterick's opinions and wishes. He made no stipulations.

"You are giving me a great prize," he told the delighted father, "of which I am not worthy, but I will try to make her happy."

And the gentle girl was happy: no tenderer or more devoted lover could the proudest beauty have desired. With truth he told her he "counted the days till she should be his." For he felt secure when by her side. The footsteps bad never followed him to Losdale Court. Just in the place that of all others he would have expected them to come, he failed to see that tiny print. There were times when he even forgot it for a season; when he did remember it, he believed, with the faith born of hope, that he should never see it again.

"I wonder he has the conscience," muttered Mr. Davis one morning, as he looked after the engaged pair. The valet had the strictest ideas concerning the rule conscience should hold over the doings of other folks, and some pleasingly lax notions about the sacrifices conscience had a right to demand from himself. "I suppose he thinks he is safe now that those feet are snugly tucked up in holy ground," proceeded Davis, who, being superstitious, faithfully subscribed to all the old formulæ. "Ah! he doesn't know what I know—yet"; which last word, uttered with much gusto, indicated a most unpleasant quarter of an hour in store at some future period for Mr. Murray.

It came one evening a week before his marriage. He was in London, in his grandmother's house, writing to the girl he had grown to love with the great, entire, remorseful love of his life, when Davis, respectful as ever, appeared, and asked if he might speak a word. Mr. Murray involuntarily put his letter beneath some blotting-paper, and, folding his hands over both, answered, unconscious of what was to follow. "Certainly."

Davis had come up with his statement at full-cock, and fired at once.

"I have been a faithful servant to you, sir."

Mr. Murray lifted his eyes and looked at him. Then he knew what was coming. "I have never found fault with you, Davis," he said, after an almost imperceptible pause.

"No, sir, you have been a good master—a master I am sure no servant who knew his place could find a fault with."

If he had owned an easy mind and the smallest sense of humorous—neither of which possessions then belonged to Mr. Murray—he might have felt enchanted with such a complete turning of the tables; but as matters stood, he could only answer, "Good master as I have been, I suppose you wish to leave my service. Am I right, Davis?"

"Well, sir, you are right and you are wrong. I do not want to leave your service just yet. It may not be quite convenient to you for me to go now; only I want to come to an understanding."

"About what?" Mr. Murray asked, quite calmly, though he could feel his heart thumping hard against his ribs, and that peculiar choking sensation which is the warning of what in such cases must come some day.

"Will you cast your mind back, sir, to a morning in last August, when you called my attention to some extraordinary footprints on the floor of your room?"

"I remember the morning," said Mr. Murray, that choking sensation seeming to suffocate him. "Pray go on."

If Davis had not been master of the position, this indifference would have daunted him; as it was, he again touched the trigger, and fired this: "*I know all!*"

Mr. Murray's answer did not come so quick this time. The waters had gone over his head, and for a minute he felt as a man might if suddenly flung into a raging sea, and battling for his life. He was battling for his life with a wildly leaping heart. The noise of a hundred billows seemed dashing on his brain. Then the tempest lulled, the roaring torrent was stayed, and then he said interrogatively, "Yes?"

The prints of those phantom feet had not amazed Davis more than did his master's coolness.

"You might ha' knocked me down with a feather," he stated, when subsequently relating this interview. "I always knew he was a queer customer, but I never knew how queer till then."

"Yes?" said Mr. Murray, which reply quite disconcerted his valet.

"I wouldn't have seen what I have seen, sir," he remarked, "not for a king's ransom."

"No?"

"No, sir, and that is the truth. What we both saw has been with me at bed and at board, as the saying is, ever since. When I shut my eyes I still feel those wet feet dabbling about the room; and in the bright sunshine I can't help shuddering, because there seems to be a cold mist creeping over me."

"Are you not a little imaginative, Davis?" asked his master, himself repressing a shudder.

"No sir, I am not; no man can be that about which his own eyes have seen and his own ears have heard; and I have heard and seen what I can never forget, and what nothing could pay me for going through."

"Nevertheless?" suggested Mr. Murray.

"I don't know whether I am doing right in holding my tongue, in being so faithful, sir; but I can't help it. I took to you from the first, and I wouldn't bring harm on you if any act of mine could keep it from you. When one made the remark to me awhile ago it was a strange thing to see a gentleman attended by a pair of wet footprints, I said they were a sign in your family that some great event was about to happen."

"Did you say so?"

"I did, sir, Lord forgive me!" answered Davis, with unblushing mendacity. "I have gone through more than will ever be known over this affair, which has shook me, Mr. Murray. I am not the man I was before ghosts took to following me, and getting into trains without paying any fare, and waking me in the middle of the night, and rousing me out of my warm bed to see sights I would not have believed I could have seen if anybody had sworn it to me. I have aged twenty-five years since last August—my nerves are destroyed; and so, sir, before you got married, I thought I would make bold to ask what I am to do with a constitution broken in your service and hardly a penny put by"; and, almost out of breath with his pathetic statement, Davis stopped and waited for an answer.

With a curiously hunted expression in them, Mr. Murray raised his eyes and looked at Davis.

"You have thought over all this," he said. "How much do you assess them at?"

"I scarcely comprehend, sir—assess what at?"

"Your broken constitution and the five-and-twenty years you say you have aged."

His master's face was so gravely serious that Davis could take the question neither as a jest nor a sneer. It was a request to fix a price, and he did so.

"Well, sir," he answered, "I have thought it all over. In the night-watches, when I could get no rest, I lay and reflected what I ought to do. I want to act fair. I have no wish to drive a hard bargain with you, and, on the other hand, I don't think I would be doing justice by a man that has worked hard if I let myself be sold for nothing. So, sir, to cut a long story short, I am willing to take two thousand pounds."

"And where do you imagine I am to get two thousand pounds?" Mr. Davis modestly intimated he knew his place better than to presume to have any notion, but no doubt Mr. Murray could raise that sum easily enough.

"If I could raise such a sum for you, do you not think I should have raised it for myself long ago?"

Davis answered that he did; but, if he might make free to say so, times were changed.

"They are, they are indeed," said Mr. Murray bitterly; and then there was silence.

Davis knocked the conversational ball the next time.

"I am in no particular hurry, sir," he said. "So, long as we understand one another I can wait till you come back from Italy, and have got the handling of some cash of your own. I daresay even then you won't be able to pay me off all at once; but if you would insure your life—"

"I can't insure my life: I have tried, and been refused."

Again there ensued a silence, which Davis broke once more.

"Well, sir," he began, "I'll chance that. If you will give me a line of writing about what you owe me, and make a sort of a will, saying I am to get two thousand, I'll hold my tongue about what's gone and past. And I would not be fretting, sir, if I was you; things are quiet now, and, please God, you might never have any more trouble."

Mr. Davis, in view of his two thousand pounds, his widow, and his wayside public, felt disposed to take an optimistic view of even his master's position; but Mr. Murray's thoughts were of a different hue. "If I do have any more," he considered, "I shall go mad"; a conclusion which seemed likely enough to follow upon even the memory of those phantom feet coming dabbling out of an unseen world to follow him with their accursed print in this.

Davis was not going abroad with the happy pair. For sufficient reason Mr. Murray had decided to leave him behind, and Mrs. Murray, ever alive to her own convenience, instantly engaged him to stay on with her as butler, her own being under notice to leave.

Thus, in a semi-official capacity, Davis witnessed the wedding, which people considered a splendid affair.

What Davis thought of it can never be known, because when he left Losdale Church his face was whiter than the bride's dress; and after the newly-wedded couple started on the first stage of their life-journey he went to his room, and stayed in it till his services were required.

"There is no money would pay me for what I've seen," he remarked to himself. "I went too cheap. But when once I handle the cash I'll try never to come anigh him or them again."

What was he referring to? Just this. As the bridal group moved to the vestry he saw, if no one else did, those wet, wet feet softly and swiftly threading their way round the bridesmaids and the groomsman, in front of the relations, before Mrs. Murray herself, and hurry on to keep step with the just wed pair.

For the last time the young wife signed her maiden name. Friends crowded around, uttering congratulations, and still through the throng those unnoticed feet kept walking in and out, round and round, backward and forward, as a dog threads its way through the people at a fair. Down the aisle, under the sweeping dresses of the ladies, past courtly gentlemen, Davis saw those awful feet running gleefully till they came up with bride and bridegroom.

"She is going abroad with them," thought the man; and then for a moment he felt as if could endure the ghastly vision no longer, but must faint dead away. "It is a vile shame," he reflected, "to drag an innocent girl into such a whirlpool"; and all the time over the church step the feet were dancing merrily.

The clerk and the verger noticed them at last.

"I wonder who has been here with wet feet?" said the clerk; and the verger wonderingly answered he did not know.

Davis could have told him, had he been willing to speak or capable of speech.

Conclusion: He'd Have Seen Me Righted

It was August once again—August, fine, warm, and sunshiny—just one year after that damp afternoon on which Paul Murray and his friend stood in front of the Ship at Lower Halliford. No lack of visitors that season. Hotels were full, and furnished houses at a premium. The hearts of lodging-house keepers were glad. Ladies arrayed in rainbow hues flashed about the quiet village streets; boatmen reaped a golden harvest; all sorts of crafts swarmed on the river. Men in flannels gallantly towed their feminine belongings up against a languidly flowing stream. Pater and materfamilias, and all the olive branches, big and little, were to be met on the Thames, and on the banks of Thames, from Richmond to Staines, and even higher still. The lilies growing around Dockett Point floated with their pure cups wide open to the sun; no close folding of the white wax-leaves around the golden centre that season. Beside the water purple loosestrife grew in great clumps of brilliant colour dazzling to the sight. It was, in fact, a glorious August, in which pleasure-seekers could idle and sun themselves and get tanned to an almost perfect brown without the slightest trouble.

During the past twelvemonth local tradition had tried hard to add another ghost at Dumsey Deep to that already established in the adjoining Stabbery; but the unshrinking brightness of that glorious summer checked belief in it for the time. No doubts when the dull autumn days came again, and the long winter nights, full of awful possibilities, folded water and land in fog and darkness, a figure dressed in grey silk and black velvet fichu, with a natty grey hat trimmed with black and white feathers on its phantom head, with small feet covered by the thinnest of openwork stockings, from which the shoes, so much too large, had dropped long ago, would reappear once more, to the terror of all who heard, but for the time being, snugly tucked up in holy ground the girl whose heart had rejoiced in her beauty, her youth, her admirers, and her finery, was lying quite still and quiet, with closed eyes, and ears that heard neither the church bells nor the splash of oars nor the murmur of human voices.

Others, too, were missing from—though not missed, by Shepperton (the Thames villages miss no human beings so long as other human beings, with plenty of money, come down by rail, boat, or carriage to supply his place). Paul Murray, Dick Savill, and Walter Grantley were absent. Mrs. Heath, too, had gone, a tottering, heartbroken woman, to Mr. Pointer's, where she was most miserable, but where she and her small possessions were taken remarkably good care of.

"Only a year agone," she said one day, "my girl was with me. In the morning she wore her pretty cambric with pink spots; and in the afternoon, that grey silk in which she was buried—for we durst not change a thread, but just wrapped a winding-sheet round what was left. O! Lucy, Lucy, Lucy! to think I bore you for that!" and then she wept softly; and nobody heeded or tried to console her, for "what," as

Mrs. Pointer wisely said, "was the use of fretting over a daughter dead a twelvemonth, and never much of a comfort neither."

Mr. Richard Savill was still "grinding away," to quote his expression. Walter Gramley had departed, so reported his friends, for the diamond-fields; his enemies improved on this by carelessly answering,—

"Grantley! O, he's gone to the devil"; which latter statement could not have been quite true, since he has been back in England for a long time, and is now quite well to do and reconciled to his family.

As for Paul Murray, there had been all sorts of rumours floating about concerning him.

The honeymoon had been unduly protracted; from place to place the married pair wandered—never resting, never staying; alas! for him there was no rest—there could be none here.

It mattered not where he went—east, west, south, or north—those noiseless wet feet followed; no train was swift enough to outstrip them; no boat could cut the water fast enough to leave them behind; they tracked him with dogged persistence; they were with him sleeping, walking, eating, drinking, praying—for Paul Murray in those days often prayed after a desperate heathenish fashion—and yet the plague was not stayed; the accursed thing still dogged him like a Fate.

After a while people began to be shy of him, because the footsteps were no more intermittent; they were always where he was. Did he enter a cathedral, they accompanied him; did he walk solitary through the woods or pace the lake-side, or wander by the sea, they were ever and always with the man.

They were worse than any conscience, because conscience often sleeps, and they from the day of his marriage never did. They had waited for that-waited till he should raise the cup of happiness to his lips, in order to fill it with gall—waited till his wife's dream of bliss was perfect, and then wake her to the knowledge of some horror more agonizing than death.

There were times when he left his young wife for days and days, and went, like those possessed of old, into the wilderness, seeking rest and finding none; for no legion of demons could have cursed a man's life more than those wet feet, which printed marks on Paul Murray's heart that might have been branded by red-hot irons.

All that had gone before was as nothing to the trouble of having involved another in the horrible mystery of his own life—and that other a gentle, innocent, loving creature he might just as well have killed as married.

He did not know what to do. His brain was on fire; he had lost all hold upon himself, all grip over his mind. On the sea of life he tossed like a ship without a rudder, one minute taking a resolve to shoot himself, the next turning his steps to seek some priest, and confess the whole matter fully and freely, and, before he had walked a dozen yards, determining to go away into some savage and desolate land, where those horrible feet might, if they pleased, follow him to his grave.

By degrees this was the plan which took firm root in his dazed brain; and accordingly one morning he started for England, leaving a note in which he asked his wife to follow him. He never meant to see her sweet face again, and he never did. He had determined to go to his father-in-law and confess to him; and accordingly, on the anniversary of Lucy's death, he found himself at Losdale Court, where vague rumours of some unaccountable trouble had preceded him.

Mr. Ketterick was brooding over these rumours in his library, when, as if in answer to his thoughts, the servant announced Mr. Murray.

"Good God!" exclaimed the older man, shocked by the white, haggard face before him, "what is wrong?"

"I have been ill," was the reply.

"Where is your wife?"

"She is following me. She will be here in a day or so."

"Why did you not travel together?"

"That is what I have come to tell you."

Then he suddenly stopped and put his hand to his heart. He had voluntarily come up for execution, and now his courage failed him. His manhood was gone, his nerves unstrung. He was but a poor, weak, wasted creature, worn out by the ceaseless torment of those haunting feet, which, however, since he turned his steps to England had never followed him. Why had he travelled to Losdale Court? Might he not have crossed the ocean and effaced himself in the Far West, without telling his story at all?

Just as he had laid down the revolver, just as he had turned from the priest's door, so now he felt he could not say that which he had come determined to say.

"I have walked too far," he said, after a pause. "I cannot talk just yet. Will you leave me for half an hour? No; I don't want anything, thank you—except to be quiet." Quiet—ah, heavens!

After a little he rose and passed out on to the terrace. Around there was beauty and peace and sunshine. He—he—was the only jarring element, and even on him there seemed falling a numbed sensation which for the time being simulated rest.

He left the terrace and crossed the lawn till he came to a great cedar tree, under which there was a seat, where he could sit a short time before leaving the Court.

Yes, he would go away and make no sign. Dreamily he thought of the wild lone lands beyond the sea, where there would be none to ask whence he came or marvel about the curse which followed him. Over the boundless prairie, up the mountain heights, let those feet pursue him if they would. Away from his fellows he could bear his burden. He would confess to no man—only to God, who knew his sin and sorrow; only to his Maker, who might have pity on the work of his hands, and some day bid that relentless avenger be still.

No, he would take no man into his confidence; and even as he so decided, the brightness of the day seemed to be clouded over, warmth was exchanged for a deadly chill, a horror of darkness seemed thrown like a pall over him, and a rushing sound as of many waters filled his ears.

An hour later, when Mr. Ketterick sought his son-in-law, he found him lying on the ground, which was wet and trampled, as though by hundreds of little feet.

His shouts brought help, and Paul Murray was carried into the house, where they laid him on a couch and piled rugs and blankets over his shivering body.

"Fetch a doctor at once," said Mr. Ketterick.

"And a clergyman," added the housekeeper.

"No, a magistrate," cried the sick man, in a loud voice.

They had thought him insensible, and, startled, looked at each other. After that he spoke no more, but turned his head away from them and lay quiet.

The doctor was the first to arrive. With quick alertness he stepped across the room, pulled aside the coverings, and took the patient's hand; then after gently moving the averted face, he said solemnly, like a man whose occupation has gone,—

"I can do nothing here; he is dead."

It was true. Whatever his secret, Paul Murray carried it with him to a country further distant than the lone land where he had thought to hide his misery.

"It is of no use talking to me," said Mr. Davis, when subsequently telling his story. "If Mr. Murray had been a gentleman as was a gentleman, he'd have seen me righted, dead or not. She was able to come back—at least, her feet were; and he could have done the same if he'd liked. It was as bad as swindling not making a fresh will after he was married.

How was I to know that will would turn out so much waste paper? And then when I asked for my own, Mrs. Murray dismissed me without a character, and Mr. Ketterick's lawyers won't give me anything either; so a lot I've made by being a faithful servant, and I'd have all servants take warning by me."

Mr. Davis is his own servant now, and a very bad master he finds himself.

ORIGINAL SOURCES

Beresford, J. D. "Force Majeure," *Nineteen Impressions*. London: Sidgwick & Jackson, 1918.

Bierce, Ambrose. "The Secret of Macarger's Gulch," *The Collected Works of Ambrose Bierce, Volume III: Can Such Things Be?* New York: The Neale Publishing Company, 1910.

Blackwood, Algernon. "The Empty House," *The Empty House and Other Ghost Stories*. London: Eveleigh Nash Company Limited, 1916.

Capes, Bernard. "A Ghost-Child," *Loaves and Fishes*. London: Methuen & Co., 1906.

Clements, Frank. "Far Too Conventional," *Ghosts and Goblins*, 1913.

Croker, B. M. "The Dâk Bungalow at Dakor," *To Let*. Philadelphia: J. B. Lippincott Company, 1893.

de la Mare, Walter. "Out of the Deep," *The Riddle and Other Tales*. London: Selwyn & Blount Limited, 1923.

Donovan, Dick. "A Night of Horror," *Tales of Terror*. London: Chatto & Windus, 1899.

Everett, Mrs. H. D. "The Crimson Blind," *The Death-Mask and Other Ghosts*. London: Phillip Allan & Co., 1920.

Galbraith, Lettice. "A Ghost's Revenge," *New Ghost Stories*. London: Ward, Lock, Bowden and Co., 1893.

Hodgson, William Hope. "The Horse of the Invisible," *Carnacki the Ghost-Finder*. London: Eveleigh Nash, 1914.

Jacobs, W. W. "The Well," *The Lady of the Barge*. London: Harper and Brothers, 1902.

James, M. R. "Lost Hearts," *Ghost Stories of an Antiquary*. London: Edward Arnold, 1904.

Marsh, Richard. "The Houseboat," *The Seen and the Unseen*. London: Methuen & Co., 1900.

Moffat, J. "Honest John," *Ghosts and Goblins*, 1913.

Morrow, W. C. "Over an Absinthe Bottle," *The Ape, the Idiot & Other People*. Philadelphia: J. B. Lippincott Company, 1897.

Mulholland, Rosa. "The Haunted Organist of Hurly Burly," *The Haunted Organist of Hurly Burly and Other Stories*. London: Hutchinson and Co., 1886.

Nesbit, E. "From the Dead," *Grim Tales*. London: A. D. Innes and Co., 1893.

Pain, Barry. "The Tower," *Here and Hereafter*. London: Methuen & Co., Ltd., 1911.

Perrin, Alice. "The Footsteps in the Dust," *Red Records*. London: Chatto & Windus, 1906.

Praed, Rosa Campbell. "The House of Ill Omen," *Stubble Before the Wind*. London: John Long, 1908.

Riddell, Charlotte. "A Terrible Vengeance," *Princess Sunshine and Other Stories*. London: Ward and Downey, 1889.

Sinclair, May. "The Intercessor," *The English Review*, July 1911.

Steele, Wilbur Daniel. "The Woman at Seven Brothers," *Land's End and Other Stories*. New York: Harper & Brothers Publishers, 1918.

Whitehead, Henry S. "Black Tancrède," *Weird Tales*, June 1929.